MY HUSBAND'S LIES

Caroline England is a former divorce and professional indemnity lawyer who lives in Manchester. *Beneath the Skin* was published in 2017. *My Husband's Lies* is her second book. Caroline England Author can be found on Facebook or you can follow her on Twitter @CazEngland

To Rosie, my beautiful big sister. Miss you.

The champagne cork cracks like a firework. Covering her ears, she shrinks away from the hotel bar, trying to remember why she's there. A reception, yes a wedding reception; she went to the ladies'.

'There you are! You disappeared. They're taking the photographs now. Are you coming outside?'

She puts down the glass and turns. It's him, it's the husband she loves far too much. His jacket is missing, his aftershave's strong.

Holding her breath, she listens. *Pitter patter, pitter. patter.* 'But it's raining.'

Staring as though he knows, his eyebrows knit. 'It stopped ages ago. Everyone else is outside. Are you coming?'

His tone is too loud, his waistcoat too bright.

He's lying, he's lying, she knows when he's lying.

And the voice is still there; she can hear it quite clearly.

Pitter patter, pitter patter, listen to the rain!

Pitter patter, pitter patter, on the windowpane.

God, she hasn't heard that rhyme for years. Not her mum,

surely? Yes her mum, before she grew bad: holding her close, singing softly and stroking her hair. 'My perfect little poppet. Such a very good girl!'

'Hey dreamer, are you—'

She jerks at the sound. It's her husband, still gazing, his eyes telling lies. She just needs a few moments to make herself *perfect*. 'You go ahead. I need the loo. I'll be out in a minute.'

She watches his strides, then straightens her dress. Oh God, what the hell? Marks on her skirt, splatters on the silk. Holding her breath, she crouches down to inspect them. They dilate, creep and grow as she stares. Surely not blood? It wasn't her fault; she didn't mean to hurt anybody.

After a moment she blinks. No, silly! Just water from the ladies' tap. Or the spray of champagne! More likely the downfall. *Pitter patter, pitter patter.* She told him it was raining.

Her mind focusing, she breathes. Everything's fine, it really is. The room key is in her handbag, she can go up and change. Not a problem, absolutely! If she hurries, she'll be back before anyone notices. Like rabbit running! *Run rabbit, run!*

Removing her shoes, she darts up the stairs, counting each riser until she's on the third floor. With a loud clatter and clang, she leaves the fire door behind, her feet smacking the carpet as she sprints to the room.

Run rabbit, run rabbit, run, run, run!

With the swipe of a card she's in, almost giddy with purpose.

She sits on the bed and time slows. Sees her heels in her hand and tries to focus, to think. That's right; she came inside for the toilet. Washed her hands at the sink, watched the water drip from her fingers to avoid looking at her face. The dress, yes the dress; she needs to change it.

Her breathing shallow and fast, she brushes her hair, lines her shoes neatly, takes off her jacket, then slips off her dress.

2

'So I feel the benefit,' she remembers. Her mum's words. Like the rhyme, the lovely rhyme, before she went bad. *Pitter patter, pitter patter. Listen to the rain.* She looks to the window. There it is, the windowpane! And she can hear it, it's raining.

Striding to the window, she feels the heat rising. She knew he was lying; she always knows when he lies. She has to tell him, she has to tell him. He has to know that she knows!

The sash window protests, but she pushes and tugs and eventually it relents, yawning wide enough for her to see him and shout.

'Stop pretending! I know the truth! I know when you're lying!'

He doesn't turn, he doesn't hear, so she climbs on the ledge, swaying for a moment as she straightens her legs. Closing her eyes, she stands tall. Feels the breeze, a lovely breeze. And the refreshing splatter of rain on her bare arms and belly.

Ah, there's the voice again, soft and reassuring.

Pitter patter, pitter patter.

She leans forward to listen.

Listen to the . . .

But a shriek spoils the moment, too loud in her ears. She looks down and teeters.

'Oh my God, look! There's someone at that window. Oh my God, quick, someone help! I think she's going to jump!'

CHAPTER ONE

Five Hours Earlier

Dan

Dan Maloney smiles wryly, a puff of air through his nose. 'A church, another bloody Catholic church.'

Unsure if the words emerge out loud, he stares at the hoary building through the spattered windscreen. Its arched windows are dark, the only sign of life a single clump of early daffodils beside its black door.

The pelt of rain brings him back. It's bouncing off the bonnet like crystal ball bearings. 'Poor bastards,' he says. 'I thought it might ease off.'

'Yeah.'

The tone of Geri's voice makes him turn with a jolt. A small furrow mars her glowing face as she rubs her rounded belly. His baby's in there. He'll be a dad, a bloody dad! Six and a half months on and he's still struggling to believe it.

Trying to breathe away the flash of terror, he smiles. 'Little Nutshell playing up?' he asks lightly.

'Just an angry kick,' she replies. The usual beam replaces the frown. 'Yeah, I know. Poor Nick and Lisa. But I guess this is what you get in mid-January. Rain and more grey rain! Aberystwyth or Manchester, same difference.' She leans across to straighten the white rose in his buttonhole. 'Should I change into my flats?'

'Nah, I like the killer heels. We'll walk slowly. Stay there and I'll come round with the umbrella.'

As he opens the door, a sleek red car hurtles towards him through the deluge, then swerves at the last moment, pulling up next to his.

Will Taylor opens his window and grins. 'Careful, Danny Boy, might get a few drops of rain on your head and spoil the lovely locks. Then you'll be banned from the wedding photographs, leaving just handsome me.'

Dan laughs. 'Good try, William, but no contest. I'm *so* the best man,' he replies.

Inhaling the briny tang in the air, Dan links arms with Geri and they slowly negotiate the gritty puddles in the car park. They are overtaken by Will and Penny and another man in a suit, his face hidden by a black umbrella.

Dan steps into the dimly lit porch. The fusty smell strikes like a familiar soft slap. A blend of incense and aged parchment, taking him back. 'Reminds me of when I was an altar boy. Every bloody time.'

Will shakes his umbrella and grins. '*You* were an altar boy? You're joking, Dan. What about *the opium of the masses*? And the bloody rest. Think you owe me a few pints for all those pub rants I had to endure.'

Dan wonders why he mentioned it. 'Strange but true. At primary school. Before we went to St Mark's.'

'Pretty boy with dark curls in a cassock? Yup, I can picture that.' Will stretches his wide shoulders and wipes the drops of rain from his close-cropped brown hair. 'It's bloody freezing in here. Think we're the first to arrive. Where the hell is Nick? His brother's old Merc was right behind us when we left the hotel.'

Geri tucks a soft afro curl behind her ear and steps towards Penny. 'Hi, Penny,' she says, kissing her cheek. 'You look nice; red is definitely your colour. Love the dress coat, bet it's silk. I had intended to take off this ugly old thing, but . . .'

Penny blinks and shakes her head almost imperceptibly. 'Maybe it'll be warmer inside.' Then after a moment, 'Great hat; it suits you.'

Geri rubs her stomach. 'Thanks, thought it would distract from, well, this,' she replies with a happy grin.

Penny nods but falls silent. 'Oh, do you know . . . ?' she starts eventually, turning to the tall man reading desiccated messages on a cork noticeboard.

'Sorry!' Will says. He unbuttons his jacket, which looks a little too tight. 'I forgot you two hadn't met. This is Sebastian, my little bro. Seb, this is Geri, Dan's *much* better half.' He looks at Dan. 'You remember Seb, don't you?'

'Yeah, of course.' Gazing for a moment, Dan takes in Seb's sharp cheekbones and shock of brown hair. Bloody hell, time flies. The fair-haired slender youth's now a broad handsome man. He shakes his hand. 'Long time, though. The swimmer!'

'Yup, that's me. Shall we go in?'

Though the church is dank and cold, a surge of heat sweeps Dan's chest. The empty silence is broken by the echo of their heels and muffled barking from outside. Will strides noisily ahead, lowering his body by the knee at the altar and making the sign of the cross with a flourish. He looks back with a grin. Seb follows with Dan bringing up the rear, shaking his head, but smiling.

Thrown back to the *pretty boy with dark curls in a cassock,*

7

Dan listens absently to the two brothers banter for a while. When his racing heart finally steadies, he joins Geri and Penny.

Penny is taking off her thin coat and folding it carefully on her lap. 'So I feel the benefit, as my mum always says,' she says quietly. 'And mums are generally right about everything, aren't they?' she adds with a small smile.

Geri laughs brightly. 'Heard that one too. I'll be saying it soon! God, Penny, you're so slim. You make me look like an elephant. It would've been nice to splash out on a new outfit, but there isn't much point until this little monster makes an appearance.' She holds out a patent-clad foot. 'I bought shoes to die for, though. Now, they are compulsory for a wedding! Dan loves them, don't you, Dan?'

'Yup, guilty as charged.'

The hum of conversation around them increases, but they lapse into silence, turning each time a blast of moist air alerts them to a new guest's arrival.

'He's very dishy,' Geri eventually comments, nodding towards Seb. 'Your brother-in-law. Sebastian, is it? He'll make Nick look bite-size! Surely he's spoken for?'

Penny doesn't answer, her large eyes are glassy and far away. Then she turns to Geri with a small jerk. 'Oh, sorry, no, they've just split up. She's French.'

'French, eh?' Dan says with a grin. 'I'd better find out more.'

Shaking himself back to today, Dan returns to the chancel step. Standing next to Will, he studies the damp people slowly filling the church. His gaze catches the photographer. Almost invisible, he's taking snaps of the guests, some standing in groups, wearing heels and hats, hushing greetings and discussing the rain, he supposes, others hitching along the wooden pews and studying the Order of Service as they wait for a familiar face. His eyes rest on Seb Taylor sitting on the front bench. His arms are folded, his long legs stretched out. He's looking back at him through striking blue eyes.

'So, you remember the swimming at St Mark's?' he asks.

Dan feels himself flushing from the intensity of Seb's gaze. 'Not much,' he says with a small laugh. 'The disgusting pool mainly. Full of urine, sweat and sh—' Bloody hell, he's sounding like his dad. 'Other things one doesn't like to dwell on!' Seb's stare is still steady, as though reading his mind. 'Yeah, and those grubby changing rooms; no wonder everyone dived in the showers so quickly, bloody freezing in there and—'

But he's saved from his blather by a slap on his shoulder and Will's deep voice. 'Bloody hell, look at the time. No priest! We'll be relying on you to don your little cassock, Dan.' He looks at the door and laughs. 'And where's the bloody groom? His mum isn't here either. We'll know who to blame if Nick's done a runner.'

CHAPTER TWO

Nick

Staring at the ribbon caught up in the windscreen wipers, Nick Quinn taps his foot. Patrick has decorated the vintage Mercedes; white ribbon on the bonnet and bumper, silk flowers on the dashboard. The handsome car was bought new by their father years ago and passed to Patrick on his eighteenth birthday. He frowns, sure he remembers his dad handing over the keys, though with the fifteen-year age gap, he'd have only been three.

'Why don't we hire a car for you and your family like everyone else does?' Lisa asked when they started their wedding plans.

'Oh, it's family tradition,' he replied with a shrug. 'The Merc is pristine. It'll look great.'

But it's Patrick's lore really. He doesn't like change. 'But we always have a turkey roast at Easter!' he'll say if their mum suggests something new.

As Patrick negotiates the sodden streets of Aberystwyth, Nick glances at his brother's greying hair, wondering how he'll cope this Easter if he isn't there. Christmas too. If he's at Lisa's family house in Wales. Or just him and Lisa at their own home. The thought of letting Patrick down makes him hot. His older brother has always been there, like a sentinel, with his peculiar and tender love.

The traffic is thick; it's still raining heavily. Nick goes to touch the small scar on his scalp, but stops just in time before messing his hair. He's surprised the caught ribbon hasn't perturbed Patrick, a lot less often does; a speck of mud on his tyres, let alone on the mats. Thank God it hasn't; they're already running late after a shrill spat between his parents, then turning back for his dad's reading glasses.

Finally arriving in the drenched car park, Nick spots Dan and Will's cars parked together like kippers. Feeling a warm spread of comfort, he jumps from the car, flicks open an umbrella and opens his mum's door. She slips out, neat and trim in her hat and tailored suit, and smiles reassuringly. Patrick does the same for their scowling father, but at a much slower pace. Harry's hip replacement was a complete success according to the consultant, but he still struggles. 'He's got a new hip. He needs to use it,' his mum says. But only in private.

The rain splattering his polished shoes, Nick walks briskly up the path towards the stone and cream church.

'Are you nervous, love?' his mum asks, tightly holding his arm. 'Big day. *Your* big day. Exciting but nerve-wracking at the same time.' At the door she pats the rain from his shoulders and kisses his cheek. 'You look very handsome. You make me so proud.'

Similar to the words she used on his first day at school, he tries to answer with a mildly sardonic quip, but finds that he can't. It's as though the soft, steady smell of her perfume is stuck in his throat. Instead he focuses on the door, pushing it hard and almost colliding with the priest.

'Sorry,' he says. 'Nearly knocked you over, Father.'

Father Garry turns. 'Just wiping my feet.' He shakes Nick's

hand and Patrick's, then his mother and father's. 'Welcome . . . Welcome all,' he says, his eyes pale and rheumy.

Glancing at his mum, he's not sure what to say. Father Garry has clearly forgotten their names, though the tense wedding run-through was only last night.

'Nicholas the groom; Harry, Patrick and Dora Quinn,' she says clearly. Then another guest arrives, bringing a fresh burst of rain. 'You go ahead, love,' she says to him. 'Your best men will be waiting.'

Dan and Will are standing at the front, chatting to Seb. Striding towards them, Nick feels the rush of release as they grin. Dan, black-haired and handsome in his cravat and his tails, makes a show of looking at his watch. Will puts his top hat on his broad chest, miming a dance.

When he reaches the transept, Dan cocks his head, his eyes dark and watchful. 'Everything OK, Nick? Feeling ready?'

'Yeah, apart from the monsoon, a divorce over Dad's glasses and the priest having dementia, everything's fine. Bloody hell, this is scary—'

'Piece of piss,' Will says, grabbing him firmly by the shoulders. 'Saying the vows is the easy bit. Wait until you're twelve months into the life sentence.' He looks at Nick's expression and laughs. 'Only kidding, mate; everything will be fine and Lisa's a smasher.'

Watching the priest light the candles, Nick tries to loosen the breath which feels jammed in his lungs. Coming back to the conversation, he turns to Seb Taylor. He's studying Dan with a mild frown. After a few moments he speaks. 'So, not just one best man, but two,' he says, nodding to his older brother.

'What I lack in hair, Dan makes up for in eyebrows,' Will replies with a grin.

'Had them blow-dried especially,' Dan quips. 'Thing is, Seb, everyone knows that *I'm* the best man. Batman's Robin—'

Will pulls a droll face. 'More like The Joker—'

Nick interrupts, the trapped air bursting out as he laughs. 'I couldn't choose. But with the grief that I'm getting from these two, I should've spread the net wider. In fact, seeing as you're here, Seb—'

'Hurtful,' Dan says with a mock-sad face. 'Don't you think so, Will?'

'Yeah, Dan.' He puts his fist on his chest. 'Gets me just here. Maybe we should leave.'

Listening to their wisecracks, Nick's heart finally slows. His mum's perfume has gone, replaced by a dank smell of old paper and wet clothes. He tunes into the low hum of conversation and turns to his guests. His parents and Patrick have settled in their places on the front right pew, Uncle Derek and Auntie Iris immediately behind them. Not actual family, but almost. His dad and Derek have been friends since school. Like him, Dan and Will, the 'A Team' as his mum always called them. Not forgetting Jen; honorary sister-cum-protector pal, all-round good egg.

Suddenly remembering it's his day, he lifts his hand towards friends, mates from school and university and work, who wave back, giving thumbs-up and grins. Lisa's Swansea contingent, he supposes, are the dozen or so chatty faces on the left, and there's a choir of five grey parishioners in pews to one side. A row of differently coloured umbrellas are drying at the back of the church, making small pools of water on the floor. They slightly lift each time the door opens, as though they're breathing.

Surprised Jen hasn't arrived yet, his attention returns to his best men. They've moved onto nurses' uniforms and big breasts, the usual when they rib him about Lisa. 'He was looking for nympho nurse porn but accidentally found a wife,' Will is saying to his brother. Nick smiles, thankful for his friends, their steadiness and their laughter. At a sudden rush of sound, he turns again, but it's another two pearly parishioners noisily removing their wet coats. The umbrellas relax, like a false start, before lifting their ribs again, but it isn't his bride or her taciturn chunky brothers.

Catching his mum's soft smile, he nods and looks away. The imperative is there, clenched in his jaw. As much as he loves her, he has to break free, has to do it today. Glancing again at the entrance, a thought suddenly hits him. Suppose Lisa doesn't come? Bloody hell. Suppose she changes her mind? What then?

CHAPTER THREE

Jen

'The sea, Daddy! The sea.'

Though the grey ocean merges with the dirty sky, Anna has spotted it from the back seat of the Kenning family car.

Ian glances at the clock, then takes a left turn towards the seafront. 'Let's take a quick look,' he replies.

'Oh God, we're going to be late,' Maria groans loudly.

Jen counts to five, then tries for her even voice. 'No we're not; and don't say *God*, Maria, you're only thirteen, not thirty.'

'We're always late and it's *so* embarrassing. If it was me—'

'Enough, Maria,' Ian interrupts from the driver's seat. 'It's Nick and Lisa's wedding day. Mum's school friends will be there, so let's try to be happy and have fun. OK, love? We're nearly there now. Just enough time to see the waves. See how they crash against the promenade.'

Jen glances at her husband. 'Think someone came to Aberystwyth as a boy,' she comments dryly. Maria is right; they will be late, but there's no use arguing. Though mostly easy-going, when Ian's mind is set, it's best to follow his lead. And besides, Maria and Holly's windows are already down, the wind buffeting their neat wedding hair.

'Tastes of fish,' Holly says, licking her lips. 'Your go, Anna.'

Anna climbs onto Holly's knee and hangs out of the window, returning after a few seconds with more than wet lips.

'OK, enough now. Seat belts back on,' Jen says, trying not to think of how long it took to plait, curl and straighten three sets of hair, but quietly pleased their diversion has thrown the smug satnav. When it finally rallies and they arrive at the church, the bridal limousine has just beaten them into the car park.

'Don't worry,' Ian grins, looking at Jen. 'You took ages to get out of the wedding car. You needed a crane, if I remember.'

'Cheeky sod,' she replies. 'You weren't even there. You were in the church longing for your beautiful bride to appear. It was the hoops at the bottom of the dress, actually. They took some manoeuvring. But you're right; Lisa won't be jumping out of the car and into this horrible weather without a million umbrellas. Park up and we'll sneak in ahead.'

Finally settled in their pew, Jen lifts her hand to Penny and Geri across the aisle, conscious that her windswept girls have accidentally sat on the bride's side.

'Why is Penny staring and who is that fat woman sitting next to her?' Anna asks from under the brim of her hat.

'She's not fat, she's pregnant, Anna. That's Geri, Dan's girl-friend. You've met her before. And keep your voice down, love.'

Her eight-year-old studies Geri for a few moments before turning back. 'She's not as handsome as Dan, but I like her hat. What colour will the baby be?' she whispers.

'A beautiful colour,' Jen replies. She leans forward to study Holly who's predictably sitting next to her dad and peering at his mobile. 'Are you all right now? Feeling better?'

Despite the fishy shower, she thinks her middle daughter looks pale. The girls had a puking virus which lasted two days, but Holly was sick again after breakfast, or so she said. Jen dashed up to the bathroom, but the toilet had been flushed, the only sign of vomit being a large wet patch on the front of the pretty satin dress Holly didn't like. She didn't quite get her wish to sport trousers, preferably jeans, but the dress she's wearing is far from the floaty creation Jen had wanted all three to wear.

'Struggling with puberty, poor lamb,' her mum says of Holly, but Jen wouldn't know. When she was twelve, she'd just started at St Mark's. She loved growing up and all that went with it, especially the attention from the A Team boys. 'The honorary boy,' Nick's mum used to describe her. 'Yeah, one with tits,' Dan, Will or Nick would quietly snigger.

The sudden rich peal of Mendelssohn interrupts her fond memories. Ian rises and takes her hand. 'Here we go, love. Got the tissues ready?' he asks with a grin.

'Cheeky sod,' she replies, smiling. But she catches Holly's slender arms as she stands. Not just the vomiting, she's spider-thin too. The sick bug, of course, the virus.

Shaking her head, she turns to the doors. Nothing to worry about. Nothing at all. Just a routine illness.

Surely?

CHAPTER FOUR

Dan

Will throws back his champagne. 'Rain's stopped; everyone smiling. All's well that ends well.' He slaps Dan on the back. 'I'll get us a top-up. Not so bad, eh? This wedding malarkey. Mark my words, you'll give in like the rest of us poor bloody . . .' But abruptly he stops and turns around with a frown. 'Was that . . . ? Did you hear that?'

Dan turns too. Two women in work uniforms are pointing to the main hotel building, their faces aghast.

'Oh my God, look! There's someone at that window. Oh my God, quick, someone help! I think she's going to jump!' one of them shouts.

Snapping his head to the scene, Dan stares. What the fuck? What the hell? Dressed only in her underwear, Penny Taylor is standing on the window ledge, her pale body and buffeted blonde hair framed like Botticelli's Venus. He gazes for a moment before adrenaline kicks in. Will is just gawping, clearly gobsmacked. Grabbing him by the shirtsleeve, Dan propels him towards the hotel door. 'Will, move! Now, Will, go now. I'll be right behind you.'

His body tingling with energy, but his mind strangely detached, Dan scans the scene. Lisa and Nick are turned away in a group with her dad and his parents, listening to the photographer's instructions. Two of Jen's kids are watching the newly-weds and not Penny, thank God. And Will's jacket, he's still holding it; the key card is there in the pocket. Grasping Geri on the way, he spins her to the window. 'Look, it's Penny,' he says quietly. 'Tell those bloody women to go in without making a fuss. Tell them everything's in hand. I'm following Will.'

The grass squelchy under his feet, he sprints to the hotel, the thought of the A Team school relays stupidly popping into his head. As he bursts through the door, the lift closes on Will, so he opens the fire door and belts up the stairs two by two, the urgency pounding in his ears but his mind still clinical: the third floor, two doors down from theirs. He has the key. Catch up with Will. Tell him to be calm; warn Will not to lose it.

He fires through the exit, but Will is already there, thumping the door with his fist. 'Penny? Answer the door. Answer the bloody door!'

Handing Will the key, Dan lifts his finger to his lips and shakes his head.

Will takes the card and with a trembling hand he swipes and swipes again. 'It's not working.' He tries once more. 'It's not fucking working!'

Dan takes it from him. 'Here, let me try.'

Fuck, Will is right. The key card doesn't work. Time is the thing. He doesn't want to alarm Penny, but she could jump. Fucking jump!

Staring at the woodwork, he remembers what his dad said about the *sweet spot* to bust open a door. Without thinking about it too deeply, he steps back, lifts his leg, and with as much momentum as he can muster, he drives the heel of his foot towards the lock. With a sickening noise the wood cracks and splinters. Kicking again, then again, the door ricochets open.

Time slows as he takes in the picture. The window is gaping, the curtains flapping in the breeze. But Penny is still there, thank God. Her narrow back towards them, she's gazing at the trees, lightly swaying and humming a tune.

Dan lets out his breath. She's sitting now; she's sitting on the ledge. Though not looking at Will, he instinctively grabs his arm. 'Easy, Will. Take it easy.'

Will clears his throat. 'Penny? Pen? Are you coming in?' he asks, moving slowly towards her.

Penny turns, surprise flashing on her face. 'Oh, Will! I wanted to tell you something.' Her forehead furrows, as though trying to remember.

His face pale and sweaty, Will's voice is hoarse. His fear is palpable; Dan can *feel* it. 'Just come in, Penny.'

'In a minute, let me show you . . .' Pushing down her skinny arms on the sill, she draws up her legs to stand.

Will steps forward, raising his arms. 'For God's sake, Penny, please just . . .'

But she's already standing. Then suddenly she's wobbling, her arms flailing like small propellers.

Dan dives. Like a rugby tackle, he lunges forward, holding out his hands to grab Penny's legs, or her waist, anything, please God, other than thin air.

CHAPTER FIVE

Nick

The first test, *for better or for worse.*

Nick gazes at the polite polished faces of his guests. A plastic bubble, he thinks. That's how it feels; he can still smell the tang of roast beef and hear his new father-in-law's heavily accented voice, but they're muffled by his thoughts.

He tries to shake himself back to his wedding dinner. The dessert bowls have been cleared and the champagne flutes refilled. Friends and family have turned their chairs, they're listening and smiling. He knows there's eight tables, but he counts them, rehearsing each label: 'St Mark's' for the school crowd, 'Leeds' for uni, 'Swansea' for the noisy Welsh, or 'the coven' as Lisa calls them . . .

His mind drifts to her prolific wedding lists and he smiles a small shaky smile. The handwritten plaques were her idea, pretty much everything else too. She was their clever wedding planner; centring every table with a potted flowering plant, rather than cut flowers, so that they'd last; lovingly decorating each invitation, each envelope; choosing the menu, the hymns and the flowers. Even the men's suits, their patterned waistcoats and plain cravats.

But no one can plan everything.

A *blip*. That's what Dan called it. 'It's only a blip, mate,' he said when he came back from Will's room. 'Will has to go home with Penny, but don't worry, leave everything with me.'

His heart thrashes. Dan caught Penny just in time. Only just in time! Moments later and she could've been dead. Bloody hell! A fucking vast blip in his regular safe life.

Feeling for Lisa's fingers under the stiff tablecloth, he tunes into her father's words. His hair is black and oiled and he speaks for some time: his birthplace of Swansea, which raises a loud cheer from his plethora of sisters; his meeting with Lisa's mum at a church dance; moving to her home town of Prestatyn; having two burly boys before his beautiful baby daughter. He says Nick will find out, if he hasn't already, that his girl is 'a bossy little Miss, a bossy little *Mrs* now, but only in a good way, men need to be told'.

As the coven make another whoop, he squeezes his new wife's hand. She turns towards him and her green eyes are shiny. He's only known her for thirteen months, but he knows without a doubt she's still grieving for her mum. He hopes Lisa and his own mum will become close, but senses a frostiness between them. 'Your mum only had boys,' Lisa says. 'Of course she's indulgent with you and Patrick, but I don't think she knows how to relax. It's different between mothers and daughters.'

He didn't recognise Lisa's description, but looking at his mum now, he can understand her mistake. Straight-backed and small, she looks timid and tense, but underneath she's quite steely. Once Will and Penny had left, she took him aside. 'It's your day, love, yours and Lisa's. No point dwelling on it, you need to put it behind you. Most people didn't notice. Forget it and enjoy yourselves.'

Though he knew his mum's words were partially a white lie, he found Lisa hiding in the ladies' and repeated them. 'It's our day, Lisa. Hardly anyone saw. We're going to put this behind us. Yes?' Looking into her tearful face, willing her to agree.

It felt like the first test, *for better or for worse*.

The guests bang the tables as Dan stands for his speech. He takes off his jacket, rolls up his shirtsleeves and loosens his cravat. Pausing for a moment, he looks around the room, then lifts his dark eyebrows and clears his throat. 'Mr and Mrs Quinn,' he says. '. . . Senior. A few words to the wise before I start. Perhaps now would be a good time to leave . . .'

There's laughter and a loud cheer. 'Dish the dirt, Dan,' a pal from university shouts.

That's it, Nick thinks, trauma over. Please God, let that be it. Please put my regular and safe life back on track.

Yet still his heart races.

CHAPTER SIX

Jen

Jen picks up the 'St Mark's' place card and studies it for a while. Though the music is blaring and people are milling and chatting near their table, she can't hear anything except the clatter of her heart. It has been racing since looking up to see Penny's pallid face at the window, and even self-medicating with champagne hasn't helped. They've been joined by Dan from the top table and though usually calm, he's agitated too, repeating himself like a record stuck in a groove. He's been brilliant all day, hurtling with Will to deal with Penny, then taking on the role as the only best man at the meal with aplomb, but it's as though the trauma has only recently set and is playing on a loop.

He's shaking his dark head. 'At a wedding of all places. I can't believe Penny did that,' he says again. Frowning, he turns to Geri. 'She was humming when we got there, but after getting her to safety, she behaved as though everything was normal. Saying she had to dress and brush her hair, check her face in the mirror. Bizarre. Did she say anything to you in the church?'

'No, I've already said, Dan, she seemed normal. Well, quiet, but she's generally pretty quiet, isn't she?' Tapping a painted fingernail on her lips, Geri frowns. 'God, it was only a few hours ago and it's already hard to remember.' Closing her eyes, she starts to describe Penny's movements, but Jen drifts, the batter of her heart still loud in her ears. She tunes in again when Geri mentions Will's name. 'She was there when Will was fooling with your girls. It was funny to see them swallowed up by his wedding tails, then racing away. Poor Holly being lugged back under his arm like a sack of potatoes did make me laugh.' For a moment she looks startled. 'God, did I really laugh and say it was one of those joyous moments everyone remembers? I looked for Penny then and she was walking inside. Then, I don't know . . . the confetti shot?'

'Bloody unbelievable,' Jen says, her thoughts popping out as words. 'I wonder what was going on in her head.'

Turning to the dance floor, she absently watches her daughters. They didn't see Penny at the window, thank God. At least she doesn't think so. Geri guided Holly and Maria inside before anyone noticed and she was on the way to clean Anna's shoes in the ladies', so she was carrying her.

She sighs. One of life's shocking turns; unexpected change in an instant. Her worries about Holly seem silly now. And besides, she looks fine. Her pretty face is flushed and she's even laughing with Maria. Dancing and music; the two things they have in common.

The only two things.

Still finding it impossible to fully absorb what's happened and shape how she feels, she glances at her watch. Bloody hell, look at the time! Enough theorising about Penny, it's time now to focus. Pinning her hair behind her ears, she turns to Ian. 'When should we take the girls up to the room?' she asks. 'It's getting late.'

He looks up from his mobile. 'Another ten minutes? I'll give them a warning.' Putting his hand on her arm, he squeezes gently. 'You stay and chat. There's no need for us both. I'll put them to bed and catch the end of *Match of the Day*.'

'Thanks, love, you're a star.'

With a surge of affection, she smiles as her husband threads his way to their girls, his red hair flashed green by the neon lights. She observes for a few moments as he negotiates their departure. Her daughters' faces go from truculent to defeated, from nodding to broad smiles. Bribery, she thinks, it's the secret of parenting and works every time: money for Maria, football stickers for Holly and swimming tomorrow morning for Anna, she guesses. Of course Ian wants to escape to watch the football highlights and review the day's scores, but he's still a bloody star.

She turns back to the table; Geri is studying her nails, Seb and Dan drinking in silence. She puts her glass to her mouth, then realises it's empty. The speculation storms back. What the hell happened today? What was going on in Penny's mind? She seemed fine for the photographs at the church. They stood together, chatting about the girls as usual, and she asked Penny if she was reminded of her big day. She was outside the hotel too, wasn't she, when Will was larking around? Was that when she caught the puzzled look on his face, when he asked if she knew where Penny had gone?

Leaning towards Seb, she studies him for a moment, wondering how he's feeling. Worried for his big brother, she supposes. She knew him so well as a boy, but she hardly knows the man. His intense eyes seem focused on Dan and there's a small frown she can just see beneath his long fringe.

'Hey, Sebi. Any word from Will?'

He turns his head sharply, looking startled. 'No, not much. Just a text to say they're home.'

26

She sits back again, the palpitations still there. 'What do you think he'll do? He can't just do nothing.'

The words emerge louder than she intends, but no one has a reply. Then Seb seems to rouse himself. 'I bought a couple of bottles of brandy for Nick. Good stuff. Think we're bringing down the tone sitting here looking miserable. How about we polish one off in my room?'

'A brilliant idea. You're a bloody star, Sebi,' she declares, standing. She grabs Geri's hand. 'Come on, pregnant lady. You can be my chaperone.'

Vertical, she sways. God knows how much she's already drunk, but she can't *feel* it yet. She pictures Penny on the window ledge, so pale and so thin, wearing only her nude-coloured underwear. Drinking more is the thing. She'll need the anaesthetic tonight.

CHAPTER SEVEN

Dan

Trying to block out thoughts of his bizarre mission earlier, Dan piles from the lift with Seb, Geri and Jen. Though unsteady on her feet, Jen takes the room key off Seb and opens the door. Almost holding his breath, he watches her close the sash window. Then she piles cushions behind Geri's back, throws off her shoes and curls her plump legs under her bum as though the bedroom is hers.

Not sure where to sit, he takes the regency armchair and Seb sits opposite, his fringe flopping forwards as he pours brandy into glasses purloined from the bar.

'I know I shouldn't,' Geri says, inhaling the honey-coloured liquid before sipping. 'But this smells so expensive that a small taster won't hurt.'

Jen's grin shows the dimples on her affable face. 'Double for me.' Tucking her dark bob behind her ears, she looks pensive. 'I wonder how Will is. Nick and Lisa too. The wedding planner had anticipated rain, I'm sure, but *that* must have been a surprise.'

Dan swirls his brandy, the prickle of amazement still there.

'Shock, you mean. Thank God we were outside. I still can't believe she did it. At a wedding of all—'

'Change the record, Dan,' Jen snorts. 'We're all pretty stunned. It's not every day—'

'Stop, for God's sake, just stop!'

They all turn to Seb. There's a crack in his voice and he's glaring at Jen. 'You seem to be forgetting about Penny. How *she* must be feeling.' He rakes back his hair. 'Can any of us imagine? To do something so extreme. In public too.' He puts down the bottle and pinches the top of his nose.

Dan stares, astonished. Seb had seemed so passive up to now, but his features look broken.

A burst of guilt spreading, he drops his gaze quickly. Penny has only been married to Will for a year or so, but of course she's still Seb's sister-in-law. Feeling he's seen that shattered look before, he automatically stands and puts a hand on Seb's shoulder. A memory from long ago surfaces, replaced moments later by Penny's pale face, her strangely glazed eyes. Thrown back to the sensation of freezing flesh in his arms, he abruptly pulls back, his heart galloping. 'You're right, Seb. I can't imagine.'

With difficulty, Geri sits forward and stretches her fingers towards Seb. 'We're all with you there, Seb. I guess it's just so surreal. You're right, absolutely, poor Penny.'

'Sorry, Sebi.' Jen climbs off the bed and though so much shorter than him, she manages to fold him in her arms. 'Me and my big mouth. You know what I'm like. Of course I'm worried about Penny too. We all are.'

The four of them change the subject eventually, even manage a laugh as the brandy is poured and time drifts.

'You did a great speech, Dan,' Seb says, sitting forward. 'Really funny. I thought Nick's mum might faint, though. "What happened in Amsterdam should stay in Amsterdam. *However* . . ." You should have seen her startled face; I doubt she's previously heard of a ladyboy.'

Dan lifts his glass. 'Cheers, Seb. I was pretty nervous. You know, without my straight man. Had to improvise.'

Geri stands and yawns. 'God, I'm shattered,' she says. 'I need my bed.' She pecks Dan on his cheek. 'You stay and enjoy that delicious brandy while the going's good. Try not to wake me when you get back.' She pats her stomach. 'One lot of kicking is enough!'

Catching her hand, he squeezes and smiles. 'Quiet as a . . . goldfish, I promise!'

'Night, Geri,' Jen mumbles as the door clicks to. 'I'm closing my eyes but I'm not asleep.'

Dan lifts his legs, stretching them onto the bed. The dent left by Geri's body is still warm. He briefly wonders what life will be like when two becomes three, before parrying the thought and turning to Seb. 'So, where are you living now, Seb?' he asks, holding out his tumbler for a refill. 'You were probably ten when I last saw you.'

'Thirteen. Swimming gala.'

'Of course.' Dan pictures the boy clutching his bronze medal, his face broken. He pushes the uncomfortable image away. 'Did you keep it up, the swimming?'

Seb rocks his head and stares at the ceiling. 'For a while. All good things come to an end though.' Then after a moment, 'I'm living back home in Withington with my mum, just for now. I was living in France with—'

He's interrupted by a knock at the door. It's Ian Kenning, his pale ginger hair sticking out on one side. 'I've come for my wife . . . Ah.' He laughs, looking at the bed. 'As I suspected! Ready to go, love?' He picks up Jen's shoes, pulls her gently to her feet and guides her from the room, her eyes almost closed.

Clearly too gone, Jen doesn't speak. 'See you tomorrow at the walk,' Ian says, closing the door behind him.

Seb pulls off his shoes and socks, then his waistcoat and cravat and lies in Jen's place. He puts his arms behind his head. 'The funny thing is that I can't work out if I dumped her or if she dumped me. Claudia,' he adds. 'Fucking beautiful, hot-tempered, impossible.'

Dan laughs. 'Not all bad, then.'

'Fantastic sex. Course that's what I'm remembering. Not the tantrums, the viciousness, the lack of support. She's a cunt, Dan. I just need to remember it.'

'Fair enough.' Dan stretches his arms, still feeling the muscular pull from yesterday's brutal game of squash with Will. Or perhaps from his fall backwards earlier, his best friend's wife like a cold mannequin on top. Surreal. He really needs a piss but his legs seem paralysed by brandy, though his head feels surprisingly fine. 'Sex?' he says after a moment. 'What's that then?'

Seb looks at him and smiles. 'Timing,' he says.

'What, with women?'

'No, your jokes. You have good timing.'

'Like the swimming,' Dan replies, thinking how different Seb looks when he smiles. From chiselled moody to an easy white grin in an instant.

They chat about sport for a while, Dan remembering Seb was a great sportsman at school. Like the A Team at St Mark's, each sport came easily, though swimming was his forte. He had a place at the University of Edinburgh to read Biomedicine, but his father died unexpectedly.

'I'm beat,' Seb says abruptly. Scraping his hair from his forehead, he stands. 'I need sleep.' He heads for the bathroom. 'Kip here if you want.'

Absently stroking the dark stubble already appearing on his chin, Dan nods. I'll go in a minute, he thinks, closing his eyes. When he opens them again, Seb's back in the room, rubbing his angular face with a towel. Broad shoulders, hairless toned chest, he's just wearing briefs. Swimmer turned model, he now remembers, his mind far too sluggish. Of course Will had mentioned it. But things had gone sour, hadn't they?

Trying to remember the story, he gazes at Seb, then pulls his legs off the bed. 'I'll just have a piss and then go.'

In the bathroom, he puts a hand against the wall to steady himself. The pee doesn't come for a while. Then he stands at the sink, drinking water, briefly catching his tousled hair in the mirror, which he rakes into place.

The room is dim when he returns. The glow from a bedside lamp accentuates Seb's sculpted face. He props his head on his hand and gazes at Dan languidly. 'Do you want to stay?' he asks. The sheets are pulled away and he's naked; his long limbs and tight torso are bathed in soft light.

Dan's impulse to make a joke is overridden by outrage. 'What the fuck? You've got this all wrong.' Backing away from the bed, he grabs his jacket, then points a finger at Seb. 'Totally fucking wrong. Do you hear me?'

His fringe falling forward, Seb sits. For a moment he stares, then shrugs and falls back. 'Whatever,' he says, pulling up the crisp sheet and turning onto his side.

CHAPTER EIGHT

Nick

The tension finally squeezed from his face, his limbs, his whole bloody body, Nick winds his way around the balmy room, chatting to university friends and their partners, to people from work, to his aunties and uncles and cousins on his dad's side. Everyone offers him a drink, but there doesn't seem to be time to accept. The evening has rushed by; he and Lisa stayed close at first, holding hands tightly as they greeted their guests. Then the coven descended and Lisa was whisked away, enveloped in their noisy cachinnations at one end of the room. He hasn't spoken to her since their first dance, but every now and then he watches for a few moments, taking in her laughter and friendly grin as she chats to the guests, still incredulous that the smiley girl he first saw on a dating site is now his wife. There was always a sense of something missing from his life, but that void has been filled like a foot in a snug-fitting trainer. The feeling of possession surprises him. 'She's mine,' he says inwardly. 'She belongs to me now.'

He approaches his godparents. 'Sorry it's taken so long to say hello. Exhausting, this groom business,' he says with a smile.

Uncle Derek stands. 'Let me get you a drink,' he says. 'You

can't be at your own wedding without a glass in your hand. What would you like, son?'

'Pint of lager would be good,' he replies, suddenly realising how thirsty he is. He takes Derek's seat and turns to Iris. Although now into her seventies, her features are pretty and petite, and with her softly curled hair she looks much younger. But her knuckles show her age as she clutches his hand.

Her eyes shine and she beams. 'Hello, lovey. Don't you look handsome. You and Lisa make such a beautiful couple. We're as proud as punch.' She digs into her handbag and pulls out a horseshoe-shaped trinket. 'Course we've got you a proper present and a nice large cheque from Derek, but here, love. It's for good luck. Remember to keep it upright.' She slips it into his pocket. 'Matt and Jamie send their love and congratulations.'

'Thanks, Iris. How are they both doing? How many grand-children is it now? I think Mum said five at the last count.'

They chat for a few minutes about her sons and their chil-dren. 'What's she called again? Jamie's wife?' Iris asks, sliding her hand into his.

Startled by the question, Nick has to think back to informa-tion gleaned from his mum. The younger son Jamie had married again, but what was her name? 'Judith? Jude?' he asks.

'No, the other wife. The one who kept our Jamie too far from home. He wanted to come back from Bristol, but she wouldn't let him. That one.'

Ruffling his hair, he tries to remember the name of Jamie's first wife, but Iris appears to have lost interest. She's nodding towards Patrick, sitting apart from Lisa's brothers who're prop-ping up the bar. 'We need to find someone for Patrick now. But I don't know who'd take him on at nearly fifty. Even when he was little and played with my boys he was a funny little bugger.'

34

The description takes Nick by surprise, but as he looks into Iris's bright eyes, he realises she's tipsy, very tipsy.

'He'd have these uncontrollable tantrums over nothing and the only person who could bring him round was your Susan,' she continues. 'She just had a way with him, even though she was so much smaller. He's talking to someone now, mind. They say people often meet a new love at a wedding. Wouldn't that be nice?'

Nick turns to look at his brother, then comes back to his godmother's peachy face. 'Sorry, you've lost me. Who is Susan?' he asks. But her shining eyes have moved to her husband. He's standing behind Nick, holding two pints of beer and a glass of wine in his hands.

'Can you take this wine off me before I drop it, son?' he says to Nick. And then to Iris: 'Harry is sitting over there on his tod. We can't have that on his son's wedding day. Shall we walk over and join him?'

Nick watches Derek and Iris wander off. Then he stands alone for a few moments, sipping his pint and glancing around. A girl from uni and a lad from work are smooching on the dance floor to 'I'm not in Love'. The disc jockey is packing up, the St Mark's table is empty, the number of guests has worn thin. The coven have stopped dancing and they've joined Lisa's brothers at the bar.

His drink almost spilling, Lisa catches him around the waist from behind. 'It's OK, we can go now. They'll be here all night.' Her voice is slurred and he realises that although he's completely sober, he's more tired and achy than he's ever felt before. But he's married now, he's done it! He's finally broken free; he has a perfect-fit-trainer lovely wife.

They bid goodnight to the Swansea clan. Lisa's father says a few words in his ear. Of advice, he supposes, he can't decipher a word. But at least his new father-in-law laughs, unlike the bouncer brothers who stare at him steadily from their whisky tumblers as though they haven't drunk a drop.

'Push them with a little finger and they'll both fall off their perches,' Lisa whispers, reading his thoughts. She holds out her hand. 'Come on, husband. Time for bed.'

As she stops to negotiate the short flight of stairs to the bridal suite, Lisa wobbles. Feeling a surge of emotion, Nick collects her gown from behind and steadies her by the waist. It's their first few moments completely alone as man and wife and he wants to freeze-frame them: the feel of the crisp silk in his hands, the innocence of her small stockinged feet on the carpet, the whispery curls of hair on the nape of her neck, the sleepy smile on her contented face.

Perfumed by a huge bouquet of white flowers, the warm room feels foreign when they go in. The lights are muted, the soft linen turned back.

'Can you help me with my dress, dearest hubby?' Lisa asks.

He fumbles with the tiny buttons as she chats. She's happy, her voice drowsy, and he's glad, relieved the blip hasn't spoiled her special day.

'I would like to consummate our marriage,' she's saying, struggling with her words. 'But I'm too pissed. As Dylan said, "Someone's boring me. I think it's me". Thomas, not Bob,' she mutters, before collapsing onto the bed, still wearing something old and something new.

Turning to his wedding tails, Nick slips his hand in the pocket and pulls out the silver horseshoe trinket. Keeping it upright, he traces the engraved names with his finger. Good luck for him and Lisa, he thinks with a smile. A little naff, but sweet of Iris. Then, with a frown as he pictures her face: but who the hell is Susan?

CHAPTER NINE

Dan

Dan is splayed on his stomach in the rumpled bed.

'Dan,' Geri rocks him gently. 'Don't forget it's the walk.'

'Shit.' He sits upright. Then holds his head. 'Shit.'

'So the expensive stuff still gives you a hangover.' Geri smiles. 'My wee dram tasted lovely, though. I can't wait until I can drink what I like, eat what I like, sleep all night.'

'Thank God I drank water before bed.' The image of Seb Taylor hits him, followed moments later with a thought: perhaps I misread it. He turns to Geri. 'Is it raining?'

'No, it's lovely. At *breakfast* it was lovely.' She pulls back the heavy curtains, revealing a glint of sunshine on the bare branches of the trees. 'See?'

'Sorry. Was breakfast nice?'

'Smoked salmon and scrambled eggs. I sat with Ian and the girls. No one else was there at first. Oh, except Nick's brother. Patrick, is he called? A little . . . strange? Then that older couple appeared. The man who has a genuine Teddy boy quiff? His godparents, I think.'

'Yeah, Nick's rich Uncle Derek.' He takes Geri's hand, pulls her down onto the bed and gently rests his head on her belly. 'Sounds like you were given an early call. Naughty boy.'

'Or girl.'

'Or girl. Can't wait either way.'

'I might give the walk a miss, Dan. I could do with closing my eyes and trying for a nap. Do you mind?'

Dan shakes his head. Sees Seb Taylor's naked body. 'Maybe I should stay with you.'

'You can't miss the walk! Think of Nick and Lisa, trying to get back on track, wiping out the blip of yesterday.'

Those Renaissance blank eyes bring him back. 'Bloody hell, what a blip. Incredible.'

'True.' Geri looks at her watch. 'Come on, Dan. Shave, shit and shower. In whichever order is the fastest. The walk starts in twenty minutes.'

Standing from the bed, he tests his head with a twitch. 'Any painkillers in your handbag? And can we escape as soon as I'm back from the walk? I don't want to hang around and I'd rather phone Will from home. Is that OK?'

Geri cocks her head and gazes for a moment as though reading his mind. 'Suits me,' she replies with a shrug.

He's surprised to find bruises on his thighs and his stomach, and despite fumbling with the shower, the soap and his walking boots, Dan arrives in the hot reception just in time.

Newly married Mrs Quinn is handing out photocopies of the route. Her fine hair is still in its wedding chignon. She keeps lifting her hand as though to check it's still there. She looks tired and her smile seems too bright. Like a jaded holiday rep, he thinks. And Nick seems distracted. He's chatting and smiling too, but it's as though there's the slightest delay, like his mind is elsewhere. But then again, who can blame them? What Dan himself described as the *blip* must still feel fresh for them both. He just keeps temporarily forgetting.

He touches Nick's elbow. 'Everything OK? How was the bridal suite?'

A slight delay before the pale eyes focus. 'Yeah, great. The room's fabulous. It's a shame there isn't enough time to really enjoy it. Come and have a look later. Geri not walking?'

'Sorry, no.'

'Oh right. So a walk could bring on—'

'God no, she's not that close to . . .' Nick's guileless face makes him smile. 'No popping for several weeks yet, Nick. She's just tired. Needs a nap.'

'Oh right.' Nick grins. 'No hot water and towels, then?'

'Only for me when you've dragged me to the top of that bloody Welsh hill.'

Inhaling deeply, Dan tightens his laces. He pictures Geri's sleeping face as he left. He's looking forward to becoming a dad, he honestly is, but the whole idea of a real baby is nebulous. Being an only child, he's never even had a sibling. He has no idea what to expect. Mostly he's fine, but sometimes the thought of the responsibility leaves him breathless.

The walkers head off towards a rocky stile. The breeze cooling his cheeks, Dan hovers near the rear and discreetly glances around the group of twenty or so adults. Seb Taylor isn't there, thank God. Popping a mint from his pocket in his mouth, he registers the weak sunshine. Then he shakes his head and smiles to himself. What was it Will said yesterday? All's well that ends well. Bloody hell, what an ending. But Penny's safe and she's home. Geri's sleeping. Everything's fine.

He pictures Seb's naked body a last time. He misread it, definitely, panic over.

A sudden touch on his shoulder makes him jolt. 'No Geri?'

a voice asks, but it's Jen, just Jen, appearing from bloody nowhere like a sniper. Slipping her arm into his, she propels him forward. 'You can be my chaperone, Danny Boy. Keep me upright.' Looking pretty rough, she slides on her sunglasses. 'That's better. I confess I was hoping for rain.'

He smiles wryly. 'Me too.'

'What, Super Dan miss a walk? You must've polished off the bottle. I should've warned you about Seb.'

'Warned me about Seb? How?' he replies, conscious his voice has emerged in a ridiculous squeak.

'Oh, he can drink anyone under the table. Despite being beautiful, honed to physical perfection, kind and sweet, et cetera et cetera.'

'You sound as though you don't like him.'

Unexpectedly stopping, Jen slips down her sunglasses and looks at him pointedly. Then she sighs. 'I do like him, but he's always been Will's little brother. Trips to Crocky Trail, Chester Zoo, Blackpool and stuff. Then suddenly he's a grown man I don't know all that well. Boy to man in a blink. It's weird really.'

Picturing the cropped hair of the swimmer, Dan wonders how to respond, but Jen speaks again.

'I wonder what happened with Claudia. Both bloody gorgeous, they seemed a good match. I only met her the once, but it was pretty embarrassing, if I'm honest.' She looks wistful. 'You know, loaded eyes, intertwined fingers, shallow attention. In love, I suppose.' Then she laughs, her tone back to sardonic. 'Or maybe it was lust, transient but delicious. Like the croissant I pinched on the way.'

Pulling a flake of pastry from the ends of her hair, Dan laughs. 'Evidence,' he says, glad of something to distract his hot jumble of thoughts. 'Back to the lab for testing . . .'

Jen doesn't seem to hear. 'I keep thinking about Will and

40

Penny. It isn't something that happens every day, is it? What would you do? What would you do if it was Geri?'

He smiles thinly. 'God knows. Ask my mum?'

'As much as I love her, Will's mum would be no use. She's . . . delicate. And pretty old these days, like Nick's mum and dad. Funny, that, my parents started young. Like me, I guess.' Raising her eyebrows, she laughs. 'Many a slip 'twixt cup and lip, as my grandma put it.'

They continue to climb companionably, breaking apart for the muddy puddles, then linking again.

Abruptly pulling away, Jen takes off her sunglasses and waves. 'Just what we wanted, there's Seb!'

'Oh right,' Dan replies. Hoping the alarm doesn't show in his face, he nods towards Nick. 'I'll leave you and Seb to it. Better check on the groom. See if he needs a push after the rigours of his wedding night.'

Catching up with Nick, Dan tramps on, his walking boots heavy on his feet. He's hungry and thirsty and nauseous, aware of Seb Taylor's head at the front, inches above the other walkers. Aware when Seb stops, aware when he turns his dishevelled head.

'Look there,' Nick says suddenly and Dan follows his arm towards the windswept coast and the grey choppy sea. 'See below that ridge? The oaks are in a sort of canopy. Apparently they've been stunted by the strong wind and they're a haven for woodland flowers and creatures.'

Dan raises his eyebrows, surprised at Nick's interest. It feels like a conversation between strangers, weird and surreal. Like the astonishing blip; like bloody Seb Taylor. 'Sounds lovely. Not exactly central minging Manchester, is it?' He smiles, tasting the salty air on his lips. 'She'll turn you into a country boy if you're not careful.'

'Nah, not Lisa. She hasn't lived here for years and since her mum died there isn't the need to visit very often. I think we've successfully converted her.' He pauses for a moment, then grins, the familiar Nick Quinn returned behind his toothy smile. 'Except the rugby. When it comes to rugby, she's Welsh.'

The oasis appears without warning, an old farmhouse building rendered white, with shiny worn cobbles and casks in its yard. 'You go ahead,' Nick says. 'Better wait for the wife!'

Real ale, hot drinks and traditional cakes are on offer at the bar. Not ready to face food after all, Dan knocks back a mug of strong tea, helps himself to another and sits.

Jen thumps down at his bench with a cup of hot chocolate and a plate. 'Welsh bakestones, apparently,' she says, nibbling the cake. Then leans in to whisper, 'I feel guilty, but I can't summon up the usual court jester stuff today, so I'm going to cheat.' She slips on her sunglasses. 'God knows I could do with the exercise, but I've asked Ian to drive up with the girls and collect me. Bloody hangover! Don't think I can face the walk back.'

Dan looks around the low-beamed room. The numbers seem thin. 'I don't think you're the only one.' He rubs at a knot in the wooden tabletop. 'Take it Seb has gone too?'

'I don't know, he was outside smoking something that wasn't a cigarette.'

He feels surprise and mild outrage. He's never done drugs, not even weed.

'Oh, don't be so square,' Jen says, laughing. 'You should see your lemon face. It's what the young ones do. They do weed instead of cigarettes.'

'We're not that much older than Seb. Four, five years, tops,' he says, thinking, thirteen, the swimming gala; Seb Taylor was thirteen.

'Maybe you're right; I lose track. God, I keep thinking about Will and what he's going to do.'

Dan nods, thinking of the quip about asking his mum. His mum is the last person he'd ask about anything, but he joked because the thought of losing Geri scares him. Without Geri there, strong and solid, he'd be lost.

A beep from the courtyard interrupts the small silence. Jen lifts her sunglasses and peers through the leaded window. 'Ian's a bloody star. Do you want a lift back?'

'Cheers, but no thanks. Catch up with you soon.'

He strolls to Nick and the remaining handful of walkers. Jen's offer was tempting, but he's still the best man, the *only* best man. He sits at a rustic table, chatting with the other guests until Lisa announces in her clear-cut Welsh tones that it's time to walk back to the hotel and that if anyone needs a wee, now is the time.

Stroking the soft growth on his chin, Dan reminds himself to shave. He takes out his mobile to call Geri, then remembers she'll be napping. 'Just texting Geri. Catch you up,' he calls over to Nick. When he looks up from his phone, Seb Taylor is sitting on the other side of the table.

'Perhaps I did get it wrong,' Seb says with a small smile. He looks different again. Like he's just out of bed. Tired eyes, messy hair, unshaved chin.

Dan feels his face growing hot. He'd rather forget it.

'Or perhaps not,' Seb adds, his startling blue eyes piercing Dan's.

Dan drops his gaze, the blush deepening. Seb's legs are touching his under the table. 'Full marks for the correct answer first time,' he says, lamely trying for a quip. 'Everyone's going,

43

we'd better get a move on. I just need a piss.' He nods to the outside door, willing Seb away. 'Don't wait. I'll catch up with you.'

The downhill walk takes less time. Trying to focus on the other walkers' conversation at the front of the group, the heat in Dan's cheeks finally recedes. It took him ages to piss. He had to sit in the cubicle and wait, like a stupid bloody teenager.

Geri is waiting on the sofa in reception when he returns to the hotel. She comes to the doorway and smiles her sunny smile. 'The miracle of fresh air! You all look much better than you did three hours ago.' She lifts her dark eyebrows in silent communication. 'My back's been aching and it's a long drive home. Would you mind if we leave sooner rather than later, Dan? We're all packed.'

'Come on, Dan, there's time for a half,' somebody says. 'We're looking forward to *dishing the dirt* part two.'

Dan crouches to pull off his muddy walking boots. He's aware of Seb close beside him, removing his jumper, kicking off his soiled trainers, peeling away his damp socks. He turns towards Nick, feeling guilty, but still ready with the apology and excuse, the need to bolt imperative.

'That's fine, Dan. You and Geri get off,' Nick says, beating him to it. 'We're all going soon. See you after Barbados!'

'God, I'm jealous.'

'I won't send you a postcard. Just pics of white sandy beaches, clear blue sky, turquoise sea. *If* I get chance between a few rounds of golf, water sports, caviar and cocktails at the pool . . .'

They joke for a few moments, the smile back on Nick's face. Dan feels Seb's body move away. 'Nice to meet you, Geri,' he hears him say. 'Back in Manchester now. Got your number. Be catching up with you very soon.'

Dan takes a deep breath before standing. The tone of Seb's words was just friendly, wasn't it? Bloody hell; bloody hell. Why do they feel like a threat?

CHAPTER TEN

Penny

Gritting her teeth, Penny knocks.

The woman is fairly young, late twenties or so, the same age as her. She puts a clipboard on the desk, holds out her hand and gestures to the chair next to hers.

'Thanks for coming in, Penny. I'm Debbie, a therapist in your care team. How are you feeling today?'

Almost holding her breath, Penny nods, 'Fine, thanks.'

She doesn't like this; she doesn't want to be here. It's embarrassing, humiliating, unnecessary, but she has to do it for Will. She wants to stop him from worrying with that anxious strange stare.

The woman smiles and makes eye contact. 'Well, fine is a good start. Do you know why you're here today?'

Doesn't the woman know she did a medical degree? Well, almost. But she has to behave and answer the questions like a very good girl. 'Psychological therapy,' she replies politely. Then, as though reading from the script, 'Helping me find out what happened and why. Helping to find ways of coping, so it doesn't happen again.'

The woman sits forward, her face open and interested. 'What did happen, Penny?'

Penny breathes, remembering the paranoia, the voice, the certainty. They feel distant now, thank God. 'A panic attack, I suppose,' she says eventually.

Far more than a panic attack, she knows. She let Will down badly. Bad, bad Penny. Did all the things she promised herself not to do. She can picture it now, like a film in slow motion. Will's shaking hand in hers, his unreadable tight face. The guests trying not to stare as he led her out to the car.

The woman nods to her notes. 'I only have the bare bones. Tell me more. Where were you?'

'At a friend's wedding reception.'

'Go on.'

'It was in a hotel. I went to the room and I opened the window to call my husband.'

The woman waits for her to speak, but she doesn't want to describe the stupid certainty, the rhythmic, coaxing tune in her head.

'What happened then, Penny?'

'He thought I was going to jump. Maybe it looked like that but . . .' Taking a deep breath, she tries for a smile. 'He was mistaken. Maybe I got too close to the window . . . I might have stood up, just to look out. You know, a beautiful view . . .'

Oh God, she's talking too much. Stop and breathe, stop and breathe.

'And then?'

'He came to the room with . . .' Oh God, the shame. 'With a friend and they kicked in the door.'

'Why did they do that, Penny?'

'They thought I was going to jump from the window, I suppose.'

She waits for the woman to ask the question, but she just nods sympathetically.

'I wasn't,' Penny says. How many times must she say it? To her mum and dad and the doctor and Will. Especially Will; her Will, her Will. 'I had no intention of jumping. I'm not suicidal. Really. That wasn't why I was there.'

Confused, delusional, she knows. But she doesn't want to say it.

'Why were you there, Penny?'

She stares at her hands. Paranoid too. Can she say that? Can she say she was convinced Will was lying? It makes her sound unbalanced. She's not; she's not. She's really not crazy.

'A nursery rhyme got stuck in my head. The one about rain.' She looks up to the woman and sighs. 'It had been raining all morning but it stopped. I don't know why, but I was convinced it was still raining. So I opened the window to tell Will.'

'Why did you want to tell Will?'

Penny turns to the window. Why *did* she do it? Why do the very thing that will push him away? She sees the fear in his eyes when he looks at her. She has to fix it, get their marriage back on track.

Going back to the woman's frown, she smiles. 'Because I tell him everything! I love him. He's not just my husband, he's my closest friend.'

And friends don't lie to each other. Do they?

CHAPTER ELEVEN

Dan

His head propped on his hand, Dan slouches at the kitchen table, unshaved. The pine table still wobbles and the floorboards feel cold beneath his bare feet. He can smell yesterday's omelette, but none of those things are the problem. The house is old and retains odours; he likes it that way.

Wearing her dressing gown, Geri stretches and yawns as she enters, then starts with surprise. 'Oh Dan! I thought you'd gone to work. Sorry, I dropped off again. What time is it?'

He shrugs and pushes his half-eaten breakfast away. The cereal was soft and tasteless. He wasn't hungry enough to make the effort with toast.

'Eight? Eight fifteen?'

'Shouldn't you be dressed by now? Is someone else opening up today?'

'Nope.'

Geri rakes her fingers through his uncombed hair. 'Then, shouldn't you . . . ?'

'None of the other staff arrive until half past nine. And why should they? No one looks at properties at the crack of dawn.

I'm just the idiot who turns up an hour before everyone else because a conveyancer's lot is not a happy one. And as for bloody Salim—'

'A sleeping partner who sleeps?' She looks at him thoughtfully. 'Are you OK, Dan? You've seemed a bit jaded this week.'

He pulls her gently towards him, his face meeting her protruding belly. Resting his head against it, he plants a soft kiss, inhaling a comforting smell he couldn't describe if he tried. 'I'm just jealous. I want to stay at home with you and Henrietta.'

'Henrietta? Very Jane Austen. So, the baby is a girl today?'

'Yes, she told me this morning when you were sleeping.'

'Well, Henrietta says it's time for Daddy to get shaved and dressed.'

He puts his hand to his chin, feeling the bristles for a few moments. He has what Jen Kenning always describes as 'Irish stubble', black and soft but persistent. He can't be bothered to shave. 'How about a beard?'

'A beard?' Geri says slowly, then laughs. 'OK. Let's see how it goes.'

When Dan arrives at the estate agency, Maya Ahmed is waiting outside, clutching her coat collar around her neck. 'Blooming heck, Dan,' she says, peering at her watch. 'This is a first. And I'm freezing.' She turns to the shop window and gesticulates to the photographs of large properties for sale in Wilmslow and the other affluent Cheshire suburbs. 'Interesting, though. Seeing it from this side. How the other half lives.'

Not in the mood for chat, Dan unlocks the door. 'Two sides to everything in life, Maya,' he says.

'A bit deep for you, Dan. Had a transformation overnight? You'll be wanting something other than tuna and mayonnaise on your sandwich next.' She follows him to the back office, watching as he disables the alarm, opens the safe and turns on the answerphone without removing his coat. 'Everything OK at home?' she asks over a prattling long message. 'Geri well? Baby still cooking?'

'Yup. Pass me that pen. Has the post arrived?'

She rolls her sable eyes. 'I wouldn't know, Dan. I've only just arrived. We walked in together a minute ago, remember?'

Ignoring her puzzled gaze, he continues to focus on the answerphone messages.

She opens his laptop, presses the start button and studies him again. 'Your overcoat is a clue of your recent arrival.' She cocks her head. 'Some men get the baby wobbles. Did you know that?'

'Been reading *Cosmopolitan* again, Maya?' He looks up from his scrawl. 'What?' he asks, looking at her gappy grin and trying not to return it.

'Nothing,' she replies with a chuckle. Two telephones peal shrilly. 'Here we go,' she says. 'Where the flip is Andrew? Why's he always late on a Friday?'

Maya pops her dark head around Dan's office door before lunchtime. 'I thought I'd better check. You know, what with the designer stubble and all.'

He looks up from the letters and searches, the plans and paperwork spread over his desk. It's always the same on bloody Fridays. The morning has flown; four residential completions already, another four in the pipeline.

His mind still on the files, he looks at Maya blankly.

'Check whether it's still a tuna and mayo sandwich for lunch?' she explains. 'And somebody is here about a viewing. Wants a big cheese. Us minions won't do, which is a pity. You'll know what I mean when you see him.'

The surge of irritation is there; why does *he* have to do everything? 'Salim can see him. He's the—'

'Property man. I know. But he isn't here yet. No idea where . . .'

The annoyance increases. 'Tell the viewer to make an appointment.'

'I already tried. He says that he knows you.' Maya looks at her notepad. 'Sebastian Taylor?'

The alarm hits immediately. What the fuck? What the fuck? He tries to think for a moment, aware of Maya's gaze as he struggles to find an excuse. Perhaps there are two Sebastian Taylors in his phone book, but he instinctively knows there aren't. 'Oh right, show him in,' he says evenly, hoping the heat hasn't risen to his cheeks.

He clears his throat.

The door opens. Maya appears first, then gawks with obvious interest. Stepping forward as though this unexpected visit is perfectly normal, he takes Seb's outstretched hand. Time stalls. Maya finally stops staring and speaks. 'Anyone need a drink?'

'Sorry,' Seb says when the door clicks to. 'I know what you must be thinking.'

The words take Dan aback. Why is he sorry? What the fuck does he mean? He tries to formulate a reply, but finds himself stunned as he studies Seb's face. He's tried to push this man from his thoughts since the wedding weekend, but finds his heart rushing.

'Just turning up here,' Seb continues. 'Nothing bad has happened.' His piercing blue eyes are on Dan's. 'To Penny. Nothing bad has happened to Penny. She's fine, at home with Will; there hasn't been another . . .'

Dan feels his cheeks colouring, wonders whether it's obvious Penny was the last thing on his mind. He clears his throat again and rallies. 'Oh, great; that's good. So she's OK? And Will? We've spoken briefly, but I didn't like to go into detail, you know, asking questions. I guess when he's ready, he'll talk.' He's still standing and so is Seb. Business mode, that's the thing. 'Take a seat. So, how can I help?'

Seb looks around the office before pulling out a chair and sitting at a distance, as one might do for an audition. He's wearing loose-fitting torn jeans, a patterned shirt and black jacket. He leans forward, his legs spread, his elbows on his thighs.

'I don't have your mobile number. You described where this place was at the wedding, but I didn't remember a name.'

'Wilmslow Property Services,' Dan replies, as though the name wasn't etched on the shopfront in huge letters.

Seb pulls a folded paper from his jacket pocket. 'Yeah, so I see.'

They both turn to the door as Maya bustles in, catching her colourful hijab in the door. She puts the coffee on Dan's desk, then peeks over Seb's shoulder at the sales particulars he's holding.

'Ah, Oak House. Not far from here. Always a shame to split something so beautiful into flats but they've done a great job. The penthouse apartment is really fab if you like a good view of the Cheshire countryside. You'll need to get in a viewing soon though, there's been a lot of interest because the rental is surprisingly low. It nearly went last week but the woman had a pet, which isn't allowed. You don't have a pug do you?' She stands back to study Seb's face, then grins. 'No, of course not. You look more like a golden retriever guy to me.'

Feeling a surge of release, Dan laughs and picks up the telephone. 'I can give Salim a bell now if you're really interested. He's the property man.' He nods at Maya. 'Or if Andrew has got a slot this afternoon?'

'He's back from his viewing. I can ask him right now.'

There's a pause for a moment; Seb's eyes are on his. 'What about you, Dan? Can't you show me around?'

'Sorry, Seb, I'm mad busy today. Friday's are always the worst. I've had four completions this morning and there's another four of the bastards before five . . .' Dan knows he's babbling and can't quite meet Seb's steady gaze. 'I would if I could. I'm sure Salim will be—'

'Let's make it tonight then. I can buy you a pint afterwards.'

Feeling hot and stiff in his suit, Dan drives straight from the office towards the other side of Wilmslow. The afternoon lurched by with little time to think of anything other than the house completions, two of which went pear-shaped.

He feels culpable as he weaves through the heavy traffic, sorry for those families whose excitement has been crushed and replaced with anxiety. He wishes he didn't care, wishes he could shrug it off. Like Salim or like Will. But then he remembers Will's face at the wedding. A look of astonishment, replaced seconds later with sheer panic.

Loosening his tie at the traffic lights, he sighs, then has to brake sharply not to overshoot the gated access of Oak House. Thinking it could do with some lighting, he slowly accelerates up a sweeping driveway enveloped by stark looming trees. The red-brick property bursts out at the top. A Victorian mansion, no less. He grabbed the sales particulars before leaving the office but hasn't had time to look. Not that he knows much about property *per se*. He's the solicitor, Salim has the surveying qualification.

Dan sighs at the thought of Salim. The anxiety is there, a disquiet he's never felt before, a need to know that everything's fine on his side of the business. How can he be sure? Geri took voluntary redundancy from the City Council when it was on offer last year and he's the sole earner. They have a baby on the way.

He parks his car next to a large flower bed of severely pruned roses. There is no sign of Seb or a car.

The February evening is dark and sharp, but Dan feels sweaty, no longer from the stress of appeasing angry clients, his rush from the office or his fear of being late, but from his thoughts, which have now kicked in. Is this viewing for real? Can Seb genuinely afford to rent something so opulent?

He stares through the windscreen. The residence is a far cry from the large semi he shares with Geri. Their house is in a nice part of Chorlton, a repossession he bought at a good price and Victorian too, but nothing compared to this grandeur, albeit desecrated by the modern trend of flats. He looks at the photographs. A discerning revamp, he supposes. As Salim points out, a tasteful renovation is preferable to a tasteless one, or even worse, a fun pub.

He pictures Geri's sunny smile. 'Are fun pubs so bad, Dan? Child-friendly food, soft-play areas for kids? Beer gardens with swings. That might be us one day.'

He'll be a father in just over two months. The thought is still incredible.

'Furniture optional,' the sales leaflet says. Would Seb need furniture? He split with his girlfriend, Claudia. They lived in France. She was beautiful, good in bed and a cunt. That's all Dan knows. He looks again at his watch, then checks his mobile for messages. They arranged to meet at seven o'clock; it's now seven-thirty. Could Seb already be inside?

He walks to the panelled front door, the clatter of pebbles under his work shoes sounding loud in the still dark. He has no idea whether the other apartments are already let, whether Seb could have gained access. This situation feels unreal; he has no idea why he's here, he has no desire to view other people's properties and he'd like to go home. Examining the keys to separate out the correct one, he turns at the crunching sound of a car approaching.

Seb dips his head to climb out of a black cab. 'Left my car in France along with everything else,' he says easily as he approaches the door. 'Sorry I'm late. The first taxi didn't come. Could've borrowed Mum's car, but no insurance.' He puts a firm hand on Dan's shoulder. 'Shall we go in?'

They stand apart in a small lift. Seb presses the button for the top floor, but for moments nothing happens.

'Reminds me of that scene from a Peter Sellers' film,' Dan says to fill the silence. 'The out-takes are famous.' He glances at Seb. His expression is blank. 'A fart scene? You must have seen it. They had to film it again and again because the actors kept laughing. Corpsing, I think they call it.' He knows he's babbling again. 'Have you pressed the right button?' He leans over Seb's chest, takes in the aroma of coconut shampoo, notices Seb has changed his shirt, then presses the button to close the doors. 'Maybe that'll do the trick.'

The lift takes them to a personal entrance hall with a vaulted ceiling, which leads to the glossy white door and the intercom. Dan knows the atmosphere smells of fresh paint and polish but he can't escape the smell of coconuts. He fumbles slightly with the keys, pleased when the heavy door opens with only one turn of the double lock. He switches on the light and they're met with cream; a carpeted drawing room with pale walls, high ceilings and two large windows looking out to the dark Cheshire countryside. The wide room is sparsely decorated with a three-piece sofa suite at one end, a glass dining table the other.

Dan stands at the door, playing with the keys. Through his peripheral vision, he watches Seb opening doors and glancing in. 'Furniture is optional,' he eventually comments to fill the muffled silence. He doesn't know what else to say.

Seb stops and stares through a window before abruptly turning. He looks as though he might speak, but heads towards the master bedroom instead.

Dan clears his throat. 'I'll wait in the kitchen. Give you time to have a proper look.'

Sitting at a high bar stool, he absently strokes the soft bristle on his chin and looks around. He and Geri were due to refurbish their kitchen, but now it's on hold. On hold until after the baby is born. It's fine and it's good. He just wishes the words *on hold* weren't quite so obscure.

Suddenly aware that minutes have passed without any word from Seb, Dan looks at his watch. He takes a deep breath before leaving his hiding place. Seb is in the drawing room, sitting on the middle sofa and gazing at an empty cream wall.

'I guess that's where you'd hang a flat-screen television or a mirror. Or maybe a Renoir if you have one spare in the attic,' Dan says, trying to lighten Seb's silence. He perches on a two-seater sofa and breathes through his nose, glad the visit is nearly over. 'Seen everything you want to see?'

Seb doesn't answer the question, but turns his focus to Dan. 'If I rented this place, would you visit?' he asks.

'Don't start—'

'Don't start what?'

The surge of heat in Dan's chest hurtles to his face. 'I'm not gay, Seb,' he blurts.

Seb smiles a small smile and looks down at his hands. 'Who said *I* was?'

Dan wants to remove his jacket to help him cool down, but fears it would give Seb the wrong message. 'OK,' he says. His throat feels constricted, but he needs to get the words out, needs to know what's going on. 'So, are you really interested in renting this place? Someone else from the office could've shown you around. Why me? What's going on, Seb?'

Seb lifts his face. 'I was in Morocco last week. On a work shoot.'

Dan nods; that's why his eyes seem so blue.

'So I would've got in touch with you sooner. After the wedding.'

'Nothing happened at the wedding. Well, not to—'

Seb's gaze doesn't waver. 'Didn't it? Like nothing happened at the swimming gala?'

Beads of sweat cool his spine. 'What gala? I don't remember any swimming gala. It's time to go, Seb. I've had a shit day. I'm knackered and hungry. Have you seen everything you want to see?' He's said it too harshly, he can see the recoil in Seb's face, but he really won't look; he doesn't want to feel the pull, that tug of *something* he's felt since the wedding. He tosses the keys in his hand and doggedly heads to the door. 'Mustn't forget the alarm and the lights. I'm sure there'll be stairs if the lift's playing up.'

The lift doors are still open, as though waiting. Dan stands to the left, keeping his eyes on the buttons as they descend, then strides out to the front door ahead of Seb. The cold breeze cools his face as he raises his car fob, then he remembers Seb came by taxi. 'Jump in. I can drop you at your mum's,' he says, climbing in.

Staring grimly ahead, he inserts the keys, turns on the ignition, slips the car into gear. But then he stops. The smell of coconut still hovers.

Turning to Seb, he gazes for a moment before looking away. 'Or how about coming to mine? Dinner with me and Geri and the bump? She usually makes pasta for a whole squadron, so

I'm sure there'll be plenty,' he says over the hammer of his heart. 'We can pick up some beer on the way. We do have brandy, but it might not be quite the standards you're used to. Might have cost more than an Ayrton Senna but less than a Bobby Moore . . .'

Knowing he's prattling again, Dan opens the window to release the new rush of heat. The aroma of coconut wafts away, but the tension's still stifling as he heads towards home. Aware of Seb's scrutiny, he chats inanely about pasta and pesto and parmesan, but the need to eat has clean gone.

The clench in his gut is no longer hunger. It's excitement; dangerous bloody excitement, tight and tingling in his belly.

CHAPTER TWELVE

Jen

Anna's green anorak at the far end of the damp playground catches Jen's eye. She briefly lifts her hand to wave before dropping it again. Holly is no longer at the primary school; she's been in high school since September, but old habits die hard. She hated having Jen there at her school. It was bad enough if your mum was a teacher, but a lowly classroom assistant! It was just *so* embarrassing. So Jen acknowledges her pretty red-haired daughter discreetly on lunchtime duties, even though she's only eight and still loves her mummy.

It's the start of Jen's second year. She's still glad of her decision to train as an assistant rather than a full-blown teacher. For now at least. She works two and a half days in a job-share, giving her time to cram in the cooking, the shopping and the bills in the remainder of the week. Though in fairness, Ian does his bit; he irons if there's sport on the television and he hoovers at weekends, pretty fair in her view. But then Ian is a good man. Except when he's watching his beloved United play football, he's an even-tempered, easy-going guy; they make a good team.

A football approaches and she runs, hoofing it accurately to a boy from her class. His freckled face colours with embarrassment. Jen should know better than to interrupt the boys' game, but she was sporty as a girl and finds herself with daughters who prefer their mobile phones, television and music to sporting activities. 'Do you wish we'd had a boy?' she used to ask Ian, pretending a boy would have been nice for him rather than her, but now that Anna is nearly nine, capable of creating a website, let alone dressing and feeding herself, she can't imagine wanting another child, either boy or girl; it would be too much like hard work.

The sudden spurt of activity has left her breathless. She knows she should lose a few pounds, but dieting feels like hard work too. Her daughters are all skinny. She wasn't ever thin, not that she minded. Girls like to be skinny for boys, but in her experience, males prefer a little flesh. But the fact is Holly is *too* thin. She eats well enough, but doesn't put on weight. Would it be weird to take her to the doctor? A sort of Munchausen by proxy? Plump mother taking skinny daughter to the doctor's? And anyway, would Holly comply with such an *embarrassing* request?

She glances at her watch, a fake designer brand bought on their last holiday to Turkey. It's Wednesday, her half-day. Toasted teacakes for lunch, she thinks. Thank God butter's back in vogue.

The doorbell rings at two. Jen licks her fingers and flings open the door, but it isn't Ian's Amazon delivery of books. It's Will Taylor, looking smart. Like a rugby player setting off on tour, the central button on his suit jacket looks precarious, as though it might pop any moment.

Her heart jumping, she steps back in surprise. 'Oh, Will.

Hello!' She glances at the kitchen, catching the breakfast disarray and the second half of her teacake on a plastic Disney plate. 'Was I expecting you? Did you text?'

A shadow passes across his face and he turns briefly to his car. 'No. Sorry, I was passing, so I thought I'd see if you were in.' His eyes come back to hers. 'Is that OK?'

'Of course. No problem, come on in.' She tiptoes in her socks and pecks him on his cheek. 'Excuse the mess. I was just having my lunch.' She examines his tense face, anxiety replacing surprise. 'Is everything OK? Is Penny OK? I've been really worried.'

He smiles but looks weary. 'I know. Thanks for your texts. I'm sorry I haven't phoned for a proper chat since the wedding but . . .' He follows Jen through, sits at the table and rubs his forehead. His hair is receding, but he keeps it cropped short. His head is the right shape, she always finds herself thinking, he suits it like that.

'Tea or coffee?' she asks brightly to cover her embarrassment. She changed into a hoody and jogging bottoms the moment she arrived home. The outfit isn't as clean as it could be and the fresh butter mark doesn't help. 'How about a teacake? Toasted or plain?' She presents the open tin with a flourish. 'You can smell the sultanas. Mum baked them and they're delicious. My fingers are still buttery.'

She makes for the kettle but Will catches her wrist. There's a frown on his face and his voice is low. 'To be honest, I'd rather . . .'

The burn of his touch rushes to her cheeks. 'Talk?'

'Yes.' He smiles faintly. 'Talk like we used to.'

She sits down on the chair next to him. Takes a deep breath. Tries to look him in the eye. 'No, Will, we promised.'

'I just need you right now.' He puts a hand to her cheek, his eyes hollow and dark. 'I never stopped needing you.'

Flinching from his touch, Jen tries to swallow the flood of emotion before speaking. 'No, Will. You're not being fair. To any of us. We said a clean sheet after your wedding.' She gazes at his face. 'It was hard, really hard, but we've done so well—'

He drops his hand, sits back and closes his eyes. 'Fair dos. I miss you. I miss us. That's all.'

She turns away to the sink and busies herself with the kettle as she steadies her breathing. His suggestion's a surprise, his lack of fight even more so. She wishes she could ignore the clutch of concern mixed with ache in her chest. She starts to count to ten but turns after five, returns to her chair and takes his large hand. 'Are you OK, Will?'

'Yeah. I'm OK.'

His drained handsome face doesn't match his words; she can feel herself falling.

'Are you really OK?'

He lifts her hand to his lips. 'You've no idea how much I miss you,' he sighs.

Will lies on his front; he always lies on his belly after sex. He closes his eyes, sighs with a smile and nods off. In the old days Jen didn't like it; his turning away made her feel slighted and used. She wanted to be cuddled and kissed, to be told how great their lovemaking had been. Perhaps it was because sex in a bed was so rare; she counted it up once: sex in a bed with Will before marriage to Ian and after. The after far outweighed the before. In her marital bed too. Yet she never felt guilt, at least not the guilt she should have. What did she and Will always say? That it wasn't really betrayal because they'd been together forever. But of course that wasn't strictly true.

She leans over, inhaling the familiar smell of mild sweat and deodorant, kissing the back of his broad shoulder. 'I have to leave at three to collect Anna from school.'

He immediately turns, his face closed and sleepy. 'But we haven't had a chance to talk.' He hitches up the bed and puts his arm around her, pulling her close. 'I shouldn't have broken up with you before uni,' he says into her hair. 'I have no idea why I did it. I should have begged you back before . . . before it was too late.'

Before marrying Ian Kenning at twenty-one. Giving birth to Maria three months later.

Like his visit, the words are a surprise; Will hasn't said them for a long time, but still she doesn't reply. There's no point reminding him that he thought the grass was greener, that he wouldn't have as much fun in his fresher's year with a girlfriend holding him back.

That he broke her bloody heart.

'Tell me about Penny,' she says instead, needing to know sooner or later. She takes a breath and steels herself. 'Tell me what happened at the wedding; tell me why.'

He's silent for a while, then he kisses her forehead. 'I had to pay for the cost of the door the other day. Thank God Dan came with me to the room. My legs were like jelly. Another minute and who knows?'

'Do you really think she would've done it?' Jen asks, but Will stares ahead, saying nothing. 'It's OK,' she adds, her heart racing with the sudden need to know everything. 'We don't have to talk about it if you don't want to.'

Will inches down the bed, pulling her with him. He looks at her thoughtfully, then leans forward with a gentle kiss. 'I don't want to talk about it, if I'm honest. But then I'm offended no one is asking me about it. It just adds to the weird embarrassment of it all. She's remarkably fine, actually. Her doctor

64

arranged a home treatment team for the first few days, prescribed medication, and now she's having counselling, on her own to start with and then with me, if she wants. Of course, it should be her bloody mother, but I doubt she'd agree . . .'

Jen's heart slows. She pictures Penny in her underwear, pale-faced and dead-eyed, on the hotel window ledge. Over the past couple of weeks, she hasn't let herself dwell on reasons why she would do something so extreme and so public, but still there's a huge sense of relief. 'Oh right, so she did it because of her mum?'

'Not directly, but in Penny's head . . . God, I don't know what goes on between them. Penny says it's bad. In her face all the time. Constant criticism, nagging, pressure. Comparing Penny to her bloody perfect brother.' He stares at the ceiling, a pensive frown on his face. 'Of course, she doesn't do it when I'm there. Or if she does, it's more subtle, disguised as concern. You know – she only wants what's best for Penny, she only wants to help.'

Jen nods, surprised if she's honest. Her girls were bridesmaids at Will and Penny's wedding, so she saw a fair amount of her mum in the run-up. She was a bit distant, if anything. Friendly enough, but mad busy with all her volunteering commitments. But in fairness, she never hid her preference for Penny's brother. 'Boys are so much easier, Jen,' she'd say. Which was a bit rich said to a mother with three girls.

'So her mum thinks she's done nothing wrong?' Jen asks eventually.

Will pauses and rubs his head. 'I don't really know if she has. Penny's an adult, not a child anymore. She can't blame her mother forever. Can she? I really don't know, Jen. We're all in our thirties. Shouldn't we be past all that parental angst by now?'

He falls silent again and Jen drifts for a while. Parental angst isn't something she likes to contemplate; thoughts of her father are best hidden deep. But her mum Nola is a star; a constellation in fact.

'I'm trying, Jen. I'm trying to be supportive.' Will's clotted voice jerks her back. 'I'm going through the motions, but if I'm honest, I don't get it. I mean, what the fuck did Penny think she was doing? At someone else's wedding? Disappearing without saying a word, going into our hotel room, locking herself in. If Dan hadn't kicked in the door, who knows?' He stares at the ceiling and rocks his head. 'But then again, even if she'd jumped . . . We were on the third floor, for fuck's sake, not the thirteenth.' Abruptly leaning forward, he puts his face in his hands. 'I didn't know it was coming, Jen. She never said a word. Just that blank polite face she's had for months. She might do it again. How will I know? I have to work; I can't be with her all the time, watching her, hiding the window keys, counting the kitchen knives. It's a bloody nightmare.' Then, with a shuddery sigh: 'I know she's the one who's ill and needs help. I know I'm being selfish, but it's doing my head in.'

Jen puts her hand on Will's back and rubs gently. 'Maybe the counselling will help you as well as Penny,' she says after a time. 'Perhaps you have to say how *you* feel, you just have to be honest.'

Will turns his head and smiles wryly. 'Not completely honest, though, eh?'

Before leaving the house, Jen opens the bedroom window and changes the bedding. Smoothing the duvet cover, she contemplates how she feels about Will's unexpected visit. Wistful, she supposes. There are other words to describe the act itself. Almost immediately gratifying would be apt today. Not that sex with

Will wasn't always satisfying in the end, but it was more routine, the slow burner of regular sex. But it has been a while since they were last together. There was a period after Anna's fourth birthday when he'd drop by almost weekly. He was auditing then and they'd go to bed for his lunch hour and chat before making love, rather than the other way around. Then he met Penny at a medics' ball; she'd gone at the last minute to make up the numbers on the table. The lovemaking seemed to intensify then. Perhaps they both knew the end was imminent. Handsome, gregarious and charming, Will had plenty of girl-friends over the years, but Penny seemed to stick.

Fighting a sudden urge to sob, she strips the pillow, puts the soft case to her face and breathes in his smell. When pregnant with Holly, Will sent her an email out of the blue. It was a period when she was consumed with the highs and lows of motherhood and she'd seen little of him for many months.

'Went to Edinburgh for a conference yesterday,' his message read. *'On the way back I napped on the train and dreamed of us at eighteen.*

Woke up very confused. You were there; you were real, in sharp focus. Amazing how a dream can bring back the past with such clarity. As soon as I got home I dug out the old Canon. Too emotional to try it, but there in its case was my favourite photo of the most beautiful woman ever, taken with said camera. I thought I'd lost it forever.

Even now I'm welling up. Just SO in love with you and captured on film.'

CHAPTER THIRTEEN

Nick

Nick pulls his car into the flagged driveway of his childhood home feeling a mixture of relief and guilt. Relief that he's left it; guilt for feeling relieved.

Being the much younger child hasn't been easy. Although Patrick visits their parents regularly, he moved to his Cheadle flat years ago, leaving young Nicky Quinn with their doting parents. Of course, Nick didn't mind then; he was cushioned and loved. But he returned after university and found himself glued, a strange sticky mixture of love and dependency.

'You need to break free from your parents, obviously,' Lisa said, not long after they met. 'But they need it too. I've seen it with other people's parents. Their kids finally leave home and they have to learn to live with each other again. You know, without the crutch of a child. Your mum and dad are getting older, so they need to adjust before it's too late.'

He moved into Lisa's small semi two months before the wedding, but spent some time each evening at home with his parents.

'I get it; a weaning period,' she said. 'But after the wedding you're all mine.'

It was how he saw it too. He knew the umbilical cord had to be cut, but felt the severance wouldn't be complete until he was married to Lisa, until he'd said the vows out loud to everyone listening in the church. But now he's done it, he suspects life isn't quite so black and white. He's glad he's left, and of course he'll always love his parents, but he craves their approval as much as ever.

He rings the bell and stands at the frosted-glass door, rubbing his hands against the cold evening as he waits. Eventually he sees the smudged outline of his father leaning down to insert the key in the lock. There's a latch on the door but his parents have taken to locking it with a key even during the daytime. It finally opens, revealing the addition of a safety chain since he was last here.

It feels like reproof.

A blast of warm air fragranced with emulsion and cooking hits his face. 'You should at least leave the key in the lock, Dad. If there was a fire or an emergency you'd have to find the key. The delay could make all the difference.'

'That's what I've been telling him,' his mother calls from the kitchen. 'He won't take a blind bit of notice. And he can never remember where he's put them. Now you've mentioned it, no doubt he'll listen.'

Breathing in the oily smell of roast potatoes, Nick thinks about crutches. The bickering between his parents had got pretty bad before he left; he can't imagine it has got any better.

His father turns away and hobbles back towards the small sitting room at the front of the house. 'You finally decided to visit, then? I believe you've been back for a week,' he says over his brushed cotton shoulder. Then after a moment, 'Arsenal and Spurs. Two nil. Are you coming to watch?'

'Hello, love,' his mother says, pulling him into a hug. 'Careful of the walls. They should be dry by now, but you never know. Oh, it's lovely to see you. How was the honeymoon?'

He looks around the hallway. Sees the usual Artexed white walls behind the Lowry prints. He opens his mouth to say something nice, but his father's voice interrupts.

'Where are you, Nicky? Watch this replay.'

'It's fine, love,' his mum says. She throws a crisp tea towel over her trim shoulder. 'Dinner is ready in ten minutes. Then the television is going off, football or no football. We can talk then.'

After a few minutes of sport, Nick takes his usual place at the dining table, his back to the manicured square of grass through the open curtains of the large window. 'How's Patrick?' he asks over the prawn cocktail starter. 'I sent him a text. I thought he might be here to say hello. I've brought him a bottle of Barbadian rum.'

'Not tonight. He still comes on a Wednesday for his dinner,' his mum replies, offering him buttered triangles of brown bread. 'You know how he likes his routine. So, tell us about your honeymoon. Was it as lovely as you'd hoped?'

Nick tells his parents about Barbados, the unrelenting sunshine, the glossy hotel and their room looking onto the almost white beach. The fabulous food, especially the soup, the cheeky small birds that begged at the table, the symphony of crickets at night. And even though he says *we*, he's conscious when he mentions Lisa's name. Lisa, who is now his wife, as though she doesn't belong. He should have brought her with him tonight; he should have insisted.

The main course is his favourite food; roast beef and Yorkshire puddings, even though it's a Friday and his parents usually eat fish. His mum puts the last two crispy potatoes on his plate and passes him the gravy. He feels inordinately full from potatoes and nerves.

'Nicky, be a good lad and find out the half-time score when you've polished them off,' his father says.

'Really, Harry. Can't we just talk? A whole meal without football?'

'It'll only take a minute.'

'He's here to see us, not the football.'

'Nicky wants to know, the same as I do, don't you, lad?'

Nick leaves the table and spends a few moments in the sitting room, staring at the muted television screen and just breathing.

'How's Lisa?' his mum asks when he returns with the goal update. 'It's a shame she couldn't join us tonight. Is her tan as nice as yours?'

Nick finds himself flushing. 'She's fine and sends her apologies. She's out with some of her nursing friends. They arranged it months ago—'

'Oh, don't worry. She has her own life. Of course she does. And it's lovely to have you all to ourselves.'

He fluffs his hair, his fingers catching the scar line on his crown, then glances at his mum as she heads to the kitchen. Does she know he's lying? Her face is warm and placid but he doesn't want her to think badly of Lisa, to assume the lie is because she doesn't want to visit. He had hoped Patrick would be here, so he could ask all three of them his burning question and watch their faces. 'Who is Susan?' he wants to demand. 'Auntie Iris mentioned someone called Susan at the wedding. "Your Susan", she said. A small girl who could bring Patrick around. Who is she and why has she never been mentioned?'

His mum's voice cuts into his thoughts. 'Your favourite for dessert, love.'

He lifts his head to an apple and blackberry tart crusted with sugar. She cuts a huge slice and smothers it in cream. And his father is talking. He's warming to a story from his school days

71

with Uncle Derek that Nick's heard before. A holiday to Scarborough, just the two of them. How he had the brains and the charm but Derek had the looks and the brawn; that between them they were a winning team, 'both on and off the pitch of life'. The story is a long one and not without humour.

Apple pie and anecdotes. His regular safe life. Nick knows he won't ask his question.

They go back to the television and Arsenal win 3-1. His mother stands, points the remote and the room falls silent.

'You can't turn it off now, Dora. We need to hear the summary.' His father's voice is high-pitched, like a child's. 'Give me the remote.'

'Nick doesn't live here now, Harry. We should be enjoying his company. I'm bringing in the coffee and we can play cards for a while. Nick has his own home to go to.'

When his mum leaves the room, Nick picks up the remote, turns on the TV, reduces the volume and places it in his dad's bony hand, then crouches at the cupboard to find the cards. But his eye catches the framed photographs of him and Patrick in chubby-cheeked school poses, fifteen years apart. They are always there on the pale wooden top, a fixture he rarely notices, but when he does he feels wistful, the whiff of loss still there from when Patrick left home.

Returning with drinks on a tray, his mum tuts at the almost muted TV screen.

'Tell you what,' he says quickly, wanting to avoid the inevitable squabble. 'Instead of playing cards, let's look at some old photographs. Have you any of Rhyl? Remember when some drunk bloke came into our hotel room one night and wouldn't accept it wasn't his room?'

He sits next to his dad on the two-seater sofa and his mum kneels at their feet, sorting through photographs from an old shoebox, each packet carefully labelled in her neat handwriting. She selects one marked 'Rhyl' and hands it to him.

'You were only three, love. Can you really remember the man in the hotel room?'

'Family lore.' He smiles, flicking through the snaps. 'I feel as though I can remember, but the story has been told so many times, who knows? By Patrick, particularly, he likes that one.' He holds up a photograph. 'I remember this beach. Playing cricket and rounders. Did we go with the cousins?'

He gazes at the snap. It's of him and Patrick on a damp sandy beach, standing next to a large sandcastle, the wind blowing their fair hair in their eyes. Then another of them between their parents with the same backdrop of the pale choppy sea. His father's hair is still brown and his mother looks young and pretty, yet he remembers a whole childhood of people assuming Dora and Harry were his grandparents.

'Whole childhood? Really? They're not that old,' Lisa laughed when he told her. It was probably no more than a handful of times, but each one had hurt because he saw the slapped look on his lovely mum's face.

His father swaps his glasses and takes the picture. 'What about when you fell from the landing? You must remember that. Climbing over the bannister when no one was looking—'

'Oh, don't, Harry. It makes me feel queasy, even now.' She puts her hand to her chest. 'Only three or four. You cracked your poor little head open and it bled terribly. You had to have stitches. It was a miracle it wasn't any worse.'

More family lore. Nick puts a hand to his hair, his fingers finding the small scar. 'No, I don't remember, though Patrick's version about me trying to be Superman makes me laugh.' He glances at his mum's wretched face. 'How about school days?' he asks, changing the subject. 'Do you still have the sports day photographs?'

That makes her smile. 'As if I'd throw them out, love. It's a shame Lisa isn't here to see your skinny legs.' She selects the top photograph from the wallet labelled 'St Mark's' and passes it to Nick. 'There we go. You were twelve then. Do you remember, we called you the A Team? You, Daniel Maloney and William Taylor. You won the relays every year.'

'Hundred, two hundred and four hundred,' his dad says, taking off his glasses and placing the snap close to his eyes. 'I could relax for the relay, but the individual races . . . There'd always be trouble. Sulking and the like when one of you boys had to win. And that was just the fathers!'

His dad tells the story with a fond smile. Nick has heard it many times before, but each time there's the slightest embellishment. All the fathers would watch their offspring and shout, bets would be laid. Alex Taylor would spend his winnings buying a round at the pub and Jed Maloney would give it to Dan.

He feeds his dad the line: 'And what about you, Dad?'

'I invested it wisely.'

It's what he always says, but today there's a pathos about him. His father's working days are over; his status as a respected bank manager long gone.

'Oh, and here is one of you, Daniel, William and Jennifer O'Donnell. Look at her pretty dimples!' Dora smiles. 'We called her the honorary boy. Thick as thieves, the four of you.'

Nick twists his wedding ring, still tight on his finger. 'And probably still are.'

His mind flits to the blip, surprised his mum hasn't mentioned it. But then again, despite her small frame and soft face, she's quite stoical and surprisingly tough. 'There's no point crying over spilt milk,' she always says when things go awry, 'You can't change the past, you just have to get on with it.'

When she'd advised him to move on and pretend it hadn't happened, she'd obviously meant it.

He feels his dad's interest drift back to the television. His mum rolls her eyes and offers the mints, followed by a selection of photographs of him as a blonde-haired plump toddler.

'Cute,' he says. 'Lisa would like to see these. How about photos of Patrick when he was that age? Did we look similar?'

His mum holds out her hand for support and then stands up slowly. 'This knee gets stiff if I kneel down too long. Arthritic, I expect.' She picks up the framed photograph of Patrick wearing his pale blue National Health spectacles and leaning to one side. 'There's this and his other school portraits. But we don't have many others. It was slides in those days. Negatives in little cardboard frames. I don't know what happened to them. You'd look at them through a projector, wouldn't you, Harry? Derek had one and we'd go round and have a film night. A shame really. Patrick had beautiful curly white hair.'

His father snorts, but doesn't turn from the television. 'Aye, Derek's film nights. Those were the days.'

Nick eventually leaves feeling soulful. Even his mum who's so fit seemed to be ageing today. He knows it's pathetic for a man of thirty-four, but he wants his parents to live forever; severance or not, he fears the trauma of their death. He can't imagine what it was like for Lisa to lose her mum. Though three years ago now, he feels her grief at the surface whenever mothers are mentioned.

He says goodbye to his parents, stands under the outdoor light and listens to the scrape of the keys and the chain before moving away listlessly. Then he sits in his car for a few moments, thinking. He doesn't want to go home to Lisa empty-handed so looks at his watch. It's quarter to ten, not too late, surely, to visit his godparents? And if it is, he'll make his excuses and leave.

It is too late, for Iris at least. She has already gone for 'a bath and to bed' when Nick arrives in their lantern-lit driveway. But at the stained-glass bungalow door, Derek insists Nick comes out of the 'bloody cold' and joins him for a nightcap and a cigar if he fancies.

He follows Derek into the spacious lounge, which smells, as always, of spirits and tobacco.

'Take a seat, son. It's lovely to see you, and it'll give me an excuse to escape from the wife's scolding for ten minutes,' Derek says with a smile.

Nick presents him with Patrick's bottle of Barbadian rum: 'A small gift from our honeymoon to add to the collection. From me and my wife!'

He wonders what he'll give Patrick instead, but he still feels miffed at his brother's inability to be even slightly flexible. Patrick lives on his own with his carefully stored gadgets and gizmos; it isn't even as though he ventures to the pub on a Friday night.

Derek examines the bottle. He's a youthful-looking man, smallish, trim and fit with a moustache and a full head of grey hair, which he still styles into a neat fifties quiff. Not at all like Nick's dad with his white thinning hair, poor eyesight and constant hobbling. Though both their accents still have a Salford twang, it's hard to believe the two men were born the same year.

'Oh, and thank you very much for the wedding gift and the cheque. It's incredibly generous,' Nick adds. He's glad he's remembered. He and Lisa actually bought Derek a golf cap and accessories from Sandy Lane resort as a thank you, but he hadn't anticipated visiting tonight.

'Not a problem, son. Glad to share the few bob I have sitting bored in the bank. If it wasn't for your dad—'

'Yeah, I know. But still it's very kind.'

Derek moves behind a leather and teak bar in the corner and offers Nick a tipple of his choice from the array of bottles on display. Nick has no doubt that nothing has changed since the Dillons had this mismatch of stone and brick built on the pricey Hale plot in the sixties. He stares at the bar, still feeling that prickle of excitement he had as a boy; kneeling on a stool behind the counter, playing barman. Though his mum would shake her head, Derek waved her worries away. 'Let the lad have some fun. No harm pouring himself half a lemonade.' But when Dora wasn't looking, Derek allowed him to pour measures of Martini, Cinzano or Campari for the adults, adding soda from a crystal glass syphon. 'Go on. Try it, son. Just a small sip.'

Nick would always cough or grimace; the cocktails were too dry.

'They're women's drinks. Take a snifter of this,' Derek would laugh, pouring him a wee drop of cherry brandy or amaretto, sweet and warming in his chest.

Gazing at the electric fire in the stone-cladding wall, the adult Nick sips his beer. The fake flames remind him of the opening credits of a James Bond film. Was it all the films or just one? Patrick would know. He loves the Bond movies. He could name each film's third production assistant or set designer if you asked him. Nick wonders if his brother ever visits Derek and Iris. It's not something he mentions, but they're his godparents, not Patrick's.

He shakes his attention back to Derek. He's still ruminating about Barbados, how he and Iris once visited Bridgetown as a port on a luxury cruise. Keen on cruising, they're trying to persuade Dora and Harry to go on the next one. But of course there's the problem of Harry's hip. There's a lot of walking on the excursions, on the ship too. Perhaps they could hire a wheelchair.

Nick tries not to show his exasperation, but the words emerge harsher than he intends. 'The doctor says the hip replacement was a complete success. The limping is just a matter of habit.' He tries again with a jocular tone. 'He's just being a grumpy bugger, Derek. Don't encourage him!'

Derek looks at his feet. Nick finds his loyalty to his father touching, if at times maddening; he's never had anything but praise and admiration for Harry Quinn. 'If it hadn't been for your dad's sound financial advice, and that first loan, I wouldn't have made my few bob,' he always says. They've been tight friends since school, nearly seventy years. It's an astonishing feat, one Nick hopes to replicate with Will and Dan. The honorary boy, too.

He thinks of Will's text: *'Sorry, man. You can't begin to know how sorry I am. I'll explain when I see you. Have a great honeymoon.'*

For the first few days in Barbados, it felt as though he and Lisa talked about nothing other than the blip. He didn't really want to dwell on it, but Lisa was intrigued. How bloody awful was it to see Penny teetering on the ledge? Why did she do it? What had gone on with her and Will? It just went to show that no one knows what goes on in people's heads. Behind closed doors too. But her interest eventually ran out of steam, thank God. Since then she's been more vocal about his current concern. 'Come on, Nick, I know it's been eating you since the wedding, you just need to ask. It's probably nothing.' But as he gazes at Derek's ruddy face, he knows he can't do it; his parents and his godparents are of a different generation. If something hasn't been mentioned, it's deliberate.

He knocks back his half-pint. 'I'll leave you to the rest of your evening. Tell Auntie Iris that the two of you must pop in any time. We're not far away. Tea and biscuits always available! And thank you again for your generosity. You really didn't have to.'

Derek doesn't move for a moment. He strokes his moustache, then nods, heading towards the open door which separates the lounge from the bedrooms, which he closes. 'You've come to ask about Susan,' he states. 'It was a slip. Iris shouldn't have said anything. It's not our place to say.' He sits on a leather-cushioned window seat and motions Nick to sit too. 'Your mum and dad . . . lost her, long ago. I know young people like to talk these days, but some things are better left in the past. Do you see what I'm saying?'

Nick's heart thrashes. 'I had a sister called Susan?'

Derek nods slowly. 'Your Patrick's twin.'

CHAPTER FOURTEEN

Penny

The therapist is sitting patiently, the clipboard on her knee.

'Let's talk about you and Will,' she says.

Like insects on her skin, the alarm is immediate. 'Why?'

'Well, he's your partner, of course. It's usual to ask at the outset, but last time we got sidetracked.' The woman cocks her head. 'Is that OK?'

Penny looks at her hands. 'Of course. What do you want to know?'

'How is your marriage? Any issues or problems?'

She thinks of Will's curious change of mood. So tense and silent since the wedding, but much chirpier this week, talkative, bright, back to the usual quips. But that's good, really good. Isn't it?

Trying to hide the breathless shudder, she uses her best mask-smile. 'No, none at all. Well, apart from this, of course. We're very close.'

The woman gazes for a moment too long. 'Any children?' she asks.

'No.'

'And your other family?'

This feels more comfortable, she can talk about them. 'Mum and Dad and a brother.'

'OK.' The woman looks at her notes. 'You described the incident at the wedding as a panic attack,' she says. 'Have you experienced them before?'

'No.'

'OK. Can you describe how it felt?'

Thrown by the change, Penny frowns. She's no keener on talking than she was last time, but knows she must go through the motions for Will. Show Will that she's fine. Not crazy at all. 'I was anxious.'

'Anxious how?'

She thinks. Where to start? Would complete honesty help? She doubts it. And anyway, she knows it was paranoia, just stupid delusion. 'Just anxious in general. But right then I had to change my dress. It was stained. It felt important that I change it.'

'You felt you should change your dress. Why?'

She almost laughs at the question. 'You can't wear something dirty in public!'

'Who says?'

'Well, my mum for starters . . .'

The woman smiles. 'Ah, mums, eh? How's your relationship with yours?'

Ha! She's prepared for this one; it's what she told Will. The grains of truth; a perfect reason why. He's no idea she knows. But what does she know? Nothing, Penny. Nothing!

'With Mum? Not brilliant, really.'

'Why is that?'

'Just the usual mum and daughter stuff.' It feels disloyal to her mum, but it's true in some ways.

81

The woman remains silent. Debbie, she's called Debbie. Come on Penny, you need to say more. Blame mother, poor mother. 'It's my fault really. I try, but I never quite . . .'

'Never quite what?'

'Meet Mum's standards.' She catches Debbie's gaze. 'When I really should. Dad's high up in the police, but Mum's the achiever. Pretty much superwoman. She's on the church committee, a Justice of the Peace, local school governor, Girl Guide coordinator . . .'

'You feel you don't meet your mum's standards. How does that make you feel?'

The graduation photos on Facebook back then. Smiles, champagne, mortarboards, proud parents. She can give an honest answer to this one. 'It makes me feel under pressure.'

'What do you mean by pressure?' the woman asks.

Anxiety, anxiety, crippling anxiety. Not to lose Will; to be the perfect wife. And fear. Fear of discovery; fear of Will lying.

She tries for a smile. 'Like most women, I suppose. A need to get everything right.'

Will used to think she was perfect. She feels the tears breaking through for the first time since the wedding, but she sniffs them away. She has to get her Will back. She'll do whatever it takes.

CHAPTER FIFTEEN

Dan

Maya pops her head around Dan's office door.

'Wasn't sure if you were still on the phone. Is Geri OK? She sounded a bit anxious when she called earlier—'

Dan smooths his soft beard and shakes himself back to Maya's voice. Geri is nearly eight months pregnant and every unexpected call makes his heart lurch and race with anxiety. He wouldn't dream of telling anyone, not even Maya. They would think he was stupid, a pathetic weak fool. 'Bloody men!' he hears Jen Kenning laugh. 'They're not the ones who have to scream, puff and push, never mind dealing with the bloody haemorrhoids.' Yet that's the problem. If he was the one puffing and pushing, he could deal with it head-on. It's being a helpless onlooker which scares him. 'Yes, she's fine thanks,' he replies automatically, but Maya still hovers, a frown on her small forehead. 'Well, she had a bit of a fright this morning,' he explains. 'The baby hadn't moved for a while . . .' The thought of losing the baby almost paralyses him. He doesn't really want to talk about it, but knows Maya has his best interests at heart. He tries for a smile, taking in her fringe, which has changed colour since yesterday. 'But it's fine. By the time I'd finished with the Hendersons and phoned her back, she said the baby was doing somersaults. So all's good now.'

Maya raises her eyebrows. 'Sounds like a lazy boy.' She hands him the second post. 'There's the signed inventory for the Oak House penthouse.' She puts her hand on a hip. 'I wouldn't mind that swanky new furniture. But then again, a cigarette burn or a coffee stain . . .' She grins. 'Then there's chewing gum, tomato ketchup, curry, hair dye. Ouch! Can you imagine the bill?'

Dan feels a prickling on his spine. 'Oh, it's gone then? Someone has signed up?'

'Yeah, your dreamy chiselled friend.' She looks for a moment at his face. 'I assumed you knew. He signed up last week, I think. Andrew sorted it out.'

'Oh, right. Great.' He picks up his mug. 'I'm parched. I don't suppose there's a coffee going?'

When Maya leaves the room, he sits back in his chair and breathes, feeling surprise, and if he's honest, slight pique. Seb Taylor hasn't been in touch, but then again, why would he? They're not really friends. He's the younger brother of a friend; just an acquaintance. Yet after the viewing they drove back to Chorlton Green. When they arrived, he could see Geri was dead beat, but she made pasta, then sat on the sofa in her fleecy pyjamas and chatted amiably with Seb for more than an hour.

Leaning forward, he doodles, picturing the scene. He made up the fire, then sat opposite them in the armchair and watched, mesmerised by their striking and contrasting beauty: Geri, her face plump and rounded, her black skin and dark eyes glowing and warm, against Seb's. His face so sculpted, his nose straight and sharp, his eyes piercing and blue. The conversation was fascinating too. Geri asked the questions he wouldn't have broached, and though Seb's face was thoughtful, he replied easily. Information about his life, a world away from theirs. The ins and outs of modelling, the sort of money he earned, the famous people he'd met or worked with. And about Claudia, also a model, how they had loved and lived and how it stopped, suddenly.

'I just fell out of love,' he said with a shrug. 'I couldn't get enough of her one day, then the next it just ended, like I was living with a stranger.'

The fire had sizzled and snapped, the conversation moved on, eventually to sport and swimming came up.

'Dan likes to swim,' Geri said. 'You should see him on holiday in his budgie smugglers. Races of course. Every blooming stroke, even butterfly. He always has to win.'

'That's just the toddlers pool,' he quipped. 'Though, seriously, there'd be no chance of beating Sebastian Taylor. A county champion, Geri. He could beat everyone. Though if it was squash or tennis, I might be in with a shot . . .'

'Sunday morning, then,' Geri replied, smiling. 'We can sign Seb in at David Lloyd as a guest. I can go swimming, at a gentle speed for once, you two can play squash and then we can all meet in the cafe for a bite of lunch. The winner pays!'

'You're on,' Seb replied, the grin back on his face. Then Geri said she was exhausted and had to go to bed. Seb ordered a taxi and they hugged at the door. An easy friendly hug, a pat on the back, see you on Sunday. Relaxed and so natural, the whole evening had felt good, really good.

The aroma of coffee alerts him to Maya's presence at his desk. He lifts his head to her questioning dark gaze, wondering if he has a smudge of ink on his nose, but she simply asks for the last tape so she can push on with the typing in time for the post.

Not friends, not really, he's thinking. Seb sent him a text the next evening. '*Sorry, squash another time,*' it read. He hasn't been in touch since.

Dan looks at his watch; the second hand jerks, much like his heart. He put on his bright confident voice when he phoned Geri back. 'A baby acrobat, eh? Sounds like my boy! Everything is fine, Geri. No need for you to worry.'

But still, better safe than sorry, and the midwife said to call any time.

He picks up his mobile and scrolls down the contacts. The midwife's voicemail message kicks in, so he leaves a reply. 'Hi, it's Dan Maloney from Chorlton Green. Everything's fine with Geri and the baby, but could you pop by this evening? Just tell Geri you were passing? A little reassurance would be great.'

Dan washes the dinner dishes absently, then takes the coffees through to Geri. She's curled on the sofa, her eyes on the television screen.

'Come on, Dan, you're missing it.'

She turns to him with an amused smile on her face; it's a comedy they both like, and he sinks down next to her, aware of sounds and seeing colours, but his ears tuned for the doorbell. Trying not to glance at his watch, one programme merges into the next.

The bell finally rings at eight-thirty. A plump midwife bustles in with the cold February wind. She's called Bernadette; she's visited before. Looking at Geri, she crinkles her freckled nose. 'I could say I was just passing, but that wouldn't wash, would it?'

Dan rakes back his hair, aware of Geri's embarrassment, the flash of irritation in her eyes.

'Sorry,' she says to Bernadette. 'I hate making a fuss. It's fine now. The baby didn't seem to move last night, then again this morning, but now I feel as though I was imagining it; he's been moving non-stop since.'

'He?' Bernadette asks, digging in her bag and extracting a number of items, much like Mary Poppins.

Geri nods her head in Dan's direction, but won't look him in the eye. 'A lazy boy, according to his secretary.'

Dan watches with folded arms as Bernadette listens to the baby's heartbeat, then manipulates and measures Geri's bump with a tape measure not dissimilar to the one in his mum's sewing box.

'Baby is fine. Head not engaged yet but a lovely steady beat,' she says. 'Now what about Mum? I'll take your blood pressure while I'm here.' She hands Geri a small container. 'Then can you do me a little pee? Mid flow as usual, please!'

'Are you still cross with me?' Dan asks later, perched on the bed in the dimmed bedroom.

Geri is tucked in and looks sleepy, thank God. Bernadette's friendly face clouded after testing her pee with a stick. Everything was well with the baby, she explained, but Geri's blood pressure was raised and there were traces of protein in her urine. She'd be back again on Thursday, but if the reading was any higher, she'd refer Geri to hospital. High blood pressure in the last weeks of pregnancy wasn't unusual, but it had to be monitored. So Geri needed to rest: no household work, no heavy shopping, no stress. She turned to Dan then. The best way of ensuring rest, she said pointedly, was for someone else to do the chores.

For the past hour Dan has taken Bernadette at her word; he's emptied the dishwasher, vacuumed downstairs and badly ironed seven shirts.

'Course I'm not cross,' Geri replies, reaching for his hand. 'In fact, you did the right thing. I don't have an antenatal appointment for five days. The blood pressure might have been worse if I'd waited.'

'Can I have that in writing? *You did the right thing.* Just to record it for posterity?' Dan laughs, but feels shaky and powerless inside. He releases Geri's hand and stands. 'Right, an online supermarket delivery next. Before you drop off, anything particular we need to buy?'

Geri rolls her eyes. 'Oh, God. It's all going to be beer, blue milk and red meat again, isn't it?'

'Pretty much.' Dan turns off the light as he leaves. 'Now get off to sleep, and no snoring!'

He struggles with the washing machine. He's put in the dirty clothes, pleased at having remembered to keep the whites separate, and he's firmly closed the door. He's guessed the quantities of fabric liquid and conditioner, hoping for the best. But as he crouches at its front and stares at the programme options, he has absolutely no idea which to select. Pre-wash or quick wash, synthetics or cotton? Of course, he could call his mum and ask her, but Annette would want to know why he was doing the laundry at this time of night and why he couldn't ask Geri. Then she'd either imply Geri wasn't pulling her weight or she'd sense imminent doom, and after checking her appearance in the mirror, she'd be round to the house clutching her rosary beads, with his poor dad in tow. Father Peter too, if she could.

Of course, Dan could be truthful and tell his mum about Geri's high blood pressure, but he and his dad have spent years not being entirely truthful with her. Nothing that really matters, but sometimes it has been easier lying low with a problem rather than facing the fuss. Like when he was caught drinking cider at school, or the time he was arrested on a march. When he bumped his dad's old banger before he had a driving licence, when he 'borrowed' coins from the swear box. Even when he was made redundant. It was better for his mum not to know.

He smiles wryly. Only child syndrome. Strong-willed, self-important, controlling and confident. Even arrogant, apparently. But he's never had to worry about that. His mum was the child in their family.

His mobile vibrates in the back pocket of his jeans. It's a number he doesn't recognise.

'Is that Daniel? Daniel Maloney?' a woman asks. Her eloquent thin voice is familiar. 'Hello, Daniel. I'm sorry to call you like this. It's Yvette Taylor, William's mum—'

'Oh, hi, Mrs Taylor,' Dan starts, thinking, Will, oh God, what's happened? I've hardly been in touch. I should've been in touch. 'Is Will OK?'

'It isn't about William, it's Sebastian. It's hard to explain on the telephone, but he's asked for you. I said I would call his brother, but he insists on you. I'm sorry to call at this time and I know your young lady is pregnant, but I'm not sure what else—'

Hearing the crack in her refined tones, he interrupts quickly, 'Don't worry, it's fine. I'll come straight away. I'll only be ten minutes.' He suddenly remembers Seb's Wilmslow flat. 'Where are you now, Mrs Taylor?'

'Sorry, of course. We're both at home in Withington. Sebastian's back with me now. He has been for a while.'

Almost holding his breath, Dan checks on sleeping Geri and leaves her a note, puts on a jacket, feels his pocket for his mobile and steps outside. He climbs into his car, then noticing the frosted windscreen, he strides out again to scrape it with a credit card. His heart thumps loud in his ears. What the hell is going on? He knows Mrs Taylor from childhood parties and occasional sleepovers and of course Will's wedding, but not that well. The A Team lived in different parts of Manchester, so it wasn't like playing with the lad next door; unless there was a sporting activity at the weekend, their friendship stayed at school. And Seb wasn't even part of the A Team. Why ask for a random friend? Why not his brother?

Arriving in Withington, he indicates left onto a cul-de-sac hidden by thick-trunked trees, then into a cobbled courtyard. His breath shallow in his chest, he strides to the last house, the only one not lit by an outside light. As his eyes accustom to the dark, he hops up the stone steps and rings the doorbell, watching the steam of his breath in the frosty night air. There's no answer for a while, so he rings again, wondering what this strange situation is about. Maya said Seb had signed up for Oak House. Why was he still here? And why the hell was he asking for him?

The door finally opens. Mrs Taylor is as tall and dignified as he remembers, but her handsome face is pale and tight and she's breathing heavily. She adjusts the scarf tied chaotically around her head. 'Daniel, thank goodness. He's still upstairs in the bathroom. I don't know what's going on.'

Dan removes his shoes at the door just like when he was a boy. 'Shall I?' he asks, nodding to the stairs, the dash up to Penny suddenly fresh in his mind.

'Yes. Please do go up. It's the bathroom at the very top.' She puts her hand on her chest and raises her chin. 'I think he might have locked it.'

The stairs cold under his feet, Dan climbs, leaving Mrs Taylor below. Turning at the first landing, he sees her lift trembling hands to her face. He takes the next flight two steps at a time, annoyance replacing anxiety. What the hell is Seb playing at? He's a grown man; he saw how Penny's attention-seeking spoilt Nick and Lisa's wedding.

He takes a breath and knocks briskly at the bathroom door. 'Seb? It's Dan. Open the door.' He raps again. 'Seb. Open the bloody door.'

Seconds pass. The anger turns to alarm, his heart thrashes. He stares at the oak door. It looks pretty solid. The police or an ambulance or even the bloody fire brigade? But he'll have a go first. Maybe oak has a soft spot. His shoulder or his foot? Instead he tries the porcelain handle and the door breezes open.

Propped against the side of an old bath, Seb's arms circle his knees. His head is bowed, his face hidden by hair. He's wearing jeans and trainers but his chest is bare.

Crouching down, Dan takes a shallow breath. What if Seb doesn't wake, if he's unconscious, even dead?

'Seb? Seb?' he asks, holding his shoulders and gently shaking.

Sebs lifts his head and opens his eyes. For moments they're glazed and confused, then recognition sets in. 'Dan,' he whispers.

'What's going on, Seb? What have you taken?'

'Nothing. A sleeping pill.'

'How many?'

'Just one, maybe two.'

'What for? Why are you in the bathroom?'

'Cheating,' he says quietly.

Dan feels strangely calm. He dips his face to meet Seb's. 'Cheating? What does that mean?'

Slowly shaking his head, Seb opens his fist. His fingers are darkly stained and it takes a moment for Dan to spot the glint of metal. 'I didn't do it,' he says. 'I knew you'd come.'

'Seb . . .' Carefully removing the razor blade, Dan wraps Seb's hand in a flannel, struggling with an urgent need to cry. 'Seb. Why would you do this?'

Seb rocks his head as the tears spill from his eyes.

'What's going on, Seb? Talk to me.'

He mumbles and drops his head to his knees.

'What?' Dan asks, instinctively pulling the wounded man into his arms and holding him tightly. 'What did you say?'

'I'm lost,' Dan thinks he hears.

He puts his lips to Seb's hair, aware of an ache he's never felt before, certain in this moment that he's hopelessly lost too.

CHAPTER SIXTEEN

Jen

'I like your blouse, Mum,' Holly says, munching her cereal at the small kitchen table. Anna nods too, her mouth crammed with toast.

'Thanks, love. Dad bought it for my birthday, but I thought it was too small. Must've lost a few pounds.'

Maria walks into the room, her school skirt rolled up at the waist. 'Holly creeping up to Mum again,' she comments. She mimics Holly's voice. '"Oh, you do look pretty, Mum. This food is really nice." Blah, blah, blah . . .'

'There's no harm in being pleasant, Maria.' Jen tries to say it evenly; she would rather give her a mouthful, but as Ian points out, it would be counterproductive, resulting in the usual retort that she does nothing right, 'perfect Holly' no wrong.

It's a question of Maria's age and personality, Jen knows, and the truth is they're alike. At thirteen she was equally as opinionated and difficult, but her mum's patience was admirable.

'I'll go to Daddy in Ireland; he loves me,' she'd frequently hurl at Nola if she wasn't getting her own way. Despite her dad's absence, she saw him often, was still his 'precious only girl'. He'd welcome her in Ireland at the drop of a hat. Not that she wanted to leave her mum and her friends in Manchester, but it was nice to know she could escape if she wanted to.

Nola snapped only once, and from the hand covering her mouth and her remorseful eyes, immediately regretted it. 'I'm sick of hearing it, Jennifer! Has it never occurred to you that he chose *her* over you and your brothers?' Then later, more softly, 'I'm sorry for snapping, love. You can't always have your cake and eat it. It's just one of life's hard lessons.'

How she had hated her mum then; she knew her daddy had only left Nola and not his precious only girl, so that didn't bother her. It was her mum's use of the proverb. Even then Jen knew she had a tendency to be greedy, to want the best of both worlds, and why shouldn't she? But now, as a mother herself, she wonders how her lovely mum managed to be so restrained. Who knows what Nola might have said to her own mother and sisters, but if she despised her unfaithful husband, she never let on to Jen or her brothers. To this day her parents are still married and her dad provides financially, but she has a 'stepmum' in Ireland she never intends to meet.

'Toast or cereal?' she asks Maria. Then notices her face; it's heavily made-up, the foundation a shade too dark for her pale freckled skin and she hasn't rubbed it in uniformly. The girls aren't supposed to wear make-up at school, but she understands Maria's need. At thirteen she wouldn't have got away with foundation, but she would've applied mascara, hoping her mum wouldn't notice. Even then she wanted to look nice for Will Taylor. Trying for an Ian sort of tack, she takes a steady breath. 'You look very pretty today, Maria, but maybe the foundation needs . . .' She makes a rubbing motion on the line of her own jaw.

'Oh, for God's sake!' Maria replies, pulling away from the table, stomping to the door and slamming it behind her.

Jen turns to her other daughters, wondering if they'll be as difficult one day. She hopes her fraught relationship with Maria isn't because she's simply crap at relating to girls. After the first few weeks grieving for Will at university, she threw herself into the social scene, doing all the things she figured she'd missed during the two years she'd dated him. But at the end of the day, there was only one thing: close female friendships. Along with Dan and Nick, Will had been her best friend. Perhaps a sister would have made a difference, but she only had brothers. She tried, but she struggled to get close to other women her own age and ended up sharing a house with men.

She sighs inwardly. Holly and Anna are looking down at their breakfast with tense faces; they don't want a scene. Plonking down at the table, she picks up Anna's toast and takes a bite.

'Well, that went well, didn't it?' she says, reeling slightly from the thick spread of Marmite. 'Supermarket this morning. Anything we particularly need?' She gives Anna a friendly nudge. 'Other than chocolate biscuits?'

As she darts through the drizzle between the boot and her front door, Jen waves to Hamid in his garden. Pruning, she supposes, at this time of year. She drops the heavy shopping bags in the hall and feels her hair. It doesn't like rain; rain makes it swell. But it's only a little damp, so that's OK.

Staring at the shopping, she tries to focus on frozen items and the time, but she's distracted by the number of plastic bags she'll have to hide. Ian remembers to recycle, taking them into the supermarket and using them repeatedly until they collapse; she has a hundred in the boot, but always forgets. She digs around for the fish fingers and peas, shoves them in the freezer, then looks at her watch. She still has ten minutes, but still, she wants to look nice, to smell nice too.

In the bathroom she takes off her knickers, has what she terms to the girls as a 'personal wash', puts on a clean pair, then brushes her teeth, applies perfume and a hint of lipstick. This meeting is planned and deliberate; Will Taylor hasn't taken her by surprise by just turning up and needing her. She has no excuse, not even to herself.

She's going to have sex with him this morning.

Her husband is a very good man; she should feel crippling guilt, but as she stares at her pink-cheeked reflection, she feels nothing but breathless excitement.

The low hum of his car filters through the open round window. He's early, which is nice. She hears his commanding 'Morning', wonders what Hamid might make of it. But Will has visited her home hundreds of times, including two weeks ago. Why would today be any different?

She doesn't bother with her tights; she skips down the stairs like the eager teenager she was.

'Mum's gone to the shops, Will. She's usually about an hour. You'll have to be quick!' she hears in her mind, but today they'll have more time than when they were seventeen. Will is officially out of the office on an audit that 'could take two hours or two days'.

'You're early,' she says, smiling as she opens the door. 'I haven't had time to put the shopping away.'

Will circles her waist and pulls her towards him; she stands on tiptoes to kiss his soft lips. She always forgets how tall and broad he is, or perhaps she forgets that she's small.

'Bugger the shopping,' he says after a few moments. 'I've been thinking about you all morning.' He looks at her face, gently raking her hair behind an ear. 'You are beautiful, Jennifer O'Donnell, do you know that?'

Absently stroking her back, Will sighs. 'You have the softest skin ever.'

He hasn't turned away, he hasn't slept. He's so different today; she wonders what he's thinking. He kissed her for much longer than usual, then pulled her on top of him and stared at her face until her moans reached a peak. Then when he came, he didn't let go but kept his arms around her body, holding her tightly against his chest. She heard the thud of his heartbeat and felt him go limp inside her, his warm semen gluing them together until she pulled away with a small laugh, saying she needed to pee. She was glad of the break; pleased to have a wash, to put on her underwear.

'I'll rustle us up a sandwich,' she now says, detaching herself from his warm body.

In the kitchen she flicks on the kettle, makes sandwiches on autopilot, fitfully putting away the shopping and thinking about Will as though he's already left. Analysing their lovemaking like she did at seventeen. She doesn't really like being on top; she's too conscious of her large swinging breasts and the roll of fat around her stomach. She feels infinitely more attractive lying down. And the truth is, she didn't come; she finds it difficult to orgasm in that position. Not that it's a certainty she won't, given time, but she felt under pressure from the intensity of his gaze. If she's honest, Will isn't like Will today. His ardour is freaking her out.

She returns to the bedroom with a large pot of tea and a platter of triangular sandwiches, crusts removed. 'My mum would never forgive me—'

'For us? For doing this?' Will asks, his face serious.

'No, silly, for not eating the crusts.' Jen laughs and climbs on the bed. 'They would make my hair curl if I ate them, apparently. Not that I wanted curly hair.'

Will rubs his head. 'Mine used to curl—'

'I know, I remember.'

They fall silent for a while, Jen eating the sandwiches, Will staring at the ceiling.

'I just wish—' he starts.

'That I'd made cheese and ham? Cheese and pickle will have to do you. Come on, eat up.' She plants a kiss on his nose, needing him to be the usual easy-going Will. She finds herself gabbling to ease her disquiet. 'Which filling do you fancy? You don't want to be responsible for me eating the lot. Talk to me. Tell me about Penny. How's the counselling going? Has she gone back to work? We exchange texts every now and then, but it's difficult. I don't know how much I'm supposed to know.'

Will hitches up the bed, takes the platter and brings Jen up to speed with information she already knew or had guessed. Penny has finally seen the psychiatrist; he's diagnosed a psychotic episode brought on by anxiety and stress; she isn't a danger to herself; if she learns to deal with the underlying problems, it's unlikely to happen again. The real danger was in bottling the issues rather than dealing with them; the anxiety had fermented, the bottle top had finally popped at Nick's wedding.

'Presumably the relationship with her mum,' Jen says, looking at the remaining triangles and wondering if she should've made just one more smoked salmon and cream cheese.

'Well, yes . . .' Will replies.

The change in his tone stops her short.

'I guess her mum has made it worse,' he says slowly.

Jen puts down her sandwich. 'Made what worse?'

Will glances at her, then looks away. 'Penny's feelings of failure. She says her mum always had, and still has, ridiculous expectations; never holds back in letting her know if she's dropped below them.'

'Bloody hell, Penny went to Cambridge; she looks down a microscope all day to prevent babies getting spina bifida,' Jen says, knowing that isn't the point, that Will is trying to say something else, something she doesn't want to hear. She continues doggedly, 'She can hardly have fallen below anyone's—'

'We've been trying for a baby, Jen.' He pulls up his knees and rests his head in his hands. 'Nothing's happened yet. I know that's not unusual, that it sometimes takes months, even years, but Penny's desperate for it to happen. She tries not to show her disappointment but . . . I tell her to relax, that I'm chilled either way, but she says her mum's on her case all the time. Wants her to have a boy, obviously.'

It feels like a blow; a terrible blow, almost physical. 'I didn't know—' Jen starts. But then why would she? Why would Will tell her he was trying to start a family? He's married to Penny; it's what people do. Yet it's something she's never contemplated: Will as a doting father.

He continues to speak, his voice soft and thoughtful. 'I suppose that's why the wedding was so difficult for her to handle. Seeing Geri's bump, watching other people's toddlers and your girls; everyone carefree and happy. Then her period came. God, I'm no expert and she's playing it down, but my guess is her feelings of failure were brought to a head . . . I'm sorry, Jen. I should have said something before now.'

She tries to keep the hurt from her voice. 'No, of course not. No reason why you should. It's yours and Penny's business, not mine.' She slips from the bed and picks up her scattered clothes.

'Nearly two-thirty! I'll top up the tea, then it's probably time for you to go.'

She hears Will enter the kitchen, but doesn't turn from the kettle. He slips his arms around her waist. 'You're crying,' he says.

Jen shakes her head. She has no right to be weeping, but the deep scratch of heartbreak is there at the surface. Like the agony of childbirth, it has come back, an indescribable pain she'd thought was forgotten. Her mum managed to hide the full truth of her dad's betrayal until she was sixteen. Nola didn't want to tell her then, but knew there was a fine line between telling the brutal truth and perpetuating an easy lie, which would eventually be found out. The misery she had felt was unbearable. A double pain. She already knew that her daddy had left her mum; now she knew he had left her as well.

Will gently turns her around and bends to look at her face. 'It might never happen.'

'It *should* happen,' she replies, covering her eyes with her hands. 'I want it to happen, for you both. You'll be lovely parents. It's just—'

'I know,' he replies.

Will doesn't want to leave but Jen persuades him to go, saying she needs to stop crying, to give her face time to recover before collecting Anna from school. But the truth is she wants to sob, to weep for her sorry self, like she did at eleven, like she did at sixteen. Then again two years later, when Will Taylor broke the heart he'd so tenderly mended.

She wipes her face and watches silently as Will knots his tie and slips on his jacket. He's filled out in the last few years, but keeps himself in shape playing squash with Nick or Dan. It reminds her of Geri's phone call last night.

'Did you know Dan and Geri want to have us all round for

a meal before their new baby arrives? This weekend's the plan. Do you think Penny will be up for it?'

'I suppose she might. More getting back on track.' Will pats his pocket. His eyes are distracted. 'So, I guess I'll see you then.' He walks from the kitchen towards the front door, then turns and comes back. 'I bought you something,' he says. He reaches in his pocket and brings out a small ivory box which he places on the table. 'It's nothing much. I just saw them and thought they'd look nice on you.' He smiles faintly. 'Something that wouldn't be noticed; something you might have had for years. See you at Dan's.'

Jen waits for the click of the front door before letting out her breath, then sits down at the table, her chest aching, her face wet. Her fingers tremble as she opens the box. A small pair of diamond earrings shine sharply from their black pillow, earrings with posts, designed for pierced ears. Closing her eyes, she feels for an earlobe. She hasn't worn pierced earrings since she was a teenager.

Jen stares at the orangey glow on her plate. Spaghetti bolognese for dinner. She tries to limit it to once a week, but still feels like a rotten mother. It's not the only dish she can cook, but it's one all three girls will devour without complaint. Anna's class did a project at school about healthy eating. She came home with a food timetable to complete and wouldn't let anyone else in the family see it. Jen thought nothing more about it until Anna's class teacher sidled up in the staffroom.

'Spaghetti bol for tea tonight, perchance?' the teacher asked before presenting her with the evidence in Anna's loopy scrawl. 'It's OK, I won't call social services this time,' the teacher laughed. 'Even I'm not convinced Anna eats it for breakfast.' She'd looked at Jen's face. 'Oh, Jen, I'm only teasing. I thought

101

a clean sweep was hilarious. Tell you what, though, you should see some of the answers.'

Jen winds the pasta on her fork, but doesn't feel hungry. The family rule is to finish one's plate of food, including the vegetables. She wonders if the girls will notice her break it today.

'What have you been up to, love?' Ian asks from the other end of the table. 'I'm jealous of your days off. Do you think a head of year would get away with a job-share application?'

'No chance,' she replies, trying for a smile. 'You're too precious, being a maths genius. Maria has already had three supply teachers since September, haven't you, love?' She looks at Maria but her head is down and there's no reply. 'Just the supermarket today, which reminds me. I bought something for you girls.' She leaves the room and returns with three Easter eggs. 'Ta-da!' she says, holding them up like a glamorous assistant on a quiz show. 'An early treat before the real Easter bunny arrives.'

Maria lifts her head, her expression scathing. 'I actually thought it would be something interesting. Easter isn't even for weeks.'

Jen takes a breath and counts to five. She hadn't intended them for today, but hoped to lighten her own gloom by pleasing the girls. 'It's just for fun, Maria. I thought it might bring a smile. Look, I've selected each of your favourite Disney movies. *Frozen* for Anna, *Ratatouille* for Holly and *Toy Story* for you. *Toy Story 3* of course.' She catches Ian's surprised face. 'It said limited edition, so I didn't want them to be gone the next time—'

'I'm not eight any more, Mum. What would I want with Disney chocolate? I've had it before. It's disgusting and tastes cheap and nasty. If you're that bothered, you can have mine. You'll enjoy stuffing your—'

Ian bangs the table with his fist. 'Don't you dare,' he roars. 'Don't you dare speak to your mother like that, Maria. Get up to your room. And give me your mobile.'

'I haven't got it—'

'Do you think I'm bloody blind? It's on your lap. You've been looking at it all through the meal.'

Maria leaves the room with the inevitable slam; Anna and Holly continue to eat with heads bowed in silence.

'Thanks, Mum, I like mine,' Holly eventually says.

'And I *am* eight,' Anna adds, breaking the tension.

'Are you all right, love?' Ian asks later when the girls have gone to bed. He pulls Jen into a hug at the sink. 'You seem a bit . . . delicate. Sorry I lost my rag with Maria, but I think she's had it coming for a while.'

She looks at Ian, then kisses his cheek. He's usually so measured and reasonable; she does the shouting. 'She's pushing the boundaries. And probably hormonal or in love. Longing for the boy at the desk behind to notice she exists. That type of thing.'

'At thirteen I was too busy building my railway set in the attic to notice girls.'

She smiles weakly. 'Not to mention the train- and plane-spotting.'

It's one of their in-jokes; Ian's a self-confessed nerd. But steady and dependable and kind.

He sighs and shakes his head. 'I see it every day at school. They're so grown-up these days. Texting, sexting, putting dodgy photographs on Instagram. So aware of, well, everything. But when it's your own . . . Tell me you weren't in love at thirteen.'

'Well . . .' Jen replies, pulling further into the hug, wishing she fancied this lovely man even a fraction of how much she still wants Will.

'Of course; Will,' Ian replies with a laugh. 'I always forget about you two.' He pulls away and picks up a tea towel. 'Did you have a nap today?'

Jen feels her face flushing. 'No, why?'

'Oh, nothing.' He shakes his head and changes the subject. 'Have we got a date for the get-together at Dan's? It's good of Geri to offer when she's nearly fit to burst.'

'Dan's on cooking duties, but I suggested we could all bring a dish.' Trying to act normal, she prods Ian at the waist, hoping the colour has died from her face. 'This Saturday. Maybe you could do your famous curried potatoes.'

'*A* dish, Jen Kenning? I don't think you're programmed to prepare only one—'

The telephone interrupts Ian's reply and Jen answers.

'Is that Mrs Kenning? Holly's mum?'

Her stomach clenches. 'Yes, it is.'

'It's Miss Fern, her PE teacher.' Her voice is terse, to the point, she doesn't sound friendly. 'Is it convenient to have a few words?'

Holly? What the hell? 'Of course.'

'It's about Holly's weight loss. Haven't you noticed?' The teacher doesn't try to keep the distain from her voice. 'To be honest, she looks half-starved in her PE kit. It's only my opinion, but if she was my daughter, I would have her checked out by a doctor.' She's silent for a moment. 'Unless, of course, that's already in hand.'

CHAPTER SEVENTEEN

Nick

Nick opens his eyes. The bedroom is dark, Lisa silent beside him. The dream has dissolved but his legs are burning with the tingling sensation he's experienced over the past few weeks. He doesn't look at his watch; he knows it'll be three, his personal witching hour.

He rewinds to his Hale visit, examining Derek's face behind his closed eyes. 'Patrick's twin,' he said, but the nod was final. That was as much as he was prepared to say. It was fair enough really. It wasn't his godfather's place, and as much as he had wanted to know more, he'd been embarrassed too, couldn't wait to get out of the stifling bungalow. It wasn't the sort of conversation Nick Quinn had with anybody. Except Lisa, of course. He'd rushed home with the news, his hand trembling on the steering wheel, pleased not to return empty-handed after all.

'Susan was Patrick's twin,' he blurted the moment he arrived in their bedroom.

Lisa pulled off her eye mask. He could tell from her sleepy, disorientated look that she'd had a glass or two of wine, but

105

she shook herself awake, patted the bed and spoke, her lilting voice infused with enthusiasm. 'Really? Susan was your sister? Wow. Jump in and tell me all about it.'

They talked for an hour, maybe more, looking at the revelation from every angle. Lisa interested, asking questions, speculating on what might have happened. A childhood illness or an accident, she concluded. Either way it was tragic. No wonder it wasn't mentioned. And she let him rabbit on, smiling and supportive and loving, until he remembered she was on an early shift. So then he let her sleep, watching her soft face and marvelling at how lucky he was to have found her, his needle in a haystack of mugshots online.

He now turns the pillow and sighs. He's never had this wakefulness in his life before and isn't sure how to deal with it. Some say to get up, have a piss, read a book or make a drink, but he doesn't want to disturb his sleeping wife. Blackout blinds, thick-lined curtains and her eye mask. And a stiff drink. He thought her bedtime routine was odd at first, but as she put it, 'You've never had to work shifts, have you, Nick? You've never had to trick your body into sleeping when you want it to. It isn't flipping easy.' And she was right. He'd never worked shifts, he'd never done anything unusual; he'd had a nice, comfortable, sheltered life. Regular and safe. The most dangerous thing he'd done was the internet dating, and even there he'd fallen on his feet more or less the first time. But then he'd been cautious about what he wanted, who he wanted. He'd chatted online with several women, but Lisa was the only one he had wanted to meet.

He sighs and turns to a thin crack of light through the curtains. Perhaps that's why he's so obsessed about the sister he's never met. Not that he's described it as an *obsession*; that was Lisa's word. They'd talked about it most evenings and then on Tuesday she'd suddenly snapped. 'Can't we talk about something other than your bloody obsession?' He was offended and hurt, put on his jacket to go out. But where would he go? For a drink with Dan would be the obvious choice, but Dan would look at him with those dark trustful eyes and Nick wasn't ready to talk about it, probably never would be. A family secret wasn't the kind of thing that went on in either of their lives. They were just ordinary guys.

Of course, there was the Penny blip. That wasn't ordinary and if he's honest he's avoided telephoning Will because he doesn't know how to handle it, how he would handle it, if he'd be forgiving or understanding, or just bloody annoyed. Once the shock had worn off he'd been fine at the wedding, relaxed about it on the honeymoon, but the discovery he had a sister has thrown him, the Nick Quinn he once knew has changed. This one wakes in the night full of resentment and anger.

Time passes and he stirs again with a jolt. Lisa's side of the bed is empty and there's daylight through the open door. He sits up and lowers his head, feeling dizzy and gluey from the interrupted argument with both his parents in his dream. The reason why has evaporated already, but he remembers the shouting, his and Patrick's shouting.

He turns to the clock. Oh fuck, look at the time. Hot, sweaty and slightly nauseous, he tumbles out of bed. What the hell? He has a meeting at ten. Why didn't she wake him?

The tiny contact lenses refuse to stick to his eyes, his toothbrush falls, spreading a line of striped paste on the floor. The shower is too cold, then too hot; he still hasn't worked out how to fix the mean temperature, the soap is soggy and the towel Lisa left on the heated rail is still damp. The team meeting's in an hour; it's in a fucking hour! He needs breakfast, that's the thing. He's hopeless without food.

His head clears and his heart slows as he spoons in the dull muesli and chews. He almost breaks a smile. He hasn't overslept since he went to a house party with Will and Dan and woke up next to an extremely fat girl. The ribbing went on for weeks. 'Except she had no ribs,' one of them quipped. The team meeting will be fine. It's his team after all. He'll take the tram, say his car's on the blink. He can text, rearrange. He's not usually late. It's not the end of the world.

'It's not the end of the world, Nick!' Jen's words, said often at school. She called him for a chat last night.

'I know the A Team are important,' Lisa said when he'd finished. 'But remember I'm a team member now. Your A plus!'

'So you are,' he replied, not sure that he liked it.

Feeling disoriented in his glasses, he climbs the stairs and pads to the bedroom. The door handle still sticks. Though he's not a bloody joiner, Lisa asked him to repair it, replace it, whatever.

Standing at the wardrobe, he smiles wryly. 'You and me both,' he says aloud, as he struggles to align the sliding door on its track. He pulls out a grey suit. He and his colleagues sit in front of computers all day, so dress code is casual, but suits are expected for meetings. Raking irritably through Lisa's clothes, which take up most of the closet, he searches for a shirt. But a white shirt isn't there, nor any blue ones. What the hell? He hasn't worn a bloody shirt all week. He stalks down the stairs to the kitchen, pulls out the ironing basket, throwing to one side Lisa's uniforms, her blouses and skirts. His shirts are at the bottom, all bloody six of them, crinkled and creased. He pictures Lisa's easy shrug. 'They're your shirts, Nick. They're not going to iron themselves.'

He immediately thinks of his mum, wonders if there's time for her to drive over and iron them now. Dismissing the thought, he shoves them into a plastic bag. He'll drop them off after work. His mum will be delighted. There's his dressing gown too. That needs a wash.

He stomps back upstairs, puts on a patterned shirt, toys with the selection of ties, then decides not to bother. He's not at St Mark's anymore, for God's sake. Then he sits on the bed, sends a text to work and composes one to Lisa.

'You could've given me a nudge before you left,' he types before deleting it.

He wants to mention her team member comment, the lack of cereal choice, the towel, the soap and the shirts. The bloody door handle. He wants to complain about the description 'obsession'. But he knows he isn't being fair. He would've been annoyed if Lisa had woken him at half past five. She works the same as him; why should she do the shopping and the ironing? The word obsession still rankles, but she did apologise; someone had died on her high-dependency unit that day. Said she didn't mean to be rude, but putting it in context . . .

He catches himself in the mirror as he leaves the bedroom. An unshaved man wearing dodgy glasses with wet spiky hair, trying to look trendy, stares back. He quickly takes a selfie. *'Things can only get better,'* he types, sending it to Dan and Will.

Scooping up his keys, he heads for the door. Then turns back to the kitchen, helps himself to a handful of biscuits and empties the bag of shirts into the ironing basket.

CHAPTER EIGHTEEN

Penny

Penny stares at the jug as Debbie pours the water. Plastic, of course, with plastic matching beakers. God, she wishes she didn't have to do this peeling back of layers. She's hardly a risk to herself or anyone. But she's being dutiful, as ever. Here to convince Will she's stable, taking the antipsychotics like a good girl, even though they make her sluggish and tired.

Drifting back to last night, she tries to block out Will's withdrawn mood, the way he stared at his mobile as though willing it to ring, then turning it face down when he saw she was watching.

Normal behaviour or secretive? Normal, Penny, normal. Don't go there again. Paranoia, that's all. Just stupid paranoia!

'Penny?' No clipboard today, Debbie leans her head on her fist. 'The panic attack you described. The psychiatrist called it a psychotic episode. I know you're a scientist. Do you think that's fair?'

A curveball question; where is this going? The usual spread of goosebumps. 'It's an umbrella term, I suppose, for various mental health problems . . .'

Debbie gazes. 'An umbrella term. Any similar episodes or issues?'

'No.'

'None at all?'

Penny shifts in her seat. 'Exam time at uni, maybe.' Then she smiles. 'But everyone gets stressed then, don't they?'

Debbie nods and waits. Then eventually: 'OK. Can we go back to the wedding, Penny?' The therapist picks up her notes. 'You mentioned your anxiety about the dress and your need to change it because it was stained. Can you tell me more about it?'

Still picturing Will's frown, Penny sips her water. On a high yesterday morning, a low when he got home. Work pressures, probably. Oh God, she hopes so.

'Penny? Why were you anxious about your dress at the wedding?'

She comes back to Debbie's soft eyes and her question. The query makes her angry and hot, but it's one she can't parry. A baby, a child, the intense need for Will's baby. She's played it down with him as usual, but he might talk about it in the family session, if one goes ahead. Then it would look odd.

She clears her throat. 'I had just been to the ladies' and discovered my period had started. The stain wasn't blood, just the water from washing my hands, but I got it all out of proportion, I suppose. Tried to focus on other things . . .'

'Like?'

Penny smiles wryly, hears the tune, but from a distance right now, thank God. 'The rain.'

'How did you feel about getting your period?'

She takes a breath, willing the words to come out normally. 'I was disappointed. Will and I had been trying for a baby since we got married.'

Debbie stays silent.

'Of course I couldn't show it, but I was . . .' Devastated, bloody devastated. Again. Watching other people's kids laugh, hug and run. Envious, deeply jealous. Wanting to scream. 'Disappointed. I thought I might be pregnant.' She shakes her head. 'Stupid, really. I think that every time.'

'You thought you might be pregnant but you weren't. How did that make you feel?'

Terrified she'll lose Will. But she doesn't say that. She tells another truth, relieved to let it out. 'A failure. A complete failure.'

Seconds pass without words. 'Penny? What are you thinking?'

Not thinking, but hearing, right now in her head.

'Penny?'

She tries not to cover her ears. To be honest or not? Would Debbie tell Will? She's never mentioned the voices to him. But she's scared, really scared. It mustn't happen again.

'There's a rhyme in my head now. Another nursery rhyme.'

'Like at the wedding?'

Penny's heart starts to slow. No, not an actual voice like the wedding, not really. 'No, just a tune.'

'Which is it?'

'Hush little baby, don't say a word.'

'When do you hear these tunes or rhymes?'

'When I'm anxious, I suppose.'

'Do they help?'

Penny thinks. 'They're soothing, I guess. And safe.'

'Why soothing and safe?'

Penny nods; it makes sense. 'Takes me back . . .'

Takes her back to the time before she *went bad*. But, of course, she won't say that. Will mustn't know. He must never, never know.

CHAPTER NINETEEN

Dan

Feeling ridiculously light-hearted at Saturday breakfast, Dan takes the last bite of his bacon and egg bap and scrapes back his chair. Tensing as usual, he checks his mobile for new messages. The texts between him and Seb have been frequent over the past few days and he's bobbed over to the Red Lion each evening for a quick beer with him, but the tight knot in his gut is still there. Of brotherly concern, of course. Fucking terror, if he's honest. But everything's fine, thank God. Seb is pretty much back to normal.

Well, as normal as life can be in such astonishing circumstances.

After the surprise call from Yvette on Tuesday, Dan didn't know what to expect, and then when he got there and found Seb in that terrible state, he found he had reserves of strength and wise words he hadn't known he possessed. He sent Mrs Taylor to bed with a reassuring smile and sat Seb in the kitchen, plying him with strong coffee and questions. What exactly had he taken? How many? Had this happened before? Did Will and his mum know?

There was a ball of anxiety in his stomach as he examined Seb's broken face. He knew then that Seb wasn't attention-seeking; his mental state was real and devastating. His heart lurching with compassion, he knew he had to do something, but what? Call an ambulance? Drive Seb to a hospital? Make him be sick? He'd left Geri asleep and alone. She had high blood pressure. Was *she* OK? But eventually Seb's eyes seemed to clear. 'You sound like the fucking Gestapo,' he said. He began to talk then and Dan was reprieved from having to decide.

Coming back to Geri's gaze, he kisses her cheek. 'Will you be all right on your own? I don't know how long I'll be or how much stuff Seb has to move.'

'I'm pregnant, not ill, Dan. Besides, I'll be glad to get rid of you and all your hovering. Not to mention the smell of fried eggs!'

'Hovering? Harsh word. I was thinking more *domestic goddess*. Who knew I was such a star. Cleaning, shopping, washing, great conversationalist—'

'Thank goodness Jen has taken control of the cooking tonight is all I can say. It isn't kind to give one's friends constipation through lack of fibre, scurvy through lack of fruit, diabetes through excessive—'

He gives Geri a peck on her cheek. 'You love me really.'

She puts her hand on her stomach and looks at him thought-fully for a moment. 'I do love you. Very much. And I'm glad you've cheered up. You seemed really down a few weeks ago. It wasn't like you.'

Dan shelves the comment. 'That's because I'm looking forward to the get-together tonight. Are you certain you're up to it? I'm sure everyone would understand if—'

Geri throws a toast crust in his direction. 'Go!' she says. 'You're driving me bonkers.'

Absently listening to the radio, he drives to Withington through light rain which might just be snowfall, then he parks on the cobbles and looks up. In the light of day the three Georgian houses are huge. He hears Salim's voice saying that if these houses were in Wilmslow they would be worth a 'fucking fortune'. Yet even in Withington they are impressive, stunning and stately and still proper family homes; he certainly wouldn't pass up the chance if one came on the market.

'Morning, Mrs Taylor,' he says brightly at her front door. 'Chilly weather. Wrap up warmly if you're going out today. Sounds crazy for February but I think it might snow.'

She takes him by the hand, holding it firmly. She's a graceful lady, her angular face hollow now, but it's clear where Seb gets his looks from. 'Please call me Yvette.' She looks at him intently, the focus for once in her eyes. 'You will look after him, won't you? He doesn't like me to ask about it, but I know he goes through low phases. Bipolar, I expect. He won't let me tell William. But he's entitled to his privacy, we all are.'

'Of course,' Dan replies. He isn't surprised at her words. He can remember the glazed look on her beautiful face when the A Team came for sleepovers and parties. She rarely smiled or fussed like his own mum. She'd silently detach herself and go upstairs to her room, leaving Mr Taylor in charge, gregarious, fun and loud.

She meanders to the kitchen, leaving him in the large breezy hall, tapping his foot on the parquet for several minutes. He considers calling Seb's name, but something makes him look up and he's there in the shadows of the first-floor landing, staring silently down.

Averting his gaze, Dan clears his throat and turns to a battered suitcase by the door. 'Yours, I assume.'

'Yup. Apart from the boxes, that's pretty much it,' Seb replies, walking down.

'Three boxes and an eighteenth-century suitcase. The sum total of your worldly possessions?' Dan asks. He wasn't aware of holding his breath, but feels a warm spread of release as he exhales: Seb's face looks healthy and fresh, the only evidence of dysfunction being the gauzy bandage on his right hand.

Seb shrugs. 'Everything's in France.' Then he smiles. 'Or was. Thrown out or sold by now, I should think.' He walks to his mum who has silently appeared behind Dan. 'You didn't really like her, did you, Ma? But too polite to say anything.' He pulls her into a hug. 'I'm only down the road. Not as far as France this time. OK?'

She drops her head on his chest for a moment, then gently pushes him away with the flat of her large bony hand. 'Food,' she says. 'It's on the kitchen table. I prepared you a box of tins and dry food, then there's meat and dairy for the fridge and I've frozen some meals. Put them in the freezer as soon as you're there.'

Dan smiles in the lift to the penthouse apartment, remembering how nervous he felt last time he was in it. A clean shirt and the aroma of coconuts. He'd supposed Seb was trying to seduce him. The thought seems silly now.

'Fart scene,' Seb says. 'That's what you're thinking.'

'I didn't think you were listening.' Dan laughs, thankful Seb doesn't know what he's thinking.

'I've seen it now. On YouTube.' He lifts his eyebrows. 'You finally make sense.'

Seb's face suddenly transforms with the huge grin Dan rarely sees. He hopes it lasts. He still feels guilty for misjudging him, Penny too. He's always been socially conscious, but never really understood that mental health problems are as genuine and damaging as any illness. Seb gave him that insight. Sat at his mum's kitchen table and gesticulating with his injured hand, the words abruptly flowed.

'It's like claustrophobia, Dan. The walls cave in without hope; there's no happiness, no desire, no fucking energy. It's as though it's sucked out.' He briefly met Dan's eyes before dropping his gaze to his palm. They had both stared at the blood seeping through the white flannel. 'You can't imagine. The need just to stop becomes overwhelming.'

Dan listened, saying nothing, unsurprised when Seb admitted to being diagnosed by a French doctor as bipolar. Prescribed stabilisers, he'd never collected the prescription; he didn't like being labelled or dependent on pills. And besides, he felt he coped better smoking weed.

Dan broke his silence and became angry then. 'For fuck's sake, Seb. My limited knowledge may only come from reading the *Sunday Observer*, but can't cannabis bring on psychosis or make things even worse? And anyway, you shouldn't be self-prescribing, look where it's got you tonight.'

Seb promised to see an English doctor; he even managed a small smile and 'Scout's honour'. Dan doesn't want to spoil his contentment by raising it now, but wonders if he's seen the promise through.

The apartment smells of polish and lemons; it's as cream-coloured as Dan remembers. Seb lugs the suitcase through to the master bedroom, then comes back to the kitchen where they drink lager and empty the boxes. With a raised eyebrow, Dan takes the piss out of the few sentimental knick-knacks Seb has brought – his album of sporting certificates, a framed photograph of him and Will as small boys, a scrapbook bursting with football memorabilia, a Thomas the Tank Engine alarm clock.

Seb lightly flushes and laughs. 'Mum packed everything but my clothes.'

'Yeah, right. I believe you, honest,' Dan replies with a mock-serious face.

They move onto another box, extracting pairs of mismatched crockery – patterned china bowls, plates, cups and saucers, bone-handled knives, ornate fish forks and dimpled serving spoons, items clearly purloined from Yvette's erratic kitchen. They line them up on the dark island like Noah's Ark. For a moment they stare at the scene.

'Yup, goes well,' Dan comments, his eyes sweeping the glossy kitchen. 'You'll only be able to invite one friend to the tea party, though.'

They laugh, but the unpacking takes only minutes. Dan swigs the last of his beer and looks at his watch.

'Don't go yet,' Seb says. 'Let's eat one of Mum's delicacies for lunch.' He dips into the cool bag, chock-a-block with plastic boxes, and extracts the first one. Squinting at the tiny scrawl on the label, he reads, 'Ratatouille with bacon. Six minutes to heat. How does that sound?' He stands at the microwave looking doubtful. 'How are you with new gadgets?'

Dan moves next to him, remembering his quip to Geri this morning. Her parents and sister have travelled up from Birmingham to take her shopping, so he knows he has time. 'Dab hand at everything. Domestic goddess, that's me.'

He programmes six minutes, then stares at his reflection in the dark oven door. Seb's shoulder is touching his. He's looking at him, not the microwave.

'That so?' Seb says and Dan turns his head, wondering if Seb can hear the hammer of his heart.

Dan takes a deep breath. 'You said you're not gay, right?'

'I did.'

Dan backs away to the kitchen island, sits on a bar stool and turns the empty beer bottle with the tips of his fingers. Eventually he speaks, his voice croaky. 'Then the night of Nick's wedding . . .' He doesn't want to ask, but he really needs to know; not a night has gone by without him examining what happened from every angle. 'You invited me – at least I think you did – into bed. Suppose I'd said yes? What then?'

Seb rests against the sink, his arms folded. 'I've no idea. I've never . . . I've never done anything further than a fumbled snog with a guy and that was . . . different.' He shrugs. 'He came onto me and I wanted to know what a kiss would be like, so I thought why not. But the wedding . . . I suppose I was pissed. Then the brandy—'

'Oh, right.' Dan drops his gaze, colour flooding his cheeks. So, he had got it wrong. He can't quite identify the strange mix of emotions fogging his mind, but at least he now knows.

Seb steps forward, leans on the granite surface and dips his head to Dan's. 'The brandy made me brave. Perhaps I thought I was in with a chance.'

Dan lifts his head in surprise. Seb's voice is warm and playful.

'I had a crush on you when I was eleven, Dan. Daniel Maloney, dark and handsome, so fit, a sporting hero. *Super Dan*, as Will used to call you—'

'Really? I had no idea.'

'I know,' Seb replies dryly. 'I was invisible. Staring at you longingly in my striped pyjamas from the top bannister when you came to see Will.'

Dan laughs unsteadily. 'Now you're taking the piss,' he replies.

'It was agony, actually.' Seb pauses for a moment, his eyes piercing. 'Then when I was thirteen. The swimming gala. You noticed me then.'

'You didn't win. Against all expectations you came fourth.

119

CHAPTER TWENTY

Jen

Jen bumps onto the Chorlton Green kerb, the loud clink of dishes dragging her back from dark thoughts. Geri's at her front door, chatting to her neighbour. She lifts her hand to wave.

Climbing out, Jen stifles a yawn. 'You are so good to us,' she hears as she makes for the boot. A rattling milk float overtakes, blocking the sound. When she turns, Geri's there in her slippers, holding out her arms to help, her broad smile lighting her face as usual.

Geri takes the proffered platter. 'That smells delicious. Thank you so much! Without you we'd be subject to Dan's attempts at haute cuisine. He's been looking up salad recipes on the internet, so be warned.' She studies Jen's face for a moment. 'Fancy a sit-down before you bring everything in? It's the least I can do.'

Jen smiles wryly. 'If I sit down I might not get up again.' She watches the milkman and thinks of her wakefulness last night; three hours of worrying about everything, from Holly's weight loss to why Ian asked about her napping, from Will's unexpected gift to accidentally poisoning the guests tonight. 'One of those nights, tossing and turning,' she explains, then focuses on Geri's huge bump. 'Listen to me complaining! At least I *can* toss and turn.' She steps to Geri and greets her with a kiss on both cheeks. 'Dan not home?'

'Not yet. He's being really sweet by helping Seb move to his new flat. Mind you, I think he was glad to escape his duties for a while—'

'Duties?'

Geri rubs her belly and looks thoughtful. 'The midwife put the fear of God in him. Not that Dan believes in God, of course.'

Jen smiles and picks up a roasting tray. 'Very true. Probably why he's the best of us all.' She follows Geri to the hall and takes the dish through to the kitchen. 'I'll get the next box—'

She's stopped by Geri's inquisitive gaze. God, she must look rough.

'Quick coffee first?' Geri asks.

Jen looks at her watch, she really doesn't have time and the smell of fried eggs makes her feel strangely sad. When she lifts her head, Geri speaks again. 'Any particular reason for the tossing and turning?'

'Holly's PE teacher phoned to say she's too thin. A neglectful mother, she all but said. I feel like a really crap mum.' The words are out before she can stop them. She hadn't intended to say anything to anyone. It's ridiculous, she knows, but the anxiety about Holly makes her nauseous, which is pretty ironic.

'You are not a crap mum, Jen! Far from it. I'm sure the teacher just put it badly. What are you planning to do?'

Not in the mood to elaborate, Jen gathers her escaped hair and threads it back in her ponytail before replying, but she's saved by the loud peal of Geri's telephone. 'Think that's yours, Geri. I'll grab the rest of the food and shoot off.'

Retreating to her boot, Jen adjusts tin foil and sighs. She scoops out the heavy platter and almost bumps into Dan.

His grin's as bright as Geri's. 'Bloody hell, Jen. There's only eight of us. We're not feeding the five thousand.'

'Bit biblical for you, Dan,' she comments wryly. She hands him the plate and nods to his open front door. 'There's a couple more in the hall.' Looking down at her clothes, she wonders how she must look. Despite washing the hoodie several times, the butter stain remains stubbornly, like a reminder of Will. The jolt of sadness is there, but she tries for her jovial tone. 'I've brought them now in my chavvy trackie so I can go glam later. And drink myself to oblivion. If I've forgotten anything, it's tough.'

Dan narrows his eyes. 'Are you coming in for a drink?'

It's tempting to let it out, but she's said too much already. 'Nah, already bored Geri, poor woman.' She climbs in the car, breathing through the sudden impulse to cry. 'Besides, you're the hostess with the mostest, Danny boy. Time's ticking. Haute cuisine salad, I believe. You've work to do.'

Dan squats down by the car door. 'Everything OK? Want to talk?'

She gazes for a moment before answering. His dark eyes are glowing and there's an air of suppressed excitement about him, but he's always had a knack of knowing when she's low. 'You're a sweetie. You know that, don't you, Dan? Not just a pretty face.'

He nods after a moment. 'OK. See you later,' he says. 'Don't forget your beautiful smile.'

Pulling onto the drive, Jen doesn't move for some time. She stares at her small semi. She loves this house; she loves the bay windows, the white render, the round toilet window; she loves the paved driveway that could do with some attention, the privet, the firs. And she loves what's inside; not just the snug dining room crowded by school photographs and the piano, the messy cushion-strewn lounge and open fire, the compact bright kitchen. She adores her family, her beautiful girls and her Ian. She wouldn't want it any other way, she really wouldn't. Would she?

She glances at her watch, not particularly registering the time, but automatically working out how many minutes of the football match have passed. She's usually checked the score by now, anticipating Ian's mood when he returns. Even if United win, he'll be cross if they don't play at their best, if they're half-hearted or let in any goals. She just ignores him, of course, lets him rant for a while before he retreats in a sulk. But that isn't so bad. What did her mum once say? 'Better football than a woman.' And, of course, Nola should know.

Loving, reliable Ian. What did he mean by her napping?

Closing her eyes, she pictures a hot noisy coach of football supporters and smiles at the memory. Fourteen years ago! How fast time has passed. It was an away match to Anfield at university and she sat next to another student, biting her nails. Other than his ginger hair, she barely noticed him, but they were sitting together again at the ground. Although she did the usual effing and jeffing, he watched the match with a rigid face in near silence. But at half-time he turned, showing a warm, friendly smile.

'You're noisy,' he said. 'Tell me, what madness made us choose to go to uni in Liverpool of all places?'

No one would ever replace Will, but she immediately liked him; he came from Manchester, his home a stone's throw away from Old Trafford, and she instinctively knew he was steady and dependable. United scored and they hugged. It turned to a clumsy kiss which became a long snog.

Steady, dependable Ian. The one thing that's certain. Oh God. Everything's fine there, isn't it?

CHAPTER TWENTY-ONE

Penny

Debbie sounds different on the phone. She said calling was fine, but still.

'Are you OK to speak for a minute?' Penny asks.

'Of course. I said to call. How are things going?'

'Much better, thanks. You know you suggested writing stuff down? Well I haven't managed much about me, but it got me in the writing zone, the scientific one, at least.' She smiles, feeling pleased and a little bashful. 'Which is a good thing. Doing nothing is driving me nuts. Just medical articles. I thought I'd send them off to some journals, see if they get published.'

She needs to get to the point; that isn't why she's calling. She spent ages in Costco, mulling things over. Tonight will be the first time she's seen the A Team since the wedding. It's important to get it right.

'Excellent!' Debbie says. 'You sound as though you're a little restless. Do you feel ready to go back to work?'

'Oh, I want to. Will isn't so keen.'

'Why?'

He still thinks I'm crazy; that I'll do something mad. 'He worries. He just wants me to get better. Do you think work would be a step back?'

'What do you think?'

'I feel really fine. I think it would help me get back on track. Get over the . . .'

'Over what?' Debbie asks eventually.

Penny sighs. 'The embarrassment of it all. It can't get much worse, can it? A psychotic episode at someone's wedding? Not just someone, but close friends.'

Feeling her chest tighten, Penny pauses before asking her question. She didn't think about it before, but she popped into Sainsbury's for milk on the way home from therapy on Thursday, and there he was in the dairy aisle, someone she knew, an old pal. No, not a pal, but an ex-boyfriend from uni. A flatmate, in fact. He pretended not to notice her, but she caught the alarm on his face before he scuttled away. So, it's important to get it right with the A Team. They're her friends, her only friends, she needs to show them she's normal.

'Are you still there, Penny?'

'Sorry, yes.' She remembers him laughing. Struggling to shake away the old memory, she takes a quick breath. 'Do you think it would be weird to apologise to our friends?'

'Is that important to you?'

'Yes, it is.'

'Can you explain why?'

Because she didn't apologise back in time. Or at least explain that it wasn't her fault. Well, not really.

'I think an apology is due and it might make the whole thing seem less . . . odd.'

'Then why not?'

'Will thinks I should leave it.'

127

'But what do *you* think, Penny?'

She doesn't reply. Pictures Will staring at his phone as though willing it to ring. Not coming to bed until he thinks she's asleep. And even then not dozing, but staring into the black night.

Debbie's voice makes her jolt. 'Are you still there, Penny? Making decisions is difficult but often a sign of progress. How would you feel about deciding for yourself?'

CHAPTER TWENTY-TWO

Nick

Nick and his wife arrive early at Dan's. He shakes hands with Dan, trying not to catch Lisa's eyes. 'Told you so!' they say.

They had an argument before leaving home. She was still in the bathroom when the taxi arrived.

'Hurry up,' he'd shouted up the stairs, 'the taxi is waiting.'

'You ordered it too early. I told you I wouldn't be ready,' she'd called back. 'We'll be the first people there, just you see.'

She came down the stairs eventually, applying bright lipstick.

'What?' she asked, looking at his face.

'Well, if you didn't wear so much make-up, it wouldn't take so long.'

He knew he'd said the wrong thing the moment it was out. Speaking without thinking, as usual. He glances at her now. Her face is so pretty, she doesn't need to wear make-up at all, let alone the amount she smears on when they're going out. He'd belatedly tried to explain it in the taxi, but she wasn't for relenting.

'Didn't your mother teach you anything, Nick?' she said

tersely, her body positioned away. 'If you have nothing nice to say, then don't say anything at all.'

The smoke from the newly lit fire catches Nick's throat and he coughs, feeling stupid. He needs something to do. 'Shall I crack open a bottle?' he asks as they wait for Geri. He brought a few bottles of wedding champagne and knows Lisa will soften after a couple of glasses. Turning briefly, he takes in her tight features. Bloody hell, the sooner the better.

Dan grins. 'Thought you'd never ask. Looks pretty good stuff. Sure you don't mind wasting it on us?' he replies. His eyes flicker from him to Lisa. 'I can hear Geri now. Shall we do the honours in the kitchen?'

He follows Dan to the kitchen, glad to talk about anything but his stony-faced wife. When they return to the lounge, Geri's sitting next to Lisa, chatting about babies. Then the doorbell rings and Will bursts in noisily with the other guests in his wake, and though Lisa smiles broadly as they take their places in the dining room, he's glad to be sitting on the lads' half of the table.

Turning to Ian on his left, he asks about the match at Old Trafford, then wishes he hadn't when he remembers the result. Though generally amiable and quiet, Ian can be morose when it comes to bloody football. It's the ref's fault, of course. It was never a penalty. The goal was offside. Nick nods and drinks, but he drifts, suddenly remembering a dream from last night. Not just yelling this time, but kicking and biting. The memory makes him hot and angry even now.

Lisa's clear voice brings him back.

'That looks flipping delicious, I'm starving,' she's saying.

Wearing his naked lady pinny, Dan has brought in the starter, something along the lines of a huge prawn cocktail.

'That's us,' Penny says. 'From Costco, I'm afraid. Life is too short for spending hours in a kitchen.' She puts her hand to her mouth and laughs a little strangely. 'Oh dear. No pun intended.'

There's an embarrassing silence, which Geri interrupts. 'Serving spoons, Dan?' Then the conversation restarts, Will dominating it as usual. Not that Nick minds. Will is good to have around, talks to anyone about anything, even if his quips are sometimes too close to the bone.

Leaning forward, he tops up Jen's glass and takes in the silky blouse which shows her deep cleavage. She smiles and says cheers, but she's quiet. Her chatter usually matches Will's, but tonight she looks pretty knackered, if he's being honest. Feeling the champagne bubbles against his tongue, he smiles a small smile. He's learned from the taxi journey that being honest isn't the best policy, so it's best to keep schtum. As he stares, Jen abruptly revives, looking at Ian and telling a story about taking Holly on a big wheel ride when she was tiny. He glances at Lisa, knowing what she's thinking. Disapproving thoughts, he's sure. 'What the hell were they doing taking a small kid on an amusement ride? That's plain stupid!' she'll say later. Of course she's right, but perhaps one shouldn't be too judgmental. His parents had a child who died. Not falling from a big wheel, he's sure, but still, what the heck did happen?

He pushes the thought away and turns his attention towards Will. The conversation has moved on to cricket, so he waits for the usual crack about his batting. It comes almost immediately.

'Third slip catch to win against Manchester Grammar. Remember, Dan? Sweet victory. And Nick's magnificent nineteen not out, if I remember correctly.' Will chuckles and turns to Lisa. 'Guess what this is, Lisa?' He makes several impressive quacking noises.

'Go on . . .'

'Nick's eight ducks in a row.'

Though Ian laughs loudly, Lisa doesn't smile. Nick wants to stand and kiss her then. 'Nick was good at cricket,' she says.

'That's what he told you, eh? The lies people tell to cop a pretty nurse—'

'Ignore Will, Lisa,' Dan interrupts. 'Nick was very good. *Spin sensation*, as he was known—'

Will lifts both his eyebrows and his glass. 'And not just for cricket.'

Hearing the name *Mouse* in his head, Nick glances at Jen. She's gazing in the distance, so he shakes his head with a grin and tops up the champagne flutes.

When he sits down, Penny stands and taps hers with a spoon. 'OK,' she says with a quavering voice.

Feeling tense, he looks at Lisa, knowing what's coming.

'OK. Rather than a toast, I'm going to embarrass everyone, particularly myself, but I think it has to be done.' She turns to Lisa, then him. 'Firstly, you two. I want to apologise for ruining your wedding day.'

She puts her hand to her chest, emphasising her slim neck which is flushed with red blotches.

He doesn't know what to say; he doesn't really want to think about it. He knows Lisa's still intrigued, but the blip came and went, as far as he is concerned. Everyone murmurs that it wasn't a problem. Then Lisa pipes up in her best nurse's voice. 'It wasn't ruined, Penny. Dan called it a blip. That's how we all see it. And it's all forgotten now.'

Penny opens her mouth again, but Will interrupts, 'A blip, eh, Mr Maloney?' He points a finger at Dan. 'You should've seen him. Super Dan. All puffed up like Sylvester Stallone, charging at the hotel door.'

'Sylvester bloody Stallone? He's a hundred and three and deformed by steroids. Cheers, mate.'

'OK, point taken. More like—'

Knowing he and Lisa are reprieved, Nick joins in the banter, 'Gerard Butler in *300*? What do you reckon, Ian?'

'King Leonidas? Yes, I see that. Dan's bit of a beard looks the part too.'

'*Bit* of a beard? Thanks, Ian. I can tell I'm going to die of compliments tonight. This beard is a bloody good effort, though I say so myself. Right, I'm laying down the gauntlet. Between now and Easter, see if you guys can do better.'

Will leans forward and strokes his chin thoughtfully. 'Ah, but are we including the women?'

Nick stands again to top up the drinks. Dan covers his glass with his hand, Penny and Geri shake their heads, but the rest of them seem to be getting through it pretty quickly. He asked Lisa if she minded bringing the bottles tonight. 'What better way than to share it with friends,' she replied, pecking his lips. 'And how about the cognac from Seb? Doubt we'll drink it.'

Seb had turned up at their house on a bicycle one evening with two bottles in his rucksack to replace one he'd apparently drunk at the wedding. 'There was really no need,' he said, but Seb had seemed affronted. When he left after half an hour of strained chat, Nick had looked at Lisa questioningly. 'When someone makes the effort to cycle from Withington to Burnage in atrocious weather to bring you a present, you don't say there's no need,' she sighed.

Getting it wrong as usual.

Dan's hand on his shoulder brings him back to today. 'Dessert? Pavlova just for you, Nick.'

'Thanks, maybe later.'

Will stretches his thick arms and laughs. 'What's up Nicky boy? Need to keep that sugar intake topped up.'

Lisa refills her glass. 'Tell me about it. I'm still trying to wean him off those bloody biscuits.' She leans over the table and squeezes him playfully. 'I blame the parents.'

Nick looks at Jen again, but she's twisting her dark hair, apparently miles away. He reaches for the brandy without responding to his wife's comment. She's only joking, he knows, but feels the dig is wearing thin. Dan puts out the dessert anyway, saying that the birds will get toothache unless someone does the honours. Then the conversation moves on as they graze on cheese, crackers and grapes, discussing the difference between cognac and brandy, whether the price of alcohol really makes any difference to taste, and he is suddenly aware he's had too much to drink.

'So, what exactly happened with Seb and Claudia, Will?' Lisa is asking, her accent more pronounced from alcohol as usual. 'I was desperate to ask when he came round, but even I thought that would be a question too far. I never met her, but apparently she was stunning.'

Will laughs. 'Tall and dark, with legs that went on forever. And French.' He fans his face theatrically. 'No idea what you mean.'

Lisa leans forward. 'Let's face it, he won't be single for long. He'll find someone equally as gorgeous with a click of his fingers. He's pretty stunning himself.'

Will rubs his cropped hair. 'Which, as I'm sure you've noticed, runs in the family—'

'But of course, William. The stunning Taylors of Old Withington Town,' Nick quips, wishing Lisa didn't have to go on quite so much about bloody Seb.

'That's what I was saying to Dan earlier,' Geri says, standing up. 'About Seb finding someone new. But I guess everyone is different, maybe moving on isn't as easy as it seems.' She taps her temple. 'Who knows what's going on in here for any of us? Nobody! Unless you're the type to fess up, of course. Hope you guys don't mind, but I'm shattered. I really need to lie down.'

Geri makes for the door, but the goodnight hugs take some time, prompting a debate about the baby's sex and comical suggestions for names.

Will gives the final hug. 'Blooming heck, Geri. You're enormous. Are you sure there's only one in there?'

'Too rude, Will!' Penny says when she returns to the table. She looks thoughtful for a moment. 'How does the twins thing go? I should really know. Identical twins are hereditary, non-identical are not. Or is it the other way around?'

'I had a twin sister,' Nick blurts, startling himself. His voice sounds loud in the small silence and he's aware of its slur. 'A sister who was a twin, I should say.'

Jen suddenly animates. 'You're joking,' she says, surprise showing on her bleary face. 'Patrick had a twin sister? What happened to her?'

He thinks how to answer, but Lisa speaks first. 'She died, apparently, so Nick can't ask his mum or dad,' she says, reaching out for his hand. 'I know it's none of my business, and really sad too, but I admit I'm intrigued to know what happened, how she died, how old she was and all that. And this twins thing. As Penny says, if it could be hereditary, Nick and I might be in for double trouble one day.'

'Aren't your brothers twins, Lisa?' Ian asks, finally joining the conversation.

'Nah, they just look it. The Welsh Kray twins. I know! Heard that one before.'

135

Jen leans across the table towards him; he can see her lacy black bra. 'Why don't you ask Patrick about it, Nick? I know he's a bit older, but he's still our generation. He might be more willing to talk about it. Just the two of you?'

He tries to listen to what she's saying, but has to focus on breathing. He suddenly feels sick, the need to vomit even worse than a boat trip on a choppy sea with the A Team long ago. He pictures Will's grin. 'Come on, Nick, don't look so green. Salute like a man. We're a nation of sailors!'

Resting his head on the table, he hears Lisa ask for a taxi number from the bottom of the ocean, then he's in Dan's car, still fighting to keep the puke down.

He's sick in the bathroom at home. He can't move from the toilet. Lisa's voice is brisk. 'Keep drinking that water,' she says through the waves. He obediently takes a slug but it comes up again.

'Sorry,' he manages.

'What are you like?' she replies, and when he looks at her face, she's smiling.

CHAPTER TWENTY-THREE

Jen

Jen drifts in the high-ceilinged dining room, the warmth of the old column radiator on her back. That and the champagne makes her drowsy. The lack of sleep too, but she doesn't want to dwell. She promised Dan to bring her smile; she's doing her damnedest to oblige.

She glances around the table. The boy-girl arrangement they had when they first gathered as couples has long gone. Now Ian and the A Team sit at one end, the girls at the other. She was piqued when it changed, she liked being in the thick of male banter, but today it's a relief not to be sitting next to Will.

Penny had telephoned to offer her and Ian a lift, but Will was driving when they arrived, thank God, so she quickly slipped in the back seat and chatted to Penny. Though a little wooden, somehow, she looked amazingly well; back to peachy-cheeked and polished, smiley and pleasant. The sort of nice woman who deserved a baby. Will's baby.

'That looks flipping delicious, I'm starving.'

Lisa's loud voice prods her back to the conversation. Dan is bringing in the starter wearing the daft apron Will bought him from Edinburgh.

'That's us. From Costco, I'm afraid,' Penny says. She lifts her hand and smiles shyly, her teeth perfect and white. 'Oh dear. No pun intended.'

Jen glances at Ian and he lifts his eyebrows. She thinks of filling the silence, but Geri gets there first. 'Serving spoons, Dan?' she says.

'And the carton of thousand island sauce which came with each platter,' Penny adds, her cheeks flushed.

Dan tugs his forelock and backs out of the room. Hearing Will's melodious voice in the background, Jen holds out her glass to Nick and drifts for a while, but Geri's chuckle brings her back. 'Poor Dan,' she says. 'I feel almost guilty. Sitting here like a beached whale barking instructions.'

'A sea lion, then,' Will replies. 'You know, the barking . . .'

The thought arouses a memory. 'Oh God, remember Portugal, Ian?' She turns to the other inquisitive faces around the table, avoiding Will's steady gaze. 'We went to one of those sea life shows, which was dreadful. Poor sea lions clapping their . . . What do you call them? Fins? Flippers? Looking back, I feel guilty about those poor animals, but at the time we were far more concerned about that bloody big wheel, weren't we, Ian?'

Ian finally animates. 'God yeah. We took Holly on with us. She was only two or so. I don't know what possessed us—'

'Maria was standing up, leaning over the side of the car and pointing to the sea. I discovered I had a fear of heights, and there was Ian in the swinging seat below—'

'Trying my best to hold on to Holly, who'd transformed herself into a bar of soap. My gorgeous little girl. I really thought she'd slip through my arms. Never again!'

138

Dan turns to Geri and lifts his glass. 'Here's hoping our baby will pop out like a bar of soap—'

'Which you'll catch with your safe hands, eh Dan?'

Jen glances at Will's face as the conversation flows about cricket; the same stories told year after year. Will Taylor the steady opening batsman, Nick Quinn the spin bowler and Dan Maloney the all-rounder. She leans towards Geri. 'Soap and cricket balls,' she says with a snort. 'Bloody men, eh? They have no idea. Probably just as well. How are you feeling about it all? Not long to go . . .'

Geri replies in her usual sunny way, but Jen doesn't really listen. She's still picturing Holly as that bar of soap and how she watched Ian from the seat above struggling to hold on to her as they reached the pinnacle of the ride. It was the help-lessness that was so petrifying, the sure knowledge there was nothing she could do other than pray.

She takes a deep breath, wondering why she brought it up; the clutch of anxiety is there, like a fist in her chest. And Ian has been quiet all evening. The football result, surely? But quieter than usual. God, she wishes her mind would stop parroting his query about the nap, the bloody nap.

Gazing at Geri's spirited face, she tries to listen to her birth plan. 'You don't know yet,' she wants to yell, 'you won't realise until he or she is born the sheer intensity of the love you'll feel, the paralysing terror of ever losing that baby, that toddler, that teenager.'

All eyes turn to Dan as he brings in the food like an obsequious waiter. The others laugh, but she stares at the food, hoping it tastes good. Risotto and pasta, quiche and the gammon. Of course Ian was right, she made far too much. And Dan has supplemented it with a salad which smells surprisingly of oranges.

'Need any help?' she asks, looking at Dan.

He puts the back of his hand to his forehead. 'Don't worry about me, Jen,' he says. 'I'm just a slave to the kitchen.'

When the laughter dies down, Penny suddenly stands and taps her glass with a spoon. Feeling the apprehension in the room, Jen gazes at Penny, taking in the simple shift dress and her pretty face. As usual it's made up in neutral tones, emphasising her cheekbones and giving her that ethereal beauty. But her neck looks red raw, as though it doesn't belong.

Not able to hold back, Jen's gaze slips to Will, but he's staring at his plate.

'OK,' Penny says with a bashful smile. 'Rather than a toast, I'm going to embarrass everyone . . .'

Picturing that doll-like girl teetering on the ledge, Jen struggles to focus on her words, but after only moments, the A Team are joking, albeit a little forced. She catches Ian's raised eyebrows before turning to Penny and rubbing her arm. 'Good try,' she says. 'But there's no stopping them now. Famous beards of the world is my guess. You won't get another word in all night.'

Even though she isn't hungry, she piles food on her plate, asking Penny if she's back at work, trying to remember what she already knows from her, rather than Will. She doesn't want to think about his visit in the week; the thought of him becoming a parent still makes her feel sad.

She studies Penny as they chat, her straightened soft hair and slim shoulders, aware of Will's gaze on her while his wife is turned away. But tonight she finds she can't look back. She knows he's wearing the stripy Ralph Lauren shirt she and Ian bought for his birthday with the blue faded jeans that she likes, she knows he'd rather be drinking beer than champagne, that he deliberately interrupted Penny's speech because he found it embarrassing, but she can't look because she fears she might cry. She can feel the tears at the surface from too much alcohol mixed with anxiety about Holly and stupid sorrow.

When Geri stands, Jen looks at her watch, surprised to see it's eleven already. Geri taps the side of her head, saying the words she's been thinking all evening. 'Who knows what's going on in here for any of us? Nobody!'

Everyone stands to bid Geri goodnight. When they sit down again, Nick abruptly speaks. 'I had a twin sister,' he says, his voice slurry. 'A sister who was a twin, I should say.'

Jen peers to see if he's joking. Though pretty gone herself, she can tell he's very drunk, but his pale face is serious. Bloody hell this is news; they've been friends since they were five. 'No way,' she says. 'Patrick had a twin sister? What happened to her?'

The thought of babies prods through the haze, but she recognises the troubled frown on Nick's face. Feeling the usual surge of motherly concern for little *Mouse*, she leans across the table, trying to help with advice.

Then Penny says it's time to leave. That's fair enough, she's the driver, after all. Trying not to sway as she stands, Jen shakes her head at Ian's knowing eyebrow. He helps with her coat and she steps outside. It's colder than she thought.

Apparently over his usual football malaise, Ian offers his arm to Penny and they walk ahead. Aware of Will behind her, she follows quickly towards the car, but his footsteps accelerate and he grabs her wrist firmly.

'What's up, Jen?' he asks quietly. 'You haven't replied to my texts. Don't shut me out. Whatever it is, talk to me. Please.'

CHAPTER TWENTY-FOUR

Dan

Dressed in a jokey apron, Dan shoulders open the door to bring in the starters, two impressive platters of pink: king prawns, shrimps and salmon, brought by Will and Penny as their contribution to the meal. With the warm radiator, the candles and its colour, the room feels festive. Geri painted the walls a deep burgundy red when she was first made redundant. He realises with surprise he's finally got used to it.

'So, what's your plan?' he asked when she volunteered for redundancy.

'Paint the dining room, then get pregnant,' she replied with a firm nod.

'Sounds good,' he said, though neither idea had occurred to him before.

Even though the baby is nearly due, he finds he's still getting used to it. But this evening his agitation is mixed with other emotions he can't quite describe, something similar to the fear and excitement he felt lining up for the Big One rollercoaster as a kid. But he's tried not to mull, it's too confusing when he does. Instead he's kept busy, cleaning the oven with a surprisingly effective fat-buster, wiping the kitchen floor and setting the table while Geri napped: knives and forks in duplicate, place mats and side plates, even remembering the candles. But that's when he noticed the crockery and cutlery were coordinated and new, not a mismatch in sight, so he went out to the shed, grateful to feel the slap of cold on his face as he collected wood for the fire.

'From Costco, I'm afraid . . .' Penny says, bringing him back from his thoughts.

For a moment he stares, picturing her hollow face at the window, but the blurred image is replaced by Seb Taylor's. Seb in his mum's bathroom; Seb in the school showers.

Geri's voice breaks through. She's asking for serving spoons, so he backs out of the room like a silver-service waiter, walks to the kitchen, leans against the sink and breathes. When he returns with the spoons, Jen turns to Ian. She's been unusually quiet all evening, but her face suddenly animates. She tells a story about a big wheel and Holly. Everyone listens politely and smiles, but he knows they are missing the point. The point is her anxiety, which she's striving to hide.

He looks at Ian's face, trying to focus on his voice, but thoughts of this morning edge in, rousing and dangerous. He'd felt the intensity of Seb's gaze, but couldn't look back. They took the steaming food from the microwave, perched in near silence at the kitchen island to eat it, then he left, his heart thrashing. He's tried to keep his thoughts shallow, but his mind has wheeled with *what if* questions since.

He wishes it would stop.

Then there's Geri's bloody insight from earlier. 'Forgot to ask. How was Seb?' she asked when he got back from Wilmslow, content and carefree. 'Was he OK? Do you think he's been to the doctor?' She looked pensive. 'The end of a relationship is always hard. Most people go through a dry run or a weaning stage which tends to help, but when you live in different countries, I guess a clean and painful break is inevitable.'

She reached up to his hair. Raked a few strands into place. He had to try hard not to stop her.

'Still,' she continued. 'It doesn't sound as though there was someone else for either Seb or Claudia. Betrayal makes it so much worse for people; duplicity by the person they trust most in the world.' She gave a bright smile. 'To be honest, I'm glad of the break from unhappy people for a while, and as for Seb, he won't be single for long, will he? He is pretty gorgeous.'

He didn't know how to reply. He hadn't thought about *that* before.

Reverting to the table, he tries to listen and laugh about cricket and catches. Then he clears plates and dishes, brings in more food, hears Penny's breathless apology which moves on swiftly to muscled actors and beards, thank God. Dominated by Will, the conversation flows as his guests eat. Geri smiles politely, but he knows that it's fixed. She's had her hand on her stomach intermittently all evening. He wishes there was something he could do other than say, 'everything will be fine'. He's been saying it for eight months, wanting to guarantee its truth, fighting off the habitual impulse to pray.

He stands again, clears the crockery, fills the sink with soapy water, brings in a pavlova he bought especially for Nick, makes a quip about birds' teeth, remembers the cheese, offers tea and coffee. When he finally sits down, Lisa's talking about Seb's girlfriend, her accent stronger than usual.

Her green eyes are wide. 'Let's face it, he won't be single for long. He'll find someone equally as gorgeous with a click of his fingers. He's pretty stunning himself.'

Will makes another joke in reply, but Dan keeps his head

down, brushing biscuit crumbs into his palm. He feels hot, unsettled and irked by the speculation, even more so by Geri who joins in with her bloody theories. But then she stands up, saying she's exhausted and needs to lie down.

Following her upstairs, he perches on the bed until she's finished in the bathroom. Feeling a surge of affection when she pads out in her pyjamas, he puts his arms around her and inhales the innocent smell of toothpaste and soap. He kisses her knitted brow, puts his hand on her stomach and uses that confident voice which isn't his own. 'You're nearly due. There isn't as much room for the baby to move, remember?' He feels a kick and he laughs. 'There you go! It's a goal! Little Ronaldo is doing his best.'

Returning to his guests, he tops up the coffee cups, wondering why he has such difficulty in equating that kick with a real living baby. Looking after a newborn won't be plain sailing, he knows that. It's just that he can't imagine what it will be like at all. He glances at Ian and Jen, his usual thumbs-up for successful parenting, but tonight they seem absent; Jen hasn't been as jovial as usual, she hasn't spoken to Will at all.

The fire peters out, Penny says it's time to go, Lisa asks for a taxi number. He turns his attention to Nick. For a slight guy he can usually put away a surprising quantity of beer, but today his face is almost white and he's swaying.

'I think it might be better if I dropped you,' he says, looking at Lisa meaningfully. 'I've only had one glass seeing as I'm on call, so to speak, so I'm fine to drive. You're only down the road. Wait here one minute while I sort out the back seat.'

Outside, the sharp cold hits his face. Leaning into the car, he pushes the empty cardboard boxes to one side. Seb's cardboard boxes. Stunning Seb Taylor who'll find someone new. Trying to push the thought away, he looks up to the black sky littered with stars, then brings his focus back to his leaving guests. Lifting his hand to wave goodbye, he watches Ian and Penny climb into her four-by-four. Will catches up with Jen, holds her back to say something, but she pulls away and climbs in too.

He checks his pocket for his mobile and nods to Nick and Lisa at the door. 'Ready to go? It's pretty cold.' When they're finally settled in the car, he turns to Nick with a grin. 'Spin sensation? Bloody horrible, isn't it. Maybe open the window? The fresh air might help.'

Lisa chats as he drives, but Dan struggles to listen. His thoughts are too scrambled. The smell of toothpaste and soap. Empty boxes and sweet words. The kick of his child.

When they arrive at the small semi, he watches Nick and Lisa walk unsteadily to their lit porch, waiting breathlessly for a few moments as they skirmish with the keys. When their door finally closes, he picks up his mobile and types in three words. He drops it like a hot potato on the passenger seat, then rests his head against the steering wheel to wait for a reply.

Only moments pass, but still he jolts at the sound.

With a shaking hand, he opens the message.

'Yes I'm up. Text when you're here and I'll let you in,' it says.

Lit by the yellow glow of the night light, Seb is waiting at the door of Oak House, his hands in his pockets, his feet bare.

'Hi,' he says, standing back to let Dan into the building.

The lift is open. 'I've got half an hour, I thought I'd—' Dan replies, stepping in.

The doors close and they're glued, kissing and kissing, then find themselves outside Seb's flat where they carry on lip to lip, hair tightly wrapped in taut fingers, bodies hard against the wall.

When they finally pull away, Dan is reeling. Breathless and stunned and aching. Burning with desire he's never felt before.

Seb struggles to insert the key with his good left hand.

'Let me,' Dan says, though his fingers are trembling.

They stand apart on the cream carpet, winded and staring. Seb's wearing a white T-shirt and grey track pants, his erection quite obvious. His soft hair is ruffled, there's a fine growth of stubble on his chin and his blue eyes are charged. Though Dan's thoughts are shattered, he's aware of one imperative, that more than anything right now he wants to continue kissing and touching this achingly beautiful man.

'What now?' Seb asks.

Dan steps towards him, lifts the bandaged hand to his lips, then laughs unsteadily.

'I really have no fucking idea,' he replies.

147

CHAPTER TWENTY-FIVE

Nick

Nick wakes with a jolt from a dream in which he's not just shouting, but screaming at his mum. Again. He's had the dream several times this week and he wakes up feeling guilty, still seeing her pale crumpled face. He turns over to Lisa, but her side of the bed is empty, which is a first when she's not going to work. He looks at the radio clock, his brain taking a moment to adjust. Fuck! Twice in one week. It's ten to twelve; he and Lisa are due at his parents' house for lunch at twelve-thirty.

Calling Lisa, he sweeps out of bed, but a pain in his head hits like a knockout blow. The bloody brandy last night; even as he drank it, he knew he shouldn't have. He's fine with beer, but he's never been able to do spirits like Dan and Will, and mixing makes it worse. He's usually more cautious, usually knows when to stop.

He finds Lisa at the sink in their small bathroom. 'Why didn't you get me up? We're due at Mum's in half an hour.'

She spits out the toothpaste bubbles before looking at him evenly. 'You were sick when we got home, Nick, several times. You needed the sleep.' She turns back to the mirror, pats the grey smudges beneath her eyes with her little finger, then picks up a soft brush and gingerly pulls it through her damp hair. 'Besides, I've just phoned your mum and put it off until two-thirty.'

'You're joking.'

'No, why?'

'What did you say?'

'Just that we'd had a late night at Dan's. She said it wasn't a problem.'

He sits on the toilet seat, hangs his head and breathes deeply. The strong smell of Toilet Duck hits his nose, almost making him retch. Oh God, he remembers now, the vomiting last night. It went on repeatedly until nothing was left except bile. Lisa was very good about it; she went into chirpy nurse mode, encouraging him to drink water even though it came straight back up.

He looks at her placid face. She's right to postpone, but still. Sunday lunch at the Quinn household starts at one o'clock sharp at the table, it always has, hangover or not.

Lisa rustles in the cabinet. 'Here,' she says, handing him a sachet of powder. 'That'll perk you up. Use a glass from the kitchen, this one's dirty. And make me a cup of tea while you're there. I'm flipping parched.'

Swinging between irritation at Lisa's interference and acknowledgement she was right to call his mum, he cautiously negotiates the stairs, enters the cold kitchen, adds water to the powder and gulps down the sweet liquid. Heading back to the bedroom, he remembers the tea. When he finally returns with a pot and two cups, Lisa turns from the hairdryer and glances at the tray.

'Very proper,' she says. 'A mug would've done. No toast?'

'You didn't say you wanted toast.'

'No matter. Probably haven't got time and I can save my appetite for lunch. What do you reckon? Lamb?'

'Look, I'm not that keen on lamb either, but Dad likes it, so we'll be super polite and eat it up with a smile. OK?'

Lisa pulls out a selection of clothes from the wardrobe. 'It isn't as though I'm ever not polite,' she says quietly. She turns to Nick and watches him for a moment. 'I can't see you smiling anytime soon, though. Hadn't you better get in the shower?'

Nick makes for the door, moving his head to test whether the painkillers are working. Then he turns. 'I had another bad dream. Shouting and screaming at Mum as loudly as I could. Wanting to shake her. They're horrible. I wish they'd stop.'

Lisa holds up two dresses and shrugs. 'You're still obsessing about that sister thing. You even announced it to everyone at dinner last night, which I thought was rich when you'd sworn me to secrecy about the whole bloody thing.'

'Did I?'

'Yes, and then Jen did her *poor you, I feel your pain* thing she does with her eyes and Will and Ian are nodding at her like those little puppy toys you see in car windows—'

The headache's still there. 'I thought you liked Jen.'

'She's OK.'

'Only OK?'

'Well, she's like the matriarch of the St Mark's family. "Let me hold you to my huge bosom, boys, and make all your problems disappear."' She studies him for a moment. 'Don't look so surprised, Nick. I'm sure it was great at school having a second mum on call, but we're all grown up now and you're mine, not hers.' She pauses, frowning. 'She does it mostly with Will, mind. God knows how Penny puts up with it. She is one bloody saint.'

Nick stands immobile in the shower, the sharp water blasting his face. He's never thought of Jen that way before. Of course all three of them fancied her at twelve or thirteen; she was one of the boys, but with a pretty face and with tits which seemed to appear overnight, starring in wet dreams more often than was comfortable. There'd been a bit of a tussle between Dan and Will over who would win the prize, but he hadn't bothered to enter that particular contest as he knew he wouldn't win. But then nothing happened, all four of them stayed friends until the leavers prom in year eleven. Will and Jen finally got together that night. They had already been voted 'the most likely couple to marry' in the yearbook and there was a collective sigh when they eventually kissed on the dance floor. 'Wish I'd been old enough to place a large bet,' Dan quipped as he and Nick watched. 'But then again the odds would've been really crap.'

Refreshed by the shower, he returns to the bedroom. 'So what exactly did Jen say?' he asks, briskly rubbing his thick hair with a towel.

Lisa shakes her head and smiles wryly. 'Mother Hubbard thinks you should speak to Patrick. I guess the idea is that if it's just you and him, he might be more amenable to spilling the beans. The annoying thing is she's probably right.'

When Harry Quinn finally reaches his front door, he does the usual before opening it, including the safety chain, but doesn't greet Nick and Lisa. He turns away in silence, hobbles towards the dining room and sits pointedly at the head of the table.

The room is stiflingly warm, two rectangular slices of pâté are waiting on the pretty patterned dishes Nick's mother has used on Sundays for years. Removed from the plastic packaging, they curl at their edges.

'Sit down and help yourselves to the appetisers,' his mum calls from the kitchen. 'The pâtés are new ones from Waitrose.

151

Smooth Brussels and one with mushrooms Dad likes. Don't wait for me.'

Though the place has been laid for Lisa, Nick sits next to his father, conscious his annoyance has stretched to not saying Grace. 'All right, Dad?' he asks, offering the basket of limp toast. He helps himself to two triangles and takes a chunk from each slice of pâté even though he still feels slightly sick. 'What did you think about the goal, Dad?' he asks. 'No way that was a penalty.'

He chats as though nothing is amiss. His father is slow to respond, but he eventually unwinds, opining on yesterday's football results for several minutes. His mum is still in the kitchen, leaving Lisa excluded and silent her end, but the imminent need is to smooth his father's irritation. It's the way it has always been; he's sure she'll understand.

His mum eventually sits at the table, helping herself to the remaining cold toast. She looks pink and flustered. 'You haven't poured the wine, Harry,' she says. She turns to Lisa. 'Red or white? Now tell me all about the honeymoon. We've heard Nick's version, so you tell us yours.'

Nick squeezes Lisa's hand and keeps her glass topped as she chats amiably about the honeymoon, the soft shallow seabed and the water sports, the duty-free shops in Bridgetown and their visit to the exclusive Sandy Lane beach club.

His mum nods her head. 'I believe it's lovely. I read that the guests put up a little flag when they need a drink.'

'Well, that's just plain lazy.'

She ignores Harry's comment. 'Michael Winner always holidayed there. Several months a year, I've read—'

'I think you'll find he's dead, Dora.'

'Did I say he wasn't, Harry?' She keeps her attention on Lisa. 'Did you see anyone famous?'

152

'Funnily enough we did.' Lisa smiles. 'At the shop we saw an actor who's on the television all the time, but neither of us can name him and it's driving us nuts.'

His father cleans his glasses with his napkin and joins in the guesswork. The tension in Nick's shoulders starts to ease. Which dramas has the actor been in? Harry asks. Just television or films too? Tall or short? Which age group? Fat or thin?

Wearing oven gloves, his mum brings in the main course. 'Harry, pass me another table mat. Hurry up. It's very hot. I don't want the heat getting through to the wood.'

Nick turns to Lisa, tops up her wine and raises his eyebrows. It isn't lamb, but a casserole of ham-wrapped chicken breasts in a creamy sauce.

'Wow, thank you, this looks lovely,' Lisa says.

His dad clears his throat. 'I take it we'll be having cold lamb tomorrow *and* the rest of the week,' he says, glaring at his mum. Through the glasses, his pale eyes look huge. 'And the roast potatoes and parsnips. I don't suppose they'll keep, though.'

'Sorry, Mum,' Nick says. 'I didn't think.'

'No you didn't,' his father fires back. 'Cooking takes time and preparation. I believe you and your brother think it's magically produced by your mother from thin air.'

His mum leans over and squeezes his wrist. 'It doesn't matter, love. Cold lamb can be quite nice with pickle and this is a recipe I was going to try in the week. I had the new potatoes in anyway, though they're not strictly new as we know it, they'll be from abroad at this time of the year. Help yourselves to the veg.'

They eat for several moments in silence. 'We met some nice people,' Nick eventually says. 'We got friendly with three other honeymoon couples, which was fun in the evenings.'

'The hotel had a babysitting service, so that was good,' Lisa adds.

His father rallies with a loud snort. 'It was a *honeymoon*, wasn't it? That's for newly-weds. Why would anyone need a babysitter?'

'Josh and Shelina had a two-month-old baby,' Lisa replies evenly.

'Surely not?' his mum says. 'I know young people do things the wrong way round these days, but taking a tiny baby with them in that heat? Now that is ridiculous.'

Nick feels Lisa's belligerence coming, but doesn't know how to stop it. 'One of the honeymoon couples we got friendly with were two women,' she says clearly. 'No baby as yet though, so that was fine.'

His father's response is immediate and loud. '*Lesbians*? On their *honeymoon*?' Looking incredulous, he puts down his fork and takes off his glasses. 'I find the idea of two women claiming they are *in a relationship* repugnant anyway, but the church allowing them to marry . . . I find it quite disgusting.'

Lisa's face colours, but she keeps her voice flat. 'No it's not. They are just human beings in love. Like you and Dora were once, Harry. Calling them repugnant and disgusting is a terrible thing to say. And they have the same right as you and I to get married. In fact I admire them for standing up and—'

Nothing wrong with Dad's hip today, Nick thinks wryly as his father abruptly stands.

Again, he knows it's coming, but there's nothing he can do, there never has been when his father's rage is ballooning.

'Get out of my house!' His face a livid red, he points his knife at Lisa. 'Don't think you can tell me what's right and what's wrong in my house. Go on, get out.'

Nick puts his hand on Lisa's knee at the traffic lights. Her body is still trembling.

'Sorry,' he says. 'That was awful for you.'

She doesn't say anything for a moment, then turns her head, her eyes fiery.

'OK, you held my hand as we left. But I note you didn't have the courage of your convictions, Nick. Barbara and Carrie are our new friends, we promised to keep in touch. On holiday you were right on, down with the lesbians, but when it comes to standing up to your bloody parents, especially your dad, you just let it ride, like the bloody big baby you are.'

'Well, perhaps if you didn't polish off the whole wine bottle, you wouldn't take so much offence yourself. Your dad isn't exactly politically correct with his "I don't approve of the Socialist Republican movement, but then I don't disapprove either". What does that mean, anyway? Let's burn down a few English people's holiday homes because we resent them? Very tolerant, I'm sure.'

'You were the one topping up my bloody wine glass and this isn't about my dad. Don't shift the responsibility from your own father's actions. He just threw his new and only daughter-in-law out of his home. We've been married five weeks. Five bloody weeks! That isn't normal behaviour, Nick. They are meant to be my family, my new parents, the people I go to if I have a baby, if I ever need help. I don't have a mother; my dad and my flipping hopeless brothers live three hours away. Remember?'

'Sorry,' Nick says again, moving the car into gear. 'I'll have a word with them both.'

But his mind has already drifted to Susan. Jen is usually right about most things, he's thinking. He'll talk to Patrick. He'll think of a plan, a way for them to chat, just the two of them.

Lisa sighs and turns to the passenger window. 'You haven't listened to a bloody word I've said,' she mutters to her reflection.

CHAPTER TWENTY-SIX

Dan

The first person in the office on Monday morning as usual, but today Dan is glad of the space and the silence. He hasn't had time to think all weekend. Not that he wants to think, really. Thinking about it scares him; thinking makes it real. Thinking about it causes his belly to flip and his groin to stir. He isn't sure if it's pleasurable or sickening.

'No baby yet?' Maya asks when she arrives. There's a light splatter of snow on her padded coat. He didn't realise it was snowing again. Snowing when it should be early spring; the world gone mad, life upside down. He glances at the corner window, but the slatted blind is closed, hiding the rusty fire escape and overflowing refuse bins from the view of his clients.

'No, so close and yet so far, as Geri says. She's eight and a half months, so the baby could arrive today or in another four weeks. They don't induce mums until they're two weeks over, whatever that means.'

'Inserting chemicals up your hooter to bring on labour—'

'Stop, Maya! I've been to the NCT classes. I know vaguely. I don't need the graphics.'

Maya cocks her head on one side. 'You're really spooked about the birth, aren't you?'

He puts his hand on a pile of work files. 'More spooked about not getting my head down and working.' Then he relents with a grin. 'I like your hair, by the way. Coffee please. And a slice of toast, if we have any bread that isn't mouldy. Just butter. And how come you know so much about it?' he calls as she leaves the room. 'You're only bloody sixteen.'

'Twenty-three,' she calls back. 'Twenty-four in four and a half weeks and you'd better not forget an expensive present for the best secretary in the world.'

Dan works through his files steadily, glancing from time to time at his mobile on the desk. The phone feels like a lifeline; it feels like a grenade. He left Geri sleeping this morning, but last night he told her to call him for the slightest concern, even for a chat. Then there was the text from Seb at midnight which contained a single X. He deleted it instantly and didn't reply.

Halfway through a lease, Dan's concentration is interrupted by a familiar nasal intonation through the open door. He looks at his watch. Eleven o'clock; not bad for Salim. He eventually appears in the back office with the usual white wolfish grin, perches on the desk and tells Dan about his long weekend away. He's still wearing his camel-coloured overcoat and Dan wonders if that's because he isn't staying in the office long enough to take it off. Dan's mind drifts from Geri to Seb and from Seb to the work pile, and by the time the tale ends, he's unsure if he's heard properly. Going away with one woman on a Thursday and coming back with another on a Sunday seems pretty unlikely, even for Salim. But then again, normal, down-to-earth and completely heterosexual Dan Maloney was given an exquisite blow job by another man late on Saturday night. The thought is incredible, as though it happened to someone else.

He stares at the documents covering every inch of his desk. 'Piece of piss' domestic conveyancing it might be in some respects, but Dan feels like a hamster on a wheel; the demands never stop: searches, small queries and paperwork, letters, constant telephone calls and people. Give him companies and corporations over human beings as clients any day.

Salim stands, taking a sheaf of papers in his wake, and makes for the door. 'By the way, I made a new useful contact who'll put us on his conveyancing panel if we talk sweetly—'

'Great, Salim. That is great.' Dan loosens his tie to release the surge of heat. 'But I can't manage it all myself. If it happens, we'll need an assistant. I'm swamped as it is.'

'Sure, we'll see. Who knows? No point getting stressed until it happens.' It's what Salim always says. He turns at the door. 'Assistants cost money, Dan. Maybe we could train up one of the lads.' That's what Salim always says too.

A rap at the door chimes with Dan's rumbling stomach. Thank God for Maya, he's starving and parched. He looks up, expecting to see a colourful hijab, but it's Seb, his hair gelled in a side parting, wearing a black leather jacket he's never seen before.

'Seb,' he says, his heart lurching. 'What are you doing here? You can't just—'

'Paying my rent, remember? Besides, I'm a friend. I've been here before. Don't look so anxious, Dan. It's fine.'

'Someone might come in. Maya might—'

Seb beams. 'I passed her as she was leaving the office. She asked about my bassett hound and said something about resisting tomato ketchup on my chips. Eating on the sofa? I think she was joking. She's nice; she told me to come through.'

He reclines against the door and holds out his hand. 'Come here if you're worried.'

Dan stays sitting and stares at Seb's face, smiling and sculpted, his handsome eager face.

What the fuck, what the fuck, beats in time with his heart.

'I've been thinking about you constantly,' Seb says, still grinning. 'Feeling unbelievably horny. It was great, wasn't it?'

Dan feels his body stirring. He continues to stare, saying nothing.

What the fuck, what the fuck, what the fuck am I doing?

Seb straightens up. 'Was it great, Dan?' The smile is falling from his face; it feels almost unbearable.

Dan stands from the desk and steps towards him. 'Yes, it was. It was great, fucking mind-blowing, in fact. It's just—'

'I thought some lunch or a pint. Just to chat.'

Dan turns to his desk, sees the buff-coloured folders, wills his erection to subside.

'I'm going away for a few days,' Seb says, dropping his gaze to the floor. 'On a shoot. Not sure how long.'

Dan nods, decision made. He scoops up his mobile, collects his overcoat from the stand, slipping it on without looking at his lover. He takes a breath and exhales. It's lunch, only lunch, it's perfectly normal.

Striding ahead, he passes the lads at their desks in the shopfront. Aware of their curious gazes, he tries for a casual tone. 'We're off for a pint. See you in half an hour.'

'Bloody hell, that's a first,' he hears as they hit the cold air.

He puts his hands in his overcoat pockets and strolls shoulder to shoulder with Seb. Through the pedestrianised shopping area, past Boots and Waterstones, Smith's and Superdrug, the shops he passes each morning without noticing. As they head towards Water Lane, littered with glassy restaurants and wine bars, he wonders how the two of them look to the outside world. Business colleagues or friends? Solicitor and his client? Like a gay couple? Or like two straight men who've become temporarily deranged. That's how he feels. Excited and nervous and sick.

'This place looks good,' Seb says, diverting to a small dingy pub, surprisingly still thriving between two new handsome buildings. He heads for the back room and orders two beers. Dan follows and sits.

'Cheers,' Dan says, briefly lifting his gaze from the copper dents in the tabletop and accepting the bottle. Then he turns to the room, taking in the stench of ancient tobacco smoke, the discoloured wallpaper, the soft wooden floor, the limp mustard furnishings. Trying to focus on anything other than the pressure of Seb's knees and his feet beneath the small table. 'The photo shoot,' he asks, finally looking at Seb. 'Where are you going?'

'London.'

'When?'

Seb lifts his jacket cuff to look at his watch. 'About an hour. Catching the train from Wilmslow station.'

Picturing Seb's bare feet in the yellow night light at Oak House, Dan turns the chilled bottle. 'Could you catch the next one?'

Seb smiles his rare grin. 'For you I could.'

'Bloody hell, Dan. Look at the time! We'll be calling you Salim next,' one of the lads says when he returns to the office.

Shaking her head, Maya stands from her desk, her lips squashed in a line. She follows him into the back office and holds out a bundle of messages. 'Six calls in the last half-hour,' she says. 'Ten if you count the five calls from Mrs Kemp. I

160

wouldn't mind, but you really need to tell me if you'll be out for more than ten minutes.' She cocks her head, frowning as she stares. 'You weren't answering your mobile either. It could've been the baby, Dan. I just need to know.'

Dan looks at his desk and sits down. The tuna and mayonnaise on granary stares at him accusingly. He hasn't eaten since the toast; he should feel hungry but he isn't. His stomach is still churning with excuses, with reasons why he might be seen travelling in a taxi on a Monday lunchtime with Seb Taylor, hurtling towards Oak House with an unbelievable hard-on, desperate to release it. Yet when they arrived in Seb's apartment, more than anything, he wanted to satisfy him, to watch his face as he came.

Just boys' stuff, he'd convinced himself yesterday. Things he'd been told by two of his uni mates who'd gone to a same-sex boarding school. Wanking each other off in the showers for a laugh, even sucking. Anything to jerk off. But today it felt different; today he wanted to please, rather than be pleased. He didn't want to leave Seb's warm bed; he had to drag himself away. And Maya is right; it could've been the baby; oh God, the baby. He covers his face and sighs deeply. What's happening? What the hell is wrong with him?

His mobile vibrates, moments before a beep alerts him to a text.

'On the train, feeling good. See you in a few days,' it says.

His finger hovers over the icon, but he finds he can't delete it. He lowers his head to his arms.

'What the fuck am I doing?' he whispers.

CHAPTER TWENTY-SEVEN

Jen

Bulimia, Jen thinks. That's what they'll say. I should have noticed, I should have seen. God, what a crap mother.

The small boy next to her speaks. She's sitting with him in the reading corner, helping him to sound his words phonetically. The teaching-to-read rules have recently changed, but not, in her view, for the better. It isn't that one way of learning is particularly superior to another but that governments don't give long enough for one idea to work before pronouncing it a failure and moving on to the next.

'Like sponges', people say about kids and this boy is no exception. He arrived at her reading table with no English at all, so his progress usually delights her, but today she's distracted, her mind stumbling from one thought to another, but landing at Holly. It's her appointment after school.

'Is it an emergency?' the doctor's receptionist had asked. Of course she wanted to say yes, that Holly's school had told her to make it, that she was a bad parent and needed absolution as soon as humanly possible. But she and Ian had agreed the best approach was to keep it low-key, there was no point freaking Holly out, making a fuss over something that was probably nothing. There was the *Munchausen Mother* problem too. Jen didn't want to charge into the surgery suggesting ridiculous diagnoses when her child might just be thin. Not that she hadn't agonised over the list of potential ailments a hundred times in her head.

She's been watching Holly's food intake over the last week, trying hard not to show it, but inspecting every mouthful. Checking the toilet too, sniffing out any traces of vomit. Her fear is the doctor will say Holly has an eating disorder, and they always start with parents, mothers in particular, don't they? She understands that isn't strictly true, but still feels responsible. She should have noticed, bloody noticed!

Checking the time again, she sighs. She knows she isn't a perfect mum, that sometimes she shouts too loudly and for too long. But it isn't all the time and she never breaks her rule of not being critical of her daughters' appearances, not overtly, at least. Her mum wasn't particularly reproving of her as a girl, but she can still recall the few occasions Nola fought back against her wilful belligerence, mostly because her mum cared ferociously about keeping up standards and what other people might think, especially the neighbours, who're still her neighbours to this day.

'Your top is dirty, Jennifer. You can't go out in that. And I can see your bra straps.'

'Well I'm wearing it, Mum, so that's that. Don't interfere.'

'A slut! That's what the neighbours will think!'

She returns to the boy. He's looking back with a beam on his face, so she ruffles his hair and turns the page, wondering about his mum, who seems to snap angrily when she collects him from school. But who knows what 'goes on behind closed doors', as Nola would say. Like Penny's mum.

'Kids struggle with high-achieving parents. More often than

not, the pressure comes from themselves,' Ian commented when she briefly filled him in about the reasons for Penny's episode. She didn't tell him when and how Will had told her. Nor about his plans for a baby. She's trying very hard not to think about that.

'Who knows what goes on in here,' Geri said at the dinner party, tapping her temple. Of course, they'd been gossiping about Seb, but Jen had glanced at Penny and a shiver seemed to pass through her slim shoulders. 'Someone's walked over her grave,' Nola would have commented.

'Perfect Penny,' Dan had called her when she came on the scene. 'I didn't think she was Will's type.' Then, after a moment, 'But there's something about her which reminds me of his mum. Not just the classical looks, but a sort of stillness. Do you know what I mean?'

'No, and what is Will's type, Dan?' Jen had wanted to demand, piqued and jealous and feeling wholly inferior to the neat and slim younger woman with the china doll eyes hanging on to Will's arm when they met at the theatre. But Penny was difficult to dislike. Fairly quiet, but pleasant and smiley when she was spoken to.

Jen turns the page, wondering what Penny's mum has to complain about. Penny is still pleasant, smiley and polite. She has a thank you text from her for providing the food at Dan's. *'It tasted so fab, could I order from you rather than Costco next time?'* it said sweetly.

And there it is, that inevitable slice of pain. How will she cope when Penny and Will present a baby to the world? She won't blame Penny, per se, she won't blame anyone, she'll just feel enormously sad.

After zipping up thirty anoraks in the classroom, Jen puts on her own and strolls to the village for her lunchtime break. Then perches on a cold metal bench next to a coffee shop to call the doctor's surgery. She's mentioned it already, but wants to ensure a note is passed to the doctor saying why she's there, so he or she already knows about Holly's problem without having to spell it out in front of her. Is she being overprotective? She isn't sure, but her own diagnosis of Munchausen by bloody *something* seems more likely than ever.

When she finishes the call, she looks again at her texts. The one from Will was sent at the same time as Penny's, like 'kissing cousins', as Nola would say. *'What's up?'* it reads. *'Why wouldn't you look at me on Saturday?'*

She's thought of a thousand ways to respond, to explain her feelings of sorrow, of longing, of ending. Of betrayal, even. But what would be the point? Neither of them are free; she's married to a good man, she doesn't want to be free. And yet she's hurting. Her facade is dry and jolly, but she bruises too easily, she always has.

Shaking away the urge to cry, she breathes deeply. She shouldn't have given in when Will turned up unexpectedly that day; it's brought everything back when they were settled, when she was settled with Penny as his wife, when she could say to herself, 'It could've been worse, she could've been another me.'

A rap from the cafe window brings her back to the sharply cold Tuesday. A prematurely grey-haired lady waves and points to a slice of gateau on a plate. She's the mother of a severely disabled child whose brother was in Maria's class at primary school. Jen and the mum used to fitfully chat outside the school door, waiting for their children to spring out. The girl would be there in her wheelchair, lovingly dressed in party clothes, her head to one side, her body immobile but her eyes alive, watching the other kids throwing themselves joyfully around the playground. Jen never asked what the girl's disability was, but year after year rumour had it the child would shortly die. It got to the point where people blithely assumed she never would, that somehow she was invincible. Then she died in her sleep without warning. Other mums said her passing was a blessing, a release. Nola said taking the child back to heaven was God's way of healing. At the time, Jen disagreed fervently, but now she doesn't know.

She waves back to the woman and looks at her watch pointedly, intending to leave, but then changes her mind. It feels as though her life revolves around idioms and cake, but this woman has suffered, really suffered. She has ten minutes spare for a chat, to listen to someone else's problems rather than selfishly dwelling on her own.

The doctor's surgery heaves, surprisingly so at half past four in the afternoon, but then again it's still the flu season, and from her glance around the newly built waiting room, Jen guesses most of the patients are students. Glandular fever, perhaps, the kissing disease, the poor sods.

Thinking back to her student days in Liverpool, she remembers the first term when she suffered badly from tonsillitis, a recurring problem since childhood. She could barely swallow, and when she peered in the mirror, her throat was coated in white slime. She dragged herself to the health centre and was sent away with a flea in her ear. 'Nothing that gargling with soluble aspirin won't cure,' the doctor said dismissively. She immediately made her way to Lime Street station and caught the first train back to Manchester, nearly dropping from exhaustion at her mum's front door. It was wonderful to see Nola's concerned dimpled face, to feel the weight of her fleshy freckled arms as she pulled her into the warm house. But it was her dad she had longed to see as she sipped water on the train. It was Seamus she needed. She wanted him to hold her tightly, to spoil her with a new soft toy and packets of cherry-flavoured cough sweets; to lie on the narrow bed and stroke her hot forehead; to tell her she was his only special girl and to whisper some Irish blarney until she finally slept.

From learning about his real betrayal two years previously, it was the first and only time she allowed nostalgia to pierce her unyielding anger.

Clearing her throat, she looks at her daughter. Why she's thinking of *him*, she doesn't know. She shrugs away the memory and offers Holly a mint from the bottom of her handbag, wondering if the girls will go to university. It was a given for her; she was bright, and at the private school it was expected. Even though they are in education, she and Ian haven't yet got a handle on how clever their daughters are, and their huge state school was in 'special measures' not so long ago.

When Maria was five, Nola presented a letter from Seamus offering to pay for her education. 'Don't cut off your nose to spite your face, Jennifer,' her mum warned. But Jen declined, saying Ian had been through the state system and had done very well, and anyway she wanted her kids to be *rounded*. But the truth was she couldn't bear to accept the bastard's blood money.

Another patient's name is called, pulling Jen away from her black thoughts. Holly's eyes are still glued to her mobile.

Expecting a boy each pregnancy, Jen is still astonished she gave birth to three girls, but then again her brother's wife had longed for a daughter. After three boys in quick succession she consulted the internet for a recipe for a baby girl; she ate white bread and bananas, had sex before ovulation and did hand-stands after. But when she was eventually rewarded with a perfectly baked female, it wasn't what she'd expected; the child wasn't a replica of herself, she was dark like her father and grew up introverted.

'It's personality which defines them,' her sister-in-law said.

'And is that from nature or nurture?' Jen asked.

'Definitely nature,' she replied, but as Jen studies Holly's rapt face, she doesn't think life is so simple.

'What's happening in the world?' Jen asks her. 'Any transfer news?'

Still flicking through photographs of her favourite footballers, Holly shakes her dark head. She's a Red like her parents, but Jen suspects her interests are more romantic than technical. Of course she wants United to win, like Ian she's devastated for hours when they don't, but Jen isn't sure her daughter could explain the offside rule like she could at the same age.

The bloody waiting interminable, Jen looks again at the clock. Trying to rise above the reason why she's here, she contemplates football and what to make Ian for dinner, thoughts far preferable to those of the father she can't seem to escape.

Holly pulls at her sleeve. 'Mum, did you hear that? They called out my name.'

She stares for a moment at her daughter's luminous eyes. Funny really; it was the one thing she and Will Taylor disagreed on – the Manchester football divide.

Taking a deep breath, she puts her hand in the small of Holly's back and leads her down the corridor, and though she knows she shouldn't, she clasps her hand at the door. With a reassuring smile, she knocks, then gently pushes her daughter in.

It's a female doctor, so that's good. But she's young, so young. Will she know what she's doing?

The doctor looks up from her screen. 'Take a seat. So, how can we help you today?'

'General check-up,' Jen starts, praying that empathy will make up for lack of experience. 'Holly has just been a bit under the—'

'The PE teacher at school thinks I'm too thin,' Holly interrupts. 'She told Mum I should see a doctor.' She turns to Jen and shrugs. 'It's OK, Mum. That's what Miss Fern said when she called me over at the end of the lesson. After asking if I was eating properly. Some girls chuck their lunch on their way to school or at break.'

The fact Holly knew about the conversation catches Jen short. Then what she said finally registers. Chucking their packed lunches! The thought of her girls throwing away food is alarming. Not just the waste, which she hates, but that she's never thought of it before. And more to the point, if it is something they do behind her back, there's absolutely nothing she can do about it.

'Why on earth would they do that and go hungry?' she asks.

'They want to be skinny.'

'And how about you, Holly?' the doctor breaks in. 'Do you throw away your lunch? Do you want to be skinny?'

Holly shrugs again and says not particularly. Then she tells the doctor about the girls at school, how some don't eat, how others make themselves sick after eating and about a few who self-harm, or so they say. She thinks they're stupid. They're all into boys and fashion and she's not. She prefers watching sport and she's learning to play the guitar so she can join a band. Jen watches them chat, incredulous about what goes on in high school and amazed at her twelve-year-old's eloquence and maturity.

The doctor asks Holly to lie down and Jen watches from the side of the couch. The teacher is right; lying full length in her underwear, Holly's stomach is concave and her knees are like knots on a twig. She finds herself holding her breath as the

169

doctor looks at her daughter's teeth, examines her limbs, listens to her heart, peers in her ears, feels her glands. 'Are your legs always so bruised?' she eventually asks.

'Suppose so,' Holly replies and Jen reels, pitching with anxiety. She'd never noticed; oh God, what a terrible mother. Weight loss and bruising. What else has she missed?

Holly dresses again, sits and glances around the room disinterestedly.

'Thanks, Holly,' the doctor says. 'I know it sounds horrible, though it really isn't that bad, but I'll need to take some blood. Everything looks fine, but blood tells us everything, you know? About what's going on inside? So if your mum makes an appointment with the blood nurse . . .' She watches Holly's face. 'I know, she's lovely though, and she hates us calling her that. She's actually called Gwendolyn, so maybe the name—'

'Why can't you take it now?' Jen cuts in.

Blood tests? She hadn't thought about that; she'd been too hung up with the prospect of a Munchausen Mother eating disorder diagnosis; she'd assumed they'd be monitoring Holly's eating habits and the like. But blood. What for?

The doctor turns to her. 'We have a specialist nurse who does the bloods?' Her voice rises at the end like a question. If Jen wasn't so anxious, she'd find it annoying. 'She's very experienced and so quick you won't believe it. I'm sure she'll fit Holly in for an appointment very soon.'

They stand in the queue at reception. 'Sorry, love,' Jen says as they wait. Her heart is beating wildly, but she tries for an even tone. 'It's a bummer having to come back again. But as the doctor said, it'll only take a minute and it's not as bad as it sounds.'

'It's fine,' Holly lifts a shoulder, her gaze back on her mobile. 'As long as it's a Wednesday, so I miss double maths.'

CHAPTER TWENTY-EIGHT

Penny

'Hi Penny. Come on in.'

Penny stares. Debbie has had her hair cut substantially shorter. Kids, she guesses, Debbie has kids. One, three and five. Girls, probably, like Jen. Jen had her hair cropped when Holly and Maria were little. No time for grooming with babies born so closely together. Penny remembers her saying it.

Debbie's voice breaks through her reverie. 'How was the dinner party? Did you make your apology?'

'Yes, it was fine, thanks. Everyone was really nice.' Nervy though, she thinks. Everybody seemed edgy, Will included. Or perhaps it was just her. When she first arrived and saw Geri's huge bump, she wanted to scream. Not from jealousy, per se, but the bloody unfairness of life. Not even married, Geri got pregnant first try. Then the way she kept rubbing her stomach. As though anybody needed a reminder. The desire to throw something was imperative for a time. Had to dig her nails in her palm. Not that she would've, of course.

Debbie is gazing. 'We talked about family therapy a couple of sessions ago. Have you and Will thought about that?'

Penny pictures him putting his mobile face down. Wishes he wouldn't do that. He knows she doesn't pry. Part of her wants to, but what might she find? The thought leaves her breathless.

'Not at the moment. He's really busy at work.'

'Maybe another time?'

Penny doesn't reply. She knows he would do it if she asked, even though he hates talking about feelings in general, let alone what happened at the wedding. He hasn't said it, but he wants to move on and pretend it hasn't happened. A good thing, perhaps. But how can she forget when reminders are everywhere? The guests at the reception. Therapy. Pills making her constipated and tired. Heavily pregnant friends who are far, far too jolly. Unexpected prompts in the dairy aisle at Sainsbury's.

'I guess therapy isn't everyone's thing,' Debbie says, as though reading her thoughts.

'That's true.' She pictures her gregarious husband when he's with the A Team and Jen. Laughing, joking, happy. 'Will's as noisy as they come on the outside, but inside . . . Well, he doesn't talk much about emotions. When something's on his mind he goes quiet. It's hard to work out what he's thinking.' She frowns. 'Sometimes what he's doing.'

'So, Will isn't good at talking. How do you find that?'

Difficult, frustrating. Heart-pumpingly terrifying at times. 'Oh, it's fine, I'm used to it. I'm not exactly good at talking about things myself.'

Debbie gazes. 'I guess it can be hard for partners to cope. How are things at home?'

Penny feels the flush and puts her hand to her throat. She's being irrational, she knows it. Will's distance is nothing, just work on his mind. 'Absolutely fine. Now Dad's retired, he bobs in quite often.'

'And the relationship with your mum. How's that going?'

God, she'd forgotten about that, blaming poor Mum far more than she deserves. But Will needed a reason; she could hardly be honest. Though he never said it, his eyes showed his fear. Crazy, they said. My wife is a loony.

Will wants her to be normal. Psychosis isn't normal. Nor is paranoia; imagining those lies.

She comes back to the question. 'Oh, Mum. She's still pretty busy with all her commitments, so I don't see her as often.'

'Does that help alleviate the pressure you described?'

Penny sighs. Pressure, bloody pressure. So much. The stress of Will's moods, the fear of hearing voices, the need to be normal and never lose it again. And having to be patient and wait for her baby. 'Not really. I don't think I'll ever quite escape it all. Not unless I move to Timbuktu.'

Debbie nods. 'And Will,' she presses. 'How are things with him?'

But Penny isn't listening. Escape to Timbuktu, she's thinking. The perfect answer to everything.

CHAPTER TWENTY-NINE

Nick

Nick takes a shuddery breath and rings the intercom at Patrick's white-rendered crescent of flats. His breath emerges as a question mark of steam in the thin and crisp air, or so it seems; he's been asking himself questions ever since his visit to Derek's. Lisa says he's building something as simple and sad as a child's tragic death into a ridiculous size, that people are entitled to grieve in their own way and that he shouldn't take his parents' need for privacy so personally. She's probably right, but he still needs to ask, then he'll leave it alone.

It takes Patrick several moments to answer. 'You're early. Wait by the lock-up garages,' he says.

Nick isn't surprised on either count. Patrick's a stickler for time and doesn't like people going into his flat. The kitchen occasionally, the lounge rarely and the bedroom never.

'No problem,' he replies, smiling wryly. He still feels culpable after all these years. At the age of nine or ten, looking for a book or a comic in his brother's bedroom, he dropped his box of flags and postcards and they scattered on the floor. He knew Patrick liked to keep the postcards in chronological order, so he spread them out, trying to glean the date from the postmark before he came in. When he did, he was furious. The whole family was banned, and though their dad often ribbed Nick about it, he didn't see the funny side; his dad hadn't let Patrick down; he hadn't seen Patrick's white angry face.

Pulling up his collar, he walks around the block. Even if he didn't know which garage belonged to his brother, he'd be able to guess from its plethora of locks and its newly painted door. Over the years he's tried to convince Patrick that so many locks could be counterproductive, as it might look to a would-be thief that there was something worth nicking, but to no avail. He shakes his head and smiles weakly, wondering if the lock thing is a hereditary condition, that he too will get on board the lock train by the time he reaches forty.

'I haven't been out in the Merc since the wedding. How about a road trip, just the two of us?' he asked on the telephone, knowing this was the best way to tempt Patrick out of his usual weekend routine.

Lisa wasn't best pleased when he said he'd be out on Saturday morning, but he argued she'd be in bed sleeping after a night shift at the hospital, so what difference did it make. 'It makes a difference to me,' she said. 'Besides I'm getting fed up of this obsession about a sister you never met. What difference does *that* make?'

'It makes a difference to me,' Nick wanted to mimic, but he knew it was puerile, that it would offend Lisa even more.

He rubs his hands as he waits, thinking back to Wednesday evening to calm his agitation about his mission today. He had a quick pint with Dan and Will in the pub near St Mark's. They always meet there; a tiny drab pub in Whalley Range, one they've used since illegally buying their first pint at fifteen or sixteen. Will has the furthest to drive from Bowden, but he kills two birds by visiting his mum first.

Of course it was Will who bought that first round all those years ago; fairly tall and muscular even then, with the authoritative voice of his barrister dad. A *dirty old man's pub*, they called it then, chosen because they thought it was an unlikely place for the Brothers from their school to frequent.

He arrived the same time as Will, but Dan was already there, his head buried in the *Guardian*. Will looked over Dan's shoulder and tapped the article he'd been reading. 'Dirty old men and Catholic teachers, hmm,' he commented wryly. 'How little we knew.'

'You weren't the one always chosen to sit on Brother Joseph's knee,' Nick replied.

Will laughed. 'I was jealous,' he started, and Nick waited for the quip. 'Truly! I used to think, why can't that be me? If only I was as small and mouse-like as Nicky Quinn.'

'Piss off—'

'Seriously, though, I had a crush on Brother Mark. Do you remember him? He was young and trendy with sideburns. He wasn't there for long. Mum said that he knocked up some young girl. I was devastated when he left. If it hadn't been for Jen keeping me on the straight and narrow, so to speak, who knows? It could've been you and me, Nick. I could've been your Elton. What about you, Dan? You were the pretty boy.'

Dan sipped his pint without the usual retort. He turned to Nick instead. 'Couldn't Jen come tonight?'

'Presumably you invited her,' Will asked, opening his crisps.

Nick had. He'd telephoned Jen, but she'd made an excuse, which was annoying because she was the one he'd really wanted to talk to, and he could hardly arrange a tête-à-tête, not with Lisa in her current mood.

'How's Lovely Lisa? Married life treating you well?' Dan asked later.

'Bet you're having loads of sex,' Will quipped with a nudge.

He thought about replacing the truth with a joke, then decided against it. 'Not this week, that's for sure. It's been a frosty nightmare, and I don't mean this weird weather.' He wiped the rim of his glass with a finger, a habit Lisa tells him to stop. In for a penny, in for a pound, he thought. 'Did you two have teething problems once you'd made all the vows?'

'Whoa, not me,' Dan raised his hands and smiled. 'I haven't made any promises.'

'Does trying to throw yourself out of a hotel window count as teething?' Will added, straight-faced. Then, after grinning, 'Not your foot-in-mouth disease again, eh Nick? Thing about marriage is that sometimes you have to bend the truth for an easy life, sometimes even lie.'

Nick now watches Patrick carefully reverse the Mercedes from the garage and smiles at the memory. The pint with Will and Dan made him feel so much better; it was a relief to be honest, to see the funny side and not feel a failure for once. It was a shame not to get more of 'Mother Hubbard's' wise words, but that's in hand, he's following them now, though the worry of how and when to ask his *burning question* makes him feel queasy.

'Where to?' Patrick asks, though Nick has already told him; Patrick doesn't like surprises.

'The boat lift near Winsford. Can you remember the way? I know we've been a few times before, but not for a long—'

'Anderton Boat Lift,' Patrick interrupts. 'A two Caisson lift lock linking the River Weaver and the Trent and Mersey Canal. Only one of two working boat lifts in the UK.'

Patrick talks at some length, describing the boat lift and its history as he drives. Nick is never sure whether the information he retains for anything remotely technical is long-term memory or swatted from the internet, but his ability to cram reams of data in his head is incredible. Nick is pretty good on sports statistics, so he's a great person to have on the pub quiz team, but that's because he's interested in sport. Ask him to list the kings and queens of England or British prime ministers and he'll have no idea. That's Dan's specialty; he was always a clever boy without needing to show it.

Listening to Patrick and staring through the window, he watches the green frosted countryside spin by. Trying to bat away his anxiety, he picks out the pieces of his childhood farm set, a game he often played with Patrick: trees like cabbages, stone walls, brown fences, black and white cows, barns, goats and sheep. Unsure if it's real or imagined, he inhales the smell of manure from their long weekend walks. A strangely comforting tang. Nostalgia, he supposes.

The low sound of the car's horn brings him back to the road and a stubborn stray sheep. He turns to Patrick, suddenly remembering how comforting it was to see his fair hair in the darkness when he was small and had a nightmare. Immediately there by his side, it was as though Patrick knew. Today his greying hair is hidden by a suede hat with flaps. Give him a moustache and he'd look like a dashing World War II pilot rather than a sad fifty-year-old keeping his ears warm on a cold March morning. But Nick knows that's unkind. Patrick's a happy soul; he's had girlfriends over the years, or maybe friends who were girls, mostly slightly odd or do-gooders. But there was one who was invited on a road trip to Llandudno. Not only that; Patrick had amazingly let her stay at the flat. She seemed smiley and normal and fun, so at seven or eight Nick had liked her. Or maybe it was because she'd given him easy hugs and let him select an inordinate amount of penny chews before going on their tour. Fruit Salad, Blackjack, Refreshers and Drumsticks. And a whole lot more.

Nick smiles wryly at the memory. The bloody story of his life! He gobbled the sweets so quickly, they made him feel sick, then he got in trouble with Patrick for stuffing the wrappers down the back seat of the Merc.

A shame that girl was binned, but hardly surprising. She'd just laughed at Patrick's paddy. He doesn't like that. Nor girls who're too clingy. Or bloody bossy. He likes being a bachelor, holidaying in the same part of France year after year, living his own life, doing what he wants, when he wants to do it. With things as they are currently with Lisa, Nick has some sympathy, but then, how would he know about living his own life? He's gone straight from the frying pan of his parents into the fire of Lisa. At bloody thirty-four too.

They arrive at the boat lift in twenty-five minutes. For all Patrick's caution, he drives the Mercedes very fast, smoothly changing from gear to gear in his leather-gloved hands like a racing driver. But he takes time parking the car, manoeuvring it several times. Nick knows it isn't just a question of protecting his beloved car's doors, it's because Patrick likes everything to be equidistant, like the position of his bed, the bookcases and the sofa in his flat. Even the smallest items in Patrick's kitchen have a specific place and Nick has always known not to pry or to move them.

When they finally stroll around the complex, Patrick chats knowledgeably about salt mining. It has changed since Nick was last here. He remembers the nature park in the surrounding area, but not the manicured lawns leading to the lift, nor the visitor centre, the cafe or the exhibition. Perhaps they were there as a boy, but he preferred to stay outside, kicking a ball towards the knotted woods, darting along the dusty paths and through the tall trees, hiding from Patrick, willing Patrick to find him when too much time had gone by.

179

They spend the best part of a long hour in the free exhibition. Patrick gazes at the control centre for some time and then studies each exhibit carefully, reading the information from top to bottom, yet not participating in the interactive content. Nick's mind drifts as he fitfully plays with the gadgets. His stomach still churning, he frets about when to ask Patrick about their sister. He'd thought he'd ask in the coffee shop over a drink and a muffin, but when he looked earlier, the cafe was light and open, people were already lined at its large window to watch the boat lift itself. Hardly the place for a private conversation.

He decides to ask his question casually in the car, or perhaps at Patrick's flat later, but by noon he's starving and needs a drink, so he suggests they take a last look around the display, then find a pub for lunch on the way home.

Nick chooses an inn on the main road randomly, and though fairly empty, it displays an award for its food. Sitting at a small table, they study the menu, but Patrick's eyes flicker. He flattens his hair repeatedly and adjusts his watch. Nick knows the problem, of course. It's only twelve-twenty, too early for lunch.

Feeling the sweat on his spine, he sighs inwardly. Bloody hell. Can't Patrick be flexible for once in his life? But he needs to hold his irritation in. They're in an empty middle room, he has to press on with his questions before it fills up.

'What do you fancy?' he asks. 'My treat. Don't look at the price. Go for whatever you want.'

Patrick puts down the menu. 'I'll have a think,' he says, sipping his half-pint.

Nick taps his foot. 'Fair enough. It'll probably take ages to come, though.' He throws back his beer, wondering how to put his question, but Patrick interrupts.

'What happened on Sunday? Mum said Dad lost his rag with

Lisa. They were arguing about it at dinner on Wednesday. She said Dad should apologise, but he was having none of it. Said it was his house, bought with his money, his rules.'

'Oh, Lisa said something Dad didn't like,' he replies hurriedly. Then, taking a quick breath, 'Actually, there's something I wanted to ask Mum and Dad, but they've never talked about it, so I thought I'd ask you.' Patrick's face looks blank, so he presses on. 'It was something that came out at the reception. Auntie Iris mentioned it. She didn't mean to. It just slipped out. I think she was a bit pissed . . .'

Nick's chest feels constricted; he knows he's going around the houses, but isn't even sure what he wants to know. And Patrick's face still looks empty.

'Anyway, Uncle Derek heard and he seemed a bit . . . I don't know, annoyed, I suppose, so—'

A young waitress in a white frilled apron approaches their table and asks if they are ready to order. Nick looks towards Patrick. His face has become starched and sweaty. His arms are folded across his chest and he's rocking gently.

'Not yet, thanks,' Nick says to the waitress. Then back to Patrick, needing to spew out the words. 'So, anyway. The thing Iris mentioned without meaning to . . .' His throat feels clotted. 'She spoke about someone called Susan . . .' The rocking becomes more pronounced but he pushes on, the thud of his heart loud in his ears. 'Look, I know from Derek she was your twin, but she was my sister too, and though I never knew her . . .' He flounders for a moment, trying to frame how he feels. In his mind he sees a small curly-haired girl wearing an oversized duffel coat, keeping her twin brother in line. 'I guess I'm just interested to know about her. What happened, Patrick? How did she die? When did she die?'

A gasp emerges from Patrick's mouth, then a tumble of

words. 'It was my fault; it was my fault . . .' He blurts something more, but he's up from his seat, his chair clattering to the floor. Then he's out of the door before Nick's sluggish mind can catch up.

'Patrick! Patrick, stop.'

His heart racing, Nick stands to follow his brother, then realises he hasn't paid for the drinks. Fumbling in his wallet, he pulls out a tenner, throws it on the table and bolts to the door.

The sharp wind cools his cheeks as he runs, but when he arrives in the car park, the Mercedes has gone.

Doubling up, he breathes deeply. When his heart finally slows, he shakes his head and smiles thinly. It really is bloody cold; a hat like Patrick's is just the thing he needs now.

Perching on a fence, he goes back to Patrick's words. His fault, his fault. What the hell did that mean? And what else did he say? Something about fishing.

Blowing on his hands, he waits for ten minutes. He knows Patrick won't return, but he gives it twenty before taking out his mobile.

Lisa's voice is croaky. 'Nick? Hi. Everything OK?'

There's an instant surge of love. 'Sorry to wake you, but . . .' He feels foolish, contrite and anxious. 'Patrick has gone. I tried to talk to him about Susan but he just started babbling, then he bolted. I'm in the middle of nowhere. Can you come and get me?'

He hears her yawn. 'Course,' she says sleepily. Then after a moment, 'What on earth did he say?'

Still jittery and rattled, Nick thinks back to the pub. 'I'm not entirely sure. It happened so quickly. But I think he said it was his fault, that he should never have gone fishing that day.'

CHAPTER THIRTY

Dan

Flitting between tingling images of Seb and breathless trepidation about the baby, Dan drives the short journey from Chorlton Green to the Taylor house, but this time it's at Will's request. There's a dispute between his mother's neighbours about boundaries and their private road. Mrs Taylor doesn't want to get involved, but Will thinks the argument will escalate and wants to be ahead of the game. He and his mum have studied the title deeds to no avail; they aren't even sure which way they should look at the plans; they need an expert and 'Dan is the man'.

He asked Geri if she fancied coming with him for a change of scene, but she said she'd had the same idea, the four walls of the house were driving her bonkers, so she was going on a walk with her friend and her labradoodle to the water park.

'Walking? Are you sure? I prefer the word stroll,' Dan said with a smile, trying not to show the alarm he felt.

'OK, stroll then, but it isn't like *Monty Python*, Dan. I'm not going to lift my leg and let the baby slither out when you're not there.' She looked at him and smiled cheerfully. 'Don't worry; I'm not fretting, so neither should you. Everything's fine.'

'Course I'm not worried,' he replied, not liking the word *slither* either. 'Have fun with the doodle. Keep your mobile with you and make sure it's fully charged.'

The title deeds are now spread over Yvette Taylor's wooden table. Its herb green surface matches the colour of the kitchen units, but perhaps not surprisingly with two rowdy boys and their friends over the years, the paint has chipped off quite dramatically. Everything in the Taylor house is old or *shabby chic*, as Salim would call it. There's the odd genuine antique, polished and pristine, but the furniture is mostly just old and often broken. Dan doesn't think it's lack of money, more a question of taste and necessity. Yvette's watercolours are dotted throughout the house. Some are postcard-sized and displayed on mantelpieces, or pinned randomly on a wall with a rusty drawing pin. Others are bigger creations, hung on high walls in overlarge or damaged frames, purchased, he suspects, from charity shops in the village.

It's a stark contrast to Will and Penny's house on the development in Bowden, furnished with contemporary furniture and fittings. Perhaps it's Will's subconscious way of rebelling, or perhaps he just likes modern houses. Dan was brought up in a semi-detached council house, so emulating was unlikely, rebelling inevitable. Yet still he bought his first and subsequent houses in Chorlton Green, walking distance from his parents. What does that say about him?

He examines the plans. 'You were right,' he says after a few moments. 'You're looking at them upside down.' He points out the boundary lines, then sits down with the old title deeds and reads the clauses about shared amenities out loud.

'You are a clever boy, Daniel,' Mrs Taylor says with a rare smile. She looks like a cross between a model from the cover of a seventies knitting pattern and a bag lady, yet the scarf around her neck looks delicate, embossed with the interlinked Chanel symbol. He remembers his mum describing Will as 'the one with the eccentric mother' when they first started at St Mark's. But then again, his mum likes everything new. Annette's clothes, her shoes and her handbag always match; she's still blonde, giggly and girly in her early sixties, still rushing to the priest if life goes awry. There's nothing to compare her and the granite-haired stoic beauty standing next to him now.

'He was always the clever one,' Will says. 'Scholarship boy.'

Dan rolls his eyes. Our Poor Relation, Benefit Boy, Super Dan, Poor but Perfect, More Please Maloney. The nicknames changed over the years, but they were always light-hearted and affectionate. If his father had heard them, he would've laughed heartily; his mother would have taken to her bed for a week; their council house was bought with hard-earned money, she would like you to know.

'Let me get you a coffee,' Mrs Taylor says. She looks lost for a moment, then turns to Will. 'The old fridge. I suppose we should move it.'

'Another complaint from the middle neighbour,' Will explains to Dan. 'One that can be remedied immediately, thank God. I'll get to it now.' He looks beyond Dan's shoulder. 'I suppose you'll be wanting a lift home too?'

Seb is standing at the kitchen door, his arms behind his head, flexing his shoulders. Dan has to resist a double take and a gape; his hair has been cropped very short, he has a dark sleeve of tattoos along his left arm.

'He's only just up,' Mrs Taylor says, as though that might explain his transformed appearance.

Feeling winded, Dan returns to the deeds; he doesn't need Yvette to tell him that: Seb's feet are bare, he's wearing a white T-shirt and sweat pants.

Will rubs his brother's shaven head. 'Bloody hell, Seb. What the hell? I can't decide. Gay icon or English Defence League.' He laughs unsteadily. 'What do you think, Dan?'

Dan lifts his head, but finds it hard to look. Without the long fringe, the full glare of Seb's sculpted face is exposed. It's like staring at an eclipse when he knows that he shouldn't. And there's a feeling in his chest, a nauseous mix of lust and danger and repulsion.

Seb shakes off Will's hand and turns his attention to the kettle, filling it at the sink, then flicking it on. He shrugs. 'Photo shoot. Not my choice. You like the tattoo, don't you, Ma?' He puts his arm around his mother. 'Coffee, Mum?'

Mrs Taylor nods. She appears to have lost focus again. 'Yes, coffee. I've a bit of a headache so I'm going to lie down. The weather, I expect. Bring it up will you, darling?'

She leaves the room, tall, straight and dignified, but with an air of acute sadness.

Will clears his throat, breaking the silence. 'Right, I'm going to the tip with the damned fridge. I'll be back in forty minutes or so.' He looks at his watch. 'It's quarter past now, make sure you're ready,' he says tersely to Seb. He walks away a few steps before turning back with a tight angry face. 'I suppose your hair will grow, but you'll never get a proper job with that monstrosity on your arm. Sometimes you're so bloody stupid, Seb. If Dad was here—'

'Well, Dad's not here and my job *is* proper. See you in forty minutes.'

Dan follows Will outside, relieved to get out. He helps shift the fridge from the neglected side garden, then heave it into

186

the back of Penny's four-by-four. But Will leaves, stony-faced, declining Dan's offer to go with him, so he waits in the cold, his feet rooted to the brick driveway, trying to settle the hot panic in his chest. He stares at his car; he'd like to escape, to work out his jumbled emotions, but the title deeds are in the house and he promised to write a letter to Yvette's neighbours.

'I'm in here,' Seb calls, when he returns to the house. 'I've made you a coffee.'

Dan steps into the lounge, his eyes sweeping the draughty room. Despite its decline, it's still noble and handsome, but there's an aura of pathos about it. The floor is covered in threadbare Chinese rugs and those parts of the parquet which show have lost their shine. Seb is slouching on a worn and scratched Chesterfield sofa, his legs stretched out on a leather ottoman, apparently doubling up as a coffee table.

Taking a breath, Dan thinks back, trying to remember if the house and its furniture was so tatty when Alex Taylor was alive. Would the child Dan have noticed? Perhaps he would; Annette is still obsessively house-proud, the furniture new, every surface sparkling and straight and clean.

That smell of hygiene, not home.

After a few moments' indecision, he sits down in the armchair. But he's unable to speak, let alone look at Seb's face. He can't grasp his strange feelings, but knows one is anger. Staring at the floor, he understands Will's irritation completely.

'You can't bear to look at me,' Seb states and Dan finally lifts his head. The short crop emphasises Seb's angular face and his startling eyes. Yet the shock is still there. And there's a prickling of anxiety in Dan's gut; he can't put his finger on why. 'The tats are temporary. They'll scrub off in time.' Seb stares, tapping his foot. 'What, that's it, is it? You've gone off me because I've got tattoos and had my hair cut. Not girly enough for you now? You're so bloody conservative—'

Dan's sudden anger takes himself by surprise. 'Don't you fucking dare,' he says, standing up. 'My dad has been a paid-up member of the Labour party all his life. He did two bloody jobs to scrape enough money together to pay for my school uniform. I didn't go on a foreign holiday until I was twenty-five.' He spreads his arms. 'What would you know with all this? Wealthy dad, Chesterfield fucking settees, spending all summer in your holiday home in Abersoch with all the other spoilt rich kids.' He stalks to the door. 'Your bloody hallway is bigger than my childhood home.'

'You know I didn't mean it like that,' Seb replies. 'I meant that you're . . .'

'What?' Dan asks, turning.

'Fucking parochial, actually.'

Dan points his finger, the anger heavy in his throat. 'You don't know anything about me.'

'And you know it all, do you, Dan? Spoilt rich kid?' Seb leans forward, his eyes blazing. 'See this lovely room, this *fucking Chesterfield* sofa? My dad died right here. I was eighteen, my whole future before me and he dropped dead on me. Literally on me, here on this sofa.'

Dan stares at Seb's face. He knew Alex Taylor had died of a heart attack when Will was in his early twenties. He'd felt unwell, went for a walk to clear his head and when he came back he had a massive coronary, but he didn't know Seb was there when it happened. He wants to ask more, but still feels irrationally hurt.

Seb speaks again. 'We were watching tennis on the TV and arguing. He said I'd gone soft and lost my competitive edge, that I'd be a complete failure if I wasn't careful. "Sometimes I can't stand being in the same room as you." That's what he said to the *spoilt rich kid*, Dan. He was angry, went out for a walk, came back and tried to apologise. But I refused to speak to him, even to look at him. Next thing, he was slumped on me and I knew. I didn't move; I couldn't move. Not for God knows how long, until Mum came in and found us.'

The sound of a door closing upstairs breaks the quietness.

Seb drops his head. 'Even now I wonder if I had moved, or called for Mum, or done something, Dad might have . . .' His voice trails off. He shakes his head and stands, his expression so similar to his mum's absent look earlier. 'Well, there you have it. It is what it is. I'd better get ready, have a shower before Will gets back.'

When Dan returns to the kitchen, the plan attached to the title deeds has tried to fold itself back like an arthritic hand. He stares for a while, sighs and pulls out his mobile to text Will. Then he waits at the table, listening to the sound of near silence.

'I'll give you a lift home,' he says when Seb reappears dressed in torn jeans and a chunky jumper. 'I told Will I was headed that way, so . . .'

Seb nods, grabs his overnight bag and follows Dan to the car.

Dan drives down the busy parkway, taking a short cut through tree-lined lanes littered with million-pound houses without speaking. Then he indicates left, accelerates up the sweep of Oak House's drive and pulls up outside the front door, the engine of his car lightly humming.

Seb climbs out, then opens the boot for his bag. Dan stares ahead through the windscreen, watching a bird pecking hope-

CHAPTER THIRTY-ONE

Jen

Jen soon discovers putting on a smile is exhausting, though it probably isn't the best description. It's more a question of not looking worried. Smiling constantly would surely alert Ian and the girls to her anxiety about bloody everything. Will's text and Holly's blood tests, Ian's frequent strange glances and frowns.

She and Holly went back to the doctor's to see the blood nurse on Friday. In fairness she was lovely, though she never stopped talking. 'Just be quiet for a moment!' Jen wanted to yell. 'Just for a moment while you insert that evil-looking hypodermic into my gorgeous girl's arm.'

'Do you pluck your own eyebrows?' the blood nurse asked Holly when they sat down. 'Of course you don't,' she continued before they could work out the question, let alone answer it. 'You're just lovely as you are. But your mum will understand.' She looked at Jen and smiled. 'It'll be less painful than that.'

Holly looked away and flinched, but only a little.

What a brave girl, the blood nurse prattled as she filled several phials. She wasn't very good at faces, but could remember

191

every patient by their veins. She was called Gwendolyn, Gwen for short. Was Holly born at Christmas? Is that how she got her name? What did she want to do when she was older? She'd wanted to be a violinist but found her real vocation when she failed her exams, which shows you never can tell. And how was Mum coping? The children are brave, it's the mums who're the trouble.

Jen had wanted to ask what Gwen thought the tests would reveal, to glean something from the doctor's notes, but there wasn't a gap in her patter.

There's more chatter now at the hairdressers, but Jen doesn't mind as she stares blindly at her reflection. It's therapeutic to listen to other people's stories, often banal, but important to them. And it blocks out her own thoughts, if only briefly.

A lilac-haired lady is describing her day out with an over-sixties walking group and Jen drifts, wondering if her mum would be interested in joining. Nola likes to keep busy. She picks up litter in the local playground, spends time with the elderly at a nursing home, helps out in a charity shop. Always volunteering, never paid. At least not since Jen and her brothers were born. It's what their dad wanted when they married; a wife who was entirely dependent on him. Their dad who uprooted Nola from her friends and family in Cork because he got work in Manchester; their dad who repaid Nola's loyalty and sacrifice by fucking some other woman in Ireland.

The heat spreads in Jen's chest. There he is again. Her bloody, bastard father. He still pays for Nola's *keep*, as she puts it. She wonders if the two of them ever talk.

Lindsay appears in the mirror and speaks, bringing Jen back to her surroundings. Jen has travelled the five miles to this salon for a couple of years now, so no longer notices the zebra-patterned chairs, the leopard-print towels or the black-haired clones who wash her hair. It's Lindsay who counts and she has a three-year itch with both employers and men, a six-week itch when it comes to hair colour.

'You could try something different,' she's saying, peering at Jen's roots. She bends down to the mirror. 'What do you think of this shade?'

Lindsay's hair is pale pink today, but it suits her pastel eyes and pale face. Jen wonders what the girls would say if she returned home with cerise hair. 'Embarrassing' or 'peng', undoubtedly; she never knows which it will be. After a feisty period at the end of primary school, Holly seems to have mellowed, but her eldest is the opposite. Jen feels she can do nothing right, from the contents of Maria's packed school lunch to the style and shape of her trainer socks, never mind the brand. There's her hair colour too; she's desperate to change it to 'ordinary brown', but Jen thinks she's too young, and besides it's a glorious shade.

'People pay good money to make their hair such a beautiful colour,' she reasons.

'You have no idea what it's like to be a ginger,' Maria replies.

For now Anna is just Anna, sunny and affectionate, not even noticing her red hair, but who knows for how long?

Having fended off Lindsay's pink suggestions and listened to her latest romantic adventure, Jen lifts her head to a small television screen. She doesn't want to stare at the mirror; she knows her face is pallid and stark, the hair dye a seeping stain on her forehead and temples. Since her teens she's had a silver line in her hair, not particularly wide, but against her dark colour it always showed. At university she didn't care, it looked funky, done on purpose, but Maria came home from primary school in tears one day, saying that a boy in her class had described her mummy as being the twin of Cruella De Vil. Jen

193

had looked at Ian in horror, but he'd struggled not to laugh. 'In the nicest possible way,' he'd said, hugging her, but the damage was done; she's had her hair dyed to uniform dark chestnut every six weeks since.

'I don't know why you worry about your hair,' Ian said after meeting Lisa for the first time. 'Her hair *is* a problem. It's so feathery, it looks as though it might fall out.'

Jen was surprised he'd noticed, more surprised when he asked if she thought Nick and Lisa were really suited. Both diminutive and Catholic, true, but it seemed to Ian there the similarity ended. Nick was introspective and shy; Lisa loud and Welsh.

'Well the website said they were,' Jen joked at the time, but she's paid more attention since. Ian doesn't comment much, but when he does it's measured. He's generally right about things, which can be annoying at times. He never goes so far as to say, 'I told you so,' but he doesn't need to, it's there in the slight rise of an eyebrow.

She thinks of Nick's call in the week. She sensed he wanted to talk, that she'd come home from the pub to face Ian's raised eyebrow, but she made her apologies and didn't go. Will would've been there and she's not ready to face him.

The earrings flash again in her mind, along with his expression when he gave them. Trying to shake the image away, she goes back to Nick. She feels bad for not going to the pub. Called 'Mouse' at their primary school, he struggled with teasing, so when they went up to St Mark's she took on the role of big sister, stopping the other kids repeating the name, telling him straight when his armpits were smelly, to take a joke and man up. Even buying him Head & Shoulders when his blazer collar was dandruff-sprinkled.

Now Lisa's on the scene she tries to hold back, but the desire to help out still remains. Like the runt of the litter, he's smaller and slighter than Will and Dan, a little fragile too. Not that they don't have their moments, but they're better at hiding it, Will behind his thickset frame. And Dan? There's a thought. She's never been sure what lies behind his humour.

'Silly Mouse,' she now whispers. She liked that special place in Nick's life, but even as a teenager she was perplexed why his mum didn't sort his BO or mention the dandruff. Perhaps Mrs Quinn didn't like to upset him, perhaps she never noticed. As an adult, Jen knows mothers do all sorts of things to protect their kids. Lies, really. Like her mum hiding the truth about her father. When Nola finally told her, she was incandescent with anger before the real pain set in, but now as a mother she can't help but applaud Nola's desire to shield her child, and admire her selfless love.

Lindsay's voice interrupts her bleak thoughts. 'Two more minutes and you're done.' She picks up Jen's mobile and squints at the screen. 'Looks like you've got a message from Will.'

'Cheers,' Jen says, trying hard not to snatch.

She holds her breath before looking. Texts from Will have never been a problem before. The messages were always routine, it didn't matter if the girls or Ian picked them up, but after Ian's odd comment about her nap, she's activated her passcode. Though strange in the context of her and Will's long relationship, it makes her feel seedy.

'*I want to have you on the floor of the bluebell woods. Remember?*' Will's text said on Wednesday night, shortly followed by another. '*Sorry, Jen. Out of order in a text. Won't do it again. You weren't at the pub this evening. Just miss you.*'

Today's text is back to the mundane. '*Just back from Withington. Seb has shaved his head and has a ridiculous tattoo. Mum seems very down. More so than usual. Would you look in when you have time? I'd really appreciate it.*'

Closing her eyes, she tries to dip under a sudden wave of grief. She still visits Will's mum regularly and almost every time she's due to leave, Yvette disappears upstairs and then returns, placing an item of jewellery or a small ornament in her palm, then covering it tightly with her large elegant hand. 'For your girls when they're older. You should've been my daughter, Jennifer,' she always says.

For years Jen protested, saying one day Yvette would have her own grandchildren, but now she accepts the beautiful pieces graciously and says she'll put them away safely. And of course she tells Will she's saving them for him and Seb, for when they have kids.

She takes a quick breath. Will's kids. It had always seemed far away and theoretical, but now it feels real.

And the bluebell woods. Of course she remembers. How could she possibly forget?

CHAPTER THIRTY-TWO

Dan

Parochial, Dan thinks, fucking parochial!

Though the stunning anger fell away before he left Withington, the word still sizzles and stings. It's undeserved, bloody undeserved. He's just a regular guy these days, not as opinionated and political as he was at university, more tolerant in many ways, but still with firm values and beliefs. Small-minded, blinkered, insular, Seb had implied. What the hell does he know anyway?

Fucking offended; the description isn't fair.

Trying to loosen the tension in his jaw, Dan hops up the steps and opens his front door. His warm house always smells spicy, even when there has been no cooking, musty aromas in the ceilings and the floorboards; a distinct contrast to the smell he was brought up in, and not unpleasant, just different.

Geri gives a small jerk when he walks into the lounge. 'I wasn't asleep,' she smiles from the sofa.

'Just closing your eyes,' he replies, remembering a similar comment from Jen the night of Nick's wedding. It seems so long ago. He was a different person then. Or was he?

Parochial, Seb called him. The hurt is still there.

'Think I'll pop over to see Mum and Dad this afternoon,' he says over a sandwich at lunchtime. 'Do you fancy coming? We could walk over if you haven't already had enough walking for one day.'

Geri smiles. 'I strolled, actually. I made a promise to some guy . . .'

Thank God for Geri, dependable Geri. He returns the smile. 'Then why don't we rock and stroll to Mum's later?'

The weather keen on their faces, they walk arm in arm from their leafy street towards the busy main road to buy flowers for Annette. They stroll past the old cinema, Leon's Fabrics, various eateries and the Co-op, heading towards the cream cemetery and the large barren council estate opposite, content in their silence.

Interspersed with irritation, Dan thought about his parents as he drove back from Oak House and they're again on his mind. His black-haired dad is super fit from forty years as a postman, a bricklayer, a gardener, any work he can lay his hands on so long as it's outdoors.

'My job is to keep your mum happy. I love her with a passion,' he says to Dan. 'But a little space helps. Know what I mean?'

The thought of him dying is unbearable. After a heated argument, even worse.

'Is Seb OK now?' Geri asks, as though reading his thoughts. 'It was nice of you to drop him home. Did he get himself sorted, do you think? You know, with the doctor.'

He doesn't want to talk about Seb. He takes up too much space in his head. But Geri is looking at him quizzically.

'Until today I didn't know he was there, literally there next to his dad on the settee when he died,' he says. He hadn't intended to mention it; hadn't wanted Geri's inevitable analysis.

'Really? My God, that's awful. How old was he?'

'Eighteen, so not a child.'

Geri shakes her head. 'I don't know, Dan. Looking back, I was still a kid at eighteen. Thought I knew it all, of course, but I didn't. It's a vulnerable age for that reason, I guess. Poor Seb. That would mess up anyone's head. Just being there, seeing it happen, let alone the feelings of helplessness and guilt. On top of grief, of course; losing your dad, someone you love. God, that's terrible.'

Dan nods, feeling hot. Of course he knows this; he was just temporarily blinded by a surge of emotions he can't fully describe. Anger, panic, hurt, danger.

Not girly enough for you now?

God, lust, bloody lust. Combined and churning in his mind.

What a bastard he was to drop Seb off without a word; he should've said something, done something, an acknowledgement, sympathy. Love.

Suddenly aware she's still speaking, he turns to Geri at the gate of his parents' house. 'Sorry, I wasn't listening for a moment. What were you saying?'

'Oh, nothing. Just surmising about Seb. Perhaps that's why he just *fell out of love*. Do you remember him saying that? You know, maybe it's a subconscious way of dealing with intense emotion? Like deep trauma, forgetting or rejecting it, rather than having to deal with it head-on?'

Her words hit a note, but before he can process it, the door flings open. The stark smell of *hygiene* seeps out. His father steps forward wearing slippers and a grin.

'Hello, love,' he says to Geri with a peck on her cheek. 'Come on in, the kettle's on. Remember to wipe your shoes!' He opens his arms and pulls Dan into the usual tight hug. 'Good job you sent a text giving us warning,' he says in a low voice. 'Gave your mum time to fix her face. Someone has made a comment about the colour of the new carpet and she's taken it badly. It's called heather but looks more like my favourite old rockers Deep Purple! I wouldn't mind changing it if it was just the one room, but she's had it laid all through the house.' He laughs. 'Thank God for Father Peter. I'll ask him to drop by with his blessing, but in the meantime, say you like it!'

The four of them sit in the tidy front room, drinking tea and chatting about the strange weather and the baby, the new neighbours and *Celebrity Big Brother*, about the football match tomorrow, the views of the lads in the 'Blue' pub. Geri admires Annette's patent shoes and comments on the lovely colour of the new carpet and how it brings out the stripe in the curtains. But Dan is only half participating. He gazes blankly at the latest framed portrait of Jesus Christ, desperate to send a text in private. He wants to say, 'I haven't gone off you, Seb. I'm just confused.' But he knows he won't say that, it's too open, too honest. Instead he'll just say he's sorry.

After half an hour he pulls away from the conversation, takes the undoubtedly purple-coloured stairs two by two, stands at the bathroom door and contemplates Geri's comment about deep trauma for a moment. Shrugging the thought away, he pulls out his mobile and sits on the loo seat. As he stares at the gleaming sink, he almost hears his mum's voice. 'I don't know what he's doing in there, Jed, and I don't like to think about it, but will you have a word?' But his long absences as a youth weren't anything shameful, it was the mirror and experimentation with some of her hair products in an attempt to control the curls. He wasn't wanking but tweaking, an explanation his dad found hilarious.

Despite his agitation, Dan smiles at the irony of today's absence as he turns on the phone. Waiting for it to load, he stares at the screen. 'Shit!' There's a text waiting; Seb has got there before he's had chance to apologise.

Anticipating anger and insults, Dan takes a deep breath and opens the message.

'*Fancy watching tomorrow's match on the big screen here?*' it says.

Closing his eyes, he exhales. '*Sounds good,*' he quickly types and presses send.

When he arrives downstairs, Geri is waiting by the door in her coat, listening politely to one of Jed's jokes.

His dad turns with a grin. 'Well you look more cheery than when you arrived,' he says. 'I'll assume it's my good company rather than having just had a good old sh—'

'Ladies present, Dad!'

His dad leaves it a beat, then makes the gag with perfect timing. 'Shedload of tea and biscuits.'

Lifting his hand to wave goodbye, Dan smiles and shakes his head fondly. Even round the corner, he can hear his dad's laughter.

CHAPTER THIRTY-THREE

Jen

Hearing a creak on the stairs, Jen snaps the ivory box shut and slips it under the pillow.

Ian pushes the door open with his foot. He's carrying two glasses and a bottle. 'I'm over it now,' he says. 'Let's have a drink and watch a film.'

'No point, Ian. You'll abandon me for *Match of the Day* halfway through.'

'Then watch the footie with me like you used to.'

It's the same whenever United lose; Ian goes from a strop to a sulk and then silence for three or four hours before shaking it off, then brings the torment back at half past ten by watching highlights on the television. Jen gets pretty sick of it, truth be told. Even when they're entertaining or at a friend's house on a Saturday night, she can feel his emotional absence.

'It's only a game of bloody football,' she wants to yell. 'There are far more important things going on!' Yet she understood that passion years ago; the word 'United' came up in the speeches at their wedding repeatedly, Ian, his best man and her eldest brother competing to use the word the most times in a non-football context. But her interest seemed to wane as Holly's grew. There was a spare Kenning family ticket today, so Holly went pink-cheeked and smiley to Old Trafford with Ian; they were dropped back home by her grandad at six, silent and stony-faced. She can't imagine what the atmosphere was like in the car, yet she was a passenger once.

She now looks at Ian's distracted features and sighs. His description of Nick and Lisa's relationship pops into her head again. Perhaps she and Ian had only a football team in common and, like her mother before her, married only because they had to.

'Taste this,' he says, pouring a glass of glossy red wine. 'It's one of Aldi's select wines recommended by the *Guardian's* wine geek. Five ninety-nine a bottle, but as good as an equivalent costing twenty quid in Waitrose, so he says. What do you think?'

Jen takes a sip. She knows he's making an effort to move on from his moodiness, so she tries for a smile. 'Might taste better with chocolate.'

He punches his fist as though celebrating a goal. 'We have chocolate! Knowing my lovely wife, I bought a selection this morning. It's chilling in the fridge. Whole nut, mint or plain?' He makes for the door, then turns back, studying her face for a moment. 'Everything will be fine, Jen. Really. You worry too much.'

She puts down the glass and puts her hands to her face. 'So why the blood tests, Ian? What are they looking for?'

'Anaemia, an infection or nothing! We've talked about this so many times.'

'But suppose it's something worse?'

'It won't be, Jen.' He pauses for a moment, then perches on the bed. 'Nothing I say makes any difference, but try this. What is the worst that could happen?'

Ian has said this before. He's been on a cognitive behavioural therapy course in the context of helping schoolkids, the 'reality check theory' as he calls it. Jen isn't sure that she likes it; it forces her to face up to possibilities she'd rather not say out loud, even though they've been voiced in her head many times.

'Suppose the worst happens? Suppose the blood tests come back showing leukaemia, for example?' He dips his head to look at Jen with a solid stare. 'I'm telling you it won't be leukaemia. But suppose it was? They zap the white blood cells with chemo and there's a high percentage of treating it successfully. Yes? You know this, Jen. Little Clare Woods when she was five? Look at her now, completely clear. Then in the very small percentage where treatment doesn't work, they do a bone marrow transplant. And one of us will be a match. You or me. Your mum, my folks, a flipping donor. I would be there like a shot; so would you. But that's way down the line of probabilities. So, you have to get a grip and stop worrying. Do you see?'

Smoothing the duvet, she nods her head. Instead of assuaging her fears, they've grown even huger. But she knows he means well. She pecks his lips and nods him away. 'Whole nut,' she says, trying for her bright voice. 'And maybe some mint. *Specially* fricking *Selected* it might be, but it won't be a patch on Cadbury's.'

'Chocolate on its way.' He stands but doesn't move. Facing the door, he clears his throat. 'Is there anything else, Jen?'

Her heart immediately races. She can't see his face but knows he's frowning. And the tone of his voice . . . What the hell is he asking?

The Princess and the Pea popping into her head, she presses further against the pillow and the treasure that's hiding there, wondering if somehow he can feel it.

'Maybe a small slice of Mum's Dundee cake,' she replies, playing dumb. 'But don't let Maria see you bring it upstairs. Her hypocritical mum at it again! I'll never hear the last of it.'

CHAPTER THIRTY-FOUR

Dan

Bloody hell, I could be a father today, Dan thinks. Since waking he's said it several times in his head, but it still doesn't feel real.

Geri became pregnant at their first attempt on a scorching Cretan holiday, but after the initial exhilaration, the pregnancy seemed to creep unbearably towards Christmas. She didn't even look pregnant; it felt like a phantom. But looking back now, it has flown. The due date falls next week. Geri has a packed overnight bag 'just in case'. It sits by the front door and stares when he passes.

He doesn't feel ready.

The warble of the Sunday birds finally piercing his malaise, he takes off his hoodie and dons the garden gloves given to him by Geri's mum. The glossy holly bush stands proudly against the dull twigs of the rose bushes and the faded hydrangea heads. It has grown out of all proportion to the small sprig Geri planted last year 'so we have some to look pretty at Christmas'.

The baby could be today. He doesn't feel ready; it still doesn't feel real.

The sound of Geri's voice snaps his thoughts. 'Geri to Dan! Coffee for you,' she repeats. Tiptoeing across the paved patio, she carries the steaming mug to one side, sweetly biting the tip of her tongue as she concentrates on not spilling it.

'Bloody hell. It's actually quite warm out here. I thought it'd still be freezing,' she says.

Dan nods his thanks as he takes the cup. 'I found white crocuses hidden under the leaves. Spring is sprung!' He puts his spare hand on Geri's stomach. It feels tight to the touch, like an overinflated basketball. 'What do you reckon? Could today be the day?'

'Hope not, not on a Sunday. Everyone says not to give birth at a weekend because there's only a skeleton staff at the hospital and I certainly don't fancy doing it without pain relief.'

'Too right,' he says, flinching inwardly at the idea of her being in pain. He replaces that thought with another uncomfortable one: the sabbath. His mum and dad will be in church right now, Annette looking her best, animated and joyous, Jed droning those bloody psalms and prayers. Catching Geri's questioning gaze, he grins. 'But the child that is born on the Sabbath day . . . How does it go?'

'Is bonny and blithe, good and gay.' Geri laughs. 'Maybe not a Sunday, then. Not that there's anything at all wrong with being gay, of course. But given a choice, you'd want to give your kid the best chance for an easy life, wouldn't you? Being different isn't always easy.'

Feeling a gush of discomfort, Dan sips his coffee and doesn't reply. But he knows she's really talking about race. Geri has always scoffed and dismissed *small-minded* people who take issue with the colour of a person's skin, but from time to time she and her sister talk about a racist PE teacher at their academy who never selected them to represent the school even though they were the best athletes. The thought still makes his blood boil, though the days of him *losing it* are fortunately long gone. Still, it was only an occasional thump and always for a cause, his passions so roused that the recipient deserved it. Not parochial at all.

'Besides,' Geri continues, 'seeing as you guys are at Seb's to watch the football this afternoon, Monica's driving Mum up and we're going for high tea at a posh garden centre in Macclesfield or somewhere. I wouldn't want to miss out on displaying my little finger as I drink from a china cup, or my cream scone! Then Jen's popping by to collect her crockery around six. I said you'd drop it off for her, but she said it wasn't a problem. I get the impression she wants to talk.' She looks down to her belly. 'So not today, Fred, OK? I'm too busy!'

Dan listens to Capital radio as he drives, singing along to block out deep thought. Everything's fine, he thinks between songs. There's no sign of the baby and even if there was, Geri's with her sister and mum. He's only watching football with the lads. He could be home in fifteen minutes. And the spat with Seb is over. Everything's fine, it's really fine.

Seb answers the apartment door before Dan rings the intercom. 'I saw your car through the window,' he says, standing back to let him through. 'Everything OK?'

'Sure,' Dan replies, his breath stuck in his chest.

Striding to the large drawing room window, Seb peers out. 'Come and look. I didn't really notice until today. But your secretary—'

'Maya.'

'Yeah, Maya. She was right about the view. Still looks pretty bleak, but this morning the sun was shining and I could see, well, I could see for fucking miles!'

He turns towards Dan but doesn't quite meet his eyes. He

208

looks healthy and his eyes are bright, but he seems unusually nervous, agitated almost. His hair is still as close-cropped as it was yesterday, his facial bones still as sculpted. A stupid thought, Dan knows, but he'd almost forgotten. He drags away his gaze and looks towards the television. Perhaps Seb is thinking about their row. Perhaps it isn't really over.

Seb rubs his head, then strides to the kitchen. 'So, Dan, a drink. What would you like? I bought in beer. But you're driving, of course. I should've bought Coke or fresh juice. Or Red Bull, maybe. I didn't think.' His back still turned away, he pauses for a moment. 'But there's food. Plenty of food. Have you eaten?' He gestures towards a pile of parchment-wrapped food on the granite work surface. 'I can't remember what I bought now. Have you been to the deli on Water Lane? The choice is fucking unbelievable! And there's bread. Bread with nuts, bread with seeds, bread with olives . . .' He turns to Dan and finally meets his gaze. 'I don't know if you like olives.' His face suddenly transforms by a grin. 'Dan Maloney, do you like olives?'

'Sure,' Dan says, smiling back. The spat's over, he knows, it's there in Seb's smile. He nods at the TV. 'It's nearly three o'clock, are we going to watch the kick-off?'

They sit each end of the long sofa facing the newly acquired television on the wall.

'Flat-screen and huge. Like Will's,' Dan comments, wondering where Will is.

'But probably cost a tenth of the price. You know Will; has to dash out and buy the latest model. Car, television, mobile phone. Headphones.' He glances at Dan. 'Did you see his new fucking headphones? A thousand quid from Selfridges! Then his laptop, of course. A dream Apple customer. Same growing up. He could never wait for Christmas. Pestered Mum into early submission.' He grins again. 'Can't complain, I did pretty well out of it.' Abruptly his face colours. 'You OK?'

'Sure.' Dan looks at his watch. 'Is he or Nick coming?'

'No, I didn't ask them.'

They fall silent for a time, their gaze on the screen, Seb tapping his foot on the soft carpet. Then he turns to Dan. 'Is that all right?'

'Sure,' Dan replies again, wondering if his vocabulary is going to be limited to the one word all afternoon. But it's because he *isn't* sure; he isn't sure about olives; he isn't sure about being alone on the sofa with Seb; he isn't sure about the bloody tattoo; he isn't sure about anything.

'Food.' Seb strides to the kitchen, then returns with a tray, lobbing two packets of deli food on Dan's lap. 'You open some too. Let's see what we've got.'

They spread the open packets across the glass coffee table. Slices of meat and salami, a whole variety of sausages, pots of stuffed peppers, cheeses and savoury pastries, the sort of food Dan would normally devour, but he doesn't feel hungry; he's not sure if he'd be able to swallow if he tried.

Seb stands again abruptly. 'You need a drink. One beer is OK. I'll get you a beer. Can't watch the footie without beer.' He starts to walk away, then turns back, his face flushing. 'Are we watching the match, Dan? Is that what we're doing?'

Gazing at Seb's uncertain face, the rush of heat in Dan's flesh tightens and spreads. His head still isn't sure, but his body stands, walks to the master bedroom and Seb follows.

There's a feeling of restraint on the bed, a slowing of time as Dan watches the graceful movement of Seb's head. He's touching his skin with only his lips. Exquisite, almost painful, he's made his way from Dan's face to his neck to his chest. Now he's following the tapering dark hair with his mouth; unbuckling his belt, kissing, still kissing with soft knowing lips.

His sensations overwhelmed, Dan closes his eyes. Unhurried, more intimate and intense than before, it feels too much like making love. He wants Seb to continue, he would like him to stop. The dull sound of the television commentary wafts through the open bedroom door, becoming more and more urgent as the action builds up to a goal.

Seb pulls away, strips off his T-shirt, then his jeans, standing naked and proud, all shyness gone. His body is beautiful, toned and tight. Dan hasn't really looked at it before, not properly, from a distance. And his stunning face, the cropped hair of the swimmer. Pulsing with desire, he reaches out.

'No, not yet,' Seb says with a grin. 'I've brought you a present. Wait there.'

Returning with a gift bag, Seb sits on the bed, keenly watching him break a gold seal and look inside.

Dan stares, confused, unsure of what he's looking at. It's a tube, like a tube of body product Geri might buy.

'I thought if you wanted to . . . Seeing as we have time.' Seb's vulnerable face is watching his. 'Only if you want to. And we'd need to be relaxed, obviously, so . . .' He puts his hand in the gift bag and extracts a small sachet of white powder. 'It's good stuff from a guy I know in London, so I thought we could do a few lines, so we're chilled before—'

The outrage hits Dan hard in the chest. He drops the tube of lubricant as though he's been punched. He knows only that he has to get dressed, out of the bedroom and away from the flat before he does something stupid. The anger pumps through his body, constricting it. His lungs, his throat, his fists, but as he reaches the door to leave, he finally finds his voice.

'What's fucking wrong with you?' he shouts, straining every

211

inch of self-control. 'That's what's making you ill, you fool. Drugs, Seb. That's what's messing you up, playing with your head.' He stares at Seb's face, realisation dawning. 'You're high now, aren't you? You were high when I arrived. What the fuck, Seb? How can I possibly trust you?'

Pushing hard at the fire exit, Dan hurls himself down four flights of stairs, bursts through the heavy front door, then scrambles to his car. The steam heaves from his chest as he finally breathes. His eyes sharply sting and his hands tremble badly as he battles with the key, but the engine finally turns and he's free, down the long driveway, out of the gates and onto the leafy lane, heading towards the safety of home.

At the traffic lights he stops, punching the steering wheel repeatedly. He wants to cry, he wants to yell; he's confused and frustrated and hurt. What the fuck should he do? He shouldn't be driving in this state. Pulling into the car park of a large pub, he stares at its sign. A drink, yes a drink. He needs a stiff drink.

The football match blares from the TV above the bar. After the third large measure of whisky, Dan smiles a small ironic smile. He's watching the fucking game after all. He tries to follow the second half, forcing out the mental image of Seb's broken face as he left, replacing it with resolve: I'm not gay; I'm not fucking gay. What the hell is Seb playing at? Drugs, bloody drugs. He's probably an addict.

Spinning a damp place mat, he tries to focus, to think. Seb was meant to be Will's best man, but he was ill. The illness was shrouded in mystery. He remembers that now. And something Will said about the world of modelling and drugs.

The match ends but he doesn't move. He orders another whisky. I'm not gay, he thinks again, I'm not fucking gay. But even so, even so, why would they need drugs? How he'd *felt* was a drug. That should've been enough.

Putting his head on folded arms, he sighs. Like a teenager in love. How pathetic. He trusted Seb; he fucking trusted him. It's him who's the fool, a stupid bloody fool.

A vibration through his jacket pocket jerks him back to today, to a Sunday and to Geri, pregnant Geri, his partner. Oh God, he'd forgotten; he'd completely forgotten. He has a baby on the way, for fuck's sake! He's a bloody, bloody fool. What the hell is he doing in a pub?

His heart thrashing with alarm, his unwilling fingers fumble for the mobile, but when he squints at the screen the call isn't from Geri. It's from Seb. Seb Taylor who needs drugs; Seb Taylor who's betrayed him; fucking Seb Taylor who he wants when he shouldn't.

He hesitates for a moment, wanting to hear his voice, wishing he had the resolve to ignore it.

'Dan? I'm scared. I don't feel well. Dan? Are you listening? Can you come? I'm fucking scared. My throat—'

The alarm is immediate and sobering. 'Seb, what have you taken?'

'Nothing. Not much. You've got to come. This has never happened before. I feel weird. I can't swallow. I'm really fucking scared.'

Dan stands and puts his hand in his pocket, extracting his car keys.

'You're not driving, right?' the barman asks.

Agitation blocks his senses. He shakes his head, trying to think. Of course he can't drive. He's well over the limit. What the fuck has Seb done? What has he taken? Some rogue drug? Or an overdose? Oh God, a bloody overdose.

Going back to his mobile, he stares. An ambulance, of course. He must call an ambulance.

CHAPTER THIRTY-FIVE

Jen

Jen drives towards Chorlton Green, glad to leave the frayed atmosphere at home. She insisted the girls accompany her and her mum to the Sunday service at St Catherine's this morning. She doesn't make them attend every week, but feels once a month is fair dos to keep them in touch with their religion. Then when they're old enough, they can decide whether to take it or leave it.

She personally enjoyed the whole religious thing as a child, especially her first communion and confirmation. Admittedly, it was for the mini wedding dress and the celebration party, rather than belief, but she liked the familiarity of the prayers and the hymns, there was something reassuring about the community of it all.

She still isn't sure about belief, but going to church each Sunday makes her *feel* better. Praying helps, especially at low times. Like it did as a girl.

'Come on, love, let go of Daddy. He has to go now. It'll be OK, Jennifer, I promise. With God's help, it will be OK.' They were Nola's words when she was eleven, when she was dragged off her father, her fists clamped onto his neck, his hair, his wrists, his shirt, any part of her lovely daddy to stop him walking through the door and leaving them forever.

She sobbed every night. 'Don't cry, love,' Nola consistently said. 'He still loves you dearly; you're still his special girl. And you'll see him lots. He's left me, love, not you.'

The heartache was unbearable for months and months. Secretly she blamed her mum for Daddy leaving, but talking to God about it helped.

She now absently stares at the traffic lights and sighs. Of course, she still prays before sleep, but likes her Sundays and other Holy Days for prayer in church. It feels more personal. Like a face-to-face meeting rather than email or text, the message has a better chance of getting through. It's a bonding time for her and Nola too. Not that they need it; living in the same village, they see each other most days, but it's nice to spend three Sunday mornings out of four, just her and her lovely mum, a coffee, chat and gossip in a local cafe after church, putting the world to rights.

But today Maria kicked off. She didn't want to go to church, she didn't believe in God and if there was a God, what sort of God was he? Famine and war, Ebola and earthquakes, cancer and childhood death. Jen could see she had a point, but as ever, her eldest took it too far. Jen was a hypocrite for going every Sunday anyway, she sneered. Look how she'd bought those horrible commercialised Easter eggs the other week. Wasn't Easter a serious religious celebration? If it was, she was hardly setting an example to her children.

Jen was on the point of telling Maria to stay home, almost relieved not to have to look at her miserable features for a couple of hours, but Ian intervened again, shouting as angrily at her for disrespecting her mother as he had the last time. So she'd tagged along towards church, her face a picture of irritation and disdain.

'Come on, love, take a chill pill,' Nola said, putting her chubby arm around Maria's shoulders as they walked.

'Grandma!' the girls laughed and it broke the ice, but by the time they got back to Ian's chilli con carne, all three were sniping, so she was glad to escape later.

Jen knocks at the solid door of Geri and Dan's house. Though technically a semi like hers, it has several huge bedrooms, an attic and a cellar. 'There are four hormonal women in our house, can we swap houses?' she has joked over the years. Hers in Didsbury is in a sought-after area, but the bedrooms are small and the girls have to share. Maria has recently swapped with Anna, preferring the tiny box room than having to share with Holly. But Anna is happy; she's thrilled to sleep in bunk beds with her middle sister. 'It's like a sleepover every night,' she confided the other day.

One daughter on cloud nine; it makes Jen's heart soar. No cares in the world. At least not yet . . .

Geri eventually opens the door, yawning wearily. Jen tries to stretch her arms around where her slim waist used to be. 'You are officially huge, Geri! How's it going?' she asks.

'Another week to go, but of course that could be three. I haven't said anything to Dan, but I keep feeling a twinge, then nothing happens, so who knows? To be honest, it feels as though he or she will never come out. A sort of pregnancy *Groundhog Day*.'

'Good description. Though I find it hard to remember now. The three pregnancies seem to blend so they've become interchangeable in my memory.'

Geri smiles wryly. 'Well, that's good, I suppose. Only another two babies to go . . .'

Jen nods and smiles. The nine months did blend, and so did the labour in retrospect. But with each baby, it all came flooding back once the contractions began. Like heartbreak. But she's not here to think about Will. Or her dad for that matter. They are on the back-burner for now; worrying about them as well as Holly would be too overwhelming.

They're still standing in the slightly tangy hallway. Jen glances at the peeling corner of the faded floral wallpaper, the urge to pick and tug there as always. She nods to a box near the kitchen. 'Is that the crockery? I'll put it in the car.'

Geri puts a hand to her stomach. 'There we go again.' Then after a moment, her small frown clearing, 'Coffee first? Or a glass of wine? Come through. I've been for a cream tea this afternoon with my mum and sister. It's funny, isn't it, how your tastes change? I used to love Earl Grey before getting pregnant, but now it's too perfumed. Will I go back to liking it? Will life in general revert to normality?' She looks pensive for a moment before coming back to the conversation. 'Sorry. Did you say tea? We ordered too many sandwiches, so I have a doggy bag of goodies. Fancy taking a look?'

They sit in the bay-windowed lounge and talk about Geri's plans for the kitchen after the baby is born, in fact her plans for everything, hallway included. Jen watches the emotions flick through her shining eyes, the impatience, the apprehension, the excitement, as she explains how she didn't expect life to be on hold for eight and a half months. Though not generally an anxious person, she feels she's been holding her breath for a very long time. From getting pregnant in the first place, to peeing on a testing stick, to scans and blood tests, more peeing in pots and for the last few weeks the high blood pressure. And of course she's still holding her breath for the big one!

217

'At least a big gulp of air will help push the little one out,' Jen replies with a smile, understanding Geri's need to talk.

'And, of course, you feel unique, special and clever growing a baby,' she continues, 'which is absurd when babies are born all the time . . .'

She breaks from Jen's gaze, looks at her hands, then abruptly changes the subject.

'Strange question, but how was Ian when you were pregnant with Maria, Jen? And after she was born?' Her eyes flicker. 'Dan isn't saying anything, but . . . I don't know. Something's not quite right.' She looks embarrassed and sighs. 'You know Dan. Whatever goes on in his head stays there. But at times he seems, I don't know, far away. Course he's still loving and kind, but distant, almost. Is that normal?' She tries for a smile. 'You know, for new fathers-to-be? Should I be concerned?'

'With Dan? God no! I'm sure it's nothing and we know what wimps men are. I expect most freak out in some way or other,' Jen replies, thinking that in fact Ian was thrilled and supportive, ahead of the game at each stage of her pregnancies, wanting to be involved and hands-on, going up another notch when each baby was born. But that was Ian Kenning for you. Steady, reliable, needed in her life.

And Will, what of Will? Her soulmate, if she's honest. Handsome and solid and so necessary too . . .

Just stop, Jen. Just stop.

'More tea?' Geri asks, interrupting her fevered thoughts. She smiles apologetically. 'Sorry, I'm rabbiting on. Let's talk about you. How is Holly after the blood tests? When will you hear? Let me top up this pot with water and I'll be right back.' Geri returns to the lounge without the teapot. Her face is what Jen can only describe as stunned. 'I'm not entirely sure,' she says, 'but I think my waters have just broken.'

Jen strides to the kitchen, looks at the pool of fluid on the floor and laughs. 'What a clever baby,' she says reassuringly. 'Easy to clean up.' She takes Geri by the shoulders and sits her down at the table. 'Right,' she says. 'First things first. We call the hospital to tell them you're on the way, then we call Dan. Then a quick mop up for health and safety and I'll drive you there with your overnight bag. How does that sound?'

Taking out her mobile, Jen takes a deep breath. Right, action needed. She smiles to herself wryly. Today hasn't panned out as she'd expected. But perhaps that's not surprising. Nothing in her life has.

CHAPTER THIRTY-SIX

Dan

Dan nearly nods off, but each time, he jolts awake, taking in the acrid smell, remembering his surroundings and reprimanding himself for temporarily forgetting. He's in a crowded room at the hospital, sitting on a hard plastic seat and waiting for news. He wipes the tears from his cheeks with his hands. He doesn't realise they're flowing until they pool at the end of his nose, then drip down to his knees. They come each time he focuses on what's happened, forced out by the crushing weight of the responsibility and the helplessness he feels.

He stands again, patting his jeans front and back, then taking off his jacket and going through the pockets, sure his mobile will be there this time. That somehow the last five or six hours will rewind and start again so he can do everything differently.

Of course his phone isn't there; what's done is done; nothing will change, nothing can.

Doors open and close, brightly dressed staff come and go. Navy tunics with a red trim, blue with white and protective green. Solid colours of reassurance, he supposes, but he's not feeling it. He's not feeling anything, he's teetering and swaying, his mind refusing to focus on what's behind the closed doors.

Making his way to the gents', he drinks from the tap and splashes cold water on his face. He rubs it dry with a green paper towel, then lifts his gaze to the mirror, pulling out the wet fragments of tissue caught in his beard, thinking, who is this person I see? This cheat and this fool. This inadequate man. Who the hell is he?

Resisting the urgent need to sob, he stares at his reflection. The boy is still there, that ten-year-old boy. He's hidden by the man and the beard, but he's there.

Closing his eyes, he covers his face and wills the memories away. For years and years he barely gave them a second's thought, but they're back, fucking back. He doesn't know why; he's afraid to think why, but he can *feel* them right now. Not just the disgust and the guilt, but the touch of *his* hand, a man's grown-up hand on his penis. And those words, evil words, soft in his ear. 'Such a special boy, my Daniel. Feels nice, doesn't it? Why, look at that! I can see that you like it.'

There's a sudden urge to puke, so he lowers his head and breathes deeply, willing it to pass.

He thinks about trauma, deep trauma. Was it really only yesterday? Geri's wise words about it. Forgetting or rejecting it, rather than having to deal with it head-on. So much better that way. And that ten-year-old did it so well. Until he was thirteen. Bloody thirteen! Too old to cry, but sobbing uncontrollably in his father's arms. Ironic really. He wasn't spilling blood and tears because of the unforgivable abuse, but for something quite different. He doesn't want to think about that. It's forgotten, it's buried, where it should be.

Lifting his chin and with resolve, he takes a deep breath. Stop, just stop. Today isn't about him. No more self-indulgence.

More important things are going on. God, far more important.

He leaves the cloying toilet and stands at the door. Time for action, stop a medic, just ask. Heading towards a blue tunic, his steps are cut short. 'Dan!' The shout comes from behind him, a bellowing voice he'd know anywhere.

'Here! I'm here.' Will lifts his hand and turns back to the counter, speaking in a deep clipped voice to the same hassled receptionist Dan spoke to earlier. Clearly Will isn't accepting 'take a seat and wait' as he had previously. But then he didn't feel qualified to kick up a fuss. He wasn't family, just a friend, the fool who'd called the ambulance.

Will finally turns. His scowl is replaced with perplexed surprise. 'Bloody hell, Dan. Hospital cutbacks or what? You've walked a long way to have a piss.'

Like a shock of freezing air on Dan's skin, the worry is instant. A long way to have a piss? He reels at the words.

Will's smile is mixed with a puzzled frown. 'I thought the maternity unit was on the other side of the building. You got all our messages, didn't you?' He studies Dan's face. 'Are you all right, mate? Jen's been calling you all evening. She thought we were together, so she called me too. We've all left messages on your mobile. Geri has gone into labour, Dan. Her waters or something. She's here in the maternity unit. Jen's with her. Bloody hell, mate, you're in the wrong place, you'd better get moving.'

CHAPTER THIRTY-SEVEN

Jen

Jen leaves Geri napping in a maternity ward of four, stalking back to the corridor to check her mobile for missed calls. It's dark through the windows, the whole building strangely silent. She's still hot and agitated. With the hospital, with Will and with bloody Dan Maloney.

No answer from Dan, she put Geri in the passenger seat of her car on a towel, drove the fifteen-minute journey to the hospital, reassuring and chatty, then ended up having a heated row with the woman on reception, who tried to turn them away on the basis of staff shortages on a Sunday.

'Labour might not start for twenty-four hours,' the woman said with pursed lips. 'Ms Hesk is better off at home until then.'

It was hard not to shout. Her waters have broken, she has high blood pressure, Jen argued, she was bloody well staying put. Of course she didn't add that Geri's partner had gone AWOL, that there was no one bloody home to look after her. She'd phoned Dan twenty times, then moved on to Seb, but there was no answer from him either. So in desperation she'd called Will, who answered immediately.

'Jen,' he said. 'Finally. What's up? Why have you been ignoring me? I've been tearing my hair out.'

'You have no hair, Will,' she couldn't help but reply.

'Now you're smiling, aren't you?' he said. 'That's why I love you so much.'

The words threw her for seconds. She had to wrench her mind back to why she was calling. Where the hell was Dan? she asked. Geri's waters had broken. She'd tried Dan's mobile a hundred times. Where did he go after the football? What football? Will asked. The football at Seb's, she explained. But Will didn't know, said he'd track down Seb and try to find out. She hasn't heard from him since. Nor Seb or bloody Dan.

Deep concern now setting in, she looks again at her mobile, briefly speaks to Ian at home to fill him in, then drops on a bench and closes her eyes, wondering what to do next. This isn't like Dan; something terrible must have happened. So, what now? Dan's parents? The police? And what the hell will she say to Geri when she wakes?

'Jen?'

She jumps at the sound. Dan Maloney is standing in front of her, looking dreadful. His face is pale, his eyebrows are knitted, the white of his eyes tinted pink. 'What's happening, Jen?'

Standing up, she lets rip, but not half as much as she would've done had it not been for his desperately anxious face. 'But Geri's fine. Her waters have broken but labour hasn't started yet, so she's sleeping on a ward,' she finishes. 'Where have you been, Dan? Why haven't you answered my calls?'

'Long story,' he replies, rubbing his face. 'But I lost my mobile. In a taxi, I think.' He pulls her into a hug. 'Thanks for being here. You're a really good person; a really great friend. We're all lucky to have you.' He releases her eventually and looks to the end of the corridor with flickering eyes. 'Which way do I go?' he asks. Then, taking an unsteady breath, 'It's fine; I'll find her. Sorry and thanks again. It's late, go home to your family.'

Jen nods, picks up her coat, fishes for the keys in her handbag, then lifts her head. She can still see Dan's retreating back. She's never seen him like that before. There was a strong smell of whisky on his breath; he looked as though he'd been crying.

After nipping to the loo and tackling her badly smudged mascara, she finds Dan staring blankly at a vending machine in the waiting area.

'They told me Geri's still asleep,' he says. 'It felt wrong to sit in the ward with the other women and their babies, so I'm waiting here.' He looks at the coins in his hand, then back to Jen. 'I thought you were going home.'

Shaking her head, Jen smiles wryly. Did she really think she'd leave Dan in this state? She stands on her tiptoes to kiss his cheek. 'Hospital coffee,' she says, selecting two pounds from his palm. 'Just can't resist it.'

They sit together in the empty room, gazing at their steaming coffees. Dan flexes his right hand and stares at his knuckles, so Jen looks too. How strange; they're red and grazed. What on earth has he been doing? She slides her hand onto his. 'You would talk to me if something was troubling you, wouldn't you?' she asks. She looks at his hollow eyes, feeling a surge of love and concern. 'You know me, the soul of discretion.'

He turns towards her, a small smile breaking the tension in his jaw. 'Like when I stole from Mum's swear box to buy sweets?'

'Yup. I was your confessional.'

'The bloody confessional,' he mutters. He drops his head in his hands and for a moment she thinks he's going to say something momentous. But he shakes his dark head and looks back, his brown eyes searching and gentle. 'Same goes here,' he says.

'Are *you* OK, Jen? Geri thought you were worrying about something. About Holly? There's nothing wrong, is there?'

'Just a mum worrying. You'll know what I mean soon enough,' she replies. But her voice is a croak, she's trying hard not to cry.

Dan stands, moves the drinks, then crouches down to look into her eyes. He gazes for a few moments before speaking. 'You can trust me too, Jen. I could tell something had gone wrong at the dinner party. I've loved you and Will for twenty-three years—'

'Oh God, is it so obvious?'

'Only to me and I wouldn't dream of telling anyone, not even Geri.'

The tears flow then. She pulls a tissue from her handbag and wipes her face. 'That isn't even it; well, not really.'

'What then?'

She takes a deep shuddery breath. She's spoken to God about it a million times, but she needs to say it out loud. 'Suppose Holly was really ill with something serious? Suppose she needed me and Ian to donate something. Blood, bone marrow, a kidney, whatever? They'd do tests, wouldn't they, to see if we were a match?'

Dan's eyes study her intently, trustful and dark.

'Suppose those tests showed that Ian isn't Holly's father? What then, Dan? What then?'

CHAPTER THIRTY-EIGHT

Nick

The images hit Nick again. Patrick, poor Patrick. His strangled words. The chair as it clattered. Every time he drifts, the film bursts in his mind like a bloody Snapchat story. If only it was; if only it would vanish. Like a snap, he needs to live in the moment and stop fiddling with the past.

He yawns, points the remote and flicks through the TV channels until he finds sport. Wrestling, but what the hell. It was Lisa's turn to make dinner over an hour ago, but she's been chatting on the telephone. Not that he minds. The first caller was his mum. She's phoned several times since the Sunday lunch spat. Not saying anything specifically, but trying to build bridges, he supposes: 'Poor Dad has been so grumpy with the pain in his hip'; 'You know how stubborn he is'; 'His bark is worse than his bite'. When Lisa has answered in the past, she's given the phone straight over to him. But tonight she shook her head and smiled, engaging in light-hearted conversation with her: 'No sign of the baby yet.' 'I'm sure, but you know Dan, he'll find it a breeze.' 'Yes, due next week.' 'Of course I'll let you know.' Then rolling her eyes. 'I'm sure Nick will love it. He can't get enough of your apple tart.'

Wishing it was right this bloody minute, Nick wonders when the pie will arrive. The current caller is Penny. Unlike the conversation with his mum, he listened disinterestedly for a few moments to Lisa's exclamations before zoning out.

'Of course we're coming! Wild horses wouldn't hold us back.' 'Glad you appreciated the pun.' 'Oh God, I've got nothing to wear! What are you wearing?' 'Are hats compulsory?' 'No, I'm still coming even if it means I have to wear my flipping wedding gown!'

His stomach rumbling again, Nick contemplates whether it's worth grabbing a biscuit to tide him over until food appears. On balance he decides not. Lisa is in his good books, not only for driving to the middle of the Cheshire countryside to collect him yesterday, but for giving him space and not prying. She pulled up in the car park and took one look at his face. 'Oh, Nick, I'm so sorry. Tell me when you're ready to talk.' Then when he climbed in, she took him into her arms and rubbed his back. 'You're flipping freezing, poor lamb.' Handing him a bag of crisps and a banana, she smiled. 'Not much, because I didn't want to delay getting here, but I thought you'd be hungry.'

He'd wanted to cry. Not just because he felt so dreadful about upsetting Patrick, not only because Lisa was being so sweet, but because he missed his mum. In that moment he longed to be a little boy again. No responsibilities at all; nothing bad in his life. Just cushioned, protected and loved. As Lisa drove away, he'd turned back to look. He couldn't put his finger on why, but he knew somehow he'd left his childhood behind in that pub.

He tries to concentrate on the wrestling, but the bloody video hits him again. Patrick's pale troubled face. And that rocking, that freaky bloody rocking! He'd never seen it before. It was as though he was the adult and Patrick the child.

Topsy-turvy, disorientating and disturbing. And what the hell did he mean about the fishing? He's tried not to speculate, but his mind has needled ever since. Then Patrick is ignoring his calls and texts, which makes it bloody worse. Well it would, if that was possible.

Lisa mentioned it before bed last night. 'Want to talk about Patrick?'

He said he was too tired and needed sleep, but predictably he dreamed, deep sticky dreams of the brook at Wilmslow Park. Tightly holding Patrick's hand and wading upstream, his wellies slowly filling with water. Getting tireder and colder. The sun no longer glinting on his brother's fair hair. Then his small tremulous voice, eventually breaking through. 'It's getting really deep, Patrick. I'm afraid. Can we go back?' 'No, Nicky, we can never go back. We're here to find Susan.'

Blocking his view of the TV, his pink-faced wife brings him back from his thoughts. She punches the air. 'Result!'

'So what was that all about?' he asks, hitching to one side of the sofa to see the end of the round.

Lisa moves too. Points two fingers to his eyes, then to hers, the usual sign to make sure he's listening. 'Short notice, but would we like to go to Chester races next Saturday. Some of Will's clients have dropped out. We'll be in the members room, there'll be a meal, champagne, our own balcony – the works!' She beams, her face glowing. 'I have flipping nothing to wear, but one can't possibly refuse a freebie and you've got your nice navy suit . . .'

'Why didn't she ask Jen and Ian?' he asks.

Lisa puts her hand on her hip. She's put on a few pounds since the wedding, but he likes her that way. 'I thought that too,' she replies thoughtfully. 'But it's short notice, as Penny said, so I expect she didn't want Jen to be in a quandary about the girls. Maria's probably old enough to look after the other two, but she can be a bit of a stroppy nightmare apparently. Still, what the heck? I don't care if we're second or tenth choice. We've got the golden ticket, Charlie!' She plucks the remote from his hand and slides onto his lap. 'I love an outing, don't you? Especially a free outing.' She leans in for a kiss. 'God, I'm flipping hungry. Tell you what, shall we order a takeout for dinner? It'll take them twenty minutes to deliver.' Cocking her head, she grins. 'Now, what can we possibly do while we wait?'

CHAPTER THIRTY-NINE

Jen

'Do you want me to call school and say you're sick?' Ian asks, already up and dressed in his grey corduroy trousers. 'You didn't get into bed until the early hours. You must be shattered.'

Jen bolts up immediately. 'Oh, God. I'd forgotten! I wonder if the baby has arrived.'

Picturing Dan's face, she goes back to last night. She stayed with him in the waiting room until a midwife appeared saying Geri was awake and asking after him. He looked pretty terrified. She guessed the alcohol had worn off with the amount of coffee they'd drunk, but still wondered what was going on in his head, and she'd hesitated before leaving. But she wasn't Dan's mum and she had her own family to worry about, so she left him with a tight hug and a kiss.

She turns on her mobile and waits for it to load. 'Oh Ian,' she declares. 'How lovely! It's a boy. No need to call the school, thanks, love, I'm awake now. Though a cup of tea would be great.'

'*Wonderful news!*' she texts back. '*Love and congratulations to you both. Tell us when you're ready for visitors. I know you won't be able to fend off family, but friends can wait.*'

She knows she's sounding like somebody's grandma, but can't help sharing her pearls of wisdom. She's been there, seen it and done it! She's aware she rubs some people up the wrong way, but she's only ever tried to help. Her brothers had kids before she did, but they didn't pass on any pearls, and her mum was of the old *better not to know* conspiracy school, so she had no idea what to expect for the birth or the aftermath. Maria was pulled out with forceps at the end of a long labour; Jen had to have stitches and couldn't pee properly for weeks. The A Team came to visit her in the hospital only hours after the birth with flowers and chocolates and the cutest pink dress she still keeps in the bottom of a chest; she had to hide the catheter bag under the bed for fear of traumatising the poor lads for life.

Dan texts back almost immediately. '*I'm still coming with you tomorrow. A promise is a promise. Don't try to talk me out of it.*'

She deletes the text quickly. Ian has asked several times when Holly's results will be available, but she's been vague. Tomorrow's the day; she's already made an appointment with the surgery to collect them in person rather than over the phone. After her confession last night, Dan promised to go with her.

Breakfast runs late, the girls asking questions, pleased and excited with the news. They pile out of the house, Holly and Maria running one way to start their school day, she and Anna the other.

'Is it OK if I tell everyone at school about the new baby? And can I take off my scarf? I'm boiling,' Anna asks after five minutes skipping.

'Course, love,' Jen replies, shaking herself to the present. She sees hazy blue sky and budding leaves. Anna is right; it's a fairly balmy day again. The frosty weather seemed to last for so long that she'd got in the habit of zipping up anoraks, helping kids with their mittens, sorting out which hat belonged to which child at the end of each school day.

Anna darts ahead to another girl from her class. There's a chunk of soft ginger hair she's missed. Jen sighs. What a crap Mum, she should've helped with her bobble. The anxiety spreads again in her chest. Holly's results are tomorrow, oh God they're tomorrow. Then another urgent thought: Dan knew about her and Will; he's always known. He could see something was wrong between them. Oh God, was it really so obvious? Has she been careless? Could Ian possibly know? What did he mean by his question?

'Morning, Mrs Kenning,' the head teacher says as she passes. He's talking to another teacher in the playground, his Mr Incredible face ridiculously close to hers, poor woman. On the occasions he engages with Jen, she finds herself backing away. Fortunately they are few; his preference for new recruits is young, slim and blonde. Being in her thirties, dark and on the plump side, Jen feels outnumbered by his clones, often wondering how she managed to get a job at his school at all, never mind her cushy job-share.

But there's someone who fancies her; someone who hasn't much hair but who is good-looking and broad and knows when it's appropriate to invade her personal space. 'That's why I love you so much,' Will said last night. He said it with a smile in his voice, so he was just being flippant. Yet still the phrase has been saved in its own special file.

Since they split at eighteen, Will has often said that he wants her, he's said that he needs her, but he's never said that he loves her before.

CHAPTER FORTY

Penny

There's a stain on Debbie's jacket. It looks like chocolate. That's a surprise. With her rosy scrubbed cheeks, she's never looked like a mum who'd give her kids candy. Jen gives her girls chocolate, more than Penny would allow. But then her girls are much older now. Thirteen and twelve? And even Anna, little Anna, must be seven or eight.

The mention of Will's name pricks her ears. 'Sorry, I was miles away.'

'Last time we had a chat about Will's . . .' Debbie smiles. 'Is the word reticence a fair one?'

Penny nods. More than reticence, if she's honest. Staring absently at the TV, not always picking up when she calls. No kisses or cuddles. Friendly when they speak but absent somehow. Still, he perked up no end when Jen called him on Sunday. Apparently Dan had gone AWOL, no one could find him. 'Then why are you smiling?' she asked when he told her. His eyes had flickered before giving her a hug. 'There'll be a new baby by tomorrow. That's always good news. That'll be us one day, Pen. You know, when you're better.'

Debbie's watching as usual. 'How do you find that?' she asks.

It takes a moment to answer. Will dashed out after Jen's call and was absent for hours. To see Seb at the hospital, of course. At least that's what he said.

She comes back to Debbie's question. 'Oh, it's fine; that's just the way he is. You know, male emotional reserve. Though . . .' Her heart racing, she pauses. She'd like to be honest, tell Debbie about her anxiety about Will's strange behaviour, the urgent need to connect and start trying for a baby again, but this woman is assessing her mental health. She doesn't want to say anything which might appear irrational or cause her to dig deeper. 'Sometimes it's nice to talk, though.' She smiles thinly. 'Like now, I guess.'

'How does *male emotional reserve* make you feel?' Debbie presses.

The word pops in Penny's head. 'Isolated,' she replies, surprising herself by saying it out loud. But it's true, very true, when your husband is everything.

Debbie is gazing. 'You feel lonely at times. How about friends?'

Friends? Not really. She had her medic pals at uni, but they dropped her, of course. Like a *bad penny*. Ironic, really. 'How do you mean?'

'To talk to. Your dinner party friends, for example.'

Penny thinks about the question. Could she talk to Jen, properly talk? Affectionate and kind, she would make it easy, but she's part of the A Team, too partial somehow. And of course there was that stupid paranoia she felt around her at the wedding; she doesn't want to think about that. Which was why she didn't invite her to the races and asked Lisa instead. She's really friendly, perhaps that would work. People from work? Heavens no. And who else is there? She pictures the dairy aisle in Sainsbury's. Not just alarm, but fear on his face. Oh God; she frightened everyone away.

She mustn't scare Will; she must never perturb him.

'No, I don't think so,' she says. 'It would be too embarrassing.'

'You talk to me. Some people like to listen and assist if they can. I'm sure there's someone out there who would help. Any harm in trying?'

'I suppose not,' she replies, but her mind has already roamed. A baby, Will's baby. *That'll be us one day*, he said on Sunday. Such lovely words; music to her ears. And a loving hug too.

But why is she certain it was to hide his lying eyes?

CHAPTER FORTY-ONE

Jen

Jen writes the word 'Tuesday' on the whiteboard as usual. She turns to thirty pairs of eyes looking at hers, some tired, some bored, some interested, but all shapes and sizes and colours. She has hazel eyes and Ian has blue; Maria and Anna have brown, Holly blue. It's what one expects, it's normal, isn't it?

She looks at the teacher's empty chair at ten, wondering how to manage the day on her own, but as if by magic, the door is flung open and Mrs Cross appears, ruddy-faced and windswept. 'Sorry I'm late, class,' she says, 'but there was an accident on the way to school. A cyclist got knocked off his bike. Fortunately he's fine as he was wearing his helmet, so that's a lesson to you all . . .'

As the morning drags by, Jen sits at her corner desk, trying to focus on reading time rather than the clock. She feels guilty and furtive, which is silly when she's doing nothing wrong. She has a long-time lover and a daughter who might be his, but today she's only going to the doctor's to find out why her middle child is so thin. She's being accompanied by an attractive man who isn't her husband, that's true, a man she loves very much, but only in the platonic sense. If she wasn't so stressed, she'd laugh. 'It's like a bad Richard Curtis film!' she'd say to Ian, and he would chuckle and say, 'Then why do you watch them so often?'

Feeling ridiculously like one of the schoolkids, she walks self-consciously to the front of the classroom, whispers to the teacher that she's desperate for a pee and could she leave early for lunch. Then she trots to the road at the side of the church, hoping Dan will be waiting so she can dive into his car without anyone seeing. He's a good-looking bloke, with those beautiful eyes, and of course his contagious smile, but even as a girl she never fancied him. Too dark-haired Irish-looking, too like her older brothers. And her rotten bloody dad. Still, it'll be an excuse if anyone comments. 'Oh, he's one of my brothers,' she'll say. No one will know that her real brothers have lost hair at the same rate as they've put on weight. Not that there's anything wrong with a balding head, so long as it's the right shape.

There's a moment's panic when she stops; she can't see Dan. Then his car pulls out of a space in the car park.

'I was a few minutes early,' he says. 'Tell me where I'm going.'

Unsure if her heavy breathing is from the dash or from nerves, she doesn't speak for a moment as she steadies it.

Dan puts a hand on her shoulder. 'OK?' he asks.

She glances at him, thinking how tired he looks. Then remembers he's the father of a new baby boy. 'Oh, Dan. Sorry, I'm miles away! How's baby Teddy? And Geri?'

As he suppresses a yawn, Dan tells her about the palaver after she left the hospital on Sunday night. How a midwife finally examined Geri and discovered the baby was breached. She had a caesarian section under general anesthetic not long after; it was all pretty scary, but everything's good.

'All's well that ends well, mother and baby are fine.' He gives a sapped smile. 'I have a son, Jen. Eight and a half pounds of son. Who would've thought?' He seems to drift for a moment before focusing again. 'They'll stay in hospital for a few days. I'm under instructions to buy all the delicacies Geri has deprived herself of for the last nine months, starting with every type of blue cheese I can lay my hands on, as well as—'

'Cigarettes and port?'

The quip emerges as a croak and Dan reaches for her hand. 'Everything will be fine, Jen. I'm sure of it.'

The journey takes only minutes. 'Ready?' Dan asks, once they're parked.

The surgery door opens with a swish and warm air. Jen tells the receptionist she's there, then they sit huddled in the waiting room looking at snaps of Teddy on Dan's mobile.

'I bet we look like lovers, which is pretty ironic,' Jen whispers.

They fall silent for a time.

'Do you know for sure?' Dan asks eventually.

She thinks about the Bluebell Woods. She'd only just recovered physically from Maria's birth, but found herself lying on a grass velvet carpet under a canopy of budding trees, surrounded by bluebells and having unprotected sex with Will. 'No,' she replies. 'Not for sure.'

Dipping into her handbag, she pulls out her battered mobile and brings up a recent snap of her wavy-haired middle daughter. She hands it to Dan and watches his face. 'She's twelve now, around the same age we first met at St Mark's.'

Dan doesn't comment. 'Does Will know?' he asks.

Jen shakes her head, the urgent need to cry stifled by the loud announcement of her name.

239

'Do you want me to come with you?'

She tries for a smile. 'Now that would be weird.'

It's the same doctor as before. There's a ladder in her tights and her hair has escaped from its bun. 'What can I do for you today?' she asks, her face weary.

It's hard not to scream with frustration. But how would the young woman know this moment has haunted her every waking moment for many days? She's not telepathic. One patient leaves, another comes in.

Jen takes a deep breath. 'My daughter had a blood test last week. Holly Kenning? The results are available today.'

The doctor asks for Holly's date of birth, then stares at her screen for some time. Jen watches her eyes move as she reads through the notes. She finally turns her head. Deep shadows beneath her eyes emphasise their paleness. 'Graves' disease,' she says. 'Also known as—'

The blow is expected, but still it's a shock. It's a punishment, of course. God's judgment for what she's done. Jen knows she's crying, but there's nothing she can do; she needs to fetch Dan so he can ask the questions she's unable to voice. She scrapes back the chair, but the doctor is dipping her head and passing a tissue.

Her face is a little perplexed. 'Of course you're concerned,' she's saying. 'But hyperthyroidism is not uncommon. There's really no need to worry, Mrs Kenning. It can be treated quite easily with the right medicines. You probably know it better as an overactive thyroid gland.'

CHAPTER FORTY-TWO

Nick

'Morning people! Lovely day!'

Nick turns to the resonant sound of Will's voice. He's wearing a mac which looks at least two sizes too small. 'Talk of the bloody devil,' Nick says. He nods to the raincoat and laughs. 'Have you put on three stone or are you wearing Penny's clothes again, Will?'

Penny appears from behind Will's umbrella. 'I know, Nick. I told him it was too small.'

Will looks down at the coat and shrugs. 'To be honest, I don't think it's mine.'

'Whose is it, then?' Penny asks, surprisingly sharply.

'No idea, must have nicked it or done a cheeky swap.' He opens the coat to look at the label and grins. 'Expensive make and thank God I did. This bloody weather.' He turns to Penny and pecks her lips. 'Right, wife delivered. Now for the train tickets. See you in five.'

'Make sure we're in the right place and that the train hasn't been cancelled,' Penny calls as he disappears again with the umbrella. She gazes at his back, a strange expression on her face, before turning with a small jerk to Lisa.

Nick watches the rain as the women chat. It's pelting down in silver stripes, even worse than their wedding day. He did the gentlemanly thing by covering his wife with the umbrella all the way from the bus stop to the railway station, but his left trouser leg is soaking. 'Worse than bloody Aberystwyth,' he says, voicing his thoughts and realising too late from Lisa's meaningful frown that it's a tactless thing to say in front of Penny.

Sighing, he turns away. He can't do or say anything right these days. To Lisa, to his parents. And Patrick, poor Patrick. Lisa tried to have one of her brainstorming sessions to analyse what Patrick had meant by his fishing comment, but hot with shame, he had to stop her. He'd tricked his big brother into talking about something which upset him. No, not upset; distress, deep distress. A grown man rocking like a child. It just wasn't normal.

Nick shakes the mental image away. It's still shocking and horrible. Thank God Jen isn't here today; she'd be bound to ask questions. He doesn't want to think about it anymore.

Will's voice brings him back. He's shaking his umbrella and nodding to the suited men on the other side of the tracks. 'Poor sods. They're on the wrong side. The train's due any minute; they're going to miss it.'

Nick watches several brightly dressed women join the race-goers on the opposite platform. They're wearing ridiculously high heels and those stupid feathery things on their heads he can never remember the name of. He glances at Lisa, glad she isn't wearing one. She tried on three or four dresses last night that would've been more suited to a nightclub than a day at the races. He knew better than to say so, but thank God she didn't choose one.

She appears at his shoulder. 'There's a train coming the other way. Are you sure we're on the right side?' she says in her nurse's clear voice.

242

Will glances at the tickets in his hand. 'Yup. Chester is south from here.'

Lisa nods to the train pulling up on the opposite track. 'But that's the Liverpool train. Isn't Chester near Liverpool?' she asks.

Will looks again at the tickets, then at his watch. 'Oh fuck! How did I get that wrong?'

Penny shakes her head, frowning. 'I asked you to check, Will. Didn't you check?' she asks, her voice unusually high-pitched.

Silently they watch the train depart. Nick raises his eyebrows and meets Lisa's eye, then opens an app on his mobile. 'No need to panic. We can catch the next train to Crewe and change there. Only twenty minutes difference.'

Unusually flushed, Will shakes his head. 'Sorry, guys. My fault. Must be losing my marbles.'

Patting him on the back, Nick laughs. 'Just bloody glad it wasn't me!'

Penny and Lisa step back to their seats and continue to chat. 'Sorry,' he hears Penny say. 'You know Will's usually on the ball, but he's been really distracted recently. He works too hard and sometimes even I can't track him down. Then when I—'

'Distracted flipping husband, tell me about it!' Lisa interrupts. 'Oh brilliant, here's the train.'

Noticing his trousers have finally dried, Nick sips the champagne. It has taken a few glasses to do its thing, but the tension in his shoulders has gone, he feels pretty damn chilled and relaxed. He's put a twenty-pound note on every race so far, and though he hasn't won, he's backed each way and his horses have been placed, so not a complete disaster.

Penny and Lisa have stayed chatting at their table mostly, but he's moved around between the bar, the stalls and the paddocks with Will and a couple of other guys, commenting on the women, the jockeys and the horses.

They now move to the damp grass, watching the sleek animals be led around a paddock. The ground is a little squelchy from the rain, but the breeze has replaced grey clouds with white, and the sun's peeping through.

'Here come the jockeys,' one of the lads says. 'I know they look small on the horses, but they're actually bloody tiny!'

Nick looks at Will, waits for the inevitable quip, which comes almost immediately. 'A job for you here if IT falls through, Nicky boy,' he says with a grin.

Shaking his head, he turns to the clusters of noisy women in the tent and watches for several moments. Mutton dressed as lamb or too tarty, he thinks. Lisa looks gorgeous today. He's done bloody well.

'Botox R Us or what?' he says when Will moves to look too. 'And what's with the eyes?'

'False eyelashes, according to Penny,' Will replies, sipping his champagne and looking at the women disinterestedly. Then he does another take, staring for a moment.

Nick follows his gaze. 'Someone you know?'

Will shakes his head. 'More losing the bloody plot.' He nods to an attractive dark-haired woman. 'Thought she was Jen for a minute.'

'Really?' Nick replies, not seeing the similarity. He comes back to Will's frown. 'Have you seen her recently? She seemed a bit quiet at Dan's. And have you noticed she's lost weight?' He grins. 'Still has the big . . .'

He does Will's usual 'big boobs' motion with his hands, but Will has turned back to the horses.

'OK, a hundred on number seven,' he's saying.

'Bloody hell, a hundred quid?'

'A chestnut beauty. I have a feeling about this one,' he replies. 'I'll put on a bet, then buy another bottle. Raise a glass to Dan.'

'God, yeah. Dan Maloney, a father! Bloody hell, a tiny newborn, that's scary.'

'Yup. Rather him than me. See you back at the table.'

Nick makes his way through the tunnel, dodging a boisterous group of men on a stag party. He climbs the steps by the stalls, turning to the sound of a siren below. A woman has been placed on a stretcher and a man is by her side with an anguished face, yet people are still milling by, drinking, laughing and chatting, oblivious to his distress. It reminds him of Patrick, his constant brother Patrick. What did he do? Why was it his fault? But there's the stab again, of disloyalty and guilt.

Climbing towards the members' lounge, he still feels the shame, but it's punctured by the sight of his wife in her emerald green dress. She's standing next to Penny on the balcony, smiling her stunning smile. It lifts his heart to the heavens.

'I've had a good look around,' he says when he reaches her.

'And?' she asks.

'You're the most attractive woman here.'

Lisa gives him a peck. 'Think you might be just a little biased. And pissed,' she says. 'But thank you, I'll take it.' Lifting her glass, she grins. 'Any more where this came from?' She nods to Penny, her eyes wide with meaning. 'We needed some fresh air, but we're going back inside.'

When Nick returns to the table, Penny and Lisa are talking, so he takes out his mobile, sending a text to a mate at work to berate him for not picking a winner, but asking for another tip nonetheless. Then he tunes into Lisa's conversation.

'You're flipping amazing, Penny. Will adores you. It'll just be work worries. There's no way he'd leave you . . .' she's saying.

Turning to Penny, he sits back in surprise. Her face is blotchy, her eyes glassy with tears. She's holding a bunched tissue and Lisa is rubbing her back.

'Everything OK?' he asks.

Pushing Penny's glass of champagne away, Lisa nods at him. 'A soft drink or a coffee would be good,' she says.

Nick stands at the bar, briefly turning back as he waits. Bloody hell, that was strange. He's never seen Penny cry before, not even when she was led silently through his wedding reception by Will. Even then she looked composed, her face like white chiselled marble. It was the blip of his wedding, astonishing when you think about it. Yet so easily superseded. His *obsession*. Oh God, poor Patrick.

A hand on his shoulder brings him back from his thoughts. It's Will, his eyes shadowy and tired. He squints at his mobile screen, then places it face down on the bar. 'I lost her, Nick,' he says. 'My own bloody fault.'

Nick turns to the table, confused. Penny's still there, Lisa pouring a glass of water. 'Lost her? How?'

Will shakes his head, looks unsteady on his feet. 'My chestnut-haired beauty.' Then after a moment, 'The horse. I mean the horse.' He straightens his shoulders and lifts his head. 'Still, what's a hundred quid? It's only fucking money. Can't buy me love . . .' Shifting his focus to the coffee, he frowns. 'What the fuck, Nick? Bloody coffee? We're here to get pissed, raise a glass to Dan's baby.'

'It's not for me,' Nick replies, not wanting to say anything out of turn, but mildly anxious about Will's strange belligerence and how he might take Penny's state. But when they reach the table, her tears have been replaced by a forced bright smile.

'Hello, Will,' she says. 'Any luck on the horses?'

Will returns her smile and kisses her forehead. 'Pretty good so far,' he replies.

Buffeted by a sea of inebriated punters, Nick catches the others up outside the racecourse. Breathing in a pleasant communal feeling, he takes Lisa's hand and listens to her chat as they make their way on the cobbles. Up the hill, past two-tiered medieval buildings and high-street shops, under the West Gate bridge and clock, dodging shoppers and cars. He squeezes his wife's fingers, still feeling good. Pissed, but not too much. No mixing, that's the thing.

The crowd finally starts to thin. Will looks at his watch, then strides ahead, Penny holding his arm. 'Twenty minutes to get there,' he calls. 'If we get the wrong train, you have permission to shoot me.'

Nick leans towards Lisa. 'What was that all about earlier with Penny? Tears one minute, then smiles the next.' He grins, the quip popping out before he can stop it. 'It was a relief when you got her off that balcony, I can tell you . . .'

'Not funny, Nick,' Lisa replies, using her reprimand voice. 'Not funny at all. You shouldn't ridicule mental health problems. It can happen to anyone.' She turns and looks at him pointedly. 'Patrick, for example.'

Although stung and surprised by her harsh comment, he goes back to the point. 'You have to admit it was weird. The way she was hiding it from Will. Why was she crying?'

'She's worried about him. Thinks he's distracted and distant. It didn't help him having to rush to the hospital to sort Seb—'

'Sort Seb how?'

'I don't know. She was a bit coy about that, so I didn't want to push it. He's back home now apparently. She's more

247

concerned about Will. Says he's super busy at work, but she's worried there's more.'

'Like what?'

Lisa pulls his hand to make him walk slower. 'I'm not supposed to say, but we're in the same boat, so I'll tell you, but you're not to say anything, Nick. You know what you're like.'

'What's that supposed to mean?'

'You blurting things out. Think first, remember.'

Nick sighs and walks on. Patrick and blurting today. What will it be next? 'So, what's the secret?'

'They've been trying to conceive for ages and Dan's baby has brought it all back. She says Will wants to be a dad and she's afraid he'll leave her if she doesn't get pregnant.'

'Really?' he asks, surprised. 'Will's never said anything to me about wanting kids.'

'Well, I don't suppose he would if nothing's happening. But even I've heard him saying stuff about carrying on the Taylor line, giving his mum a grandchild, not seeing Seb as father material, things like that. And Penny desperately wants one. Reading between the lines, my guess is she thinks it'll gloss over the blip. Course, I didn't want to say anything, but mental illness is like any other ailment, it takes time to recover.'

Digesting the information, Nick strolls on in silence, then a thought strikes. 'Why are we in the same boat?'

'Trying for a baby, of course.'

Still holding her hand, he stops. 'Yeah, but not yet. We've only just got married—'

Lisa turns. 'It's what we agreed, Nick, cracking on for a baby before we get older. I wouldn't have gone for a flipping wet January wedding if we'd planned to hang around—'

The words are out before he can stop them. 'Other things are going on, Lisa. My parents and Patrick and . . .'

But she pulls away and stomps ahead before he can mention money, the house, her shifts and a whole host of other reasons not to rush into something so huge.

'Typical selfish Nick,' he hears on the breeze. 'Still just a bloody big baby.'

CHAPTER FORTY-THREE

Penny

Wanting to get straight to the point, Penny takes a deep breath. 'Thanks for seeing me twice this week.'

'No problem. It was good to meet Will on Tuesday and talk through coping strategies for you both. How are things today?' Debbie smiles and cocks her head. 'You look as though you have something on your mind?'

Penny feels herself flushing. It wasn't something she could raise in front of Will. 'Just a question, really. Of course I know the answer, but wondered what you thought.'

'Go on.'

'I'm feeling fine, really fine. Back at work part-time, keeping busy and getting out and about.' Debbie gazes, saying nothing. 'Sounds silly, but I'm putting on weight and you wouldn't believe the . . . Well, I'm not as regular as I was, if you know what I mean. And I get sleepy. So I was thinking about easing off the medication. Still carrying on with the CBT of course, but . . .'

She has to say it, she just has to say it. The absence from Will is unbearable. If they start intimacy again, it'll put their relationship back on track. And she doesn't want to fall behind. Jen has three kids and Lisa confided she and Nick are hoping to start a family this year. Even Dan has a kid. 'I want to start trying for a family again. The research is divided, but I wouldn't want to take anything that might harm a pregnancy. What do you think?'

Debbie sits forward. 'You'd need to discuss the medication with your doctor, but my guess is he'll say it's still very early days to come off it.' She spreads her hands. 'You know as much as anyone that the antipsychotic drugs are there to help, to stabilise your moods, reduce the anxiety. A comfort blanket, if you like.'

Like the bloody nursery rhymes, Penny thinks. They're still there, but that's fine; they're only tunes, not a voice.

'I know that, of course,' she replies. She takes another breath. 'But I wonder if they're really necessary. I've never been a danger to myself or anyone else. I had a temporary leave from reality, I admit, but even the psychiatrist thought it was most likely an isolated episode brought on by stress.'

Debbie looks at her intently. 'And the stress? Has it gone?'

Penny thinks of her concerns about Will. Amazingly it helped to cry on Lisa's shoulder at the races. Thank God Will didn't notice, but Lisa was right. His strange behaviour was just stress about work. He talked to her last night about his job, a new opportunity and the things he has to think through before applying. So nice to chat and be close again, to get him onside about the future, even though she had to really stretch the white lies about her mum. She gave it a name, a syndrome in fact, so that made him sit up and listen. She knows he's nearly there, she's almost convinced him. If they could start again for a baby, life would be perfect.

CHAPTER FORTY-FOUR

Dan

I'm a father; I have a family, Dan thinks.

The piquant sweet smell of cooking from next door's kitchen window brings him back to his waking garden. He's strolling around it, holding his son in his arms and chatting quietly. He's shown Teddy the daffodils and the crocuses, the holly and the little robin who has stayed since Christmas Day. Geri is still asleep after feeding him twice in the night. He wishes she'd give Teddy formula milk so he could help rather than just watching, but he knows not to ask. She's pleased to be feeding him herself; the first twenty-four hours were a very tearful struggle before Teddy latched on. 'A little breast baby,' he joked, trying to bring a smile to her face. 'Now he's got it sussed, he doesn't want to let go.'

It's the final day of his two-week paternity leave. Maya has given him daily telephone updates, mostly funny stories about Salim and his pitiful attempts to keep the conveyancing clients happy. But at least she's kept an eye on his files, smoothing things over, buying him time. He would like to stay away from the office and Wilmslow forever, but the need to earn money is more paramount than ever; he has a family to support.

Looking at his fingers, he notices the blue emulsion embedded in his nails. His heart quickening, he stares for several moments, seeing his dad's hands. Jed painted his bedroom blue, a special treat when he was ten. A good man, a good father, his only weakness: love.

He looks up to the open nursery window. He's been doing the same for when Teddy moves in. He and Geri had painted it a pale apple green, a unisex colour, but Jed made his disapproval known once Teddy was born. 'Come on, give the lad blue. Blue for a true Blue!' He looked at Geri and grinned. 'You've got a beautiful boy. Milk it for all its worth. Then next time, when it's a girl, no one will give you a hard time when everything's pink.'

'Gender stereotyping, Dad?' Dan laughed. The word *parochial* slipped into his head then and it's still hidden somewhere in his mind even now. He's tried hard not to think about Seb. His feelings are confused when he does. From speaking to Will he knows Seb is fine, that he was discharged from hospital the day of Teddy's birth. But that, he tells himself firmly, is the end of the matter. Trust is everything and Seb can't be trusted, not even as a friend.

Looking up to the sky, he squints at a neat line of birds on a telegraph wire. Every few moments one appears to bicker with another, flies off for a few moments before slotting back. It isn't just that Seb was high on something that afternoon, it's that he managed to harm himself after Dan left, something he shouldn't have taken, more drugs, an overdose even. It feels like punishment for him leaving, blackmail almost. Dan can't take on that responsibly any more. He has a son to care for now. And besides, there's been no contact from Seb at all, no congratulations, not even a sorry.

Teddy's eyes droop and his thoughts drift to Jen. After

sending a round-robin text to tell everyone the news about Teddy, he'd spent a few moments with his brand new baby in his arms. He'd examined his glowing skin, his button nose, his tiny ears and dark eyes, his ten fingers and ten toes, his miraculously perfect child, wondering how he would feel if he discovered Teddy wasn't his. Grief and outrage, he'd supposed. But it was difficult to be objective. Together with Nick, Will and Jen were his closest friends; he loved them all very much. And anyway, who was he to judge anyone? He'd unforgivably betrayed Geri. He'd let his heart rule his head. Or was it his genitals? He'd felt so emotionally drained from lurching from one scare with Seb and his overdose, to another with Geri and the need for an emergency section, that he'd never expected, or wanted, to feel sexual desire ever again.

He and Jen sat huddled in the doctor's waiting room like lovers, which was pretty ironic, as she said.

'Do you know for sure?' he asked as they waited.

'No,' she replied. 'Not for sure.' She brought up a recent photograph of Holly on her phone and watched his face. He knows her kids pretty well, but the mugshot brought Holly's features into sharp focus: a curly-haired child, boyish in looks, the spit of William Taylor when they first met at St Mark's.

'Does Will know?' he asked, but Jen shook her head as her name was called out. He'd never seen her face so pale and so taut, gaunt almost, as she walked stiffly towards the doctor's room. Then when she came out, she fell into his arms and sobbed. Tears of relief, thank God.

Now the blood results are through, he wonders if Jen wishes she hadn't confided in him. Watching her and Will talk, noticing small intimate touches or eye contact, he'd suspected their affair over the years, but in all the time he's known little Holly, he'd never spotted the resemblance. Now that he knows, it is obvious and in plain sight. He's sure he'll never breach her trust, but secrets have a way of coming out. Not always verbally, but in some other way. He was on the point of disclosing his own that night, and part of him wants to do it even now. Letting it all out, stopping the whir of his thoughts. Like the confessional, which feels pretty ironic. *Forgive me, Father, for I have sinned.* Returning to God, like the prodigal son.

But what would he say? That he stumbled into something with Seb he doesn't understand? That he had intimate contact with another man; not what Seb had suggested on the eve of Teddy's birth, but still intimacy that went beyond a game or boyish sexual larks. Pleasurable and intense; an attachment that felt like love. And if he's honest, the thing Seb suggested, well, he can't deny that he's thought about it.

Teddy stirs in his arms, his tiny face filling with colour. Dan smiles as he heads back indoors. Who would've thought it? He's become a dab hand with nappies and wet wipes, though changing Teddy's clothes is more problematic with the small press studs. Even worse, the tiny pearl buttons on the cardigans knitted by Geri's grandma. One in every colour of the rainbow. Or so it seems.

He lays his son on the changing mat, letting him kick his bare legs in the air for a few minutes. It's hard to equate this real baby with Geri's pregnancy bump and yet as he looks at him now, it's as though he's known him forever.

Father and son, an unbreakable love.

Picking up the outfit Geri has left hanging for today, he grimaces. It's a miniature sailor suit and he isn't convinced about it. He knows Will and Nick will be sure to take the piss. The A Team are finally visiting this afternoon to wet Teddy's head. He didn't understand what Jen meant about visitors, but she was absolutely right, the last thing he and Geri needed immediately

'You can tell he's single with bags of space in his home,' Jen says wryly. 'But it is really cute, I have to say. Anna will be jealous. She still reads the Paddington books.'

Stepping towards Dan, Seb Taylor holds out his right hand. His hair has grown a little longer, his face is clean-shaved, the tattoos all gone. 'Congratulations, Dan,' he says with a polite smile. 'Hope you don't mind me turning up. Jen gave me a bell and said there'd be food.' He holds out a rectangular parcel held together with string. 'Here's something from Mum. She's been working on it for weeks. And she sends you her love.'

Dan takes his warm hand, thinks about the razor and Seb's broken face. 'Course not. Good to see you. That's really kind of Yvette.' He nods to Geri who's holding an enormous soft toy. 'And thanks for the teddy bear. At least I think so!'

As the minutes fall by, Dan walks from person to person and chats, aware of Seb's presence like ice on hot skin, talking to Lisa and Penny, laughing with Nick and Will, cradling his son.

'Should we be eating by now, Dan?' Jen asks at some point. 'I've taken off the cling film and foil. Everything's ready . . .'

Will tops up the adults' champagne glasses and they stand back in the burgundy room to allow Jen's daughters to help themselves to food first, then they tuck in to meat and cheese, to sausages and savoury pastries from blue paper plates.

'This is fun. It feels like a baptism celebration,' he hears Lisa say.

'Do you know, I'd really like that,' Geri replies.

'Yes, do it! I flipping love a party. Though can you? With not being married?'

'I don't know,' Geri says. 'A blessing, maybe? Some churches aren't all that strict. Do you know, I'm going to look into it.'

'Nappy change needed!' someone calls. 'Where's the Daddy?'

Dan carries Teddy upstairs to the nursery, the smell of fresh paint reminding him of a shameful memory he tries hard to forget. He feels sluggish and tired from too much champagne and too little sleep. Surprised and unsettled at Geri's suggestion of a baptism too. She's never said anything to him.

'Need any help?'

'No, everything's in hand, thanks,' he replies without turning from his task.

'It wasn't what you thought, Dan. Come and see me at the apartment and I'll explain.'

'Look, it's fine. Everything's fine. It's all forgotten.' He looks up and meets Seb's intense stare briefly before looking away. 'He's lovely, isn't he? My son? But he takes up all our time, so—'

'At work, then. In your lunch hour.'

'I'm only back in tomorrow after two weeks off. Salim is hopeless. I'll be mad busy catching up.'

'OK, fair enough.'

Dan changes Teddy from the sailor outfit to a stripy blue sleepsuit knowing Seb is still there. He hears him clear his throat.

'Fair enough,' he repeats. 'But if you change your mind, anytime, it would be great to see you.'

The door finally clicks to and Dan breathes, letting out a gulp of air he didn't know he was holding.

CHAPTER FORTY-FIVE

Nick

Nick is eating his lunch early, just because he can. It's a bowl of spicy prawn and feta salad, bought from the sandwich shop below his office. The double-glazed window blocks out the sound of busy traffic below, but bright sunshine creeps through the slatted blinds, highlighting a few grey streaks in his hair.

His mobile trills from the desk drawer. He considers for a moment not answering, then pulls it out with a sigh and looks at the screen. To his surprise the call isn't from Lisa.

'Hello love, it's Mum. We're at the hospital. It's Dad's hip. He fell and, well, I'll let you know the details when I see you, but Dad needs you to go to the house—'

He pulls away from his game of laptop Sudoku and frowns. 'What? You're at the hospital. How did you get there?'

'I was going to drive, but Dad was in a lot of pain, so I called an ambulance—'

'Why didn't you call me?' He almost says, 'or Patrick', but his mental image of Patrick's distress the other week puts paid to that.

'Well, I knew you'd be at work, love. I didn't want to worry you . . .'

Nick closes his eyes, quelling the urgent need to shout. He's bloody thirty-four, not thirteen. He's a grown man, perfectly capable of dealing with fucking worry.

'So why are you calling me now?' he asks, visualising his mother's undoubted panic as she searched for the keys to the front door, then the embarrassment of having to try each key to see which one fitted in the lock as the ambulance people waited through the obscured glass.

'Dad says we need the paperwork for his private health policy. I don't really understand it, but he needs to see if he's covered for his hip. Something about pre-existing conditions, he said.'

'OK,' Nick says as he reaches for his jacket. 'I'm on my way. Now start from the beginning as I walk. When exactly did Dad fall?'

As he waits for the lift, his mum explains that his dad didn't fall as such, but when he got out of bed this morning he collapsed on the carpet, screaming out in pain. She thought it was the usual, Harry griping over nothing, so she said that he'd have to wait until she was dressed and she'd take him to the doctor's in the car. Naturally she didn't want to make a fuss by calling an ambulance. But when she got back from her shower Harry's face was white with the pain; he'd tried to move and said something had popped. Of course she phoned 999 then. An ambulance car came within minutes with a lovely paramedic who said it was Harry's hip and that the proper ambulance would be just a few more minutes. He was put on a stretcher later, Nick should've heard the cursing! Still, he's settled now. They've given him pain relief and he's back to telling her that he knew all along something was wrong, so he's perfectly well in his head.

Nick cuts the monologue short, feeling the rage hot in his chest as he flags down a black cab outside the office building. He's still having nightmares, waking from them in the early hours with a thrust of relief, but unable to sleep again. The dreams are always violent and he lies there feeling guilty for the retribution he extracts. Against his mother, and now Patrick. He doesn't need a psychologist to tell him he's angry. He's perfectly aware of that.

He and Lisa argued on Sunday night. Not just the usual sniping or pointed comments, but full-blown shouting. They'd come back from wetting the baby's head at Dan's house and admittedly he was moody. He'd watched her drink the champagne steadily all through the afternoon and into the early evening, but of course couldn't say anything in front of the other guests.

'Why are you so grumpy?' she asked when they got home, but in a playful way. 'I know what I can do to cheer you up.'

Perhaps at another time he would have welcomed her inebriated advances, but at the party Jen had asked how things had gone with Patrick, whether he'd found out anything more about Patrick's twin and how was he feeling about it. He'd managed to shelve the whole question of Susan after the awful embarrassment of the road trip, but Jen's questions, and the loving way she'd asked them, brought it all back.

So he stopped Lisa at the zip of his flies and pulled away. 'I was thinking about Patrick and what he meant—' he managed before Lisa verbally lashed out. It was obvious to everyone except Nick and his stupid bloody parents that Patrick was 'on the spectrum', she yelled. 'What spectrum?' Nick asked, genuinely bewildered. 'The autistic spectrum,' she replied, rolling her eyes. She went on to say in a patronising voice that everyone knew about autism these days. Asperger's Syndrome? Didn't he read any books or the newspapers? There was a novel and even a flipping play about it. If he didn't have his face stuck to a computer all day, or occasionally just listened, he'd know more about the world.

Lisa stomped to the kitchen and snapped open a bottle of white wine then. Nick asked why she was drinking like a bloody fish when she wanted to get pregnant. Fat chance, she replied, with Nick's current libido, and anyway, why would she want a Quinn child, they were all crackers. She was sick of his weird family, sick of his obsession with the whole sister thing and sick of him.

He'd never felt so enraged. 'Well thanks very much for your support, Lisa,' he said sarcastically through gritted teeth. 'A good job I have Jen Kenning to talk to.' That's when Lisa threw the wine glass.

'Twelve pounds forty, please.'

The taxi driver's voice brings him back to his parents' house. It looks like a scalene triangle; he's never noticed that before. He takes out his wallet, then looks up. The driver is squinting at him through the car mirror. 'Are you all right, mate? You've some blood . . .' He demonstrates on his chin and Nick feels his own. The small cut from the wine glass bled like buggery on Sunday, but had scabbed since then. He must've been picking at it absently.

He unlatches the side gate and strides across the grey flags to the back door. Lifting up the outdoor mat, he scoops up the key, as ever wondering about the way his parents' minds work; two locks and a chain on the front door, a free-for-all at the rear.

His throat clogged with heat from the burning radiators and the taste of prawns, he bolts up the stairs two by two, hoping his father isn't in too much pain. His artificial hip had snapped out of its socket, his mum had said, 'no wonder it hurt'. He'd been given morphine, so was 'happy as Larry' for now while the staff worked out if he was covered for private treatment. But still, Nick wants to hurry; the memory of each time he chivvied or ignored his father's complaints about 'this damned hip' feels like a small dig in his gut.

Searching for a few moments in the bedroom, he finds the bureau key in his dad's coin pot, darts back down the stairs, settles himself on the leather chair in the study, then inserts the tiny piece of metal to lower the desk lid.

The small drawers of the wooden bureau seem to be organised. Top left, insurance. Bingo first time! He spends a few minutes going through the documents. The insurance is current, but he can't discern from the schedule whether it'll cover his dad's hip. Still, it's Harry who's the expert; he'll order a taxi to the hospital.

Looking down at the green leather chair, he holds onto its padded arms and spins on its wheels for a few moments. When his mum and dad were out, Patrick used to indulge him playing Daleks, pushing him around the carpeted loop between the hall and the lounge. He smiles at the fond memory, remembering the squeal of pleasure he always made during the final fast scoot across the kitchen lino.

Shaking the recollection away, he checks the time, lifts the desk to close the bureau, then pauses. The thought of a death certificate pops into his head, Susan's death certificate. Everything is so organised, it's sure to be there.

He finds the certificates in the large bottom drawer, neatly folded in an old cigar box. The smell of tobacco hits his nose as he opens it. Harry gave them up years ago, before he was born, but the aroma reminds him of Uncle Derek, who still smokes them occasionally when 'Iris isn't looking'.

His hands tremble as he picks through the parchments.

There's his mum and dad's wedding certificate and a bundle marked 'births', but no death certificate. He feels a jolt of disappointment, goes to put the bundle back, then glances at his watch again. Of course he knows when Susan was born, same date as Patrick, but it would still be interesting to see her name written down. Perhaps it would show who was born first.

He unfolds the documents one by one. They start with his paternal grandma and go down in order through his parents to Patrick and Susan, their certificates folded together. There's a wave of sadness as he unfolds the thick paper and reads. Susan Quinn, Patrick's twin, born eight minutes before Patrick, a long fifteen years before him.

The thought of Patrick's school photograph hits him; the way he leant to one side. He hadn't really focused on the twin aspect before, the special bond from the womb and forever after. How desperate must Patrick have been to lose her. He'd felt responsible somehow, that was clear from his spluttered words in the pub.

Feeling ashamed, Nick shakes his head. Bad, very bad; it was wrong to have hoodwinked his brother, to make him talk about something he clearly found distressing. He'd make an effort to see him this weekend, go on a genuine road trip and make amends.

Still thinking about Patrick's protective love over the years, he idly unfolds the last certificate. His of course, Nicholas Quinn. He stares for a moment, confused. The section for the name and surname of the father is blank. But realisation dawns an instant before his eyes reach the name and surname of the mother. Of course. God, of course.

Susan Quinn.

CHAPTER FORTY-SIX

Jen

'You haven't been having illicit sex again have you?'

Jen looks up sharply from her coffee in the staffroom, but it's only her pal Clare.

Clare's eyebrows are raised. 'You look more cheery than you did last week. You have colour back in your cheeks. I only saw you from a distance, so didn't get the chance to ask if you were all right. But looking at you now, you are all right. In fact, better than all right!' She laughs. 'Sex, yup, it has to be sex.'

Clare is only joking, but it doesn't stop the piercing jab in Jen's ribs. On the Sunday before Holly's test results, she made a pact with God in church. If Holly was fine she would never sleep with Will Taylor again. Ever. And Holly is fine; she may be on one, or possibly two medicines to balance her thyroxine production for life, but she is OK. In fact she's massively picked up already; not as listless as she was, nor complaining about aching legs, she simply looks healthier. She's also wearing her *illness* like a badge of honour at school, suddenly popular with the crowd she'd previously labelled *the chav and slag* group. Maria has been eye-rolling constantly since, but in fairness, she has a point. Jen isn't sure which will be for the best: Holly's continued popularity with the chavs and slags but possibly becoming one, or being dumped mercilessly by them and still being her unique little self. Either way it will be one of life's tough lessons, she supposes.

She puts a finger on her chin. 'Sex? Now remind me.' Then, smiling at Clare. 'Remember Anna is eight.'

'I could give you a personal briefing. You know I'm always on offer, dear Jen.'

'Tempting, but you don't have a willy.'

'True, but there are very effective ways and means. Besides, who needs a willy? Isn't that what little boys have before they grow into *pricks*? Like our dearest head teacher?'

Jen laughs at Clare's pun. She's one of the blonde, slim and pretty candidates appointed by their lack-of-personal-space head. Jen adores her for making her sexuality loudly known whenever he's in earshot.

The word 'willy' reminds her of Teddy's party. It was such a lovely day. Dan and Geri were so content with their stunning little boy. After a quiet start, Penny seemed happy too; she was back at work and was thrilled that two scientific articles she'd written were to be published in a medical journal.

'Bloody hell, Pen, you make the most of your time, don't you? You were meant to be resting!'

'I know. Manic crazy woman. To be honest it's a curse,' she replied, but she said it easily and with a smile. So measured and calm, it was hard to believe she'd been the woman at the window.

Nick seemed tense. She asked how his chat with Patrick had gone and how he was feeling about it all, but his reply was interrupted when Lisa stepped over. Then later Seb arrived. His hair reminded her of how he'd had it in the days Yvette got up

270

at the crack of dawn to drive him to swimming training before school. He looked a little sheepish, probably because he'd bought a ridiculously huge teddy bear from some posh toy shop in London.

The girls had stared at her with dagger eyes. 'You'd never let us have anything so big, so plush or expensive in our bedrooms,' their eyes said.

'We have a small house and I'm only a poor lowly teaching assistant!' hers replied.

Lisa was animated and chatty with everyone as usual, but Nick's gaze followed her around the room. It looked as though he was monitoring how much she was drinking. She hopes Lisa doesn't have a booze problem, but then again who doesn't, to some degree? No one likes a drink as much as she does and there have been one or two times she's wondered about her mum, when she's phoned her late at night and Nola's voice has been undeniably slurred and teary.

'Are you OK?' she asks her mum when this happens.

'Just jumbled up inside,' her mum replies. 'I'll be back to myself by tomorrow.'

'OK, sweet dreams,' Jen always says, knowing she should take her concern further, but ending the call nonetheless. She's never properly broached her mum's loneliness or her heartbreak. She feels guilty at times, but even now, even after all these years, her father's betrayal still feels too personal.

Then of course there was Will at Dan's house. It was lovely to see him smiling and joking, mucking around with the girls as usual. Though she knew the frostiness had been of her making, the phone call on the eve of Teddy's birth had broken the ice. They hugged tightly at the door when he and Penny arrived, and as she milled around the party, feeling that life was again on an even keel, she tried to picture herself at a celebration to wet the head of his and Penny's baby. 'I can do it,' she said positively to herself. 'I can be happy for them both.' But when they were saying their goodbyes and Will gave her another hug, he whispered in her ear, 'I need to talk to you about something important. I'll text.'

Will's *something important* will be revealed when he visits this afternoon. Jen's guess is that Penny is pregnant, and although she's trying very hard to be happy for them both, she finds the practice of her positive words is far harder than the theory.

CHAPTER FORTY-SEVEN

Penny

'Penny?' she hears. Then suddenly too loud. 'Penny?'

She shakes herself back to the bright whitewashed room. 'Sorry, miles away.'

Debbie cocks her head. 'What are you contemplating?'

Will's emotional absence at home. His distant gaze, lack of appetite, furrowed brow. Saying he needs time to think. Living on eggshells too. Waiting and hoping and praying when she really wants to shake him and scream: What's to think, Will? What's to think?

'Nothing much. Sorry, I'm just tired. We had a busy weekend. I didn't sleep that well.'

Debbie waits.

'Some friends of ours had a baby recently. They had a small party to wet the baby's head on Sunday. It was nice.'

She pictures Dan's baby, his gorgeous little Teddy. He was passed from person to person, but Will didn't seem interested. As ever, he larked around with Jen's kids. That's fine, really fine, of course it is. Some people are better with older children. He always seems drawn to Holly, but she's musical like him, that's all.

Debbie clears her throat. 'Did you talk to your doctor, Penny? Are you still on the meds?'

God, it's bright in the room. Pulling up her handbag, she fishes for sunglasses. 'Yes, still on them for now.' That's what she told her dad; that's what she's told Will. And she's fine, really fine. No one needs to know. And pills are most definitely not always the answer. They can make things a whole lot worse. She knows that better than anyone.

'If you did decide not to take your medication, you'd need to show you were managing well. If you weren't, there could be intervention. Forced intervention. You do understand that, don't you, Penny?'

She hears Debbie's voice, but doesn't reply. She's back at Dan's party, watching her husband. It's her imagination, it really is. That same stupid paranoia from the wedding. Loads of people look similar. It would've been well before she and Will met, so he would have told her. He would most definitely have told her. He's not just her husband, he's also her best friend.

Friends don't lie. Do they?

And they're going to escape; they *have* to escape.

She comes back to Debbie's question. 'Yes, of course I understand.'

Gazing through the sunglasses, she smiles a reassuring smile. Everything's fine, absolutely. She's coping perfectly. And anyway, she convinced them she was 'managing well' last time. They let her out, didn't they?

CHAPTER FORTY-EIGHT

Nick

All fingers and thumbs, Nick texts his mother to say he's on his way, then meets her at the hospital entrance to hand over the insurance envelope. She looks over his shoulder, her eyes showing surprise. 'Is that my car, love? Should you be driving it? I can ask your father, but I don't think you're insured.'

He explains it'll be fine, that a work emergency has cropped up, that he'll be back to the hospital as soon as he's free. He tells Dora to keep in touch about the medical insurance and to think of anything she wants him to bring later. Food, newspaper, clothes, he says, but he's finding it hard to concentrate as he gazes at her soft quizzical face. This woman isn't his mother. This woman is his grandmother! He has a desperate need to know more and the only person he can think of asking is his godfather. And he can do that right now; Derek is retired, he's bound to be home.

Swallowing down the fiery combination of bile and prawns, he drives back the way he's just come, to tree-lined central Hale this time. Alert to his mum's disappointment if he was caught speeding or scratched her beloved car, he consciously stops his foot pressing down hard on the accelerator.

God, not his mum. She isn't his mum! The words pump through his veins. Not his mum, not his mum. Unbelievable. Bloody unbelievable.

Then another breathless thought, almost gripping his wind-pipe: Harry Quinn's not his dad. Then who the hell is?

The Dillons' crazy-paved driveway is lit by the sun. The front door of the bungalow immediately opens and Iris steps out. 'Hello, Harry,' she says brightly, her blue eyes shining. 'I saw you through the kitchen window. I thought it was your mum. It's her car, isn't it?'

'Oh, I'm just borrowing it,' Nick replies, not liking to correct his name. 'Is Uncle Derek in?'

'Sorry, lovey. He's just popped out to do a bit of shopping, but he'll be back soon. Come on in. I'll put on the kettle.'

He follows her into the bungalow, noticing she's missed a pink curler at the back of her head. It's like a furnace inside and yet she's wearing a thick knitted cardigan over a floral summery dress and smart patent shoes.

Iris busies herself at the kettle, pouring boiling water in the teapot, swilling it around, then pouring it out again several times. He watches silently, fluffing his hair, fingering the scar on his cowlick, tapping his foot.

Dora isn't his mum, not his mum. Bloody hell, what the fuck? Does Iris know? Does everyone know? For God's sake, where's Derek?

He takes a deep breath. 'You look nice. Are you going out?' he asks.

She blinks, baffled. 'No, I don't think so.' Then sits down at the table opposite him without finishing her chore. 'Now tell me what you've been up to, young man,' she says with her neat warm smile. 'You're working now, aren't you? No more late

276

nights at university and lying in bed until noon! Nice to earn a few pounds here and there, but still . . .' She reaches for her handbag and brings out her purse, fumbling for a few moments with her knobbly fingers. 'Never hurts to have a little extra, does it?'

Her small eyes are bright and her hand slightly shakes as she hands him a crisp ten-pound note. Nick takes a deep breath, knowing it's wrong, but needing to use her apparent confusion.

'Thanks, Auntie Iris,' he says, his heart pelting. 'I was talking to Patrick about Susan the other day . . .'

Iris chuckles. 'A right pair those two. She bossed him around like billy-o. No wonder he never smiled. He'd have these tantrums and there was nothing anyone could do to stop them except your Susan. "Stop it, Patrick!" she'd bark crossly and he'd stop misbehaving, just like that. He adored that girl.' She sighs. 'But then, so did my two.' She stands up abruptly, a small frown on her face. 'Did you say you'd like tea, lovey? Or perhaps a nice hot chocolate? I might have some cream and marshmallows.'

'When will Derek be back?' Nick asks. The bitterness is stuck in his throat and he's thirsty, but the urgent need is to extract information while he can.

'Oh, golf takes time, love. It'll be a while.' She looks doubtful for a moment. 'Eight holes? Is that right? Or did he say nine?'

Nick nods, glancing around the bright kitchen as he loosens his thin tie. His eyes rest on a glass-fronted unit displaying ornate china plates for every month of the year and some framed photographs of small children. 'Are those the grandchildren?' he asks. 'I don't suppose you've got any photos of your boys from when they were little? With Patrick and Susan, maybe?'

He follows Iris into the lounge where she kneels on the floor and extracts box after box from the low sideboard cupboard. She opens the lids, but her photographs aren't labelled or in packets like his mum's, so she tips the contents of each box onto the mustard and brown carpet swirls, spreading them out with her arthritic hands and peering at each photograph in turn. As she pushes the rejects away, Nick collects them and puts them back in their boxes. He feels sweaty and nervous, aware that he's somehow taking advantage of her.

'Here's one,' she says after some time and passes it to him. It's a snap of a thick-haired blonde girl and a boy holding hands. They're standing next to two taller boys who are both looking away from the camera and towards her. Iris taps the photograph. 'See what I mean? She was probably only eight or nine here but she was the boss of them all. My two adored her, especially our Jamie.' She plays with the beads around her neck and chuckles, her eyes bright. 'They had that little spark going on, I could see it. When she grew into a beauty, he couldn't drag his eyes away. I caught them having a cuddle once or twice, but he went on to marry . . .' She looks blank for a moment. 'What's she called? Our Jamie's wife? Not the one now. The one who took him away?' Her eyes cloud with tears. 'She kept him from us, you know. He never came home. Well, not really.'

She abruptly recovers herself, pulls out a few more photographs and hands them to Nick, but time is passing and he wants to study them properly. 'Could I borrow these?' he asks.

The photographs are cleared away and they're back in the sweltering kitchen when Derek returns with shopping bags. He looks surprised to see Nick.

Nick covers his agitation with a smile. 'I know, Mum's car. I just popped round to let you and Iris know that Dad's in hospital with his hip. It sounds pretty painful, so I'm feeling

278

guilty for all that chivvying! Better get back with the items Mum's asked me to buy from the supermarket. No news yet of when they're operating, but I'll keep you posted.'

Keeping his hand in his pocket, he makes for the door, anxious that Iris might mention the photographs or ask for them back, fearful that he'll somehow lose the treasure that's hiding there.

'It's like an oven in here. What have you been doing with the bloody heating, Iris?' he hears Derek say as he closes the front door.

'Little Harry Quinn wasn't complaining,' comes the reply. 'When on earth did he learn how to drive?'

After returning to the hospital with the shopping and settling his parents, Nick returns his mum's car to her garage and waits for a bus home. It isn't just to avoid the expense of another taxi fare. He needs the thinking time, and weirdly, the privacy and the anonymity to study the photographs. Like a nettle sting, they smart and itch in his pocket. He feels strangely guilty; perhaps it's Patrick's comment from the road trip, or perhaps it's his feeling of duplicity having taken them from Iris. Or maybe it's the surge of secret and fearful excitement, the sort that made you want to pee as a kid.

As the bus trundles towards home, he carefully takes out the photographs. There are only three snaps, each time of Susan and Patrick Quinn, Matt and Jamie Dillon, but they seem to span the years. Five years of age, nine and fourteen or fifteen he guesses, but it's the last one he studies with great care, trying to see if there's any resemblance, not between him and Susan, that's a given, but between him and Iris's younger son Jamie.

The blend of sweat and goosebumps stays the length of the journey. What had happened back then? Susan was fifteen when she gave birth. Did Jamie Dillon know? Did Dora decide to pass off the baby as her own from the moment she discovered her daughter's pregnancy? It wasn't unknown in strict Catholic families to cover up the shame, but this was the nineteen eighties, not the fifties. Had Susan died in childbirth? Or was it something more sinister, as Patrick implied?

The bus drops him near Tesco, half a mile away from home. He walks briskly up Kingsway with resolve. After a sure and stable existence until his marriage, life has become uncertain, unsteady, downright precarious. Perhaps he is boring, perhaps he's a predictable slogger, but he needs to restore some certainty in his life and Lisa is the start. She's either with him or against him, it's as simple as that.

The bedroom curtains are drawn when he arrives at the semi. He'd forgotten about Lisa being paged in the night, so lets himself in, sits on the sofa, then stands; paces the carpet, glances at Lisa's novels on the bookcase, her pictures on the walls. Spots a small glint of missed glass, remembers the cut, looks in the mirror, sees *Mouse's* face. Shaking his head, he leaves the room, considers walking out, but heads towards the bathroom for a pee.

Finally settling at the kitchen table, he stares through the window. The daffodils have appeared in bud, not yet opened, but the rest of the small patch is a mass of overgrown grass and weeds. He idly thinks about going out there at the weekend and imposing some order, but suddenly realises he doesn't want to. It isn't his bloody garden. He looks around the kitchen. The cups aren't his, the plates aren't his, the washing machine, the scrubbing brush, the flipping chair that he's sitting on isn't his either.

Wearing her slippers and a fluffy dressing gown, Lisa shuffles in, looking sapped. 'I heard the toilet flush. You should be at work. How come you're here, Nick? Is everything all right?'

The mutinous resolve he felt on the bus starts to fade as he studies her features, sleepy and concerned. He puts his hand to his chin, his fingers finding the small scab.

The words burst out. 'I don't think we're going to make it, Lisa.'

As though he's slapped her, she jolts back. Seconds later, her face crumbles. 'Don't say that, Nick. Why would you say that?'

There's no going back. He takes a few moments to work out his anger. 'This house for a start. It isn't my home, it's yours. I feel like I'm a guest, having to ask for permission to have a bath or change the towels—'

'When have I ever asked for permission?'

'You haven't, but that's how it feels . . .' He tries a different tack. 'My parents. You've completely distanced yourself from them. You're not even friendly when Mum calls . . .'

She sits opposite him, her face pale and stunned. 'That isn't true. We chatted the other day. But your dad . . . He shouted me down and threw me out of his house. There has never been an apology. That isn't nice, Nick.'

Slipping his hand in his pocket, he touches the photographs with his fingertips, not ready to share, still bewildered about his discovery this afternoon.

'Then the Susan episode,' he says, feeling another surge of heat. 'It matters to me, but you haven't even bothered to hide the fact that you're bored of the whole thing, then when someone else takes an interest, when *Jen* takes an interest, you fly into a temper and throw a glass.'

'You know I didn't aim it at you. We have bouncy walls . . .' She takes a deep breath. 'OK, I get a bit touchy about Jen, and I apologised about the glass, but you're not being fair, Nick. I was interested, I *am* interested about Susan, but you made me feel left out. You've been incredibly moody and when I've tried to be friendly, you've pushed me away. You know that's true.' She stops talking, wiping away the large tears on her cheeks. 'Being pushed away and rejected by someone you love really hurts. How would you feel?' she says quietly.

The indignant resolve slips from his chest. 'I know, I'm sorry.'

'And you never talk things through. You're so buttoned up at times that it's difficult to know what you're thinking. I'm not a mind reader, Nick. I try, but sometimes it's impossible. And you know I'm a bit bossy. I'm a fixer, I like to fix things, but I can only help if you let me—'

He slips out the photographs then, laying them out side by side on the kitchen table. 'This is Susan,' he says, pointing to the pretty fourteen-year-old girl. 'She was my birth mother. How do we fix that?'

CHAPTER FORTY-NINE

Jen

'Hi,' Jen says when Will arrives at her door.

'Hi,' he replies, coming in. His face is pale and serious, his jaw tight. He stands for a moment, looking down at the floor before recovering himself and following her into the kitchen.

Jen sits and tries for a smile. Composes herself mentally. 'Just tell me, Will. I'll offer you a drink later.'

He stares through the window, then sits, spreads his large hands on the table, looks at her briefly, then takes a breath. 'You know we've been to this counselling—'

'We?'

'Yeah, I went with Penny last week.'

'Yes, you said you might. How was it?'

'Not my thing, if I'm honest.' He pauses for a moment, as though reordering his thoughts. 'Well, you know how counselling isn't a miracle cure, how it's all about the therapist helping you to help yourself? You know, looking to the future, making a doable plan and having coping strategies for when things go wrong. The sort of thing Geri used to do?'

283

Jen nods. 'Yes, and Ian with the kids at school.'

She stares at his face. The conversation isn't what she expects. She wonders where it's going; wishes she could stop herself from interrupting.

'Well, it's all about identifying and then tackling the underlying cause of the problem – in Penny's case, the anxiety. Remove that and life's hunky-dory.' He smiles thinly and looks at her. 'That's the theory anyway.'

'So the underlying cause is?'

'Penny's mum.'

'Ah, as we thought. Maybe try assassination?' she quips, still wondering what Will is trying to say.

'If only.' He absently rubs the table with his hand. 'So Pen and I had a long talk. She thinks her mum is narcissistic.' He glances at Jen. 'Not the guy who falls in love with his own reflection. It's a personality disorder, a syndrome, apparently. Seems an extreme description to me and I can't see it, but what do I know. It's Penny who matters and she feels it so strongly that she needs to—'

Jen remembers Ian mentioning high-achieving parents; he probably knows about this syndrome too. Her husband, who's a star. 'Oh, right.'

'Anyway, the person with it doesn't recognise it, apparently. They think they're great . . .' He smiles wryly. 'Which is self-explanatory, I suppose.' He takes another breath. 'We can't make her mum vanish into a puff of smoke or change her. Penny says there's been no sympathy or love since . . . just more criticism. Turning up unexpectedly, on the phone every day. Hurtful, unkind comments. You know – Penny has embarrassed not only herself but the whole family, God knows what her fellow JPs on the bench would make of it if they knew, that type of thing. Basically that Penny has let *her* down.' He places

284

his hand over Jen's, so hers completely disappears. Then he stares at her face. 'Her mum won't ever change, Jen. So, the answer is for us to remove ourselves from the problem – to distance ourselves. Penny can't see any alternative but to move away—'

Jen knows he hasn't finished, but can't help herself. She's back in her eleven-year-old body. It's the summer before starting St Mark's and her daddy has told her he's leaving, that he's going back to Ireland, not just for work, but forever. There's shock, disbelief, desperation.

'You can't move away, Will! You love your house. Seb's here, your mum's here . . .' Not able to voice the real reason why she needs him to stay, she urgently searches for humour. 'Manchester City are here for goodness' sake. You can't move down south. That's betrayal!'

Will curls his fingers around her palm. His eyes are on hers, dark and sad. 'An opportunity came up. Pen was really keen for me to apply for it. Same firm, new position. She can work pretty much anywhere. She's really enjoyed writing, so she's thinking of a book. She's eager to go, thinks it would be good for us both . . .'

London, Jen thinks. Will's going to bloody London.

She comes back to his gaze. His eyes are welling. Oh God, they are welling.

'The job's in Grand Cayman, Jen.'

She tries to withdraw her hand, but Will grasps it tightly.

'But,' he says, staring at her intently. 'But, just say the word and I won't go. Tell me you want me to stay and I will.'

Pulling away from his grip, she stands, her chair clattering to the floor. 'That isn't fair, Will. You're not being fair. Don't ask *me* to decide.'

The volume of Will's voice makes her jump. 'Do you ever

think about how *I* feel?' he bellows. 'In all these years you've never said, "I love you, Will". How do I know how you feel, Jen? We get on like a house on fire, we have sublime sex, but what does that mean? I've been your bit on the side for twelve or more years and while I wouldn't change that for a moment, have you ever wondered how that's made me feel? Going back to an empty flat, sleeping with some casual acquaintance just for a bit of company? Wanting to wake up with you next to me, getting drunk with you, going for a meal or on holiday? Marrying someone I love, but not the way I love you? Wanting kids, not with Penny or anyone else, but with *you*?' He stares helplessly at her face for a moment before gathering her in his arms. 'Oh God, Jen. Don't cry, please don't cry.'

She shoves him away. 'Of course I love you. I've always loved you. How could you possibly think otherwise?' She pushes him again. 'Go away. I need to be alone.'

Will doesn't move. He stands there, strong and solid, pulling her back into his arms. 'I'm not going anywhere until we've talked this through.'

'You came *this* time,' Will says, later in bed.

'How did you know?' Jen replies with an embarrassed laugh.

'I didn't at the time. It was only when I thought about it afterwards. Like I always think about it afterwards.' His face clears and he grins. 'Still, I was touched you'd made the dramatic effort.'

She feels herself blushing. 'I did nearly—'

'Yeah, but today you did big-style. Apart from the clues of noise and pink cheeks, you're exhausted; you can't move, can you? You're not hopping out of bed to make posh sandwiches and tea.'

286

'Hmm, am I so transparent?'

'Just the once, and only in retrospect.'

They fall silent and Jen wishes she could doze, sleep all day and all night spooned by Will's sturdy warm body. But today is a swansong. She hopes God will forgive her.

'We both know you have to go to Grand Cayman,' she says eventually, still turned from his face. 'When will it be?'

'A month, maybe two, I suppose. I need to say yes to the offer, then arrangements will have to be made, accommodation and so on. Penny's work too. I guess she needs to give notice, wrap up whatever she's working on.' Pulling her hair to one side, he kisses her shoulder. 'Will you look after Mum for me? Keep an eye on Seb?'

She's desperate to cry. 'Goes without saying.'

He twists and releases her hair for some time. 'Will you visit us?' he asks eventually.

She's glad she's turned away; her face would betray her. 'Damn right we will. You need a big enough pad for all five of us, and a swimming pool is compulsory.'

Will strokes her arm softly. 'I'll miss you though, terribly. Your soft skin and your smile. And I'll miss this, us.'

She tries to breathe back the tears. You can't have your cake and eat it, Jennifer, she thinks. The words repeat in her head, but like an oncoming tremor, she can feel the quaver in her false positivity. She badly wants to be greedy, wants the best of both worlds. But she holds onto her firm voice by a thread. 'I will too. There's FaceTime and texts and the telephone. We'll be OK.'

'Are you sure?'

'I am sure.'

Will is silent again for a while. 'Deal.' He gently turns her body towards him. 'But before I go . . .'

Jen lifts her lips to his, the tears silently falling. She takes in his smell, that mild combination of deodorant and sweat, wishing she could bottle it. 'Yes please, one last time,' she whispers.

CHAPTER FIFTY

Dan

Dan opens the sunlit agency at eight, stumbles to the back office, sits at the desk and drops his head to his arms. His brain feels fluffy and weightless, but his legs are leaden. He eventually lifts his head, yawns and turns on the laptop.

His eyes sting as he stares at the screen; he's never felt so tired and drained before. For the past two weeks he's been incredibly busy at work, barely stopping for a bite of lunch, then the moment he gets home, Geri passes him the baby, saying she needs a break for half an hour. She disappears into the lounge, turns on the television and closes the door, or sits in the garden if it's warm enough, puts on huge headphones and listens to music on her iPod.

Dan understands; it isn't a problem. Geri needs time out to relax, and he loves his one-to-one stretch with his boy, but by the time she gives Teddy a last feed and puts him to bed, he realises he's only had a sandwich at the office all day. So he cooks them some shepherd's pie or a lasagne, which takes far longer than he anticipates. He brings it through to Geri on a tray and they watch a half-hour programme or the news. They're

289

both shattered, go to bed, hurtling into deep sleep. Then Teddy wakes them for a feed in the night, sometimes two. As he watches Teddy suckle, he longs to sleep, but he can't drop off. That's when his mind drifts.

After the initial flurry of hands-on assistance from family, it feels as though everyone has abandoned them. Dan could ask his mum to help with the cooking and cleaning, but can't bring himself to do it. Besides liking his peppery-smelling house as it is, she'd fuss and worry, calling on his dad or Father Peter at the drop of a hat. He's not sure if Geri would see it as interference. He's not sure what she thinks about anything anymore. Since he returned to work, they've barely spoken.

'You look shattered,' Maya has said every morning this week, and today is no exception. She bursts into his office at nine and stares. 'Blooming heck, Dan. You look even more knackered today than you did yesterday.' She opens his diary, reads for a moment, then sits in the chair opposite and folds her arms. 'As I thought. Even though it's a Friday, we're pretty quiet today. No completions and I can sort Mrs Herring. And we have mobile blooming phones! I'll call if I need you. So, why don't you turn around and go back home? Chill out, have a nap, a day out in this lovely weather?'

Dan rakes his hair, thinking back to last weekend. Geri went out for several hours each day with her mum and her sister who were staying. She's been able to express her breast milk, which is great. The pleasure of feeding his child is immeasurable. He loves cradling his son, smelling him, talking to him, walking him to his parents' house in the pram, but at times he can hardly keep his eyes open. When he fell asleep for a few moments in the armchair on Saturday afternoon, he awoke with a jerk, dashing with a racing heart to Teddy's cot to check he was breathing.

'Going home would be more demanding than staying here!' he wants to say, but that would sound disloyal and unfair to Geri who has Teddy eight to six every weekday. Instead he smiles faintly, 'I might put my head on the desk, sleep and dribble. Don't wake me if I do.'

'Right you are,' Maya says, taking his attempt at humour seriously. She starts to leave the room, then turns back with a small frown. 'What about escaping to your mum's for a few hours? Or a friend's house? I'll cover for you if Geri calls. My lips will be sealed!'

'How come you're so wise?' Dan asks with a small smile, feeling he's said those words before.

Maya smiles back, looking pleased. '*Cosmopolitan* magazine?' But then she blushes. 'And maybe because my kid brother is only four. My stepmum is white and my dad couldn't cope with all the hands-on dad stuff. Culture shock big time. She didn't understand his . . . distress, I suppose, when she was the one who had to push the baby out and do all the hard stuff, but I could see how difficult it was for him, even though I usually stand up for the women.' She smiles shyly. 'But he is my dad, after all.'

He looks at Maya thoughtfully. Father love and forgiving their weaknesses; that he understands. 'You're a good kid, you know that? I'm lucky to have you.'

'I'm not a kid, I'll be—'

'Twenty-four in a week. Huge present expected.' He summons a smile. 'See, I was listening.'

He stares at his diary. A couple of hours wouldn't hurt. A bed would be brilliant, but he hasn't slept in his parents' house since he left for university. God knows how his mum would react if he turned up on a Friday morning with a 'don't tell Geri' when he's supposed to be at work.

Maya's still hovering, a small frown on her face. Perhaps he could drive to Wilmslow Park and have a nap in the car. He stands, slinging his jacket over his shoulder. 'OK, you win. I'll go out for some air, a walk or a drive. Call if you need me.'

A sudden April shower begins halfway to the car. Stopping to look to the sky, he debates whether to run on or go back to the office. By the time he climbs into the car, his shirt plastered to his chest, he feels wholly awake. What the hell, he thinks, Seb said to call anytime.

Driving on autopilot, he decides to text Seb at the traffic lights to check if he's in, but red lights turn to amber then to green each time he approaches. He hasn't had chance to think about Seb properly, at least not his words: 'it wasn't what you thought.' Now time has passed, he's having difficulty remembering why he was so angry, why he acted out of character, getting blind drunk on his own when his baby was imminent. But other things about that afternoon he does remember, the things he contemplates in the dead of night.

He parks at the side of Oak House, climbs out of his car and inhales the fresh smell of mown grass. With a warm nostalgic surge, it takes him back to cricket matches at St Mark's. He stretches his hamstrings with a smile, then glances around. The neat flower beds and the trees are glossing into life and lit up by bright sunshine, the handsome red building looks welcoming. The rain has finally stopped, leaving the pebbles with a multi-coloured gleam.

As he goes to press the intercom at the entrance, a woman opens the door with a wide white-toothed smile. She holds it for him. 'After you,' she says. 'Thank goodness it's stopped. Looks like you got caught.' She's very attractive, Dan knows, and possibly flirting, but finds he's stopped noticing the way he used to.

He walks to the lift, wondering if he'll ever be able to stand in an elevator without the same thought. It used to be a fart scene from a film, now it is something a great deal less funny, but pleasurable all the same. He feels a stirring of anticipation break through the fatigue. It'll be nice to see Seb. Only as a friend, but he likes his company, he's missed him.

He rings the bell and waits for several moments at the apartment door, then looks at his watch, registering for the first time that it's early, far too early for Seb if he's home. Feeling a mix of disappointment and relief, he strides to the waiting lift, then he hears the door open.

A woman is standing at Seb's doorway.

Holding his breath, Dan stares. Not really a woman; tall, freckled and skinny, she's more a girl. Her blonde hair is tousled and she's wearing a vest top and knickers. For a second he wonders if he's come out of the lift at the wrong floor; for another, he reasons Seb's moved out, a new tenant moved in. But he knows he's kidding himself.

The girl is still looking at him, her dark eyebrows raised.

'Sorry,' he says. 'I was looking for Seb Taylor.'

'He's still in bed,' she replies. 'Come in. I'll tell him you're here.'

Dan wants to bolt; to make excuses and leave, but he knows it would look odd. An older man in a suit turning up at your boyfriend's door and then running away again isn't normal. He doesn't know what Seb tells his girlfriends about his sexual proclivities; he didn't know Seb *had* a girlfriend.

'Sebastian, there's someone for you,' the girl calls. Then, turning back to Dan, still looking at him inquisitively, 'I'm just making a cuppa. Do you want one?'

'No, you're fine, thanks. I won't be . . .' But the girlfriend lifts her hand and disappears in the kitchen.

293

Rubbing his face, Seb emerges from his bedroom, then stops abruptly. Like the girl, he's wearing a white T-shirt and underpants. 'Dan,' he says, raking the short fridge from his forehead.

'If this is a bad time—' Dan starts, not knowing what else to say.

The girl appears from the kitchen with a mug and heads to the bathroom. 'I've made three,' she says over her shoulder.

Dan follows Seb to the kitchen. He feels foolish and needs to leave.

'It's not a bad time,' Seb says, handing him a mug. 'She's going in a few minutes. Her lectures start at half ten.'

Dan sits on a bar stool, then shakes his head. 'Sorry, Seb. I'll go. I should have called or texted. This was stupid.' He gestures towards the bathroom. 'I just didn't think.'

Seb stares for a pulse of time. 'It isn't what you're thinking.'

It wasn't what you thought. The words resonate, but he's left it too late. 'It's fine; it's none of my business.'

'You're here, so it is,' Seb replies. He rubs past Dan and walks into the lounge. 'Come here and look.'

Dan doesn't move. The exhaustion is back. If he had the energy, he'd feel ashamed.

'Dan? Come and look for yourself.'

Feeling lost and weary, Dan follows eventually. Seb is standing at the entrance to the second bedroom. A purple rucksack leans against the wall, women's clothes are draped on the small sofa and there's a neat pile of toiletries and make-up on the bedside table.

'Lorna's a pal. Pretty tidy for a model, I must say. A crowd of us were out last night for my birthday and she kipped here. She's a student. Her digs are near the university.'

Lorna emerges from the bathroom, a fresh smell of mint and lemon in her wake.

'And anyway . . .' Seb grins, nodding her way, 'You don't fancy me, do you, Lorna?' He looks back at Dan. 'I'm too old, apparently.'

'Too right,' Lorna replies. She turns to the glass dining table and points to a small pile of birthday cards with her bitten fingernail. 'Now that you're in your thirties, old man. Give me five minutes and I'll be gone.'

A sense of relief piercing the tiredness, Dan sips his tea. Then Lorna appears, her rucksack thrown over a shoulder. 'See you,' she says, and with a friendly wave she leaves.

Dan follows Seb and sits heavily on the opposite sofa. Returning Seb's gaze briefly, then looking back at his hands, he breaks the silence eventually. 'Happy birthday. You're thirty. I didn't know.'

'Thanks. You've shaved off your beard.'

'Yeah.' Dan feels his chin. 'Stupid really. Now I have to shave each morning and it's either shaving or breakfast. There's no time for both.' He smiles a small smile. 'Including the shit and shower of course.' Trying for humour, trying to be the Dan Maloney he used to be.

Seb continues to stare; he doesn't smile back. 'Is it tough?'

'You wouldn't believe it. No bloody sleep. Not that I don't love Teddy to bits.'

'You look terrible.'

A small smile again to cover the sudden urge to cry. 'Cheers, Seb. Still, at least I have an excuse. What did Churchill say—'

'Go to bed, Dan.' Seb nods to his bedroom. 'I mean it. Go to bed now, get some sleep.'

High cream-coloured walls, a soft yielding mattress and the smell of bacon. It takes Dan several moments to work out where he is. He props himself on an elbow. Seb Taylor is sitting crossed-legged on the small sofa in the bedroom, holding a paperback and wearing thick-framed black glasses.

'What's the time?'

'Nearly two o'clock. You hungry? Tea and a sandwich?'

Dan pulls himself up and swings his bare legs from the bed. He's wearing his work shirt like an old-fashioned nightdress. It's surprisingly uncreased. He feels groggy and slightly nauseous, but mentally so much better after four hours of black sleep.

Standing from the sofa, Seb holds out his palm. 'Nah, you stay there. Hope you like a BLT.' He turns at the door. 'Ma would be proud; I've been super polite and waited.' He grins. 'To be strictly truthful, it's actually a BT as I didn't have lettuce in. Strong Yorkshire tea coming up.'

Dan pees in the en suite toilet, throws cold water on his face and briskly rubs it with a towel. He looks like shit and his hair is still curly on one side from the rain. As he stares, his thoughts travel back to the A&E waiting room. That horrible clash of two lives he'd found himself living. Both foggy and clear, it feels like it happened a hundred years ago; it feels like yesterday.

When he returns to the bedroom, Seb's back on the sofa, mugs of tea and two large floury baps on a tray by his side. As though guessing Dan's mirror thoughts, he flushes and speaks immediately. 'We need to talk about the last time you were here.'

He passes Dan a mug, puts the tray on the floor and the words tumble out.

'It didn't really occur to me what you might have been thinking at the time. You know, when I called you. I was too fucking panicked to be honest, too relieved when the ambulance came and I knew I wasn't going to die. But then in the morning one of the nurses on the next shift came in and asked if I would like to talk to the psychiatrist on duty. I was like, what the fuck, but after crossed wires and confusion it turned out I was booked in as an overdose case.' Boyish and embarrassed, he smiles. 'Thank God they realised what had happened before they pumped my bloody stomach.'

Dan is still standing, his hand around the mug. He looks blankly at Seb. 'What are you talking about?'

Leaning forward, Seb frowns. 'I was having an anaphylactic shock, Dan. That's what it was when I called you. It was an allergic reaction to something I ate when you'd gone. The nuts from the deli bread probably. I had a peanut allergy when I was a kid, but nothing serious, so this attack came out of nowhere and I had no idea what was happening. My fingers started tingling, then my lips and suddenly my throat swelled up. I could hardly swallow. I was really shit-scared.' He stops, his sharp eyes on Dan's face. 'You thought I'd done something stupid, didn't you?'

Raking his hand through his hair, Dan drinks his tea without comment as random thoughts float by. Trust and honesty. Truth.

'I didn't and I won't, Dan.' Seb's face is taut, he continues to stare. 'I'm on the meds as I promised. It won't be plain sailing, but if I need help I'm going to ask for it before the walls cave in.' He abruptly drops his head before lifting it again with charged eyes. 'I've spent a whole childhood watching Mum. Wanting to help, to make it better. Praying for a smile, even a whole conversation. Wanting to fucking shake her at times. Feeling impotent and frustrated. Fucking frightened too. Of turning into her.' He takes a deep breath. 'But I'm not going to; I'm not going to hide away like she does.' He stands, walks towards Dan and puts a hand on his arm. 'Yeah? Dan, are you listening?'

Dan nods and takes Seb's hand, turning it over to examine his palm. The razor scar is still there, like a lifeline. It's a reminder, not of Seb's despair that night, but of something else, something stuck in his chest or his heart or his head, that won't be dislodged.

Standing back, a deep blush floods Seb's face as he doggedly continues. 'Then the other stuff. The blow. I got that wrong. I know that's not you. I knew it then, really. I just misjudged the whole situation.' He shrugs his shoulders. 'I was nervous.'

Dan looks at his face and can't help but smile. It's open, apologetic and vulnerable. And heart-rendingly beautiful. 'Your hair has grown longer,' he says, feeling a surge of desire. 'You have a quiff.'

'Do you like it?'

'I like your hair however you have it.'

Seb drops his gaze. 'And the lubricant. In a gift bag, for fuck's sake! That *is* embarrassing.' He sits down and shrugs again. 'I wanted to please you.'

'Fuck, Seb. You do.'

He sits down next to Seb at the end of the bed. Shoulder to shoulder, they are silent for some time. Then he sighs.

'When I was ten, something bad happened.' He clears his throat. 'Came home, confused, distraught, guilty. Told my mum. She said I was lying. She put a bar of soap in my mouth. To wash away the dirty lie. Dad was in the house but didn't ask.' He turns to Seb and smiles thinly. 'But the next day he painted my bedroom blue. The whole house was white, so that was really special.'

Seb is silent for a time. 'This bad something?'

'At church in the vestry. The local parish priest. Father Peter. Pretty old now.' Dan smiles wryly. 'Family friend. Mum's crutch. Still visits them to this day.' He sighs again. 'It was only the once, it was nothing. I don't think about it; it's forgotten. I just wanted to tell you.'

Seb nods, takes Dan's hand and puts it to his mouth. 'Are you ready for your sandwich?' He grins. 'Looks tasty, don't you think? Domestic goddess, that's me.'

Dan closes his eyes. No inquisition. No prodding nor prying. Just silent acceptance. Thank God for this man. When he opens them, he smiles. 'It does. Maybe in a while.' And then, turning to Seb. 'Do you still have the gift bag?' he asks.

It's dusky through the window when Dan wakes. He's naked and warm and exhausted; he knows where he is. He looks across at Seb, back on the sofa with his book.

Seb takes off his glasses. 'It's nearly five o'clock. I guess you need to get going.'

Dan sits and shakes his head. 'Not yet. Where's my mobile? I'll speak to Maya. She'll sort me more time.'

He feels inordinately sad; it wasn't what he expected. Exciting and embarrassing, funny and painful and exquisite, yes, but he hadn't expected to feel so intensely connected. And so guilty.

He looks at Seb for a moment, the longing still sharp. 'Seb. This can't happen again,' he says quietly.

'Why not? What's the difference?'

'You know it's different now. I mustn't see you any more.'

'Don't say that.' Seb kneels on the bed, his expression falling. 'My heart was fucking breaking. I thought I'd messed everything up. Then a week or two later, Will mentioned you'd been at the hospital that night. That you seemed pissed and confused, that you were in the wrong place. Then I knew it wasn't hopeless.'

'But it is hopeless, Seb. I feel utterly hopeless. I love Teddy, I love Geri. I never want to leave them, but how can I be an honest father and partner if I'm . . . making love with you?' He wipes away Seb's tears with soft fingers. 'And you, Seb. You have

299

your life to live. You're thirty. It's marriage and kids now, stability. That's what you need. This'll just be a phase, like Claudia.' Struggling to hold in the anguish, he pauses for a moment. 'You'll be much better without me holding you back.'

Seb stares, his eyes blazing. 'No, you're wrong. I've fucking loved you since I was thirteen, I'm not going to stop now.' He holds him by the shoulders. 'Being with you is like coming up from the bottom of the ocean. I don't want anybody else. I have a good life. I get out and about, go abroad for shoots. I meet people, go to parties. That won't last forever, so I've spoken to Will about setting up my own agency. That's fucking stability! Just you and me when we can, that'll be enough for me.' He clasps Dan's face. 'It's more than enough, Dan. To feel *this*? You know it is. Yes, Dan? Say yes.'

The curtains are closed through the leaded bay window when Dan arrives home. He finds Geri on the sofa, waiting in the dark.

'Sorry I'm so late,' he says. 'Where's Teddy?'

'In bed,' she replies, nodding to the baby monitor. 'It's past eight.'

He sits next to her. 'Shall I turn on the lamp?'

She shakes her head and turns; her eyes glint in the dusk. 'What's going on, Dan? Maya called and gave me a mouthful about how hard you're working, that you're nearly asleep at your desk, that we should be asking for help, and perhaps she's right. But it's not just that, is it?'

He hears the quaver in her voice, the deep breath of her resolve to push ahead with her speech.

'I haven't asked you before; I thought it didn't matter. But . . .' She straightens her back, folds her hands in her lap. 'The night I went into hospital for Teddy's birth, where were you then? I called and Jen called. We left messages. You didn't reply. You were missing for hours. Then when you arrived, you smelled of strong alcohol. I put it down to nerves about the baby, but there's more, isn't there? I know you're tired, we're both tired. But what is it? It started before Teddy was born. I felt you slipping away.' She takes a shuddery breath. 'Have you stopped loving me?'

'No, absolutely not.' Taking both her hands in his, he registers how small they are, her soft woman's hands. 'Absolutely not. I love you and I love Teddy—'

'But?'

He feels a strange calm. There was a moment on the way back from Wilmslow when he thought about driving his car into the front of a speeding lorry, jumping off a bridge, hurling himself towards a racing train, whichever would be the most effective way of ending the conflict and the uncertainty he's felt for weeks. He finally understood Penny's and Seb's urgent need for the internal pressure to just stop. But Geri has given him a gift, that of letting it out, an opportunity of finally being honest. Honest with her; with himself.

'I love someone else too.' He's become accustomed to the dark. He can feel her sharp recoil, see the pain in her eyes. 'I'm sorry, I'm so sorry. It just happened. I don't love you any less. I don't want to leave you or Teddy. You're my family. I love you. But I also love—'

She quickly places the tips of her fingers on his mouth. 'No. Stop. I don't want to know.'

Putting her hands over her ears, she bends her head to her knees, breathing deeply.

Dan waits in the silence, listening to the sound of his sleeping son through the monitor, barely thinking, barely there.

Then suddenly Geri screams, a long high-pitched howl.

Pouncing towards him, she slaps his face once, then again and again. 'You bastard, you bastard, you bastard,' she shrieks. Her arms wildly flailing, she thrashes his chest, his face and his head until there's nothing left. Finally falling to her knees, she curls in a ball.

Knowing each blow is deserved, Dan stays frozen and waits.

Geri's voice is muffled when she eventually speaks. 'Will you still see this person?'

'No. I don't know. I will try to stop. I have tried to stop—'

She lifts her head and gazes through anguished eyes. 'But still you will love them.' Then quietly and thoughtfully, 'Until you fall out of love.'

As though glued there forever, Dan sits silently until roused by the pelt of heavy rainfall against the bay.

'What do you want me to do?' he asks, shaking himself.

He feels numb and detached and unbelievably tired. Without Geri, solid and strong, he knows he'll be lost, but right now he can't feel it. But there's a sense of release. Not only the palliation of the confessional, but that he doesn't have to decide, that it's out of his hands.

Staring at the heap of black coals laid ready for the next cold snap, he finally speaks again. 'I can move out, tonight, tomorrow, whenever. If that's what you want. I'll pay the bills, give you money, anything you need. Just tell me what you want.'

Geri sits up and sighs. Studying his face, she lifts her hand and strokes his new growth of stubble. 'We need you. I need you. I want you to stay.'

CHAPTER FIFTY-ONE

Penny

Debbie gazes for a moment before speaking.

'Hi, Penny. You have a lovely glow in your cheeks. How's life?'

'Great, actually.'

And she does feel great without those blasted pills. In fact high as a kite! Already a little slimmer and pooing every morning, thank God! Not that Will noticed her weight. He was glad just to be back to normal, relaxed in their bed, watching TV, sleeping and snoring. Not that they've done much dozing of late. She's felt unbelievably horny for the past couple of weeks, not just because of the amazing surge of energy, but because Will finally said yes to Grand Cayman.

Distracted for a moment, she stares at the hole in her tights. Watches for several seconds to check this one's not growing.

'Penny?'

She comes back to Debbie's inquisitive gaze. What were they talking about? Will, of course, her Will. What else matters? 'Well, if I'm honest, I was a bit . . . a bit worried about Will. He was working so hard, not really talking, distracted. I knew something was on his mind but not knowing was . . .' She smiles brightly. 'Work, of course, the demands of that job! So I encouraged him to apply for a different role. Less pressure and stress. Just what he needs. Abroad, actually.' She pictures him gazing listlessly at his phone for bloody days before finally deciding. 'But he needed time to think it through.'

'Was he doubtful?'

'Yes, and in fairness understandably so. For me it's just perfect.' She smiles wryly, feeling a little guilty about blaming her mum again. Still, only white lies. Or exaggeration, perhaps. Her mum is sort of narcissistic; the disapproval of her only daughter is there, she's certain of it. 'Getting away from my personal stress, an opportunity to delve into books and my writing, not to mention the prospect of sunshine and sea! But it's a bigger wrench for Will because . . .'

The A Team, of course. That weird paranoia about Holly. Then there's Jen, always Jen. But she isn't going to let that spoil her happiness. They are escaping. Escaping! Will was seriously wavering, she's sure of it, but she got him back on track, upping the *Mum stress* before someone else applied for the job. It worked like a treat. Everything is panning out perfectly.

'Penny? You were saying about Will . . .'

She knows Debbie is speaking, but her mind can't move on. It's her imagination about Holly, it really is. Will would have told her; she trusts him implicitly, just like he trusts her.

'Penny?'

'Sorry.' She catches the hole in her tights. Definitely growing. Pushing hard to come back, she lifts her gaze to Debbie's soft eyes. What were they saying? Yes, Will, her lovely Will. 'Sorry, yes, Will was hesitant, but he came home from work one day and said he'd given them a yes. Put in a demand for a swimming pool and enough bedrooms for visitors.' She beams, she can't help it. 'A new start! In Grand Cayman of all places! I don't know if you've seen the film *The Firm*? Well, in one scene there's a red phone box just by the sea. Will's office will be a stone's throw from there. I've watched it ten times!'

'Sounds really lovely, Penny. I'm pleased for you,' Debbie says. But her face isn't matching the words. She's picking up some notes off the table. 'Your care team had a review this week. We touched on it before, but I thought it might be helpful to visit it again. Your final year at university.' She's pausing and staring. 'You spent a period of time on a psychiatric ward. Shall we talk about it?'

CHAPTER FIFTY-TWO

Nick

Lisa offers him a mint and he grins. Not at the offer of a humbug, but the feel of her stockinged foot against his groin. They are sitting on a train, heading towards Bristol with strangers either side who're both reading newspapers and taking up more than their fair share of space.

His beautiful fixer smiles back across the carriage table. He can't believe he doubted her, that he marched up Kingsway towards home with *marry in haste, repent at leisure* thumping in his head, that he'd gone so far as to say the two of them weren't going to make it. But thank God they talked. He finally told her how he felt about the house that wasn't his, his offence at her *obsession* description, the deep trauma he'd felt discovering Dora wasn't his mum; she explained how difficult it was to know what he felt about anything because he didn't *tell* her. They spent the rest of that afternoon in bed, plotting and planning, making lists between cuddles and kisses, talking everything through several times.

He gazes at the passing green countryside through the window. There's a mild anxiety about their mission today, but his heart feels so light. He and Lisa have managed to check off four out of five items on their list: his dad has a new hip; he and Lisa visited the private hospital and his father apologised for 'generally being a grump'. Lisa accepted it with grace and a grin, nodding pointedly at Nick and saying she didn't blame Harry for being out of sorts, anyone would've been more than just grumpy with such a painful hip and being surrounded by doubters. They've put Lisa's house on the market and have spent the last few weekends viewing houses in Chorlton and Didsbury. They've had lots of sex and Nick has replaced his moodiness with talking. And now they're tackling number five, hurtling towards Bristol on the pretext of a weekend away in Bath 'so we have an excuse to pop in', as Lisa puts it.

Nick telephoned Jamie Dillon before turning up at the black door of his tall and thin home.

'Hi, Jamie, it's Nick Quinn. Lisa and I are having a weekend in Bath,' he said, trying not to show his nerves and speaking as though it was a routine call, rather than a chat with someone he'd not set eyes on for years. 'Seeing as you're so close, I thought it would be nice to introduce you to my new bride . . .' Put that way, Lisa thought it a request Jamie couldn't easily refuse.

He'd had to breathe very deeply, but Lisa was there by his side, knowing what to say and what to do. Thank God for her, his beautiful little fixer.

The phone was passed to Jude, Jamie's second wife. 'The house is upside down,' she said warmly. 'But if you promise not to look, it would be lovely to see you.'

Nick is now sitting with her at the bottom of the sloping garden in weak April sunshine. The grass is still damp from light showers through the morning. Jamie's standing at a brick barbecue turning sizzling sausages, burgers and steak.

'I promised the kids the barbecue last night,' he's saying. 'Gabe is five now, you'd think I might have learned not to make promises. You'll know what I mean if you and Lisa have kids. They do not forget anything.'

It's lovely to be outside and will on summer, to drink rosé wine in a garden desperate to burst with colour, to breathe in the smell of charcoaled food and early blossom, but there's a distinct chill in the air from both the climate and Jamie.

Nick ruffles his hair, his fingers catching the thin scar on his crown, glad he's brought a thick jumper. He offered it to Lisa, but she said she was fine. She's been crouched in the wooden playhouse with Jamie's boy and girl for a good half an hour. She was solemnly handed a purse stuffed with pretend notes and coins to do her weekly shopping. Grinning at Nick, she presented her basket: soap powder, soup, spaghetti and cereal, all miniature-size. Now she's being served high tea from tiny china cups and saucers, with a side dish of plastic toast, fruit and sausages. The clever replication of a whole host of food items has made his wife laugh. 'Look, Nick, bacon and fried egg. And a bunch of French fries!' she said a few moments ago.

He wants to thank God for her love.

Though nervous and distracted, he's tried to pay attention to the kids too. They're both cute and chubby, their faces glowing and innocent. For ten minutes or so, Gabe leaned against his legs, lifting train engines with fat fingers, patiently explaining each name, rolling his bright eyes when Nick got it wrong. But he's finding it difficult to concentrate on anything other than Jamie's 'Mouse' features and finding an opportunity to speak to him without his heavily pregnant wife in earshot.

'Lily, Gabe. Food's up! Come and get yours before the grown-ups eat everything,' Jamie calls. The children collect theirs, taking a couple of bites before abandoning their plates and going back to their busy play.

Her baby bump huge, Jude stands with difficulty, stretching with a hand in the small of her back. Nick wonders how old she is. Late thirties, early forties, he guesses, at least a decade younger than Jamie. She rubs Lisa's arm. 'You're freezing. You must need a jumper by now. Let me get you one of mine,' she says. 'I'm going up anyway and it's nippy out here. I insist!'

Nick watches her slowly climb towards the patio doors, then turns back to Jamie. How old would he have been when Susan conceived? A year or two older than her, but still very young. Perhaps he never knew about the pregnancy; perhaps it'll be a shock. He studies him discreetly. A neat sharp face, slight but sinewy, with greying hair and blue eyes.

There's a resemblance; there's definitely a resemblance.

Glancing at Lisa, he takes a quick breath. 'I'm sorry, Jamie. I don't know how else to say this. I think you might be my father.'

Jamie stares at him. He's deeply frowning. 'What?'

His heart beating fast, Nick finds himself scrambling for words, Lisa looking on and biting her lip. 'I found out about Susan. I discovered she's my birth mother; I saw the birth certificate. But the details of my father were blank. So I went to see your mum. She showed me photographs. She said that—'

'That I had a crush on Susan? I did. Since I was about eight.' He continues to stare. 'But I'm not your father.' Pallid and taut, Jamie's face looks shell-shocked. He puts his plate on the table, his burger untouched, then lets out a long surge of air. 'Sorry, Nick. I did wonder when you called . . .' He briefly meets Nick's eyes before looking away. 'I haven't thought about this for a long, long time. I haven't wanted to. But I can tell you that I'm not your father.'

They silently watch the two children in the playhouse, one drawing the floral curtains in the panelled window of the cottage, the other opening them again. Then Lisa leans forward. 'We're sorry too, Jamie, for bringing up the past. But Nick needs to know more. He's desperate for answers and there's no one he can ask. When did Susan die? How did she die?'

Jamie turns to the sound of the patio doors closing. 'She isn't dead,' he says hurriedly. 'Not as far as I know. She did a languages degree at Manchester uni, went abroad for her second year and never came back. France, I think.' He finishes quickly. 'I'm sorry, Nick. This must be shocking, a lot to take in, but it isn't something I want to think about, let alone talk about, especially in front of Jude or the kids, so . . .'

Jude hands Lisa a jumper, then sits down heavily. 'Oh, aren't you all sweet,' she says, glancing at the table. 'There was no need to wait for me. Come on, eat up before it gets cold, there's plenty more.'

Nick chews his burger and politely answers Jude's questions about his parents and work, but he finds it difficult to swallow. He's reeling with shock. Susan is alive; his birth mother lives. He would have been three or four when she left the country. He glances at Jamie's children. Little Lily is three, she's in the nursery class at school, she chats, walks and sings. Plays shop, serves tea. Surely he should remember something?

Then other thoughts: how could his mother abandon him? Kids at that age are gorgeous; loving and loveable, innocent and so appealing. And what about his mum-grandma, Dora? How had she felt when her daughter left Cheshire and didn't return?

Jamie remains silent and stony-faced. 'I'll open another bottle of wine,' he eventually says, standing up.

Lisa stands too. 'I'm desperate for a pee, I'll walk up with you.'

Nick watches them stroll to the patio doors, sees Jamie's head dip towards Lisa's as he listens to her speak, then he turns back to Jude, forcing out polite strangled questions. The area, the neighbours, the garden, the weather.

After a few minutes Lisa and Jamie return. He refills the wine glasses, she squeezes Nick's hand.

Jude looks up at her husband. 'Aren't you having a top-up?' she asks with a smile. 'I thought you were drinking for me too while the going is good!'

'An offer I can never refuse,' he replies, putting a hand on her shoulder. 'But I thought I'd drop off Lisa and Nick at their hotel later. It's only thirty minutes away, save them catching the train. I can get sozzled after.'

They speed towards Bath in the dusk. Nick sits in the front at Lisa's insistence, but he doesn't know what to say; he has no idea what she said to Jamie in the garden, so he stares silently through the window, his breath shallow and tight in his chest. Jamie doesn't speak, but after several miles, the car brakes abruptly and he indicates right, pulling into a dark lay-by. He turns off the engine, removes his seat belt and lowers his head. When he lifts it, his voice sounds loud in the silence.

'Sorry, I would suggest we go to a pub for a drink, but I can't be too long. Bedtime's a nightmare with the kids. It'll be even worse fairly soon.' He looks briefly at Nick. 'Lisa says you need to know, good or bad, that the uncertainty is worse than knowing the truth. I'm not so sure, Nick. Cans of worms . . .'

'The can is already open though, isn't it?' Lisa says clearly from the back seat. 'We both saw that look on your face, Jamie. A look of hurt and pain. Please tell Nick what you know about his father.'

Jamie looks fixedly through the black windscreen, then takes a shuddery breath. 'Derek is your father. My father Derek is also yours.' He continues to stare, his eyes glassy, his voice flat. 'I know this because I saw them. Him and Susan.' He clears his throat. 'I was going fishing with Patrick and Matt, but we'd forgotten the bait so I offered to cycle back. It was in the garage, the bait, it was in the bloody garage. I would've been none the wiser, but I decided to go into the bungalow. Knowing Mum wasn't there, I thought I'd please Matt and Patrick by stealing some custard creams, bourbons, maybe even crisps, whatever I could lay my hands on. I heard noises, grunts. Went to look. Susan and my father were in my parents' bedroom. They were . . . well, they were in the act—'

Even though Jamie's appalled face tells him otherwise, there's a feeling of disbelief. 'But she was only fifteen when she had me,' Nick says. 'He was, well, he was—'

'An adult, a husband, a father? A forty-one-year-old man? I know. I never forgave him. I distanced myself, got stuck in my studies, came here for university and stayed. I would've cut myself off completely had it not been for Mum.'

They're quiet for moments. Then another thought hits, like a slap. Nick takes a shallow breath before asking. 'Was it . . . consensual?'

'Can sex with a child ever be that?' Jamie replies sharply. Then he sighs. 'I don't know, Nick. I didn't want to know. I was angry with them both.' He lifts his hands. 'She was the star of his film nights; every other slide was of her. And he was always charming, generous behind that damned bar, a sweet liqueur or three on offer every time. I saw them and I bolted. Puked in some bushes, then cycled back to Matt and Patrick as though nothing had happened.' He still doesn't turn. 'I dream about it sometimes. Even now. Standing at the door, her fair hair spread on the pillow. Her silence and stillness, his grunting, his white bum. Pumping, pumping hard.'

The image making him retch, Nick covers his mouth. He needs to escape, he needs air. But as he gropes for the door handle, a car pulls up beside them, so he winds down the window, thankful for the breeze.

'Need any help? Have you broken down?' the driver asks. 'I have some jump leads in the boot if that helps,' he says in a light West Country accent.

Jamie leans forward. 'Cheers, mate, but we're good,' he replies.

Revived by the chilly air, Nick absently watches the car drive away. 'So, you and Matt are my half-brothers,' he says, one fact surfacing from the sludge of his thoughts.

'Nothing personal,' Jamie replies, turning on the ignition. 'But I don't want to think of it like that. I love my mum dearly. It would kill her if she knew. I've never told Matt. I don't want my wife nor my children ever to know, even when Mum dies.' He turns to Nick, his voice laced with disgust. 'Consensual or not, Susan was only fourteen; he was no more than a paedophile.'

The word takes moments to sink in. Stunned by revulsion, Nick barely registers the soft squeeze of Lisa's hand on his shoulder. Paedophile? Yes, Jamie is right; their father is a paedophile. Oh God, oh God, what the fuck?

Indicating left, Jamie steers the car back onto the dark road, then he drives for a while without speaking. When he does, he sounds weary. 'Did my father know that I saw them? Did your mum and dad realise who the father was? What did Susan tell them? And what about poor Patrick? What did he know? He never visited us again. Ever. No more days out or fishing. No more film nights, thank God. A whole host of worms I stopped thinking about a lifetime ago.'

Yanked back from his bleak thoughts by the mention of his brother, Nick turns to Lisa and stares. Patrick, God Patrick;

he'd temporarily forgotten about his distress. What did he say? His fault, he said. He should never have gone fishing that day.

They lie on the bed, Lisa with a glossy magazine from the coffee table and Nick with his thoughts. He feels guilty about spoiling her weekend. They splashed out on the hotel, never thinking for a moment that the outcome of their search would be this, lying in silence on a luxury divan, when they should be enjoying the bath house and spa, then strolling into town for dinner.

Lisa sips bottled water and turns the page. She looks at him from time to time with a reassuring smile. He knows she's giving him space and he's grateful. Overwhelmed with shock and fatigue, he's having difficulty concentrating on any one thing. Like the paper game of consequences he used to play with Patrick as a child, each answer he unfolds takes him in another unexpected direction.

He rocks his head to Lisa. 'Turn on the television if you want,' he says again. It's flat-screen and large, but takes up a fraction of space in the lofty room. There's a fireplace and a desk, a coffee table and an armchair. Bang in the middle of the Georgian Royal Crescent, the hotel cost a fortune. But what does money matter? All the wealth in the world couldn't change his sheer devastation right now.

'No, it's fine. I'm enjoying reading how the other half lives.' Then a glance of green eyes. 'Anything I can get you? Do you want to talk about it?'

He finds the scar on his crown. 'No thanks and no.'

He goes back to the mental game. How does the consequence start? Nick met Dora. Dora, his mother-grandmother. She has a daughter who lives; a daughter erased, cut out of a photograph, out of her life. Pretending it hadn't happened. Can people really do that? The thought is incredible. Clearing away the spilt milk? No point looking back?

Feeling febrile and restless, he stands. Feels the radiator, then draws the heavy curtains to open the sash window. He stares at the inky view, wondering whether to walk it off at the park opposite, but his legs feel too heavy. Like his mind, his body is a paradox. It's blowing hot and cold; it wants to move, it wants to stay still.

In Hale Barnes. That's where they met. In a triangular house. Not a bungalow.

'Oh my God, here's a thought – what about the wedding money?' he asks, turning.

Lisa puts down the magazine, tightens the belt of her towelling robe and pats the bed beside her.

'That's a tricky question. I don't know, but if you give it back it'll look very odd. He'll know that you know, surely?' She peers at his face. 'Would you want that?'

'God no. I doubt I'll ever want to see him again, let alone acknowledge . . . The thought of what he did makes me sick.' He scrunches his eyes. 'But then again—'

'He's the godfather you've loved. He's also your dad. Part of him is you.'

Nick unfurls another slice of paper in his mind. 'I was only three or four. Why did she abandon me? Why did she never come back?'

'Because she was so young? Because she was at uni and wanted a life? Maybe she intended to come back but met a—'

He jolts upright. Thinks of Patrick rocking, his obvious distress. Susan must have told him; who better than her twin? 'Or because when she looked at me, she saw *him*, her rapist?'

Lisa puts a hand on his shoulder. 'Perhaps. We don't know how she felt. Who knows, maybe she loved him. I know she was very young, but still, there are other sides of love not everybody understands.' She kneels by the bed to see his face. 'Perhaps one day you can ask her. Would you want to contact—'

The scar's hot and it itches. 'No, of course not. Why would I?'

'Because she's your birth mum?'

'That means nothing, nothing.'

The consequences game starts again in his head. Nick 'met' Susan. But it didn't begin then. Dora 'met' Susan. Dora cut her out. Why? There has to be a reason why. He picks at the scar, the scar from the fall. The fall, the bloody fall. How did it happen? He climbed over the bannister and plunged. Cracked his head, needed stitches. That's what Dora said. How old was he then? Three or four. Oh no. Was Susan around then? Was the tumble her fault? Is that why she left? Oh God, oh God, did she *push* him?

Closing his eyes, he tries to go back. Nothing, there's nothing. He doesn't know, can't remember, but finds himself swaying, listening to a tune. Didn't someone sing? After nightmares? He can remember those. Someone immediately there; fair-haired, loving and gentle. He'd always assumed it was Patrick. Maybe it was *her*; perhaps she loved him once.

He opens his eyes to Lisa's; knows the last thought is the one he'll hang on to. 'Even if I did want to find her, how would I? Without asking Mum or Dad, without letting them know . . .'

'What about asking Patrick?'

'No, never. You should have seen him that day, I couldn't do it to him again.'

They talk intermittently for several minutes, unwrapping the tight folds of paper, skirting and analysing, projecting and dodging. About Patrick, the fishing trip and what he knew. His yearly holiday in France. His secret box of postcards. Could it really be possible he's kept in touch with his sister? About Iris and her boys, who're now Nick's half-brothers. They have kids, he's an uncle. Then Susan, what of her? Is she married with more children? Would she want Nick in her life?

Then they're silent for a time as he unfolds another thought. 'Why didn't Mum and Dad tell me? Patrick too? They let me live a lie for thirty-four years.'

Lisa sighs and smiles. 'That one's easy. They clothed you, supported you, kept you safe, played with you, praised you, read you stories at night. They nursed you when you were ill, protected you from harm, paid for your education, only ever wanted your happiness. I could go on, but the answer is pretty obvious.'

So, there's the consequence. 'Love?'

Lisa nods and grins. 'A funny old thing, isn't it?'

Safe in his wife's arms, his mind lets him float with that nice thought for a while. Then the game starts again.

Derek met Susan.

In Iris's bed.

He said, 'Such a pretty girl. My own movie star! So relaxed by sweet sherry. Let Uncle Derek have you.'

She said . . .

His heart whips as he stares at the ceiling.

She said no, she said no. Oh God, she said NO.

CHAPTER FIFTY-THREE

Penny

Stepping from the car, Penny stares at the huge yellow and blue sign on the warehouse building.

Stop and breathe; stop and breathe, she says to herself.

It's a Tuesday morning; she's come early as planned. It won't be busy. No need to panic, just buying crockery, it'll be a breeze!

The list in one hand, her handbag in the other, she counts the metal stairs, then stops at the beginning of the walkway. Oh God, she's been here before. It's like a run, a long sprint. But that's fine, really fine. Just get on the starting block. Wait for the gun. Follow the track. Round and round, round and round.

Like a teddy bear.

She takes a deep breath, looks left and then right. Living space, it seems, sofas, wardrobes and beds, curtains and candles. She doesn't need those and it's fine, really fine. It's not a race, no. More like the yellow brick road; she just needs to stroll and follow the path.

A mirror, a mirror. Don't look in the mirror!

That's silly of course; she knows that. She just made a mistake when she looked at her reflection this morning. Thought she saw specks of blood, moving and crawling. But when she leaned closer, nothing was there.

Debbie's fault; stupid Debbie. Got her thinking about *that* when it was all in the past. *A bad penny.* Not that she was bad. Just exam stresses, that's all. Letting off steam in the student kitchen.

A loud crash brings her back to today with a jolt. A serving bowl rocks on the floor, but it's not broken, thank goodness. That's why she's here. To buy crockery! Ironic when you think of it. She only hurled plates, really. Maybe some cutlery. A few glasses too. Whatever came to hand. But she didn't aim them at anyone. Not deliberately, at least. Except *him*, of course. Just stress, exam stress. It didn't make her a bad person; that's what Dad said. Mum didn't understand, but he did. *Bad Penny*, that's what *she* thought. Which is why Will doesn't know; why he must never know!

Breathe Penny, breathe. It's fine and he doesn't. The sessions are confidential and everything is perfect. They are escaping! Very soon! Letting out the house and going to Grand Cayman. A red telephone box! Sand, sea and sunshine, just the two of them together. And, even better, her period is late. She just needs to get the house organised. Twelve, the agent said. A dozen of everything for the new tenants. She can't use the Denby, it was bought for their wedding. That's why she's here. Time to concentrate, Penny!

Shielding her eyes from the glare of bright light, she stares at the crockery displays. Bowls, plates and side plates. Mugs, cups and saucers. So many shapes and sizes. Oh God, what about egg cups and serving dishes? And the colour? White, yellow, blue or green? What if everything goes wrong? Like Debbie, nice Debbie. Debbie who frowned, deeply frowned. She didn't like that. She won't go again.

Stupid, stupid woman, bringing *that* back. Violence, she said, a delusion with violence. Not a nice word, not a nice word at all.

Wickedness, as if! Bad Penny didn't mean to hurt anyone. Exam stress, that's all. And it wasn't her fault. The pills were the fault! Ritalin, Adderall, Dexedrine, Modafinil. Whatever was going.

'Mother's little helpers,' some people call them. Definitely some irony there. But then again . . . Now there's a thought. Packing is so stressful. Perhaps they'll help now . . .

'Need any assistance? Those plates are pretty heavy. Shall I get you a trolley?'

A young man's voice brings her back to the china department at Ikea.

'No, thank you. I'm not sure now. I think I'll start again.'

Breathe, Penny, breathe. Everything's fine, really fine. What did Will say? 'Don't worry so much, Pen. Whatever you organise, it will be perfect.'

CHAPTER FIFTY-FOUR

Dan

That broken, anguished face, oh God.

Trying to shake the image away, Dan looks at the moody sky through the windscreen. April showers in May; it's been a long time since sunshine.

After a busy day at work, he drives past the glistening swings in the park. Unlike when he was a kid, they're empty today. He and his dad didn't worry about the weather. Come rain or shine they'd be in that very park after tea, kicking a ball, throwing a frisbee, practising batting and bowling. Then onto the swings with a lolly, Jed fooling about on the slide or the roundabout, making him laugh. That's what he wants for Teddy.

At the sound of a shrill beep, he looks in the mirror. The driver behind avoids a dog in the road. Quickly averting his gaze, he comes back to the windscreen, but he's caught it already. His face, his sad face, the one which morphs into Seb's the last time he saw it.

Though only moments from home, he flicks on the radio and turns up the volume. He doesn't want to think of that night, nor the choice he made, but he does. After showering and dressing, he searched for Seb in the lounge and the kitchen. He'd left, Dan initially supposed, but he found him in the guest bedroom, staring at the black night through the window. He didn't turn when Dan called his name. He didn't turn when he said goodbye. But he finally appeared when Dan opened the door to leave. With that face, that broken, anguished face.

'What are you going to do?' he asked.

'The right thing,' Dan replied. 'I have no choice.'

Seb's voice broke then. 'There's always a choice, Dan. No one needs to know about us. We'll carry on just like this. Don't decide now. Just think about it.'

And Dan did think about it as he headed home, already feeling the weakness, the pull, the need for Seb Taylor. He sped down the motorway desperate, uncertain and torn, finally recognising he'd fallen in love for the first time, but knowing his duty lay elsewhere. The conflict was unbearable, the onus of having to decide overwhelming, but he was reprieved by Geri, strong certain Geri. 'I want you to stay,' she said and he knew then he'd do the right thing.

He now parks the car, hops up the wet steps and opens the front door of his home. With a small jolt to his chest, the smell of hygiene greets him, then his mum, wearing her Marigolds.

'Nearly finished,' she says. 'I'll put the fish pie in the oven and then I'll be off.'

Organised by Geri, Annette comes twice a week to help out with the cleaning and cooking. His parents turned up at the door one evening with a warm casserole and a new mop.

'Why didn't you say, you silly sod?' his dad said with a laugh, once Annette was out of earshot. 'She's been waiting by the phone for the call. It's what grandmas are for. It should've been you who asked her, mind. You'll have your work cut out smoothing that one over.'

Geri now appears from the lounge holding Teddy. 'How was your day?' she asks, giving him a peck.

'How was yours, more like,' Dan replies. 'Everything all right at the check-up?'

'Yup, mother and son healthy and hearty. I'm all healed up and allowed to drive again, and Teddy's on the 100th centile—'

'Which means?'

'He's going to be a big boy.' She smiles her sunny grin. 'Like his dad.'

Dan takes Teddy and kisses his soft curly hair, grateful for his beautiful son, for Geri, her smile and her positivity. Though he occasionally glimpses a wary sadness behind her chestnut gaze, it's almost as though their personal blip didn't happen. If it wasn't for his guilty thoughts, he could believe it hadn't. He hasn't seen Seb. He hasn't contacted him at all. He sent a single text late that night saying 'sorry' and Seb didn't reply. But he's been there, an ache in his chest, a blemish on happiness, almost constantly. Like Seb's temporary tattoos, Dan knows the stain will wash eventually, but it's hard, especially in the silence at night.

Geri puts Teddy to bed, then they sit in the kitchen to eat the fish pie and drink wine. Geri chats about her day, the visit to the doctor's, Teddy's loud protest when his hips were checked, the new cafe she tried with her mum friends, the appointment she's made with the priest.

Dan listens quietly, thinking back. The childhood blip had been erased; his teenage and twenties loathing of the church and its hypocrisy was intellectual, not personal. Other than his disbelieving mother, he'd never told anyone about Father Peter. But he'd needed to tell Seb, so perhaps it was personal. He'd tried to analyse that need in the dead of night. Fear, he supposed. Fear he was damaged somehow. And trust. Giving it and needing it.

323

Geri's still chatting. 'I think he'll say yes to the baptism, Dan. Perhaps he's just keen to increase the numbers in church, but who cares! He's young and trendy and seems open-minded. Of course, he needs to see us together before he decides.' She's looking at him earnestly, and for a second he sees that hurt in her eyes before it disappears. 'Are you listening, Dan? It's still a yes from you too, isn't it? You're OK with the idea of a christening?'

'Absolutely,' he replies, trying to sound enthusiastic, wondering what more he can say to convince her when he's not sure if he can do it, but the peal of his mobile saves him. He answers and listens for some time as Geri watches, her head cocked to one side.

'What was that all about?' she asks.

His breath is shallow. 'It was Penny,' he says, endeavouring to sound normal, trying to hide his tumult of emotions at the mention of Seb's name. 'Yvette's had a bad fall. Will's abroad and she can't track down Seb. She said his mobile number isn't recognised, wondered if I had a new number for him.'

Reaching for her phone with a frown, Geri scrolls down her list of contacts, rings Seb's number and listens. 'Same, number not recognised. How strange. What's happened to Yvette?'

Dan realises he didn't ask. 'I'm not sure. She's in hospital. They're doing tests, apparently.'

Geri gazes for a moment, then nods. 'Then you need to find Seb.'

His heart races, sweat cold on his spine. 'I'm sure Penny will find him. Jen will know where he is. Besides, it's Friday, I'm home early for once, I should be chilling out with you—'

'Come on, Dan. It's Will's mum and she's getting old. Anything might happen. And Seb's become a good friend too.'

She dips her face to his, her forehead still furrowed. 'Hasn't he? He'd do it for you, wouldn't he?'

Dan drives towards Oak House, trying to keep the surge of his thoughts and anxiety at bay. There's no point projecting, no point looking back. His mission is simply to see if Seb's there. If he is, he'll tell him about Yvette. If he isn't, he'll go home and carry on with his life. Simple.

Climbing the sweeping drive, he looks up to the attic. Seb's windows are in darkness. He knows he isn't there, but still he parks on the sparkling pebbles, stalks through the open front door to the lift, rings the intercom at Seb's flat, rings it for longer, then knocks and knocks louder. Tapping his foot and trying to block out thoughts of the razor blade, he takes out his mobile, tries Seb's number again.

Staring at the open lift, he endeavours to focus, to summon someone else he could call. The only one he can think of is Seb's modelling friend Lorna, but he doesn't know her surname, let alone her number. He texts Geri and Jen. *'Nobody in at Oak House,'* it says. *'Going to wait for a while. Then I'll come home.'*

He crouches at the door. Drowsy from the dinner wine, he drifts, eventually jerking awake with a shiver. The hallway is cold; his fingers are numb.

'Time's up,' he says, realising with a pang that he couldn't have contacted Seb over the past few weeks even if he'd tried; that resisting those strong desires just to text him had all been in vain. He's been cut off, blanked out from Seb's life. Chances are he's on a shoot, getting out and about, meeting people, having fun, just like he described.

Heading towards the motorway, the drizzle finally clears. Dan thinks of Will organising his new life in Grand Cayman and Penny's shaky voice on the phone. If it was his mum in trouble, they'd look out for him, for sure. So he takes the slip road and makes his way to the hospital.

The car hums as he waits at the car park barrier, but it doesn't lift up, so he parks where he shouldn't. He strides over the wet grass instead of taking the path. He drums his fingers on the counter as he waits at reception. The computer's on the blink; they can't locate an Yvette Taylor, and when they finally do, it is the ward furthest away.

The lights are dimmed in the unit, a single nurse sits in the office, her face lit by a computer screen. Dan knocks quietly at the door, conscious of the mud on his shoes, and she turns.

'I've come to see Mrs Taylor . . .' he starts, feeling the need to whisper. 'Yvette Taylor.'

She looks at him curiously. 'Visiting time's over. Are you family?'

'No, just a friend of the family.' He feels his face colouring. 'Is any family here?'

'No, she's asleep.' The woman stands and steps forward, gazing with a frown as though she knows. 'But she's fine and settled. No need to worry. I'm sure tomorrow . . .'

Retracing his steps without thought, Dan finds himself back in Chorlton Green eventually, but instead of going home, he pulls up by the park. Sitting in his car, he gazes at the black night enveloping the playground. He's deflated and tired, knowing perfectly well why he diverted to the hospital, but trying not to focus on his hope, his disappointment, his inescapable weakness. He climbs out, lifts his collar and strolls to the swings. Sits down on the plastic seat, wondering how many times it has been replaced since he was a boy.

A blind eye. His dad was weak. He turned a blind eye. The ten-year-old buried the blip, found a football team that clashed with Sunday church, said hello to Father Peter when he had to, got his scholarship to St Mark's, made new friends. It was forgotten, all forgotten. Then at thirteen, alone with his dad, the usual comment about something or nothing: 'Best not mention it to your mum.' Out of nowhere, it came thundering out. The hurt, the anger, the outrage. The crushing disappointment. Pumping from his heart to his fists, he lashed out wildly, hitting and punching and shouting until realisation dawned that his father was accepting every blow, doing nothing to defend himself. Staring at his knuckles, Dan had found blood.

Now, wiping the tears, he returns to the car. Too old at thirteen, he'd sobbed in his dad's arms. Sobbed and couldn't stop. That day he made a vow never to cry again. Yet look at him now.

Finally home, he puts his key in the latch, hoping Geri has gone to bed, but he hears the sound of the TV escaping from the lounge. Taking a deep breath, he pushes the door. Geri's in the armchair, her feet curled up. 'Oh, Dan,' she says. 'I think Teddy is smitten. He woke up and as you can see he's having too much fun to contemplate sleep any time soon.'

He turns to the opposite chair. Teddy is on Seb Taylor's lap, exploring his face with damp chubby fingers. Seb's poking out his tongue, Teddy's chortling.

Geri lifts her eyebrows and smiles. 'They've been doing it for ten minutes. What can you do?'

He finally finds his voice. 'Clearly nothing.' At the sound, Teddy turns and lifts his arms to his daddy. Scooping him up, Dan kisses his soft cheeks, glad of an excuse to hide his relief and breathe.

'Jen told Seb you'd been to the flat,' Geri's saying. 'She was at the hospital when he arrived. Yvette's doing fine. A broken ankle, which as Seb says, is better than—'

'Her wrist,' Seb finishes. 'No painting; that would really piss

327

her off . . .' Dan feels his gaze. 'Sorry about the mix-up,' he says. 'New phone, new number . . .'

They fall silent for a while, watching Teddy's head droop as Dan gently rocks him.

'Bedtime, I think,' Geri says.

Seb stands. 'Yeah, right, I'll get going. I'll just call a taxi—'

She peels Teddy from Dan's arms. 'Don't be daft, Seb, I didn't mean you. Stay and have a drink. We haven't seen you for ages.'

'No, it's fine. It's late, I didn't think of the time. I just wanted to thank Dan. I'll get going.'

Dan shakes himself back to Geri's gaze. 'It's no problem. Look, you don't need to get a taxi. I can drive. It only takes twenty minutes at this time of night.'

'I wouldn't want to put you out, but if it's no trouble—'

'No!' The men turn towards Geri. 'No,' she says again more quietly. 'It's been a long time since we've seen you. Stay, have a few drinks. We have several spare bedrooms for heaven's sake. I'm sure we could dig out a toothbrush.' She walks to the door, then looks back with a smile. 'Tell him he's to stay, Dan. You can drop him at the hospital in the morning, save taxi fares here, there and everywhere. A beer for me, please. Back in a mo.'

Dan follows, watching her climb the stairs. 'Beer,' he says, his feet stuck to the floor. 'Beers.' He walks to the kitchen eventually. Opens the fridge and stares, the blast of cold air clearing his head.

He returns with three lagers and hands one to Seb without really looking. He's still dazed that he's here. Relieved and stunned and nervous. Perching on the sofa, he puts the bottle to his lips. He knows Seb is staring, knows he'll have to lift his head at some point and look back. When he finally does, Seb speaks.

328

'Look, I'm sorry about my mobile,' he says, leaning forward. His face is sincere, bashful. 'I spent so long staring at the screen, willing a text to arrive . . .' He shrugs. 'It seemed easier to chuck it.' After a moment, he smiles wryly. 'It wasn't.' He looks to the door. 'Are you all right with this? With me being here, staying tonight?'

Silent for a moment, Dan pictures Teddy's chuckle as he explored Seb's face. It's a beautiful image, one he knows will stay with him forever.

He shakes his head and smiles. 'Sure,' he says.

CHAPTER FIFTY-FIVE

Penny

Penny yanks open the curtain. It's sunny, really sunny, a perfect day for a christening.

'Yeah, it is,' Will replies, hitching up from the bed. He shields his eyes. 'Still feels early, though. What time is it?'

Surprised she'd spoken aloud, Penny looks at her watch. 'Only six, but I've so much to do. You go back to sleep.'

Will doesn't move. 'Are you OK about today?'

She turns back to the window. 'Course, why wouldn't I be? I just have lots to do before we leave.'

'I thought that was all done. You finished work two weeks early especially.'

'It is done. I just need to check . . .'

Her voice drifting off, she heads for the en suite. She doesn't want to tell him how full on it has been. Going round the crockery floor of Ikea again and again, trying to make decisions, colours and shapes and textures, expensive or cheap. Eventually deciding on something, then finding herself back at the start of the loop. Coming home empty-handed and having to nap from sheer exhaustion. Finally buying everything online from John Lewis, thank God.

She steps in the shower. Just a few hours to go, just a few hours to go! Was it odd that Will asked if she was OK? Has Debbie contacted him and spoken about her stay in hospital? Course not, just focus! Those sessions are confidential. Stop and breathe, stop and breathe, everything's fine.

Absently turning the tap, she goes back to the long wakeful night of her house-letting worries. 'Twelve of everything,' the agent said when she signed up. 'Four double bedrooms and four extra of everything for guests.'

Of course she didn't have twelve. She only had half; six of everything. And anyway, they were all Denby, bought for their wedding. They've gone into storage. Everything has gone into storage. Except Will's guitar.

'You've forgotten your guitar, Will,' she said when the removal van left.

'I'm going to give it to Holly,' he replied. 'With the amp.'

She didn't want to ask, but found the words popping out. 'You love that guitar! It cost you a fortune. Why would you do that? Why Holly?'

Will frowned. 'Because Holly can play the guitar. Maria and Anna can use it too, of course, but I don't think they're very musical.'

A reasonable reply; it had been a normal reply, hadn't it? But when she mentioned putting it in the car, he said he'd drop it off at Jen's when the girls were at school tomorrow, didn't want it to appear that Holly was his favourite. 'Is she your favourite?' she asked. 'No of course not,' he replied. 'I just wouldn't want Maria and Anna to be put out.'

It's fine, absolutely. A sensible thing to do. But she caught his expression, those hidden hooded eyes. He was lying, he was lying. She always knows when he lies. And why did he ask if she was OK about today? Are the two things connected somehow?

Turning to the warm spray of water, she takes a deep breath and rubs her tummy. Escape very soon. Very, very soon. A tune, a comforting tune to help her relax. That's all she needs. And if that doesn't come, it's not a problem at all. The internet came good and they're safe in her handbag. She's already popped two. Ironic name, really, her mother's little helpers.

CHAPTER FIFTY-SIX

Jen

Happy, Jen thinks. Everyone's happy. I have to be too.

The June sunshine streams through her bedroom window. The household has felt joyous all morning, the girls bickering excitedly over who'll give baby Teddy his christening present first, who will hold him and who'll feed him.

Dan turned up unexpectedly with an invitation. '*You're* getting Teddy baptised?' she asked with surprise.

'It's what Geri wants.'

'And the priest has allowed it?'

'It's the child who's being invited into God's family, not the mortally sinning parents, apparently. So that's OK.' He smiled wryly, his face lightly colouring.

She gazed for a moment, not able to read him. 'Is it what you want too?'

That seemed to throw him. His dark eyebrows knitted, then he grinned. 'Sure. Might be pelted with fire and brimstone, of course. Which is why I'm here; will you do us the honour of being a godparent?'

The pleasure was inordinate, an unexpected fillip to lift her

333

despondency. 'Me? Really? Oh, that's lovely. Not Will or Nick?'

'I'd love to ask you all if I could, but I think it's considered a bit flash to have a football team of godparents.'

'Royalty does it.'

'Well, you're my royal choice, Jen. Of course, an insurance policy too – you're the only bloody catholic among us who actually goes to church. When the day of reckoning comes . . .'

Jen was pleased to see him joking; she'd popped in to visit him and Geri from time to time over the preceding few weeks, but he'd seemed soulful and tired, emphasised by Geri's over-chirpiness. But she understood new babies are hard work, especially the first.

'Who else will be godparents?' she asked. 'I need to know who my competitors are!'

'Geri's sister and Seb.'

'Really? Strange combination.'

'Geri's choice. She really likes Seb. Women eh?' he joked. 'There's me worrying about Teddy's spiritual well-being and she's thinking about cash, Seb being the most likely to succeed, as they say. You know, fame, fortune and wealth.'

'Well, she has a point. There doesn't seem to be a girlfriend on the horizon either. When I asked at Yvette's, he said he was done with women after Claudia. So, I can see Geri's made a good move. A rich and generous godfather like Nick's Uncle Derek. Possible inheritance in the longer run. Or maybe she's trying to get her sister off with Seb, keeping it in the family.'

Dan's laugh seemed thin. 'I'm rubbish at working out what goes on in the female mind, but I never thought of that one.'

Jen now turns in her long bedroom mirror, chuffed with what she sees. She splashed out on a fitted cream suit and it's a size smaller than the outfit she wore for Nick's wedding. Like a best man, being a godparent feels special; she's still flattered to be asked. Dan joked about the religious angle, but she'll do a proper job. Nick's creepy godfather gave him £50,000 for his wedding present; £500 might be stretching it, even by the time Teddy gets married. But money isn't the point; she's lovingly wrapped a children's Bible and a prayer book for today, the girls have each chosen a special gift and of course she's made the cake. It took days to perfect the icing and decorations. It looks professional and bloody brilliant, though she says so herself.

She leans towards the mirror; the dimples are there, but her cheeks seem much slimmer. Her make-up is neat and she's pleased with her hair, a shorter style, shaped into an inverted bob. Looking good, she feels, just needing the final touch, one she promised herself for today. She hasn't seen Will since their final lovemaking. After today she won't see him again for some time, at least not unless the family go on holiday to Grand Cayman. But will that really happen? Wasn't she just saying it to help him decide? For him to do the right thing, have a family with Penny, even though her heart longed for him to stay.

The earrings sparkle from their black silky pillow. She has no idea if the diamonds are real, but the plush box is embellished in gold with the name of a London jewellers. Perhaps she'll know when she wears them, like *The Princess and the Pea*.

She spends several minutes at the mirror, then hears the door open and Maria's bright voice. 'Wow, Mum, you look stunning!' Then Maria comes closer, quickly passing the tissue box. 'Careful, Mum. Your earlobes are bleeding. You don't want to stain your lovely jacket.'

Jen pads her ears, then the corners of her eyes. 'I can't get them in, Maria. I wanted to wear them today. I thought they'd look nice with this outfit.' Taking a deep breath. 'Oh well, never mind.' Trying not to show her disappointment and tears.

'Let me try,' Maria says, holding out her palm. 'Tell me if I need to stop.' She spends a few moments gently inserting the studs. 'There we go. They're so pretty, Mum. When did you get them?'

Jen waits a beat, wondering how she'll answer. Will she ever really say, 'They were bought by my lover. My lover, my man, my beautiful Will Taylor. I love him, I love him, I'll never stop loving him. Even when my babies were placed in my arms, he was there in my heart, in my gut, in my soul.'

But Maria is sweeping a finger over the gold lettering on the box. 'Very posh. Let me guess. Another gift from Mrs Taylor? Gosh, I do hope neither Will nor Seb have children. Then all those lovely things will be ours!'

'I know you're joking, love, but that's not nice,' Jen replies automatically. But the comment takes her back to the usual visit this week. With her ankle in a boot cast, Yvette Taylor had sat opposite her at the kitchen table. The rays of sunshine through the window had lit up the dust; fine powder on the pine dresser and its assortment of chipped china plates, jugs and cups, on the fridge and the windowsill, on the photographs of her sons and her long-dead grinning husband.

She seemed in good spirits. 'I'm glad Sebastian is settled. He seems happy with his flat and his new career plans. And he has a good friend in Daniel, a steady influence, I feel,' she said with a smile. 'Of course I didn't say so to him, but he and Claudia weren't suited. Beautiful, certainly, but too wrapped up with herself. He's always been a little needy, not as resilient as his brother. William is more like his father, of course.' Her eyes clouded then. 'I'll miss him when he goes to Grand Cayman, but it's probably for the best.'

'We'll all miss him,' Jen replied.

She put her hand on Jen's arm. 'But you will particularly.'

The sincerity in her face took Jen's breath, bringing on that urgent need to sob. She looked away from Yvette's gaze, towards the thin yellow start of a watercolour resting on the easel, but Yvette waited until she had eye contact again.

'You'll always be my daughter, Jennifer. Holly's mum.' Her piercing eyes shone. 'Don't worry, I've never said anything, have I? But from the moment you brought her to see me at two or three weeks old, I knew. So, you'll understand about the jewellery. Not just for her, but her sisters as well. We're all family.'

Of course Jen cried then, wept into a nearby tea towel and couldn't stop. Yvette's gaze flickered and she took a breath as though to say something. But instead she shook her head almost imperceptibly, stood up and give her a tight hug.

Jen now sighs at the memory. What was Yvette going to say? She should have asked, she should have spoken. Instead she's been left with imagined words and the smell of her delicate perfume.

Jen steps from the people carrier, stands at the wall and studies the neat church lit up by sunshine. Five months since their last celebration, there's no rain today; the sky is clear blue, the trees decorated with pink and white blossom. Yet there's still a feeling of déjà vu as she watches the photographer walk discreetly between small clusters of family and friends, taking snaps.

Cradling Teddy, Geri's standing to one side with her family, chatting and smiling as she poses for photographs with aunties and uncles. As Jen gazes, she abruptly turns towards the St Mark's crowd, watching for a few moments with a faraway frown. Then she lifts her hand to wave at Dan with the brightest of smiles.

'Jen, are you coming? You're miles away today.'

Jen turns to the sound of Ian's voice. He's offering his arm. 'You OK, love? You seem a little . . .'

'Watch it,' she replies. 'Only compliments allowed. These heels can do damage.'

Ian kisses her cheek. 'You look fantastic, by the way. Sylph-like. I'm very proud to be yours.' He rubs his hair, his face slightly flushed. 'It seems daft now, but I did wonder a few weeks ago . . .'

Jen's heart almost stops. Oh God, he knows; how will she handle it? 'Wondered what?'

'Crumpled sheets. Crumbs.' He shakes his head, the blush deepening. 'Well, that happened last time. You needing daytime naps, grazing to stop the nausea. Money and space in the house would've been tight, but I wouldn't have minded . . .'

The relief surges out as laughter. 'You thought I was pregnant?' She prods him playfully. 'Oh, Ian, you're a star. Come on, lovely husband.'

The girls dart ahead as she tiptoes along the grassy path holding onto his arm.

'It's The Godmother!' she hears in an Italian accent.

The hat hinders her view, so she turns. Dan lifts his hand. He's grown a soft beard and he's standing next to Seb. The two of them look a picture, both tall, slim and handsome in smart navy suits and colourful ties.

'You two are a loss to the pink pound,' she quips when she finally reaches them. 'You look bloody gorgeous. I'd give you both a kiss but I can't work out how to kiss and wear a hat at the same time.'

Dan smiles. 'Then I'll have to catch one later. You look fabulous too. Jennifer O'Donnell, the honorary boy. Who would've thought she'd scrub up so well?'

Will breaks from his conversation with Nick. 'Some of us did,' he says, smiling. He takes Jen's hands and kisses both cheeks. 'That's how you do it. You look knockout,' he says. The grin slips, he clears his throat. 'Lovely earrings too.'

Despite Ian looking on, the rush of emotion is immediately there. Oh God, she'll miss him; she'll miss him so much. She looks at her feet, tries for her wry tone. 'I can't walk in these bloody shoes though.'

She feels Dan's watchful gaze. 'No taking them off, now. Killer shoes are compulsory.'

'Even Seb's wearing them,' Will says. He puts his arm on his brother's shoulder. 'They look like spats, little bro.'

'That's because they are. High fashion, I'll have you know. And in keeping with the theme . . .'

'Yup, The Godfather, I get it. Beats those bloody tattoos . . .'

There's a pleasant smile on Ian's face, but England are playing and Jen knows he's itching to look at his mobile to check out the score.

'Go and read it. Discreetly,' she says. 'Or you'll drive me bonkers all afternoon.'

Nick turns back to Will. 'So, you were saying about having to slum it in Grand Cayman. Poor you, my heart bleeds. Seriously, though, how did you manage that? I'd have got bloody Margate. You are one jammy sod. When are you leaving?'

Jen drifts away. 'Tuesday from Gatwick, so we need to leave Manchester tomorrow,' she hears. She doesn't want to listen. Tears have been near the surface for weeks, but today her head feels like a bowl of liquid. If she's not very careful to keep her balance, the water will splash over the edges and spill, big time.

She heads to Dan's parents, as ever thinking what an odd couple they make. Annette, still attractive and bottle blonde, wearing tight clothes a much younger woman might wear, nervously holding onto a white clutch bag with one hand and to her husband with the other. Then Jed, with his curly black hair and his hands in the trouser pockets of a baggy suit which looks as though it's had twenty years of special outings.

'Here she is,' he calls. 'My appreciative audience. I've got a couple of jokes for you. Try this one for size . . .'

She listens to a joke, toilet humour as always, then another about Teddy never forgiving his dad for putting him in a 'daft dress'. Annette doesn't smile, she looks tense and tearful.

Jen nods to the church. 'Maybe a wedding next time?' she asks her.

The expected smile doesn't appear and Jed replies instead. 'Looks like that's the way it's going.' He grins at his wife. 'A smashing new outfit, eh? Mother of the groom. Really pull out all the stops? Wouldn't that be nice?'

Annette seems to relent with a small smile.

'No Father Peter today?' Jen asks her.

She puts a hand to the silver cross around her neck. 'He wasn't invited—'

'Because he's not very well,' Jed interrupts. 'Bit doddery these days. None of us are getting any younger, mind.' He turns to his wife and kisses her cheek. 'Though looking at this beauty you wouldn't think so, would you?'

Lisa and Penny are chatting in the shade of a tree, and as she joins them, Jen takes a deep breath. 'Not long to go, Pen. So exciting! Everything packed?'

Her eyes like Lady Penelope's, Penny blinks. 'Yes. Bit of a headache, though. Going to find the ladies,' she says.

Watching Penny walk away, Lisa briefly touches her stomach. Peering carefully at her face, Jen sees dark smudges under her eyes and pallid skin beneath her make-up.

'Oh, Lisa!' she says, squeezing her hand, the words out before she can stop them. 'Don't worry, I'm not saying a word, but I know you don't have family in Manchester and that Nick's parents are a bit long in the tooth, so if you need anything, any time, just ask.' She pauses for a moment, looking into Lisa's face. 'But do ask. Really do. I know I have a tendency to be a bit full on at times, but I'm trying hard not to be, so—'

Lisa cuts her short with a friendly smile. 'Full on would be great. Thank you, Jen. I'm pretty full on myself. We're so excited, but we're keeping it quiet for now. You know, early days.'

They're interrupted by giggling on the blossom-patterned grass. Will has one arm around Holly's shoulders as though making an arrest and he's pulling Anna along with his other hand. 'Beautiful young ladies for sale!' he's calling. 'I need a camel. Will anyone do me a swap?'

Her eyes dart involuntarily towards Penny. Her face is frozen for just a moment before it relaxes into a pleasant smile. Déjà vu again. She's seen that baffled expression before. At Nick and Lisa's wedding? Or perhaps Teddy's party? She's not sure, but she'll shelve the thought for now, the water level in the bowl-head feels precariously high.

Nick approaches from behind and puts his arms around Lisa's waist.

'Jen has guessed,' Lisa says with a smile.

'Sorry,' Jen replies. 'But even if I hadn't dragged it out of Lisa, I would have worked it out looking at you two love-doves. Anyone would think you were newly-weds. Any development with Patrick and the sister thing?'

Lisa turns to Nick, bites her lip and looks at him questioningly.

'On the back-burner,' he replies. His pale eyes flicker and shadow, and for a second Jen glimpses *Mouse's* face. Then it clears and he pecks Lisa's nose with a kiss. 'More important things going on just now. Oh, and we've sold the house above the asking price. Just need to find somewhere we like.'

'Next door is up for sale. Wouldn't it be great, popping in and out, borrowing sugar . . .' Jen starts with a straight face.

341

Then she laughs. 'Don't worry, I'm only joking. But please remember my offer. You're going to have your work cut out. Finding a house that you love, making it your own. Any time for a holiday?'

Nick shakes his head. 'Nah, holidays are on hold this year.'

Lisa is still looking at Nick. 'I've been thinking,' she says, her face flushing. 'I know we've got to find a flipping house and then do it up, but we can fit in a weekend if we need to, can't we?'

Nick's eyes widen with alarm. 'What? To Bristol?'

'No, of course not.'

'What? Grand Cayman?'

'For a weekend? Don't be daft! It's nothing, just a thought.' Her eyes flash to Jen's. 'Men, eh? Now if it was a boys' weekend away with beer and sport . . .'

Ian appears from nowhere, his face more relaxed. 'Roll up everybody,' he calls. 'The priest has arrived. It's time for Teddy's big moment.'

Rushing to Dan's downstairs loo the second she arrives, Jen looks in the mirror. As expected, her mascara has badly smudged beneath her eyes, so she washes her face with soap and cold water, then applies some hand cream in lieu of moisturiser. It gives her a strange glossy glow but it's an improvement. She's already embarrassed herself hugely; she doesn't intend to again.

Inevitably she cried at the font, but that was OK, everyone expected her to. But the crying had a knock-on effect. By the end of her choking attempt to say the baptismal vows, half the congregation were laughing through their tears as the young priest looked on in surprise.

When she emerges from the toilet, one of Geri's elderly relations clasps her greasy hands between papery palms. 'Oh,

342

the joy of a good old cry,' she says. 'I wish I could do it more often.'

Jen wryly smiles. 'It's not out of choice.'

'How does it go?' the woman asks. 'That saying about tears? "The messengers of overwhelming grief, deep contrition and unspeakable love". Yes, that's it. They're the things that make us human, though, aren't they?' She releases Jen's hands. 'Lovely to meet you. Perhaps next time we meet it'll be at Geri's wedding. If I'm still here to share another tear. Wouldn't that be nice?'

Jen almost weeps again, but busies herself in the kitchen glancing with pleasure at her cake, removing tin foil and cellophane. Dan ordered the party food from a delicatessen in Wilmslow and it was delivered prepared and displayed on silver platters, but the girls are earning money as mini waitresses, so she supervises them. Not that she needs to. Maria has been a revelation the past few weeks. Loving and kind, maturing so beautifully.

No more excuses to hide, Jen finally mingles. Some guests are in the lounge, others outside on the patio. There's a strong smell of honeysuckle and the paved area is dotted with terracotta pots of bedding plants dazzling with colour – deep blues, rich purples and bright pinks. Jen bobs from guest to guest offering fizz, wine or beer, listening to snatches of conversation, or joining in for a few moments before moving on. She can breathe and balance this way; she knows Will keeps trying to catch her gaze, but she can't risk a head-on collision.

She absently eats food, peers at Annette's photo album; chats to Geri's family and takes turns with Teddy. She hears Will tell a story of how Dan, pissed and confused, ended up in the wrong hospital department on the eve of Teddy's birth; she notices Penny knock back a paracetamol with a whole glass of champagne; she listens to a tale Jed Maloney tells about the A Team fathers placing bets at Sports Day; she sees Seb place his hand on the back of Dan's neck as he cuddles his son; she spots Ian watching sport on the TV when he thinks no one is looking. Then suddenly it's time for Will and Penny to leave. The afternoon has disappeared. She doesn't feel ready.

The A Team gather in the hall. Jen turns to the kitchen. 'You can't go yet, you haven't had any cake!'

'It's beautiful, Jen. You are clever. Too beautiful to spoil by eating,' Penny replies. Her eyes seem dark and huge; they flicker to Will. 'Sorry, guys, but we really must go; we have loads to do at home before we leave. I've been so excited over the last few days, I haven't been focusing on the packing as I should've, so . . .' She turns back to Jen, her face pale and tight. 'Did I say? We're letting the house fully furnished. Will didn't fancy getting tied up in a long lease, so it'll be more a temporary home from home type of let . . .' She looks at the girls. 'So you never know, we might get an actor or a footballer living there!'

Jen's tears spill again as she stiffly hugs Will. Yearning to return his tight grip, she quickly moves on to Penny. 'Sorry, I'm such an embarrassment, I know. I'll just miss you both so much.'

'But you'll be coming to visit us soon. You gave the office the order, didn't you, Will?' Penny says. 'Minimum four bedrooms and a swimming pool.' She looks to her husband, but his head is bowed. Then she turns to the girls, a desperate smile on her face. 'You're all set to come, aren't you, girls? Bikinis and pool games. Sandcastles and the sea. It'll be such fun!'

The girls nod solemnly and Anna bursts into tears. Then Will beckons them to one side, slips them each a tenner, then opens his arms to give a group hug, jostling until they laugh.

Jen pulls back as the others say their goodbyes. She hears her mum's words. 'It's OK. With God's help it will be OK.' They pound in her head as she makes for the garden and fresh air. By the time she returns with a steady smile and dry face, Penny and Will Taylor have gone.

CHAPTER FIFTY-SEVEN

Nick

Lisa opens the front door, picks up a pamphlet from the mat and turns to Nick. 'Weird, isn't it? This has been my home for five years, but now we have an offer I feel odd coming in, as though I don't belong anymore.' She gives a tired smile. 'I'm going up for a bath. Bring me up—'

'Hot water with one dunk of a decaf tea bag.'

She pecks his lips. 'Please. Who'd have thought I'd go off flipping tea, of all things. Give it ten minutes, I'll be soaking by then.'

Nick flicks on the kettle and flops in a chair. After the champagne, he had one sip of brandy at the party, but the moment the heat touched his lips, the gloopy smell of Toilet Duck came flooding back, so he moved on to beer. He drank several bottles of strong lager, so he should be pissed, but he just feels deflated, sad to see Jen crying like that, downcast that Will has pretty much left them forever.

Life shouldn't change; life should stay the same where it's comfortable.

Going back to Lisa's comment at the door, he breathes out

the flash of irritation. Not belonging anymore; not fucking belonging anymore! He knows it's not her fault and he's trying very hard not to take out his frustration on her, but his brother is his uncle, he has half-brothers, nephews and nieces. His parents are his grandparents, for God's sake. He pops round to see them as usual, but his attempt to act normal is exhausting. He still loves them and doesn't want to be unkind, but there's a slight feeling of revulsion when he visits. It has been in plain sight, but they're old. His father's eyes are puckered and rheumy, his mother's bony hugs and her perfume feel cloying. But at least Patrick's still Patrick, thank God. He drives over in the Merc on a Saturday afternoon for high tea and Scrabble. He seems to enjoy his new routine.

Nick snorts softly. But then Patrick would; the highest word score ever and he always bloody wins.

He hears the kettle click, but doesn't move. However hard he tries, it's there in his head and his chest. Breathless uncertainty. Life has shifted irrevocably; there's no solid ground. He has a mum he's never met. A mum he's never met! At least not since she pushed him over a bannister. Or did she? Was she singing a song, a sweet loving tune for her precious little boy?

Like a pendulum, his mind swings; one day she's the devil, the next day a saint. And as for Uncle Derek, the bloody paedophile . . . Well, there'll never be scope to forgive him.

He met Dan and Will in the week for a goodbye drink at their usual haunt. No one mentioned Jen and he was relieved she wasn't there; she might have asked questions, not just in passing like today, but one of her gentle interrogations, that glowing iris of concern which always makes him spill.

He laughs wryly to himself. Perhaps that's the cure to his constant anxiety. Maybe he needs Jen and the sweet-smelling stench of Toilet Duck to help him to spew it all out. But can he really say it? Can he say it out loud? 'I might be the product of rape. I might be the result of a grown man forcing himself on a teenager. Taking her virginity, her innocence, her life. What does that make me?'

'Nick! Nick? A drink anytime soon?'

His wife's lilting voice breaks through his malaise. Thank God for Lisa. Thank God for her. He has no right to be irritated or frustrated with her. She's been patient and kind. Listening to him when he's needed to talk; occasionally pressing him when he can't. 'Better to talk, Nick, to let it all out. Keeping fears in just makes them worse, makes them bigger than they are.'

But what can be bigger or worse than rape? That the constant thought of Derek's *film nights* and Lisa's advice were doing his head in. He'd dreaded the words coming, but knew that they would sooner or later: 'I'm worried about you, Nick. I think you need to know the truth, good or bad,' Lisa said. So he had to draw a line. He did it only last week. Sat Lisa down. Said he understood she meant well, but the past was the past. No more enquiries at the university, no more prodding and poking on the internet, no more gentle probing Patrick over coffee about postcards and France. They had a baby on the way. The future was their focus; she was banned from his past.

'About flipping time!' she now says from the bath.

Passing her the mug, Nick finally smiles. Her pink naked body looks beautiful. Though it's too early for the pregnancy to show, he feels drawn to her soft belly already. A new baby is on the way. His baby! The thought is amazing, exciting, and though he did very little, he feels inordinately clever. And it's reassuring too; something in his life that's normal and real. Makes his firm decision the right one. Burying the past. Looking forward, not back.

Lisa soaps the sponge and hands it to him. 'My shoulders please! A good old rub.' Then after a moment, 'Jen was sweet today.'

'Oh yeah?' he replies, smiling to himself. In the past he'd have agreed and said that Jen was bloody brilliant, but his foot-in-mouth disease seems to be getting better. With Patrick too. Reading up on autism has helped, but it isn't just that. It's the thing Lisa mentioned about love. Growing up, Patrick was always there, constant and patient; he has an aching desire to repay it somehow.

'She was,' Lisa continues. 'Really thoughtful about me having no family locally, offering to help when the baby comes.' Turning her head, she smiles. 'Much as I hate to admit it, Mother Hubbard isn't so bad . . .'

Nick laughs. The words 'I told you so' fight to pop out, but another thought emerges. 'Oh yeah, I forgot. What was all that about the mysterious weekend away? I thought we said the house would come first, that we wouldn't have time. Or the money, for that matter.'

'That's true.' Lisa pulls the plug, stands and holds out her hand to step out, but she doesn't meet his eyes. Instead she wraps herself in a towel, her expression terse. 'Bit chilly out here. Be a love and get my dressing gown, would you?'

He gazes at her face, her rigid pale face. She's Lisa, his wife, but he doesn't recognise her right now. The open honesty is missing.

Heat sweeps his whole body. 'Lisa? What's going on? Why won't you look at me?'

She lifts her eyes to his. 'See, I am,' she says, smiling. But the green is flecked with . . . what? Apprehension? Sorrow? Fear?

Nick doesn't move. His legs are heavy, his feet stuck to the ground. Something is wrong, very wrong. Oh God, Susan. The one thing he can't face. He told her to stop. 'What have you done, Lisa?' he asks quietly. Then he finds himself yelling, even louder than his dreams. 'What have you done? What the fuck have you done?'

She flinches away. 'Nothing, nothing much.'

His scar throbs as he stares. 'What's that supposed to mean?'

'Let me past, Nick. You're scaring me. I'll tell you when you're calm.'

'Tell me fucking what?'

The tears fall as she mumbles. 'I'm sorry, I stopped like you asked me but . . .'

He can't hear her voice. He can't focus on anything except the room caving in, getting smaller and smaller. Slipping down to the floor, he bends his head to his knees. He lifts it eventually. 'Just tell me, Lisa.'

Covering her mouth with trembling fingers, she takes a step back. Then she lifts her chin and holds out her hand. The open honesty floods back to her face. 'Come on, let's sit down. We need to talk properly.'

Almost not breathing, Nick perches at the kitchen table, looking out to the black night as he waits for Lisa to sit down.

His mind is in overdrive. A weekend away, she said at the christening. What did that mean? And though she's banned sugar, she's adding it to his tea. Oh God, oh God, she's found Susan, hasn't she? His bannister-pushing singing angel wants to see him. The thought scares him shitless; he wants to punch the bloody air.

He knows he should wait for Lisa to speak, but the words fire out. He can hear his own excitement. 'We're going to France to see Susan, aren't we?'

Lisa sits, her face solemn. 'No Nick, not Susan.' Then taking a deep breath. 'But her grave. Susan is dead, Nick. I'm sorry, so sorry.'

The words make him jolt. That's not the right answer. 'No, you're wrong. She isn't dead. Jamie told us. She lives in France. We worked it out, remember? Patrick's holidays in France? He goes to meet her.'

'He does go to France, Nick, but it's a . . .' She seems to search for a word. 'A pilgrimage, I suppose. She died twenty-five years—'

But Nick's mind has jumped to the vision of his brother, rocking, distressed, tormented. 'Patrick, God, Lisa, you haven't . . . Please tell me you haven't forced Patrick to . . .'

She puts a hand on his arm. 'I haven't, Nick. He came to me. You told me to stop and I did. Then Patrick turned up on Thursday when you were at the pub. He wanted to talk, so I listened. I'm so sorry, Nick. I didn't know whether to tell you, but I thought it through and decided I would, but not today, with the christening and Will leaving . . .'

Willing away the sudden nausea, Nick takes a deep breath. 'What did Patrick say?'

'Not much, I didn't want to pry. She died when she was twenty-four. A teacher, he said. Many friends but no husband or kids.' She clears her throat. 'I thought visiting her grave might give you some certainty, some closure . . .'

There's nothing to say, so Nick doesn't reply. Until now, he didn't know he'd had it, but the shattered hope is devastating. The feeling of loss too. How can you miss something you've never had? But it's there, an ache in his chest. And even worse, the unanswered question he'll now never know: his mum abandoned him; why didn't she love him?

Lisa's moist eyes are troubled. 'Nick? Are you OK? What are you thinking?'

'Not once,' he replies. 'That's what I'm thinking. She didn't visit me once.'

Lisa is still gazing, but her eyes flicker, uncertain.

'Tell me,' he says.

'She did, Nick. She came to see you and stayed with Patrick, but—'

The tingling is there on his scalp. 'But what?'

'That's when she died. On the ferry back to France. She drowned.'

Silent for moments, Nick takes in her words. Drowned, his mother drowned. Can it get any worse? He takes a deep breath. 'What happened? Did she—?'

'No one knows. It was left unexplained.'

He covers his face. But she came to see him. Lisa just said. Susan visited and stayed with Patrick. The realisation is sudden, but he's certain, completely. Fruit Salad and Black Jacks. Refreshers and Drumsticks. The road trip to Llandudno when he was nine. The smiley girl with the hugs and the sweets wasn't Patrick's girlfriend. She was his mother.

Then other thoughts clamouring at the door of his mind. Her unexplained death. Did she jump or did she fall? She stayed with Patrick, not Harry and Dora. And what about their plethora of locks? Were they locking her out or locking themselves in?

Coming back to Lisa, Nick finally exhales and lays a hand on her belly. 'Sorry for shouting. I didn't mean to scare you. I'm back to normal now.'

He is, he really is. The past doesn't matter, they have a child on the way. And Lisa is right. Though the ache is still there and will take some time, there's a feeling of closure from *knowing* already. A chink of light too. The girl he spent a day with in Llandudno was affectionate and fun. Though difficult to remember what she looked like, she loved Patrick, she loved him, he'd *felt* it. Perhaps there was sadness behind her friendly smile, but she wasn't a bannister-pusher, not for a moment. She was the sweet and loving songstress. He can live with that.

CHAPTER FIFTY-EIGHT

Jen

He's gone; he's gone. I have to move on.

Like a mantra, Jen thinks. It's been repeating in her head since she returned to Dan's hallway to find Will had already left. Pointless though it was, she'd wanted to meet his steady gaze one last time. The anguish had been so acute she'd wanted to howl and run after him, but right now she's exhausted, almost every last drop of emotion wrung out. Almost. Like a damp window leather, she knows there's some left.

It's late. The girls have gone to bed and Ian is downstairs watching the sport highlights on the television. Wrapped in her dressing gown and ready for bed, she's sitting on the quilt, weary and contemplative.

He's gone; he's gone. I have to move on, she says again inwardly.

But she isn't ready to take out the earrings. From time to time she glances in a small compact mirror, catching their glint and sparkle.

The Kenning family stayed until the end of the party to help with the clear-up. 'All right?' Dan asked her several times. Then as they left he pulled her back and took her hand. Smiling wistfully, he spoke quietly. 'We can't always choose who we love, Jen. Or stop loving them when we should. I understand that as much as anyone.'

It was a strange thing for him to say, and the words now play in her mind, evoking thoughts of her dark-haired handsome dad.

Nearly twelve when he left; same age as Holly. She hadn't thought of that before. But she still saw him often, thrilled to be taken out for meals, to the cinema and the shops, excited to be spoiled with toys and new clothes whenever he was in Manchester. It made up for his absence; spending time, just the two of them, her daddy and his *special girl*. But when she was sixteen, Nola told her the truth: still happily married to Seamus and living in Manchester, her mum had found out by accident. He'd been working in Ireland and had a minor car accident. Nola happened to be in Dublin too, visiting her sister, but when she arrived at the local hospital she was told by the receptionist that Seamus O'Donnell's 'wife and his daughter' were already there by his bed.

Jen had a half-sibling in Ireland, a sister born the same year as her. The lies, the hurt and betrayal were unforgivable. She wasn't his only special girl; she never had been.

'We can't always choose who we love,' she sighs, looking again in the mirror and seeing herself as her father for the very first time. Like him, she's been unfaithful; like him, she's lived a lie. Perhaps he couldn't choose who he loved either.

She closes her eyes. Maybe it's time.

Time to forgive.

A surge of sound from the living room below interrupts her thoughts. She gives a small smile; even though Ian already knows the result, he can't contain his excitement. He's a good man, a star; however much she's loved Will, she's never stopped loving him.

She catches a last twinkle before closing the compact. Maybe love can be shared. Seamus still writes her a letter from Ireland every birthday, news of his life, his daughter's and grandchildren, saying how much he still misses her and how he'd love to meet the girls.

That he hopes this year she'll forgive him.

Taking a deep breath, she lifts her hands to her ears to slide out the earrings. But the studs won't come, it's as though they are stuck, as though her skin has grown around them like a child's fist, refusing to let go.

There's a soft knock on the door. 'Hi, Mum,' Holly says, creeping in slowly. 'I went to the loo and heard you crying. What's happened, Mum? Are you all right?'

'It's these earrings,' Jen says between sobs. 'Maria had to help me put them in and now they won't come out.'

Her eyes damp with concern, Holly spends a few moments examining the earlobes. 'Tell me if it hurts,' she says, gently easing the posts out.

He's gone; he's gone. I have to move on.

'They do hurt, love. Very much. I won't be wearing them again.'

Taking the diamonds from her daughter, she carefully lays them on their dark pillow and, like a final goodbye, she closes the lid.

Holly looks thoughtful. 'Not ever, Mum? They're so pretty and sparkly and . . .' She thinks for a moment. 'Sort of special.'

Jen stares at her face, her lovely daughter's face. Sees Will Taylor gaze back. Just say the word, just say the word. That's what he said. 'Just say the word and I won't go.' She can smell Yvette's perfume. What was she going to say? And Will, what did he say about children? 'Wanting kids, not with Penny or anyone else, but with *you*?'

Coming back to Holly's worried frown, she covers her mouth. I love Will, I love Will, your father, Will Taylor. The words want to erupt from her gut, from her chest, from her throat, from her lips. But her daughter is only twelve. She can't tell her now, maybe not ever. But she can tell Will. Tell Will before he goes; she just has to say the words.

Unsteady and breathless, she hurries Holly to her bedroom. 'It's late, love, go to bed. Try not to wake Anna.' She kisses her soft hair. 'No more crying, I promise. I'll be back to myself by tomorrow.'

Jen closes the door, quickly climbs in the bed clutching her mobile. Takes a deep breath to compose the text. But her words to Holly abruptly bounce back. *Be back to myself by tomorrow.* Her steady mum's words; they slipped out unbidden. Her selfless mum who did everything to bring her up happy and safe, protected from sorrow and heartache for as long as she could.

Aching with uncertainty, Jen turns off the lamp.

He's gone; he's gone. I have to move on.

Sort of special.

Back to myself by tomorrow.

Just say the word and I won't go.

What to do? What to do? Has she left it too late?

Her mobile screen glows in the dark.

I love Will, I love Will, I love Will Taylor, beats in time with her heart.

CHAPTER FIFTY-NINE

Dan

Dan sends the text, puts down his mobile and sighs. Trying to live two lives was never going to last forever, he knew that. But today brought it into sharp focus. His beautiful son, his mum and dad, his friends. And Geri and her family; a really lovely bunch.

It was Geri's day, and wonderful. Everything she wanted, he hopes. He enjoyed it too; the friendship, the love. And though the church service was intense and emotional, it was for all the right reasons.

Feeling light-headed and insubstantial, he drifts from room to room like a ghost, picking up the odd paper plate and abandoned serviette, a champagne flute next to an ornament, a wine glass hidden behind a plant. He listens to the groan and the creak of the old floorboards. Takes in the warm spicy smell. Looks at pictures and paintings and books. Enjoying his home.

It feels strangely empty. Ironic when it's pretty much full, every bedroom in use from Geri's granny to her cousins. People sleeping, people snoring and people dreaming. Flawed human beings, he supposes; surely nobody's perfect?

Like Jen, poor Jen, the heartbreak etched on her face. Was he the only person to see it, to *feel* it? And Will, of course. With tears in his eyes.

Flopping back on the sofa, he thinks back to the pub in the week. He met Will and Nick to say goodbye. 'The Last Drink', as Will put it, genuflecting with a grin. But he could see the sadness behind his forced bonhomie. And it wasn't just Will. It felt like a play, the three of them acting the parts of the lads they'd once been in that very pub, twenty, ten, even a year ago.

Perhaps they'd all finally grown up.

He walked to the pub as usual and looked forward to the empty thinking time on the way back, but Will caught him up. 'Want a lift?' he asked

'Sure.'

Dan climbed in, but Will didn't move. Instead he stared ahead through the windscreen before finally speaking. 'I offered to stay. I offered her my heart.'

There was no need to pretend, to feign surprise. So Dan remained silent.

Will rubbed his face. 'I don't know why I hoped she'd say yes. She has three daughters, for fuck's sake. Let alone a bloody husband.' He turned to Dan. 'She was always going to do the right thing, wasn't she? That's how we were all raised. That's what we were taught. To do the right bloody thing even if we're only living half a life; half breathing, half eating, half sleeping, half shitting.' He put his head on the steering wheel and gently banged it. 'Fuck, you'd think I was used to it by now.' Rousing himself eventually, he looked at Dan and grinned. 'How's life for you, mate? We never really ask, do we? And on the rare occasion we do, no one listens to the answer.' He shrugged and put the car into gear. 'Maybe it's better that way.' He nodded to show the conversation was over. 'Lift home or do you want to walk?'

Feeling a sudden surge of tiredness, Dan now looks at his watch. The sofa is tempting, but he can't stay here all night. Still hearing the echo of Will's words, he takes the stairs slowly, reflecting on the plethora of encouraging and affectionate *marriage* comments made through the day, willing him to conform, to do the right thing.

Inhaling the tang of emulsion, he stops at Teddy's open door before quietly stepping in. Blue paint of course. For a boy, for a male, for a man. He's not sure if the smell is real or imagined, but it's always there when he thinks of his dad. A paradoxical scent of delight and love, but devastation too. However exciting it had been to have a blue bedroom, it would never make up for his dad not being there when he needed him, for standing by passively, for not fighting his corner, for being half a dad.

His eyes filling with tears, Dan gazes at his son. Much bigger now but still perfect. Perfect hands and nose, perfect eyebrows and toes. For the last few nights he's slept through until morning, but tonight Dan would like him to wake. Like Will's 'Last Drink', he needs a final cuddle with his son before he leaves. Leaves this house, this home forever, because it's the right thing to do. Not just because he's been living a lie, not only to own and declare his love for Seb, but for Geri and Teddy. Geri deserves someone who can give her his all, sexually, emotionally, exclusively. And most importantly his son needs a mentally strong and happy father. One who might not live under the same roof, but one who'll be there for him always, protecting him, loving him, fighting his corner. A whole dad, not a half.

A beep from his mobile pulls him back from his thoughts. He reads it and nods.

'Text when you're here and I'll let you in,' it says.

CHAPTER SIXTY

Penny

The living room is in darkness, the television reflecting a green glow on Will's face.

'It's late. I'm off to bed. Can I get you a drink before I go?' Penny asks. 'I think we have some beer left in the fridge.'

Will lifts a bottle, but doesn't move his gaze from the screen. She supposes that's an answer. He's barely said a word since leaving Dan's. Still sulking, probably. She wishes he wouldn't do the silent treatment, it's so hard to interpret what's going on in his head.

'Did we really have to leave so early?' he said tersely in the car.

'Well, yes,' she replied. 'There's still so much to do. I have to finish the packing and everything needs listing for the agents.'

He glanced at her and frowned. 'You said that was all done.'

'It is done. I just need to check a few things. You know I want to get everything right before we go.' Her voice drifted off.

It wasn't just that. There was the blood too; she'd sat on Dan's toilet and there it was in her knickers. She'd wanted to sob, but of course she couldn't make a scene. She'd had to breathe very deeply: a period and not a baby. Again.

Now heading to the kitchen, she idly pushes the door. Breathless terror slaps immediately. What the hell? What the hell? The room has been trashed; bar stools are upturned, shattered crockery is on the island, shards of glass on the floor. And the walls, the white tiles are smeared with brightly coloured food. Glistening green peas, yellow egg yolks, burnished orange baked beans. And ketchup. Splatters of dazzling red ketchup are everywhere, turning into handprints and reaching for the door.

Penny blinks. Bends double for several moments to let the dizziness pass. When she finally looks up, it's just her kitchen in Bowden, perfect, gleaming and neat. Not her university digs, no. No humiliation today. No cowering flatmates, their faces speckled with blood. No *him* with his sneering. No one to corner, no one to stop.

'Silly Penny!' she says aloud when the confusion recedes. It's fine, really fine, all in the past. That astonishing anger, the energy, the strength. Hurling and flinging, glass after bowl. Like the ancient Greeks and their plate *killing* for bereavement, she needed everything to stop. And it did, *he* did. At least for a while. Not bad Penny, really. Just concussion and lacerations, brought on himself. Covered in blood, a glossy cherry red. His own fault, absolutely. He should never have dumped her; he shouldn't have laughed.

Shaking herself back, she takes a deep breath. Not a bad person. Letting off steam in the student kitchen. She didn't mean to hurt anyone. Just exam stress, that's all. That's what her dad said; that's what he told the police. And Will doesn't know; he'll never, never know.

She turns to the units. 'Cater for twelve, the agent said. One last check before bed.'

One last check. Can she do it? Weary, so tired. But with a little help . . .

The pills stick but she swallows, then she opens the first cupboard. Dinner plates, side plates and soup bowls, neatly stacked. She knows there are a dozen, she's counted them before. But still, better safe than sorry.

One, two, three, four, five . . . Once I caught a fish alive! Six, seven . . .

Tightening the belt on her dressing gown, she smiles at the voice helping her to count. Finishes that storage and opens the next. Cups and saucers and mugs. Twelve when she last counted, but best check again.

Six, seven, eight, nine, ten. Then I let it go again.

Stopping for a moment, she listens. A guitar is playing along with the voice! Will's guitar, the one he's giving Holly.

Because she's the only one who can play it, of course.

A rational reply. She didn't give it another thought. Well, not really. Not until Annette brought out her photo album at the party. Competing with Geri's family, making up for the lack of Maloneys by brandishing photos of Dan as a baby.

'Doesn't Teddy look just like his dad?' she said to anyone willing to listen.

Of course Penny did, dutifully making the right noises as she studied the snaps from Dan's birth through his infanthood and eventually to St Mark's.

'Look, here's one of the A Team,' Annette said. 'You can hardly recognise Will with all that dark wavy hair. He reminds me of someone.' That's when she looked odd, when she turned and gazed around the room. 'I can't put my finger on who,' she added.

Going back to the inventory, Penny stares at the words blurring on the paper. Roasting trays and saucepans, serving dishes and tea towels. Six of those, check. The knives too, a wedding present from Jen and Ian. Funny, that. Slotting them in and out of the knife block, Penny catches their gleam and names them aloud: 'Bread knife and carver, parer and cleaver, utility and chef's . . .' Are six knives enough? Yes, surely enough.

He reminds me of someone. All that dark wavy hair.

So like Holly's. Little Holly. Holly, Holly, Holly. As she watched, Annette dashed off and whispered to Geri's granny. Then the aunties and cousins, the nephews and nieces. Nick and Lisa too. Every time she looked, they were staring right back. Sniggering, sniggering. Laughing at *her*.

That's silly, Penny. Silly Penny! Focus, just focus.

She just has to focus.

Opening the cutlery drawer, she lets out the trapped air in her chest before starting again. Twelve teaspoons, twelve forks, twelve knives, big and small. The missing dessert spoon throws her for a moment, but it's there in the sink with a bowl. Will's nightly cereal.

Hey diddle diddle,
The cat and the fiddle,
The cow jumped over the moon.
The little dog laughed,
To see such fun,
And the dish ran away with the spoon.

The sixes still troubling her, she takes off her robe to cool down, ambles to the lounge and quietly pushes the door.

Quietly she stares. Her husband is dozing. Will, *her* Will. Then his mobile snaps the silence and he jerks. Scooping it up from the sofa, he smiles at the screen. Takes a deep breath, then lifts his finger.

'Will?'

Dropping the phone in his lap, he looks up in surprise.

'Penny! I thought you'd gone to bed. You made me jump.'

'Who were you texting?'

'No one,' he replies with those lying hooded eyes. He turns the mobile face down. 'A text just came this minute. Not got round to reading it yet.' His gaze focuses and he frowns, another bloody frown. 'What are you doing, Penny?'

The tears burn her eyes. 'You're lying, Will. I know when you're lying. I've always known.' Does she say it out loud? She's not sure.

The furrow turns to alarm. 'Are you OK, Penny? What's going on?'

It's her period, not a baby. Again.

Breathe, Penny, breathe. She tries to concentrate on her task. 'Is six enough, Will? The agent said to cater for twelve.' She studies the sharp carver. 'Will six knives be enough? There isn't time to buy more.'

He's staring; she doesn't like it. And all those lies, bloody lies.

'For ages I didn't know,' she whispers. 'Not for sure, but now I know what you did.' Picturing Annette's gleeful face, she inches towards him. 'You should have told me, Will. Everyone knows, don't they? Everyone but me? Stupid Penny. Stupid, stupid Penny. They were gawking and sniggering. You've made me look a fool . . .'

Will's face is pale, his eyes hollow and flickering. Speaking very slowly, he holds up his hands. 'It's fine, really fine, Penny. Nobody knows. You don't look a fool. And it was only once, really. After your . . . after Nick's wedding. I'm sorry, Pen. It was a difficult time for us both. I just needed someone to talk to, so I went to Jen. It just happened. It wasn't planned. We didn't mean to hurt you . . .'

But Penny's counting, this time in years. Twelve. Coincidence again! A dozen, how funny. 'Holly is twelve.' She pauses for a moment and looks at the knife. It glints like a wink. 'Does that mean I should buy twelve?'

'What? *Holly?*' Will sits up, perplexed. 'What about Holly? What are you on about, Penny?'

Oh Will, her Will. His lies are so good. He's very, very good. 'Holly is your daughter, Will. Don't pretend. Everyone knows.'

His lying face is a picture of incredulity; she wants to laugh, really laugh. But his words from just now finally reach her. *I went to Jen. It just happened.*

Her heart thumps as she thinks. Focus, Penny, focus.

It's her period, not a baby. Again.

Nick's wedding was in January, January this year, when they were trying for a baby.

And *only once, really.* What does that mean?

'You went to Jen? What did you mean, Will?'

He's her Will; he's *hers.*

'You didn't mean to hurt me? What does that mean? You promised me a child.'

Jen, Jen. Jen, bloody Jen. He's been fucking Jen! Affectionate, kind Jen who already has kids, who has bloody *everything.* She's not having Will; he's hers, he's *hers.*

Realisation flaring, she gapes at his mobile, then finds herself lunging, flailing and shouting. 'It's from her, isn't it? The text is from her? Let me read it, let me see.'

Penny wakes. Her head feels heavy, her limbs achy and sore. As she yawns, she glimpses the bedside clock. Oh Lord, look at the time! Gatwick today! They've overslept when there's so much to do. She turns to Will to wake him, but his side of the bed is empty, the duvet neatly nestled against the pillow.

Sitting up, she tries to think, but her mind feels fractured. So difficult to focus, to piece together last night. She was ticking off the inventory, wasn't she? Will was in the lounge, watching TV. He must have slept on the sofa.

Hearing his deep tones, she slides on her slippers and pads down the stairs. At the bottom she stops in the hallway and stares. Blinks, then blinks again. Oh God, Will's guitar, his beloved guitar, its white veneer smeared and splintered and cracked. And its neck, its poor neck, limp and broken like the dead swan she once saw on the riverbank.

The guitar was for Holly. Why would Will do that?

She turns towards the sound of his voice, but it isn't just his. It's a hum of conversation, wafting from the kitchen; they must have visitors.

Standing at the kitchen door, she straightens her shoulders and neatens her hair. Then pushes it open. 'Hello?'

They turn to the sound of her voice. But it isn't Will after all. It's her father with their old family doctor, of all people. They're sitting at her table.

'Oh, how come . . .' she starts. Then she catches the shadows beside the back door. She stares for a moment before blinking them away. But they're here, really here. A man and a woman in dark uniform. Their arms folded, they're gazing right back with cold hostile eyes.

'Hello, love,' her dad says. 'Did you have a good sleep?'

He's drinking from a mug, a mug from the cupboard. The doctor is too; he's rudely staring, his eyes moving to her nightie.

No need to look down. It's her period, not a baby; it's only her period.

She comes back to her dad and the cup. 'The mugs, Dad. The agent said twelve; there has to be twelve, you really can't use . . .' she begins, then notices his expression. His eyes are wet. Did she call him? Why does he look sad?

'Can't what, love?'

Stepping to the gloss cupboard, she goes to open it and count, but her eyes rest on the knife block. Five, there's only five. The carver is missing. There has to be six! Where is it? Where is it? She looks at her hands, her trembling soiled hands. And her nightie, so slimy and stuck to her chest.

'Dad? Why are you here, Dad?'

'You called me. Not long ago. Do you remember?'

'What did I say?'

'That you'd been a good girl.'

A good girl? She squeezes her mind to last night. *Hey diddle diddle.* The inventory, the lounge, the plates *round and round.* A silly row about Will's mobile. He put it face down. Wished he wouldn't do that. But everything was fine, really fine. Cuddled him on the sofa until sleep, silent sleep.

Dormez-vous. Dormez-vous.

Her Will. *Her* Will forever.

The guitar, poor guitar? Not her fault, no. She had to silence the sound.

But a good girl? A *good* girl? Not bad Penny, please no.

Ah yes! Jen's text, Jen's message to Will. Though streaked crimson red, she could read it quite clearly.

'Absolutely!' she says smiling, relief flooding her cheeks. She nods to the sink. 'I *have* been a good girl, Dad. I really have! I stopped the dish running away with the spoon.'

ACKNOWLEDGEMENTS

A big thank you again to so many people:

To my gorgeous girls, my husband and the Lanigan family, for their affection, loyalty and support. To Elizabeth for finding time to counsel and chat, even on the other side of the world! To Charl for putting up with being my twin and buying me Ted Hughes poetry volumes I didn't know existed. To Emily for her beautiful sunny smile and four o'clock news bulletins. And to Jonathan for his love, humour and free publicity!

To my writing pals, old and new, for their solidarity, feedback and friendship. Particular thanks to my fantastic writers' group in Didsbury and the Psych Thriller Killers, AKA Carolyn, Libby and Samantha.

To Hazel for reading yet another novel!

To all my school, university and work friends scattered across the world. From Australia to America, from Switzerland to the

Bahamas, your warmth and big-heartedness has been amazing. From Clare's London hospitality to Jo's insightful WhatsApp messages; from Sara's constancy to Liz's eternal enthusiasm and Margaret's lunch treats.

To my lovely book-club-without-a-book friends, my fabulous cake-date mums, my supportive writer ladies who lunch, the Didsbury prosecco trio and my girls' night out faithfuls.

To the dinner-date couples and their delicious cuisine, the Hawkins and the Herrings, the Bakers and the Gammons, the Molloys and the Taylors (save for the frogs' legs!). And, of course, the Mahers for their spectacular Christmas dinner feasts.

To Belinda, my friend with the slow dog, for her wonderful generosity in too many ways to count.

To my literary agent, Kate Johnson, for her continued encouragement, patience and frequent words of wisdom!

Finally to the fantastic, hard-working team at Avon, with special thanks to my brilliant editor, Phoebe Morgan, for her invaluable input.

You can't run from the past forever . . .

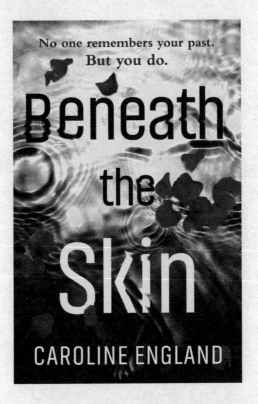

No one remembers your past.
But you do.

Beneath
the
Skin

CAROLINE ENGLAND

It will always catch you up.